CW01477038

# LIARS AND LIGHT

## The Valmenessian Chronicles
## Book One

Rebecca Camm

Printed in Australia.

ISBN: 978-0-6453455-1-3

Special thanks and acknowledgements to:
Editor  Chloe Hodge,
Proofreader; Emily Morrison,
Cover artist; K.D Ritchie at Story Wrappers,
Formatter; Imagine Ink Designs

This book is written in British English

## Content Notes

Liars and Light is an adult fantasy novel. It contains cursing, sexual references, violence, assault, and other adult themes. A full list can be found on my website, www.rebeccacamm.com or by scanning the QR code below.

*For Mitch*

# Valmenessia

The Frozen Sea

Rabben

The Great
Northern Forest

Sailor's Peril

The Perlyborn
Mountains

Forest's
Edge

The Mines

Misfortune's Forest

Fallben

Sorbg

Mibdopas

Grenlab Woods

Giland

Cressog

Blessed Reef

Revton

Royal
Brig

Donjvet
Harbour

Ocean's
Harbour

Penston

The Dividing Waters

## Nora

*14 Years Ago*

Nora stood before the king, her hands clasped behind her back and head held high. The only outward sign of her nervousness came as shallow breaths that had her chest rubbing against the soft fabric of the powder blue gossamer and lace gown her father had dressed her in. King Dominic sat in an oversized iron chair, flanked by two broad-shouldered guards fitted in sleek black uniforms that appeared to absorb the light around them, matching their fellow sentries who were stationed around the room. King Dominic stared down at Nora. His presence filled the expansive room, his aura exuding power into every crevice. Nora twirled her fingers through the ends of her hair, the dark brown waves flowing down her back. She straightened her spine, hoping to appear taller than the small six-year-old that she was before the king.

"Impress the king. Nora. Don't hold back," her fath... before their meeting with King Dominic. He had knel... outside the castle gates, one hand squeezing her... adoring. "Make me proud."

They had arrived at the castle that mor...

journey from their home in Giland in the hopes of having an audience with King Dominic, and Nora wanted so badly to do as her father had asked. They had only just found each other, and she would not let him down. Even if this meeting had her feeling unnerved.

Nora and her father had been ushered to the underground room as soon as they stepped foot on the castle grounds. The space was mostly dark, the few sconces adding eery shadows more than bright light. Glass cabinets lined the walls filled with vials, books and sinister looking things Nora was unable to identify, and she suppressed the desire to flee. Peeking over her shoulder, Nora looked to her father for reassurance. The man stood a few paces away, dressed in his finery and looking completely at ease. He offered Nora a quick smile and she attempted her own in return before she turned back to the king.

"Let me see, then," commanded King Dominic with a wave of his hand, gesturing for her to begin. She swallowed hard under the scrutiny of his hazel eyes, her smile disappearing instantly.

Summoning a small flame to her palm, Nora urged it to fly from her hand and grow in the space between herself and King Dominic. It crackled and sizzled as she transformed its shape, illuminating the gloomy room. First she moulded a lion, the fire mane lapping around the animal's snarling muzzle as it reared back ready to pounce. The lion launched, then split into three arrows that sparked and shot through the air. The heat was a welcome presence on Nora's skin, the blazing arrows filling her with confidence.

With a flick of her wrist water rained down, drenching the occupants, and extinguishing the fire with a hiss before collecting in puddles on the stone floor. Nora spread her arms wide then drew them together, revelling in the feel of her magic as the puddles gathered to form a snake whose body was that of a rushing river. The water serpent coiled, then made to strike the king, stopping mere inches from his face before splashing to the floor. Guards moved towards Nora but were waved off by the king, who eyed her intensely before encouraging her to continue.

With her brow creased and beaded with her magical rain, she twirled her wrists slowly, summoning the air around her to create three swirling whirlwinds. Nora grinned, relishing working with her wind magic. It was the element she was strongest in, and she felt her magic radiate throughout her body whenever she manipulated the air around her. She began twirling her wrists faster and faster as the whirlwinds spun around her in a dance, blowing her long hair around her face. Nora watched as King Dominic gripped the arms of his chair, his knuckles paling, and the sentries around him steadied their feet against the wind.

The cabinets rattled then shattered with a loud bang, spraying glass into the room. Gasps rang out as the shards tore through the air, sharp as daggers, one slicing Nora's cheek. She winced at the sting, blood trickling down her face, and drew her hand to the wound, halting the whirlwinds.

Panting, Nora looked around. The cabinets' glass doors were all blown out, their contents thrown to the floor. To her left, a guard knelt, clutching his stomach as red seeped through his fingers. Nora glanced away quickly, ramming down her distress, and met King Dominic's inquisitive gaze, her chin high and proud.

"Interesting," he said, running a hand through his drenched charcoal hair. He clicked his fingers and a golden-haired woman dressed in black appeared at his side. She leant down towards the king as he whispered in her ear. After mere moments she stepped aside, and the king waved his hand dismissively in Nora's direction. "You may go."

Nora's stomach dropped. Hadn't she impressed him? She made to turn towards her father, her head downcast as she held back her tears. She had done her best, but it was not enough.

A hand gripped her shoulder, stopping her from taking a step. "Not you." Nora looked up to see the woman from the dais next to her, gazing down at Nora with her close-set brown eyes. "Come."

"What about my father?" Nora asked worriedly.

"That man wasn't your father," the king smirked, his calculating eyes watching Nora. "He brought you here purely for a purse of golden coins."

Nora turned to where her father had been standing, the room now empty of all but Nora, the woman and King Dominic. The guards had seemingly vanished into thin air, and so had her father. The man who had brought her there was her father… wasn't he? She bit her lip to stop the tears that were desperate to fall.

"He brought you to me because he wanted to get paid," King Dominic told her.

"But he… he told me…" Nora began, her voice straining against the rising sob that threatened to escape. "He was so happy he found me."

"Of course he was. You are worth a lot of coin," King Dominic's voice was firm as he stood. He strode towards the door, his shiny black shoes splashing in the puddles that had pooled on the stone floor. "This is your home now."

He departed, the air growing colder in his absence. Nora sniffed, her shoulders sagging, but she refused to let a tear fall.

"Come," repeated the woman by her side, her grip tender but firm on Nora's wet shoulder, drawing Nora out of the room.

Nora was ushered down a thin darkened corridor, the woman's hand pressed gently against her back to guide her through the unfamiliar passageway. Their footsteps thumped dully as she was taken farther below, and she instinctively moved closer to the woman. Nora rubbed her arms to warm herself, the thrill from using her magic no longer preventing her from feeling the cold.

"It'll be alright, Nora," the woman told her with a soft voice that soothed some of the butterflies in Nora's stomach. Some, however, were not easily subdued by gentle voices.

A mild caress of heat enveloped them, tingling Nora's skin. The woman lowered her hand; both she and Nora were now dry. They descended a set of stairs that spiralled downwards, and Nora took her mind from the man she thought was her father and focused her attention on not tripping.

Stopping at the bottom, the woman turned, her brown eyes alight with purpose.

"Nora, my name is Rana and I need you to listen to me very carefully," the woman told her, her tone gentle but firm. "No more tears. King Dominic values power so you need to be strong. I will train your body and mind, but you must train your heart. Do you understand me?"

Nora was not sure she fully understood but nodded anyway. She had nothing else to lose. Squaring her shoulders, she jutted her chin, earning a small smile from Rana before turning to take in the room they had entered. Nora was faced with a dreary foyer with sharp lines and darkened corners. The stone walls were bare except for sconces that burned sombrely. There were no decorations or belongings as far as she could see.

"Hi!" exclaimed a boy, jumping into her path as though appearing out of thin air.

She recovered from the shock quickly, her wide eyes turning into a scrunched nose that she directed at the scrawny boy with a mop of blond hair and missing front tooth. His pointed ears stuck out on the sides of his head and his strange eyes seemed much too big for his face.

"Nora, this is August," said Rana, placing a hand on the boy's shoulder. "You two will be sharing a room." The boy's face dropped but Rana continued, ignoring his change in expression. "Why don't you show Nora where it is?"

August shoved his hands into his pockets. "No thanks."

"It wasn't a request," Rana looked down on him with stern eyes.

"Fine," he grumbled, shrugging out of Rana's grip, and taking Nora's hand, leading her away.

Nora looked to Rana with pleading eyes and an open mouth. She did not want to go with the boy, but he dragged her away before she could utter a protest. He led her through the gloomy foyer and down a set of steep stairs, guiding her to another lamplit hallway, however this one was lined with doors.

"This is my room," he said, stopping at a doorway that opened onto a cramped space with two simple beds. Letting go of her, he pointed to the bed on the right. "You can sleep there."

It was a sad room, Nora thought, looking around at the lack of possessions. "Is this an orphanage?"

August puckered his forehead. "No. I'm the only child… well, now there's you too, but there are mostly teenagers and adults living here."

"Oh, are they nice?" Nora's fingers twirled in the fabric of her dress, twisting it tightly.

"Sometimes," he replied, scuffing one of his shoes on the floor. "But mostly, no. They're soldiers… but the mean kind. Rana is nice though."

"Are we going to be soldiers?" she asked hesitantly, releasing the now creased fabric from her grasp.

August bobbed his head enthusiastically and spread his arms wide. "This is the home of King Dominic's best soldiers, and when we are older, we will be one of them."

"I don't want to be a soldier," Nora frowned, tears trailing down her cheeks. She just wanted to go home. Back to yesterday when everything seemed warm and bright.

"Don't worry, you're not one right now. You have to do a lot of training," he said before smiling. "The king chose us. We're special."

Nora wiped her eyes with the back of her hand as her heart thumped in her chest, her brown eyes wide at the revelation. *She was special.*

"Does your cheek hurt?" August asked, studying her face. "Is that why you're crying? What happened?"

"I cut it," she sniffed. "Can you heal me?"

August shook his head.

"But aren't you an Alv?" Nora eyed his pointed ears.

"Yeah, but…" he stammered.

She pouted. "Don't you want to help me?"

August tilted his head to one side, chewed his lip, then touched the wound on her cheek. At first, she thought nothing was happening and maybe his magic was weak, but then he shut his eyes. Suddenly, Nora felt the overwhelming urge to curl up on her new bed and fall asleep. She had been healed by Alvs before but didn't remember it feeling like this. Her body became heavy, her eyelids drooping, then, just like him, she closed her eyes too.

# 1

**Nora**

Present Day

"**H**ow dare they!" King Dominic flung his arms out, sending the contents on the table—as well as the oak table itself— flying across the room with the force of his wind magic.

Glass vials shattered against the wall, spattering green, violet, indigo and straw-coloured concoctions onto the stone, some steaming while others emitted pungent odours as they trickled to the floor in a rainbow mess. The table crashed with a resounding bang, hurtling splintered wood around the room. None of the Alta dared move, enduring whatever injuries were inflicted from the flying debris.

The eleven Alta currently in Royal Bay stood like statues in formation as King Dominic resumed his pacing up and down the room. The king had been stomping and bellowing for a good while now, halting his tirade only to direct his wrath at one of us, or to strike an object in the room. Nora and August had been the cowards behind when they first arrived, the cowards behind—

King Dominic's ire.

"The Alta are supposed to be some

on the continent!" King Dominic bellowed. "You're all trained to be fierce fighters! How in the Goddess Thyra's name was one of you taken?"

Smack! *The sound of a hand hitting flesh filled the room and Nora glanced to her left, careful not to move her head. One of her peers was rosy cheeked, his visible eye watering. The man towered over the king, pure muscle and magic that intimidated the fiercest of criminals, and yet he did not move. That was the power of the magical shackles tattooed to their wrists.*

*"Rana. Who have you chosen to right this wrong?" The king's words were like icy daggers, cutting through his blazing rage.*

*The golden-haired woman stepped forward; the Alta leader's focus was unwavering as she stared ahead of her. "August and Nora, my king."*

*Nora's gut tightened. King Dominic prowled the line, looking down his nose at the Alta before halting abruptly, drawing his shoulders back and puffing out his chest.*

*"You will find Felix," King Dominic snarled, his face crimson with rage as his stormy eyes flicked between Nora and August. "Dead or alive, I want him returned. No one leaves my service." He turned his back to them all, tension hanging taut in the air. "You two stay. Everyone else... get the fuck out."*

"Are you listening?" Rana asked, drawing Nora from her memories of earlier that day.

Nora still felt the king's anger through the bond and did her best to not rub the shackle tattoos connecting her to King Dominic. The urgent need to find Felix as he had commanded, grating at her.

"Mmmhhmmm," Nora lied unconvincingly, refusing to make eye contact with the leader of the Alta. Rana sat in a leather chair opposite to where Nora and August stood, a mahogany desk dividing the space between them.

Sighing dramatically, Rana continued, "As I was saying, I've been collecting information on a little group who have ill intentions towards

King Dominic. They've become louder of late, and my network informed me of possible trouble, so I sent Felix to the trades district to gather intel."

"Maybe he shouldn't have gone alone," commented Nora, trailing a finger along the edge of the desk, her eyes grazing over the collection of papers piled there.

"It's not your job to question me," Rana scolded, her hands clenching into fists, crinkling the paper she was holding. "And he was merely there to observe, not engage. It was a low-risk assignment."

Beside Nora, August remained silent, his pointed ears listening intently to their leader. He towered over both Rana and her, with his hands clasped behind his straight back and muscular legs shoulder-width apart. He never questioned Rana to her face, only ever sharing his opinions on her behind closed doors. He respected Rana enough to keep his thoughts between him and Nora, even if he disagreed with the woman. August would never disobey Rana's commands.

Rana flicked through the various documents, sketches, and maps with deft fingers, retrieving a slip of paper and handing it to Nora. "Here: the address I gave Felix."

Nora took it, then halted mid-turn, August already at the door. "Why did you choose us? If we don't find Felix…" Nora glanced at August, then back to Rana. "You know what King Dominic will do to us."

"You will find him," Rana replied, her focus unwavering from the collection of papers before her. A clear dismissal.

Nora merely nodded, following August from the room into the dark hallway. There would be no point arguing with Rana. She was the leader of the Alta, and her word was final.

Alta were King Dominic's personal warriors; powerful magic wielders trained in combat, assassination, and various forms of persuasion. Obtained by the king during mid-adolescence to serve him—August and Nora being the exceptions, having come into King Dominic's possession as children—the Alta were bound to him through the magical shackles tattooed on their wrists.

The shackles forced them to follow every command the king gave, and Nora was happy to oblige. He had wanted her, had given her a home and a purpose. If King Dominic wanted Felix found, then she would have to do just that, even without the punishment she would endure if she failed. Nora shook her head; she would not fail her king.

"Why is she sending us to look for the arrogant ass?" Nora grumbled, skulking through the narrow hallway. Sconces provided a warm light to the otherwise dark space. "Felix thought he was too good to spend much time in our presence. I don't know what makes Rana think we have a better chance of finding him than anyone else. Surely there are Alta she hates more than us?"

"She doesn't hate us," August sighed as he sauntered beside her.

Nora scrunched her brow. "Then why not give one of the others this dead-end job?"

"Rana has her reasons." He scratched his head.

Nora reached out a hand to stop him, gripping his bicep, her fingers barely able to curl around his arm. "Not like you to have no questions."

"I do, but I think there's more important things to be questioning than being chosen for this job," he replied, gently prying her fingers away.

"Like?" she asked, releasing him, and stepping back to lean against the stone wall, her face slightly obscured by the shadows.

"Like why was Felix sent on his own? If these people are rebelling against King Dominic's rule, wouldn't Rana or the king have expected something like this to happen? And why are these people working against the king? What is their motive? Maybe they are justified in their actions—"

"I'm going to stop you there," she said, holding up her hand. "You started on the right track but veered way off course. You know you can't question King Dominic. How you're even toying with the idea is beyond me, but enough. Stop twisting things in that head of yours to work around the commands. You believe what the king tells you. End of story."

August frowned but did not argue, even though she could see the fight in his dark eyes. "Where are we off to?"

Nora passed him the scrap of paper with the address Rana gave her and grumbled. "The centre of the trades district."

"Don't sound so excited," he chuckled, offering her a warm smile.

"An afternoon stuck with you, trying to complete an impossible job? Sounds riveting," she replied, her smirk looking villainous in the lack of light.

$$\Diamond$$

Nora crept through the alley, careful not to disturb anything, whilst August sketched the scene and questioned their only witness. Rana had given them the address of Felix's last location, and after speaking with a few locals they had found themselves here. The narrow passageway was littered with broken crates, overturned barrels, and shattered bottles. Even though Felix had disappeared the day before, no one had thought to tidy up. Whether that would prove lucky for Nora though, was yet to be seen.

"There was definitely a fight, but I can't find any blood, so we can assume no one was mortally injured," Nora commented loudly, narrowing her eyes as she crouched to further inspect the broken crates after hearing a rustling sound coming from their location. She dropped her voice, whispering to herself. "If only the walls could talk."

"Are you sure you saw a man matching our description here?" August asked the blacksmith who stood beside him.

"Yes," replied the short burly man. "He was arguing with another man I could have sworn was wearing a potato sack."

Nora raised an eyebrow, leaving the crates after failing to uncover the source of the sound. "A potato sack?"

The man nodded. "Couldn't see his face though, wore a hood just like you." He gestured to August. "As I said, the two of them were arguing loudly then it sounded like they got physical. I could hear things crashing about. Scared my customer away with that racket. That's when I came out here to see what was going on and I find the potato sack man standing over the man you described. The alley a mess. I went to call for the Royal Sentries, but by the time they turned up, the two you're interested in were gone."

"What did the sentries do when they arrived?" August asked.

"Nothing," the man cut his hand through the air. "Just told me to clean up."

Nora came to stand next to August, peering at his sketch. As well as the alley, he had drawn the blacksmith's workshop on the left; the oak door was wide open, under an iron sign that hung overhead with "Ethan's" and five squares interlinked and resting on their points. To the right of the alley, he had drawn the leather merchant; its wares were draped over the front windowsill and a sign was nailed into the closed door, the store's name barely eligible on the old wood.

"Does it pass your standards?" August joked.

"It'll do," she said, knowing full well that his sketch was more than adequate. "It's no work of art but that's to be expec—"

Movement on the rooftop caught her eye, and she spotted a gibbon scampering away, its ash grey fur shimmering in the sunlight. Nora took off, racing down the alley in the direction the Anima was headed. She knew they were an Anima—a race of people that could shift into animals. True animals did not have such calculating expressions, nor were gibbons native to this area.

Weaving through pedestrians, she chased after the gibbon, her eyes darting between where she was going and the Anima until she reached a stack of crates. Summoning her wind magic to give her an extra boost, Nora leapt up the wooden boxes and landed lightly on the terracotta tiled roof. Ahead of her, the gibbon turned to see her land. Eyes wide, the Anima then bolted, with Nora close on their heels.

The Anima moved swiftly, leaping from tiles to chimneys and over narrow alcoves and passageways, their arms and legs propelling them through the air. Determined, Nora followed, launching herself from one building to another with her wind magic aiding her agility and distance.

Nora was an Elementum – a race of people who were able to wield fire, water, or air, sometimes more than one – and a strong one at that. Flicking her wrist, Nora directed her wind magic ahead of the gibbon to slow the Anima down. They cried out in frustration as she gained on them, her Elementum gift giving her the advantage. She summoned a few orbs of fire the size of marbles and shot them at the gibbon, singeing their fur and causing them to stumble. She wanted to question the Anima, after all, not kill them. Nora took the opportunity and lunged for the gibbon, catching hold of the Anima's leg, and yanking the Anima firmly to her chest. Swinging her arms around the gibbon to restrain them, the Anima flailed their arms and legs before biting her hard on the forearm.

Nora growled, summoning the air from the gibbon's lungs. Their jaw slackened, and she groaned as pain fired up her arm. Blood dripped from the bite wound, the gibbon's teeth having sunk deep into the flesh. The gibbon shifted, revealing a petite woman with plaited white-grey hair and a button nose, gasping for air in Nora's arms.

Nora flipped the woman over, straddling her and pinning her wrists against the tiles near her head. Nora eased her wind magic, allowing air to return to the woman's lungs. The woman gasped in quick succession, her blue eyes darting around wildly.

"Who are you?" Nora demanded, leaning over the Anima.

"No one important," the woman replied, looking up into Nora's eyes.

"You were in the alley," Nora growled. "Why?"

The woman flinched at the edge to Nora's tone. "Shortcut."

Nora scowled, crushing the woman's wrists against the roof tiles. "Don't play with me."

"I was observing you," the woman's voice came out rushed. "That's all. I swear."

"Why?"

"I was told to," the woman bit her lip, her eyes glistening.

"By whom?" Nora was quickly tiring of this woman and her evasiveness. As much as she appeared to be frightened, she was making Nora fight for each answer.

"I don't know," whimpered the woman. "Please, let me go."

Nora summoned her wind magic once more, using it to restrain the woman's arms so that she could retrieve one of her daggers. Sitting back, Nora toyed with the weapon, a gleam in her brown eyes. The woman shivered beneath her, watching Nora intently. With the power of her wind, Nora summoned one of the woman's wrists towards her and gripped it tightly in her hand.

"Let's see if *you* like to have your arm punctured by pointy things," Nora smirked devilishly.

Before a reply could be uttered, Nora forced the tip of the blade into the woman's forearm. Crying out, she thrashed against Nora's hold, but

Nora just summoned more magic to keep the woman still.

Nora removed the blade then drove it in again, this time slower, drawing out the pain. Blood dripped onto the woman's heaving chest, staining the lilac shirt. Nora's lips pressed in a firm line as she waited.

"I don't get a name," the woman sobbed. "I've never even seen who writes the letters."

"Letters?" Nora withdrew her dagger but kept it poised above the woman's wrist, ready to strike.

"I get letters telling me what to do," the woman explained through her gasps.

"Show me," Nora demanded.

"I don't have them." The woman's eyes went wide, her voice panicked. "I'm told to burn the letters after reading them."

"Fine," Nora growled, stabbing the point of the dagger into flesh once more and giving it a wriggle for good measure. Nora watched as a strangled cry spilled from the woman's lips, then withdrew the blade. "You're going to give me a list of names and descriptions of the people you know are involved."

"I don't know anyone," the woman claimed, tears falling down her cheeks. "I swear. I was told to watch and wait for further instructions."

Nora shrugged, unmoved by the tears that tumbled down the woman's face. Using her wind magic, she restrained the woman's arm once again to the roof tiles then positioned her dagger against the woman's shoulder, slicing through the fabric and exposing the golden skin beneath. The woman flinched as Nora lined up the dagger.

"Well, you haven't been very helpful," Nora deadpanned. "I'm going to remove your arm now."

"Wait!" begged the woman before Nora could drive her dagger forward to make a more permanent cut. "Kaldom."

"What about it?" Nora growled in irritation, her fingers twitching on her weapon.

"That's where the letters come from. That's all I know. Please," the woman begged. "Please, let me go."

Nora stared intently down at the woman, deciding whether she should let her keep her arm, let alone live. Apparently, she was feeling generous today. She slowly dragged her blade along the woman's arm, spilling blood onto the already red tiles.

"Don't seek a Lys Alv," Nora commanded as she stood, towering over the woman, and casting a dark shadow. "I want you to remember me."

The woman whimpered, unable to move against the wind magic Nora still held against her, but Nora took it as a sign she'd cooperate. Lys Alvs were skilled healers, with pointed ears and golden eyes, and the ability to take on the injuries of others. Without the help of a Lys Alv, the woman would have to heal naturally, which would be painful and result in a scar.

"If you ever follow the instructions of one of those letters again," Nora said, her brown eyes alight with a threatening violence, "I will find you and kill you."

The woman trembled, biting her lip.

With a scowl, Nora strode away, releasing her magic from the woman once she was out of sight. She needed to find August, tell him what she had learnt and discover if the blacksmith or the alley had provided any further information.

Climbing down from the roof, Nora hissed through gritted teeth at the pain in her arm. As far as she could see, the damage was not too bad, but the punctures from the bite hurt like   it  . She tore a strip from her shirt and wrapped her forearm in the fabric. Her sleek black uniform was now on display around her midriff, not that any passer-by would recognise it.

Once wrapped in her makeshift bandage, she kept her arm still, the throbbing pain heightening every time she jostled the limb. She would need to see a Lys Alv for healing soon.

Making her way back to the castle, Nora moved through the orderly streets full of civilians going about their business. Royal Bay was always busy; the city never sleeping. Even at night, there was always something happening that drew the people from their homes and into the street.

Nora hoped that August had found a better lead than the one she had uncovered. The idea of going to Kaldom irked her. The city was far north and suffered from a perpetual Frost Season. It was a miserable place with a low population because who in the Goddess Thyra's name would want to live there?

Nora held her arm to her chest and wove through the crowd, veering left from the main road towards a path she had regularly trodden. It took her through darkened side alleys that snaked between the mansions of the elite district before spitting her out under the bridge connecting the mainland to a small island in the bay. The island housed the castle, a barracks for a special regiment of the Royal Sentries, The Makers' Temple, and the hidden location Nora was heading: The Alta Quarters.

Above her, Royal Sentries stood in silver armour that glistened in the sunlight. These guards were not like those of the standard Royal Sentries; they had proven their loyalty and were an honoured group, cherished by civilians, but even they did not know who the Alta were. According to the general population, the Alta did not exist in Valmenessia.

She took the hidden tunnel under the bridge, jogging through the wet, murky passage that eventually stopped at a thick door. Unwrapping her arm, she pressed the bite up against the cold stone, the magic in her blood unlocking the door, and pushed through to the Alta Quarters. Sealing the passage, she trudged downstairs to find August in their room. He lay on his bed, a muscular arm slung over his eyes.

"Where did you end up?" he asked as she sat on her bed, the mattress creaking from her weight.

"Chasing a lead," she replied sarcastically. "Literally."

"And?" August prodded, unbothered by her tone.

"And apparently the little rebellion are more organised than we anticipated. They receive letters of their orders from Kaldom, which they burn. The Anima I chased down swore she didn't know anyone else in Royal Bay, which leads me to believe she is fairly low on the ladder," she huffed, scrunching her nose. "So, we can either try and find out who's standing on a higher rung in Royal Bay, or we go to Kaldom and see who's at the top. But, I really hope you have something better to go on because I do *not* want to go there."

August sat up, his gaze snagging on her arm. He frowned in concern. "What happened to you?"

"I was bitten." She twisted her arm to show him the bloody bite mark.

"You should see a Lys Alv," he said, his lips tugging up at one side once it was obvious her injury was only a flesh wound.

"Oh really? I never thought of that." Nora rolled her eyes and wrapped the makeshift bandage back around her arm. "I will once you tell me whether you have something better to go on."

"I wish I could say yes, but unfortunately the blacksmith had nothing more to say once you'd left." He dragged a hand through his chin-length, dirty blond hair. "Looks like we're going to Kaldom as soon as you've been healed."

That was definitely not what she wanted to hear. Groaning, Nora stood to find a Healer. "I fucking hate the cold."

2

## Nora

Fastening her pack to the mare's saddle, Nora slipped the leather strap through the buckle, pulling it tight, then stepped on the stone block and lifted herself on the horse. She ran her fingers gently through its mane, the brown hair silky in her hand, before gripping the reins and nudging the horse out of the stable.

"Cheater!" August called from where he stood with his own horse, feeding the animal a carrot whilst his free hand rubbed the horse's neck.

Nora smirked and urged the mare to run through the gate and out into the bustling street without looking behind her. She wanted to beat August, and if getting a head start helped her do that then why shouldn't she take every advantage she could? If there was one thing she'd learnt from life, it was that it was never fair.

Racing up the street, she directed her horse northwards, weaving deftly around the people and other obstacles in her path. Nora's horse moved with precision as she sped on, putting more distance between her and August. The sound of cheering echoed around Nora, and she slowed her horse to a trot to see an excited crowd lingering around the fountain, blocking the intersection. The people were completely distracted by the woman who stood on the raised stones before them, shouting her interpretations of what the stories of the Gods and Goddesses meant.

There were five Gods and Goddesses in Valmenessia. Frode, the God of Wisdom and Perseverance; Thyra, Goddess of Nature and the Elements; Aren, God of Stewardship and Creatures, and the twins; Jord, Goddess of Balance, Truth and Passing; and Nyssa, Goddess of Mercy, Healing and Help. Each deity represented the five races of Valmenessia: Human, Elementum, Anima, Mors Alv and Lys Alv respectively. Their stories and teachings were always being used to either enlighten or manipulate.

Shit.

Nora's eyes darted around, and she chewed her lip; she needed to keep moving if she was going to stay ahead of August. She didn't know what the woman's intentions were behind her proclamations, not that Nora was waiting around to find out. Nora took a turn onto a narrow walkway, much to the protest of the current occupants, then pushed her mare onwards and up a set of narrow paved steps before reaching another main road. The little detour was costing her time. She could hear August and his horse gaining ground, the sound of hoofbeats coming from behind her.

"Come on," she whispered to the seal brown mare, leaning forward in the saddle. "Run, beautiful, run."

The mare took off, speeding through the street alongside the startled cries of those she passed by. Buildings became more spread out and paved paths turned to compressed dirt as she raced on. She was determined to make it to the city boundary before August. The competition was their thing; every time they had been sent on missions outside of Royal Bay, they would race to the edge of the city, and whoever was last owed the other a favour—something Nora did not want to give to August.

A loud neighing came from behind and Nora glanced back to see August pulling his horse's reins hard to avoid a collision with a man carrying a crate of green fruit. The horse reared back, snorting in irritation as August struggled to maintain control. August mustn't have seen the man with his hood drawn—a happy side-effect of his necessary fashion choice.

Nora chuckled over her shoulder, guiding her horse away without slowing. There was no way he would catch her now.

Ahead of her, the towering walls marking the entrance to Royal Bay grew taller with each gallop. Royal Sentries patrolled atop the stone barrier, pacing up and down its line with swords resting on their hips and bows strapped to their backs. Unlike the silver-armoured sentries guarding the castle, these men and women wore a plain grey uniform with the king's crest over their chests.

The gates to Royal Bay were wide open, providing a view of the vibrant green land beyond. It was a stark contrast to the yellow stone city she was about to leave in her haste. She eyed the exit, the wind blowing through her hair as she grinned at the victory mere seconds from her grasp.

"Nice try!" August shouted, racing past her. Dirt kicked up into her face as he pushed ahead, and she growled at his back.

"No!" she hissed through gritted teeth. "Come on, we can't let that asshole win!"

The mare sped up but there was no use, August rode through the gates before her, halting his horse in the grass beside the road, just beyond the Royal Sentries' line of sight. Nora slowed, swearing colourfully as she took her time to reach him. She hated listening to his gloating.

"You cheated and still lost," August tutted as she approached, pulling her horse up beside his. "What would Rana say of your shitty riding?"

"There is nothing wrong with how I ride," Nora scowled at him, his face concealed by his hood. "I just choose not to crush people in my path unlike you."

"I missed that guy," he protested, sounding genuinely concerned by almost colliding with the other man.

Nora pouted her lips. "If you say so."

"You're just a sore loser," he scoffed jokingly, setting off along the road. "And now you owe me a favour."

"What do you want," she sighed, riding beside him, and joining the flow of people leaving the city.

"Nothing," August said innocently.

"You forfeit your favour?" she asked, eyebrows raised. "That's strangely nice of you."

"No, I'm just saving it for later," he replied. "I like the idea of holding it over you."

Nora groaned, patting the mare. "See, girl, I told you he's an asshole."

"Don't listen to her, Nora is a terrible judge of character," August laughed, reaching over to stroke a hand down the mare's neck.

Slapping his hand away, Nora mumbled a profanity under her breath and turned her attention to the road ahead instead of her cocky travelling partner. She and August had been inseparable for the last fourteen years. Whether it was training or undertaking missions set out by Rana, it was always the two of them. Even though she hated when he won anything against her, there was no one else she would rather spend her time with, especially when she was commanded to travel from home.

Nora and August were journeying north towards Kaldom, much to her dismay. After consulting Rana about the events of the previous day and her run-in with the Anima, the leader of the Alta had agreed that venturing to the frozen city was the best plan they had from the minimal information they had obtained. It wasn't ideal and set Nora's nerves on edge. She hated not being confident in her direction, but what other avenue could they take? King Dominic wanted her and August to find Felix and so that was what they had to do.

Guiding their horses down the road, the sun shone overhead, persistent in its endeavour to provide warmth to those below, even though the clouds continued to try and block its glow. Passing through farmlands and rolling emerald fields, farmers laboured away tending to their crops, and smoke bloomed from the chimneys of stone cottages dotting the hillsides in small clusters. They stopped briefly in villages to rest, water their horses, and gather more supplies, but mostly kept to the road to lessen the gossip. Whether or not the general populace knew what an Alta was did not matter when travelling with August.

August was tall, muscular, carried a sword at his hip that gleamed in the sunlight, and wore his hood drawn, concealing his forbidden heritage. Both his appearance and his attitude turned him into a beacon of sorts. A dark, foreboding beacon. Staying in one place for a long period of time was not ideal while on the road. At least in Royal Bay there were so many unsavoury sorts that she and August could go unnoticed and even wear their uniforms in public. But on the road it was a different story. Townspeople tended to talk, and gossip was best avoided. So, they kept moving, stopping for as limited a time as possible. Even if August didn't draw attention, the urgency in the king's commands to find Felix made it hard for Nora to stand lingering.

The view was unchanging as the days wore on, until their approach to the city of Giland provided them with the only difference in surroundings since they first departed Royal Bay. Orchards ripe with colourful fruits stretched on as far as the eye could see, their growth spurred on by Elementum magic. Giland was known for its large population of Elementum, the city prospering on their citizens' gifts. How they managed to grow and store food here was almost an art, the craft passed down through generations and remaining somewhat of a mystery to outsiders. The industry kept Lord Gudrid swimming in coin, so he protected his people's secrets in turn.

Nora spotted a familiar cottage nestled amongst the orchards. Memories rushed into her mind before she could stop them, like an unexpected flood she had no time to prepare for. She bit her lip. Fire tearing up walls and blocking her path flashed through her mind as black smoke filled the space around her. Fear gripped her chest, squeezing it tightly until she could barely breathe. She was trapped. Cries of anguish rattled through her ears, adding to the consuming noise of the crackling flames, her heart beating all too quickly.

"Nora… anyone home?" August teased, waving his calloused hand in her face.

She blinked and shook her head, the vision immediately fading, and she smacked his hand out of the way before tugging on the reins and pulling her horse to a stop in the middle of the road. Grumbles sounded around her, but she ignored them, instead focusing all her attention on pushing the haunting memories from her mind.

A cool breeze caressed the sweat on the back of her neck, providing a welcome relief to the overwhelming heat that felt all too real once again.

"Nora?" August asked, his voice filled with concern as he turned his horse around and stopped beside her. He faced the direction they had come from so now they were almost eye to eye… if his weren't hidden in shadows that is.

"Yes! I was just thinking," she replied defensively, scowling at him.

"About?" he pushed.

"About… about whether we stay in Giland tonight or if it'd be better to keep moving," she lied. A white lie, but it *was* something she had wondered as they drew closer to the main city. "I'm craving a soft bed and warm meal, but the longer we take to get to Kaldom the less reliable our lead becomes. Going into the city adds unnecessary time to our journey."

August placed a hand on hers. "I think you worry too much. There's no point racing to Kaldom and being exhausted. Plus, what's one night in a nice comfy bed?"

"I'm sure we can find a village further on," she said, ignoring his question because a comfy bed did sound amazing to her.

"Maybe," he shrugged. "But why risk another night on the ground if a village isn't as close as you hope?" He moved closer, his hand squeezing hers. "I know why you don't want to stay here, but what are the chances you'll run into the man who pretended to be your father? He may not even be in Giland."

Seeing her imposter father was not the reason she didn't want to stay in Giland, but she'd never voiced the truth aloud and had no intentions of doing so in the future. Running into the man she'd called father was not something she wanted to do either. Mostly because she'd like to take her time punishing the man who lied to her; really enjoy their reunion. Alas, she had commands to follow, and the probability of him being in the city was slim anyway. He was most likely off scouring the country for something or someone else of value to sell to the king.

Nora sighed, her shoulders dropping. She was not completely sold on the idea of stopping in Giland, but if she pushed too hard to stay away August might ask her about her feelings, or worse, think her a coward. There was no way she'd stand for that.

"Fine," she grumbled.

"Say it," he ordered, practically bouncing in his seat.

"Say what?" she asked with an exaggerated sigh.

"You're right, August," he teased. "What would I ever do without you?"

"You're right, August, whatever would I do without you," she mimicked, her brown eyes aglow. "How else would I feel better about myself than having the constant daily reminder that it could be worse, and I could be an oaf like you?"

"You're unbelievable," he chuckled, shaking his head.

Her sickly-sweet smile was her only reply as they set off once more. Nearing the edge of the orchards, the canopy of trees thinned around them to reveal the city beyond. Long red-bricked buildings sat in rows and sentries patrolled the outskirts, wearing a mix of King Dominic's and Lord Gudrid's colours—grey coats marked with the king's crest and red pants for their lord. Lord Gudrid's crest was very similar to the king's, almost to the point that it was hard to differentiate the two if one didn't know what to look for.

Drawing closer to the city, the road grew busier. Anima in various forms moved through the crowd or flew overhead as Nora and August joined the people entering the city. Other than the few Lys Alvs Nora had spotted—their pointed ears and golden eyes distinguishing them from the other races—those traversing the road were seemingly either humans, Elementum, or Anima in their human form. Except, of course, for August... not that anyone would have been able to see the features of his race with his hood drawn. The other travellers gave them a wide berth because of his mere presence, opting to stare from afar and whisper with those nearby.

August tugged Nora's horse to the side of the busy street and rummaged through his pack, pulling out a few rolled-up pieces of paper. After reading the city names scrawled on them, he handed her the one titled Giland. She unfurled the hand-drawn map—one of many items they had taken before departing Royal Bay—and held it before her, getting her bearings. It was a magnificent map, and looking at it, she wondered if the cartographer would have made a living from his skill had he not been trained as a member of the Alta. It was a shame that cartography was not a skill the king valued.

The orderly city laid out before her had the expected streets and landmarks, the taverns, markets, and residential districts, but the map was also annotated with a key specifically for members of the Alta. Buildings were marked to show low-profile accommodations, safe houses where supplies could be found or items stashed, and locations of interest where information could be easily obtained, or allies called upon. Nora traced her finger over the inked paper and frowned.

"Give it here, you're terrible with maps," August teased, seizing the map from Nora. "I'll pick somewhere for us to stay."

"Then why did you give it to me in the first place?" She narrowed her eyes and flipped him off.

"It's fun to watch you get confused," he laughed.

"Ass," Nora ground out, following him as he set off down the road.

"I vote we stop at The Kindred Spirit for the night, get a warm meal and a bed," August announced, his focus ahead of him as he manoeuvred his horse through the streets.

"And what made you choose that place?" Nora asked, an eyebrow raised.

"It has a nice name and one of those fancy symbols scrawled on it," he replied over his shoulder.

They turned a corner and then another, and Nora felt a little like they were wandering in circles. The buildings were all uniform, the factories barely distinguishable from the shopfronts and residential homes of citizens. The larger windows, extra doors, or signage being the only features that told them apart. There was no way she'd be able to get back to the city gate without August's help if she wanted to avoid wandering around aimlessly for hours.

August stopped his horse abruptly, inclining his head towards a building to her left. "Hungry?"

She turned to see a magenta sign above one of the many doors of a long red-bricked building, The Kindred Spirit scrawled on it in elegant lettering.

"You could have just said we've arrived," she groaned dramatically, leaving him to take the horses to the adjoining stable as she strode towards the inn.

## 3

## Nora

Nora pushed open the stained wooden door—its newly painted surface slightly sticky to touch—and was embraced by a cosy warmth and the scent of roasting meats. Inside, she made her way to the burly man at the bar. He was tall and muscular with salt and pepper hair and a matching thinning beard.

"Welcome to The Kindred Spirit. What can I do for you?" he asked, leaning his elbows on the glossy oak bar.

"I would like a room for myself and a friend," Nora replied. "And dinner, too."

"I have one free room. Meals are served down here," the barkeep replied, returning his attention to wiping the bar with a well-worn rag.

"Are you sure there's nothing I can say to persuade you to eat in the room?" she asked, batting her eyelashes at him.

The man paused mid-wipe; his gaze swept over Nora's body. Nora clenched her teeth to stop herself from smirking as the barkeep shook his head almost regretfully. "I don't think so, but thank you. I am spoken for, and my wife would kill me if I so much as looked at another woman in that way, much less let one stay up here."

"I guess I'll take it," she blurted out, cheeks flushing a deep red.

"Ten silvers," he coughed, rubbing the bar a little more vigorously.

"Ten silvers? If you want that kind of coin you should be bringing my dinner to my room... Four," she countered.

"Eight."

"Five," Nora raised her brows and tilted her head.

The man scoffed. "Seven."

"Five," a grin spread on her face.

"Six."

"Done." Nora dropped the small pile of coins onto the bar at the same moment August strode inside the inn.

Nora and August squeezed their way through the crowded dining room towards an available table near the stone fireplace. She took the chair nestled in the corner—closest to the fire—the flames beckoning her Elementum magic. August sat opposite, stretching out his long legs and knocking into her own. She kicked him beneath the table, earning a groan from August.

"That wasn't very nice," he said, rubbing his leg.

"I'm not nice," she replied with a closed lipped smile.

At first, they received a few inquisitive looks from other patrons, but their gazes soon turned away either to gossip about who August was or to become more subtle in their staring. It was a better response compared to the one August would have received if he did not have his hood drawn.

Nora observed the several patrons in the dining room; a few were enjoying meals with some form of reading material or companion, and she found her stomach growling at the mouth-watering scent of roasted meat that wafted her way as a waiter walked by. A lanky boy who appeared slightly younger than herself reluctantly approached her table. His short curly brown hair looked in need of a good comb, the ringlets dangling across his eyes. He took their order, even though it was obvious he would rather have been anywhere else, his distant gaze making her feel certain that he wouldn't remember what she wanted. Once he had left, Nora and August sat in silence, listening to the gossip currently being passed around the nearby tables.

The conversations around them were of little interest: mundane daily tasks, business transactions and petty chatter. Nora spied one woman beside them who appeared to be talking to herself, only to glimpse a chipmunk scurry out of her bushy hair and onto the table. Whether the tiny animal was an Anima or whether the woman was simply talking to a pet rodent, Nora couldn't tell.

"Nothing of significance happening around here," August commented, sitting back in his chair, and folding his arms over his chest. "Giland's light on the gossip."

"Mmm," Nora pouted. "It's strange there is nothing of note. Even small towns usually have something exciting to talk about, but these people are as bland as a bowl full of flour."

August chuckled and Nora couldn't help but grin, the expression quickly fading as she tilted her head to the side. The conversation at the table in front was piquing her interest. The trio had only recently sat down and were now leaning in closely as they spoke.

"The poor child found her dead in a pool of blood. Throat slit and the Makers' Mark drawn in blood on her forehead," stated a slender man with a neatly trimmed moustache.

His companion's eyes widened as the man's skin paled. He was already rather white, so to pale further was a rather impressive feat. "Shit." He shook his bald head. "What a pity."

"Indeed," agreed a curvaceous woman, sitting back in her chair and frowning. "That poor boy will forever be traumatised by the sight of his mother like that."

Nora pictured the scene: a plain woman's face staring at the sky with the crimson Makers' Mark—a sun and moon surrounded by a large circle—the blood a stark contrast on her forehead compared to her grey skin. The Makers—Solari and Lunia—were the parents of the five Gods and Goddesses of Valmenessia yet were mostly a mystery to the people. There were no accounts nor stories about the Makers other than The Dawn, the tale of the Gods and Goddesses' births. The Makers' Temple in Royal Bay may have been named for them, but inside, the five Gods and Goddesses adorned the walls and were sought by the people. The Makers were not worshipped, nor were they prayed to, making the Makers' Murders even more strange.

"From what I've been told"—the slender man sat up, like a peacock on display— they haven't caught any suspects yet, but they believe it's multiple people committing these heinous crimes. This is the seventh case in Giland alone."

"I assume you've been speaking with your connection in Lord Gudrid's sentries? I bet the Anima are behind these attacks—multiple from what you're saying," said the pale man, tersely tapping a chubby finger on the table. "The Anima are out of control, even King Dominic knows that."

"I heard it's not the Anima, but the Mors Alvs," the woman said, leaning in further, her tone conspiratorial. "My neighbour mentioned seeing a man with eyes like the night skulking around in the dark. The Mors Alvs have come to punish us all for the deaths of their kin."

"But they have been extinct for two decades," argued the pale man. "After Queen Helen's death, King Dominic made sure to rid the continent of the Mors Alvs. And, even if there were a few who escaped the king's wrath, their magic enables them to steal health and magic from others, the strongest Alvs being able to kill with only a touch. Why would they bother violently stabbing people or cutting throats, not to mention the Marks?"

"To hide that it's them?" suggested the slender man, his hand resting on his chin as he ran a finger over his moustache. "Two of the seven murdered were Anima, and the Mors Alvs definitely have motive."

"They don't exist anymore in Valmenessia," grumbled the other man. "You both are being ridiculous even entertaining the idea. It was the Anima, mark my words."

A waitress appeared beside Nora carrying two pints of lager and two plates piled high with meat and vegetables balanced on her outstretched arm. "Roast lamb, my dears," she said by way of greeting as she placed their dinner and a key marked with the number four on the table.

Nora strained her ears to listen to the conversation at the next table. Unfortunately, the trio had moved on to more mundane topics. The woman had impeccable timing…

"Thanks," drawled August. "I don't think I've ever been called dear before."

The woman nodded, her kind smile thinning, wary of the dark

figure before her. Clasping her hands over her round stomach protectively, she quickly retreated to serve another guest.

Nora looked down at the roast lamb and breathed in its aroma, using her wind magic to guide the scented steam to her nose, making her mouth water. "Let's not get thrown out for frightening the staff," she said without looking up from her plate.

August protested half-heartedly. "She didn't see my face."

"A cloaked figure can still have the same effect."

"I'll be on my best behaviour from now on," he promised, then tilted his head towards the plate in front of him. "Smells delicious."

Nora grinned at what lay before her; it had been two days since her last warm meal and this one looked worth the wait. She ate the lamb, savouring the rich flavour of the meat that had been soaking in a rosemary and garlic gravy. Sighing with contentment, she began devouring her food more earnestly.

August chuckled. "Enjoying yourself?"

"Yes," she said, drawing out the word. "As a matter of fact, I am."

"So, Makers' Murders that sound a lot like those Rana briefed us on in Royal Bay," August commented, sticking his fork into a piece of roasted carrot.

"Enacted by the ghosts of vengeful Mors Alvs, murdering people in the name of their long dead kin," Nora added, taking a bite of her meat.

"Apparently," August replied, scratching his chin. "I didn't know the murders were occurring outside Royal Bay."

"Me either." She pursed her lips, tapping her fork on them in a steady rhythm. Rana was known to keep secrets. Nora didn't expect the leader of the Alta to tell them everything, but it would have been nice for the woman to give them a little more information every now and again. "Rana would have known about these murders happening in other cities and just didn't tell us. There is no way something like this would be occurring without her knowledge."

"Nothing gets past her," August agreed.

"Unfortunately, the trio's little conversation over there is useless," Nora said between mouthfuls.

"Not entirely," he said, "the Makers' Murders—"

"Are irrelevant to finding Felix," she interrupted. "Unless he was

31

murdered, which there is no evidence of, they are Rana's problem."

"And the Anima they spoke of? Should we look into them?" August asked.

"Why?" Nora scrunched her brow. "Both the Anima and Mors Alvs being suspected murderers doesn't have anything to do with Felix."

"They could…"

Nora shook her head. "Mors Alvs are not killing people and as for the Anima… their population is huge, it's like saying that everyone with brown hair is a suspect." She pouted her lips. "I think connecting the murders to Felix is a stretch."

August inclined his head stiffly then turned back to his meal before him, not pushing the idea any further which Nora was grateful for. She couldn't be bothered entertaining farfetched possibilities when the lead they were following to find Felix was already shaky at best.

They ate the rest of their dinners in comfortable silence, consuming their meals quickly. She could feel the strain from their days of travel ebbing from her shoulders, leaving her muscles as if drawn out by the food and the heat of the dining room.

"I needed that," Nora declared once she had scraped the last morsel of food from her plate and licked her fork. Leaning back in her chair, she patted her full stomach.

August laughed and downed the rest of his drink, placing the empty mug in front of him. "I don't know about you Nora, but I think it's time for bed."

He yawned and stretched his arms above his head before rising from his seat and collecting both their packs and the key for their room. Nora followed August out of the dining hall and past the sign hanging from the ceiling near the bar that pointed towards the accommodations. They walked upstairs and through a narrow corridor to a dark teal door with the number four painted near the top in similar script to the sign outside. The lock clicked and August turned the handle, gesturing for her to enter first.

"Not too bad," whistled Nora, stepping into the room and glancing around with her hands on her hips.

She had stayed in a few rented rooms but this one was among the nicest. For one, it appeared to be clean. Secondly, there was a bench with a mirror and pitcher of water, and, best of all, there was a fireplace. Kneeling next to it, she piled in some kindling from the tub provided before igniting a ball of flame in the stack of wood. It caught easily and she added a few bigger logs to the pile.

Nora turned towards the bed to find August spread out like a starfish on top of it, snoring softly. He had removed his travelling cloak and sword, having dumped them in a pile near the door along with their packs, but that was it. How he had always been able to fall asleep so quickly was beyond her. She and August had shared a room in the Alta quarters in Royal Bay since she was six, and she had become accustomed to drifting off to the sound of his breathing. They had never requested separate rooms at home, and even though Nora inquired about two rooms when they travelled, she was always content when they had to share. August's constant presence was a comfort to her, not that she would voice the thought aloud.

Nora retrieved her pack and searched through its contents for a well-worn shirt. She quickly undressed, the removal of her daggers slowing the process as she tried to limit her time exposed to the cold. Pulling her shirt on over her head, Nora frowned as she stared at her reflection in the mirror. Her long, wavy, chocolate-coloured hair drooped in what was originally a high ponytail, and her upturned dark brown eyes stared back at her—both features further emphasising her pale complexion. She ran a finger gently over the thin white scar on her right cheek, a constant reminder of the day her life had changed.

Turning side to side, she inspected her lean body. The sinewy muscles framing her figure were the kind that were formed after years of tough physical training, yet her shoulders sagged uncharacteristically. Even though they had stopped to rest each day, the constant travel was tiring. Padding over to the bed, she roughly shoved August over to one side, not caring if she woke him as she lifted the floral-patterned covers and climbed in. Nora shivered at the touch of the cool sheets on her bare legs, but luckily the fabric was soft, and it was not long before she gave in to sleep.

## Nora

Nora awoke with a start, nightmares chasing her from sleep, and she turned to see August still slumbering, drool forming a puddle on his pillow. She shuddered at the ache in her chest, her heart attempting to slow itself after her dreadful dreams. They were always the same; Nora standing in a blackened field, smoke billowing from the ashes as she shook uncontrollably in her drenched nightgown.

Palming her eyes, she shoved the images away. Minimal light crept in through the gaps in the curtains as Nora dragged herself from the cosiness of the bed. It was earlier than she would have liked to wake but the unwanted dream had left her alert and needing to move. She slipped on her uniform, the soft black fabric clinging to her skin and co[...] every inch of her body from her ankles and wrists to her ne[...] than providing free movement, Nora thought the uniform [...] useless. It did little to protect her from the weather, let [...] not to mention black was not the best colour for cam[...] felt that whoever designed it cared more about [...] body than anything else.

Retrieving her daggers from the tab[...] them to either side of her hips; their pre[...]

in case her magic somehow failed her, which was not something Nora felt was possible. She was confident in wielding her Elementum gifts.

Finally, she pulled on her civilian clothes—black slacks, navy blue shirt, knit sweater, and leather boots—over her uniform, then tore the blankets from the bed. August rolled, falling to the floor with a thud and swearing loudly.

"Time to wake up," Nora sang, folding her arms over her chest and looking down at him sprawled out on the floorboards. "Let's get moving."

"Have I ever told you how much I dislike you?" He grumbled, his voice husky as he gripped the bed to help him rise to his feet.

"Many times," she grinned. "And the more you say it the more I want to torture you. Now up, let's go!"

August grabbed his boots and sat on the edge of the bed. "What time is it? Why are we in a rush?"

"King Dominic wants us to find Felix," Nora stated matter-of-factly.

"Oh really?" August raised his brows. "I just thought he wanted us to go on a little holiday."

"You're so simple," she replied, waving off his sarcasm and collecting her pack. "Lucky you have me to help you."

"Fucking lucky indeed," he mumbled.

Nora stood by the door, tapping her foot impatiently. "Take your precious time why don't you?"

August flashed his middle finger then stood, running a hand through his hair, and collecting his belongings before following her out of the room.

"Everything okay? Are you still worried about seeing your fake father?" August asked, strapping his sword to his hip before shrugging on his cloak and pack as they walked downstairs. "Is that why we are leaving so early this morning? Goddess Jord knows I would have loved to sleep a little longer, but I'd let the early wake up go if you wanted to talk."

"No," Nora shook her head. "There's nothing to say so you'll have to hold a grudge. I just want to do as the king commanded. Every minute longer it takes to find Felix grinds at me. I don't know how it doesn't bother you."

"I'm special, remember?" August teased, nudging her playfully, his tone losing its note of concern.

They left The Kindred Spirit and August dragged her into the bakery opposite, the sweets displayed in the front window catching his eye. He ignored her protests about wasting precious time and how they could easily eat breakfast on the road.

"A large slice of every cake you have and a pot of tea for us to share," August told the waitress—a dainty tanned woman with golden eyes and pointed ears.

Nora raised her eyebrows at him as the waitress left their table. "And how is tasting all the cakes they have to offer a good idea for breakfast let alone a necessary use of the king's coin, may I ask?"

They did not receive a wage. Alta had no need for their own money as everything was supplied to them. When sent on missions, they were provided with a large sum of coin. Their shackle tattoos prohibited them from purchasing anything the king would deem unnecessary, so it was a safe bet that the money would be spent properly. At least, that should have been the case; August always seemed to be able to rationalise so many things that Nora would have thought impossible.

"Cake is food. I need food to live, and the king wants me alive," August replied smugly. "As for eating cake for breakfast, I believe you once told me cake was suitable for every meal."

Leaning back in her chair, Nora folded her arms and narrowed her eyes. Her tattoos felt like thorns pressed against her skin. At this point they were only mildly irritating— warning her about bending the rules—but they threatened of the pain they could cause if she continued down the wrong path. "You shouldn't do that… it's not right to manipulate the king's commands."

"I'm not manipulating anything," he said, unable to hide the subtle rub of his own wrists, clearly not as unaffected as he pretended to be. "His commands are open to interpretation."

"They're not and you know it. Plus, I believe I was talking about ice-cream." She smiled mischievously.

"How could I confuse the two?" August chuckled, one hand placed on his chest mockingly. "If it will put you at ease, I was thinking of doing the parade…"

The waitress approached, precariously balancing a large tray on one hand. Resting it on the edge of the table, she unloaded a serving plate with six generous slices of cake, a pot of tea, and two cups. "You two sure do have a sweet tooth."

"Have you ever heard of The Great Valmenessian Cake Parade?" August asked, cutting the corner of the chocolate cake with his fork.

"No, I haven't." The waitress slid the tray from the table and rested it between her hip and wrist. "Mind you, I haven't been working here long."

Perfect. Nora suppressed a wicked grin and scoffed, "It is only the most prestigious cake grading society in all the country." She inclined her head towards August. "So prestigious, in fact, that one judge must conceal their identity at all times in case of sabotage or bribery."

"Oh dear," gasped the waitress, golden eyes bulging.

"It is a perilous job, but someone must do it." August held his fork up at eye level as though scrutinising the cake wedged in its tines. "How else will the citizens of Valmenessia know where to experience the finest cake?"

"And not just anyone can do it," added Nora. She placed a hand on her chest as though swearing a vow. "There is a whole system."

"Yes," agreed August, nodding. "The system."

"The system?" the waitress asked, tilting her head to one side.

"You haven't heard of it?" Nora gasped, her brown eyes widening.

The waitress shook her head, chewing her bottom lip.

"Colour, texture, flavour, shape, scent…" listed Nora, lifting a finger at each descriptor.

"Don't forget moistness," said August.

"Ugh, I hate that word," groaned Nora dramatically, rolling her eyes as she helped herself to some apple cake.

"Hate it all you like, but it is one of the most important elements of the system," chided August, waggling a finger at her. "Do not get me started on the classic sponge!"

The waitress glanced at the piece of sponge cake she had served them, her fingers tight on the tray she held. "What's wrong with the classic sponge?"

"Obviously, the layers of sponge are split with cream, but do you put fresh strawberries or strawberry jam in between the layers?" asked Nora, pointing at the waitress with her fork.

"Clearly fresh!" declared August, waving his own fork theatrically, flicking crumbs of chocolate cake at Nora.

Nora stifled a laugh as well as the urge to splatter cake all over him in return. "Wrong! The answer is jam." She all but yelled, wiping herself down with her napkin then throwing it at him.

"But the cake is moist enough without adding jam," argued August, catching her napkin with his free hand. "No one wants a soggy cake."

"Oh dear, I'd best leave you to it then," declared the waitress, looking a little flustered as she interrupted their well-rehearsed rant. She pressed a hand to her neck and offered them a strained smile before leaving them to return to the service counter.

"Think she believed us?" August asked, grinning through a mouthful of sponge cake.

Nora's lips twitched up at the side. "We'll just have to wait and see whether we get a bill."

◇

Nora stirred her tea, her arms folded over her chest with only a finger moving to direct her wind magic. "Time to go."

"Fine," August groaned, chewing the last bite of cake, and dropping his fork to the plate. The metal clattered loudly as it hit the ceramic.

Nora downed the rest of her drink, donned her cloak, and collected her pack from the floor near her feet before following August outside. The golden-eyed waitress wished them farewell and refused to let them pay.

After having their cake filled breakfast, they decided to stop at the markets to collect supplies before leaving Giland. As they approached the market, the streets came to life with people and the scent of spiced foods, baked goods, and florals. The stalls were eclectic, selling everything from pastries and stews to trinkets and statues of the five deities, all owners hoping to lure in those strolling by. One woman, working at a stall selling weaponry, shifted into a cougar and bit down hard on a man's arm, demonstrating the strength of the armour for potential buyers.

Nora's eyes darted over the wares of what the other stalls had to offer—leatherbound books, colourful potions, and garments that glittered as they fluttered in a breeze summoned by Elementum stall owners—the scene catching her eye as August dragged her towards the stalls selling food.

Nora had been to markets before, but there was something about this one and the way the sellers went out of their way to catch the attention of the travellers. It was a spectacle as much as a marketplace.

"What do you want?" August asked her, stopping in front of a man selling baked goods.

"I'll get a couple of pastries and let's get some bread for later too," she said, eyeing the delicious looking spread before them. "We should also grab some fruit; I heard they grow Alv specialities here."

"You can't eat Alv food," August reminded her, putting the bundle of pastries and bread into his pack.

"I know," she frowned, thinking of the time she was dared to eat a fruit that looked like a purple apple but had the texture of an orange once she'd bitten into it. The endeavour had resulted in her being sent to a Lys Alv for healing after she was unable to stop herself from giggling for three hours.

They purchased a selection of non-Alv fruits and vegetables, but as they headed out of the market they found their way obstructed. A crowd had formed in the street, the atmosphere loaded with an intensity that had Nora alert and flexing her hands. Her wind magic danced at the tips of her fingers, ready to be let loose. She peered around those gathered to see three of Lord Gudrid's sentries dressed in their pressed grey coats and blood red slacks, arguing with a dishevelled looking man.

"I am not dangerous!" cried the man as he hunched over, the palms of his hands pressing together as he begged. "Please! I have never harmed anyone in my life!"

"Not my problem," replied the tallest of the sentries, turning his bulbous nose up at the man before him. "By the decree of His Majesty, King Dominic, for the safety of the citizens of Valmenessia, all Anima whose shifts are of a predatory nature are not permitted to live in large cities."

"But—but I have done nothing wrong! I rarely even utilise my shift!" The man implored desperately, kneeling on the ground.

Nora glanced at August; King Dominic had only recently signed the new law. Anima violence had steadily increased, so the king had moved swiftly, banning all threatening shifts rather than searching for the few.

"As well as residing in a high-density area," the sentry continued, pacing in front of the man, "you have failed to provide us with your registration papers."

"These laws are misguided," August murmured to her as the Anima was hauled away by the guards, his incessant pleading drowned out by the comments of the crowd now gossiping among each other. "First, Anima have to register themselves, and now they are being convicted for the crimes of others, purely based on race."

"Not everyone is being hauled away by the sentries," Nora said. She pointed to where the cougar from the market stood in the shadows of her stall. "It appears some are still free to roam Giland."

"So, the rules don't affect those with money," August stated, a tightness to his tone.

She refused to look him in the eyes. "If Lord Gudrid's sentries are being prejudiced in their arrests, that's on them. Not King Dominic."

"Last night you said we shouldn't look into the Anima link to the Makers' Murders because it would be like being suspicious of every brunette in the country," August said, "but now you're saying that the king's law marking all Anima as violent are good. How does that make any sense?"

"King Dominic is trying to protect the people of Valmenessia," Nora replied, narrowing her eyes. "I don't know why you are twisting all this into something it's not."

"Stop sticking your head in the sand," August scoffed.

Nora stormed off, not bothering to reply. They had no say in what they were to believe, and she liked it that way. King Dominic's word was golden and that was good enough for her. She urged the hollow feeling that had crept into her gut away. They followed the king's commands; it was not her place to think beyond that. Sure, there had been an increase in Anima arrests, but if that was what it took to keep order then so be it. They were the ones committing the crimes after all. Nora stretched her neck to each side and rolled her shoulders. King Dominic was just trying to protect his people.

They headed back towards The Kindred Spirit to collect their horses from the stable next door. Finding her mare in one of the stalls, Nora offered her horse a juicy red apple then mounted the animal before she and August went on their way.

As they rode through the streets Nora eyed a spotted leopard bounding along the rooftops. She opened her mouth to point out another Anima flaunting the king's new law to August, but the leopard disappeared before she could utter a word.

"Let's get out of here," she said instead, urging her mare to pick up the pace.

August's horse met her speed, and it wasn't long before the city of Giland was a speck in the distance.

## 5

## Nora

Nora was freezing her ass off atop her mare. Shivering, she folded her arms to her chest, jamming her leather-gloved fingers under her armpits. An iciness lingered under the tree canopy, uninhibited by the sunlight creeping through gaps between trees. The three layers of clothing she wore and the orb of flame she had summoned provided little protection from the winds whirling between the trunks. It had been almost two weeks since they set out to Kaldom—one week from Giland—and she missed her home in Royal Bay. Nora cursed the weather as they drew farther north; Frost Season was supposed to be at another month away at least, yet here the cold was already making itself known.

"Ready?" Nora called without turning. The crackling ball of fire floating around her burned with earnest as it attempted to chase away the chill. "I'm going to lose an extremity soon! I'm surprised you haven't lost that one with how long you're taking!"

August's laugh boomed behind her as she diverted a piece of breeze with her wind magic, directing it towards where he stood behind a tree. He swore and she grinned, stifling a snicker.

"When nature calls, you answer," August sm

appeared at her side, fixing his cloak over his broad shoulders, and climbing atop his horse.

Nora rolled her eyes. "Doesn't mean you have to have an in-depth conversation. Maybe stop drinking so much water."

"Okay, stop pissing, stop drinking..." he tapped each finger as though making a list. "Anything else? Stop eating? Maybe stop sleeping?"

"Sounds perfect. Add stop talking, too."

"You're so pleasant," he mocked. "I just love spending all my time with you."

"You *are* unusually lucky." She winked, setting off.

They were halfway to Kaldom, riding through the Grenblad Woods towards the city of Midskopas—the midway point between Royal Bay and the frozen northern town. They had stopped in the woods late the previous night to rest, choosing not to wake anyone in the village they had passed. Well, August had decided, and Nora had felt too tired to argue. She had regretted the decision to be so compliant when she had woken up cold and sore that morning.

"Give me the sketch of the alley," Nora said, wiggling her fingers at August.

He leant back and rummaged through his pack, pulling out the drawing he had made in Royal Bay and handing it to Nora. She had gone over the scene multiple times since they left their home city, always searching for something she may have missed and coming up short. Chewing the inside of her cheek, she inspected the drawing once more. Nothing new appeared as she stared at it; there was still the overturned alley, the leather merchant's shop on the right and the blacksmith on the left. She frowned at the charcoal sketch.

"I'm guessing nothing new has appeared magically before your eyes?" August joked, riding beside her.

"No," she sighed. "But I still feel like we are missing something."

She handed the sketch back to August as they neared the edge of the wood and joined those travelling along the main road. They were making good time. It took them half a day of riding but soon they drew closer to Midskopas, the road becoming busier. People appeared to be in lines, slowly trudging toward the city's entrance.

Nora frowned as she and August joined the queue. "I wonder what this is all about?"

"Is there some event on that we didn't know about?" August asked, glancing around at the mass of people.

"I think we should just go around the city," she suggested, turning her horse from the road. "This is going to take too long and there's no reason for us to go in there anyway."

"Wait," August grabbed her reins, halting her horse. "I'm calling in my favour."

"I was beginning to think you'd forgotten about that."

"You wish," he laughed.

Nora scrunched her nose. "So, you're wasting your favour on making me wait in line?"

"No, the favour is that you have to agree with me for the rest of the day," he said mischievously.

"That's not a favour, that's slavery," Nora rolled her eyes.

"Next time you should clarify the rules a little better," August said. "My first decision is that we go into the city."

"Ugh," she sighed, failing to hide her grin. "Why?"

"I've never been to Midskopas," he shrugged. "Can't we try to enjoy the trip to Kaldom? How could it hurt having a little fun on the way?"

Nora narrowed her eyes.

"Plus, I don't want to sleep on the ground again tonight," he added, rolling his shoulders.

She chewed her lip. They needed to find Felix, that was their number one priority, but...

"Fine," Nora sighed. She'd hated sleeping on the dirt too. "But we leave as soon as the sun comes up."

"Deal," August held out his hand and she shook it.

The line moved slowly, those walking practically dragging their feet, but time passed relatively quickly thanks to the entertainment from those around them. Some people had taken the opportunity to show off their wares and make a bit of coin, whilst others got into arguments. The more heated disagreements turning into fist fights. Eventually, Nora and August neared the front and were met by two vandalised stone pillars bordering the road, welcoming travellers to Midskopas. Nora angled her head to see wild cats carved into pillar tops staring down on those who passed by with narrowed eyes.

The felines represented Lord Akedale of Midskopas, who had been born into a long history of powerful feline Anima, with his own shift revealing a large black panther. The Akedales were a proud family who were known for boasting about the unbroken line of powerful male Anima heirs who became stronger and stronger with each generation. As part of her training, Nora had sometimes been stationed as a hidden guard to King Dominic. On occasions when Lord Akedale would visit the castle, his bragging had been insufferable. Luckily, she had never had to engage with the man. Nora had been delighted to hear that his son had shifted into a tabby cat and his daughter into a lioness.

"State your reason for entering the city," barked a sentry. He held his plump hand before the horses, bringing them to a halt.

Scrunching her nose at the man before her, Nora eyed his uniform. Steel grey fabric trimmed in black, with the king's crest—a three-pointed crown with a flame, droplet, and swirl over each tip—embroidered over his chest. Royal Sentries. King Dominic had a small contingent of his sentries in each city as a way of establishing his presence all over the country. However, unlike in Giland, here there seemed to be many more of the king's sentries than Lord Akedale's, in fact, the lord's sentries were nowhere to be seen.

Nora fought the urge to frown. She'd known entering the city was a bad idea.

"I'm here to visit my aunt. My father deemed the roads too unsavoury to travel alone so he hired that brute to escort me," she lied, rolling her eyes dramatically and jabbing her thumb in August's direction.

The sentry eyed her and August suspiciously. "Is that so? Off with the hood," he nodded towards August.

"Don't bother," Nora pouted. "There's nothing good to look at under there. He's not much of a conversationalist either. You'd think my father could hire a handsome knight to travel with me, but no. I get this grumpy man. Please, will you help limit my time in his company and let me pass?"

"Does your aunt have a name?" the sentry pressed.

"Veronica," Nora lied.

His jaw twitched. "Last name?"

Nora pursed her lips and tilted her head, twirling her fingers through her ponytail. "To be honest, I have no idea. She just married, you see, and my father sent me here to meet her new wife but for the life of me I can't remember her wife's last name." She peered at him through her lashes. "If you see my aunt, you won't tell her of my forgetfulness, will you?"

He huffed exasperatedly. "What is her address?"

"I have it here somewhere." She rummaged through her cloak pockets in search of the non-existent piece of paper with her made-up aunt's address.

She could hear the voices of disgruntled travellers behind them, upset about the delay due to her conversation with the sentry, but the stubborn man would not budge. Silently cursing August, she tried to decide how to get them out of this mess. The sentry was not going to let them in without fact checking her story, and she doubted he would let them walk away either. Stupid August and his stupid favour.

"I don't have all day." He gestured to five younger sentries behind him. "Take these two into custody until she can give you an address."

"Sir," said the one closest, pointing to the small crowd forming as a blush crept up his neck. "Is that really necessary? The line is getting quite long, and I highly doubt she is a threat."

The older sentry fisted the shirt of the younger man, drawing their faces closer. "How dare you question me," he growled, flecks of spit flying from his lips. He shoved the younger sentry away. "Take these two now!"

The sentry's blush deepened until it resembled a tomato skin. He nodded hurriedly as the four other sentries the man had called almost fell over each other as they rushed to take the reins of Nora and August's horses. She shot August a quick scowl then dismounted, allowing the sentries to escort them and the horses away.

Passing through the entrance and into the organised chaos of the city, Nora took stock of the Royal Sentry unit. There was so many of them, and as she glanced around she failed to find a single sentry of

Lord Akedale's.

As they were escorted further into the city, Nora took stock of where they were. The architectural style of the buildings in Midskopas were in some ways like their home in Royal Bay, yet the colour tones were a contrast. Where the buildings in Royal Bay were predominately pale-yellow sandstone with reddish brown terracotta tiled roofs, the buildings in Midskopas were made of dark blue stone and the roofs were tiled in charcoal grey. Nora was surprised by the lack of general upkeep of the city given Lord Akedale's pride. Midskopas smelled of sweat, decay and cinders. Many of the buildings were vandalised or in need of repair, and a few seemed abandoned, which was odd considering how busy the city was.

The streets were not paved like Royal Bay. Instead, the horses trod upon crushed rock. Nora could not imagine it being ideal when it rained, and she doubted the gravel would do much to prevent the streets turning to mud. Perhaps that was why there were a multitude of wooden bridges hanging over the streets, joining one roof to another. An alternate way to travel when it rained? She doubted the prospect of walking twenty or so feet in the air during a storm would be preferable.

A spotted leopard stalked precariously along the edge of the roof to her right before stepping onto a bridge, swaying ever so slightly with its movement as it stared down at those walking below. Their eyes met—the leopard's a cloudy grey—and Nora held its stare before it turned and leapt away. She could have sworn she'd seen the Anima before…

"Your idea is off to a terrible start," Nora whispered to August, her side brushing up against his as they walked. "How do you suppose we get out of this without causing a scene?"

"Yellow snow?"

"That's not subtle or quick," Nora rebuked. "What race are they?"

August lifted his hand slightly and she could sense his magic moving through the air, like an invisible coil of smoke.

"Humans," he said after a moment, lowering his hand. "All five."

"Hmmm," she bit her lip and kept her voice low. "I'm not doing yellow snow. It's immature and unlike you, I have some semblance of class."

August barked a laugh, earning a glance from the sentries

surrounding them. "Fine. Unrequited love it is."

Nora smirked, focusing on the sentry closest to her, specifically the blood flowing in his veins. Manipulating fluids within a person was difficult magic, something she had spent years training for. It took a lot of her power, and she would need to let her Elementum gifts have time to recover. Nora wouldn't usually use her gifts for something so tasking, but as she had to agree with August for the rest of the day...

Drawing on her magic, Nora scrunched her brow, urging the blood in the sentry's veins to race.

"Ahh," groaned the sentry, stumbling as he clutched his chest.

"Are you alright?" asked one of the other sentries, as she placed a hand on his back.

Before the man could reply, Nora clenched her fist, calling his blood to his heart and flooding the organ. With a strangled cry, he dropped to his knees, his face twisted and glistening with sweet. His hand gripped his shirt tightly and he let out a final gasp before falling face first onto the ground. Just like an unrequited love that had one's pulse racing, the man's heart eventually broke.

"He's dead!" called the woman as she leant over his still body, her fingers pressed to his neck.

As another sentry moved to inspect the fallen man, Nora took the opportunity and pushed her magic forcefully into him. The sentry dropped to the ground, crying out in a twist of pain as his heart gave out too. Behind Nora, August spun, knocking out the other two sentries with expertly aimed hits to the head before either could blink. August had always moved crazily quick, something that surprised many given his size.

"Stop!" shouted the woman. The last sentry stood beside her fallen companions and slowly drew her sword, pointing it towards Nora. Citizens passing on the street hastily scurried away at the commotion with their heads downcast. "Don't move."

"Or what?" Nora scoffed, summoning the last of her magic.

With a flick of her wrist she threw a gust of wind at the woman, tossing the sentry against the nearest wall. With a sickening crack, the woman's head hit the stone before she crumpled to the floor where she lay motionless. Without hesitation, Nora and August moved swiftly, dragging the five sentries into a darkened alley.

"What now?" Nora asked, looking down at the sentries resting against the wall. It looked as though they had all simply fallen asleep if one didn't take into consideration the blood trickling down a few of their faces or the way two of them were eerily still.

"We need to get out of the city before these guys are found," August said, leading her back towards their horses. The two animals stood alone in the street, sniffing the ground for scraps.

"No shit," Nora scoffed, gathering the reins of her mare. Rather than climbing onto the animals, they proceeded on foot, guiding their horses down side streets and away from the sentries. "Still happy to call all the shots?"

"Yes," he flashed her a grin. "I like being in charge."

Nora rolled her eyes. "And you're doing such a fine job."

## 6

**Nora**

Tiles creaking beneath her feet, Nora surveyed the Royal Sentries stationed at the city walls before turning towards August, who was leaning against a stone chimney. They had left their horses at the first stable they passed and had been making their way along the rooftops around the edges of the city, scoping out possible exits.

"We won't be able to leave without being stopped and questioned" Nora said, a frown creasing her brow. "It looks like the Royal Sentries are posted all along the perimeter, not just at the gates."

"You're not usually one to turn away from a chance to show your skills." August teased. "You could incapacitate a few with a hand tied behind your back as you demonstrated a couple of hours ago.

Nora crept in his direction, using her wind magic to carefully placing her weight evenly on the tiles. "Without unrequited love took difficult magic. I'd have to wield and that's messy. Rana didn't want a big sc Dominic be pleased if I killed a bunch of his easily be forgiven, but I'm not keen on alternative."

"So, we lay low for a while,"

neck then looked to the sky. "Looks like it will rain soon. We could investigate some of the markings on the city map. Find shelter and someone to aid us that we can trust."

"I know just the person," came a male voice from behind Nora.

She turned to see a tall man with coffee hair and pointed features climbing onto the roof. The man looked only a few years older than her, his light blue eyes the colour of a cloudy sky, dancing with a confidence only youth could give.

"And what gave you the impression we wanted your opinion?" Nora asked, staring up at him as he moved closer.

He towered over her, yet his lanky appearance held very little threat. Not that she would have felt intimidated if he were broad and muscular either. August straightened but didn't move any closer, watching the interaction from over her shoulder.

"This," he replied. He undid the first few buttons of his shirt to reveal a smooth chest marked with the tattoo of the King's Guild. A three-pointed crown with a flame, droplet, and swirl hovering over its tips rested on his pale skin. The mark of the King's Guild was inked willingly to the king's most devoted followers. Unlike the Alta tattoos, the Guild tattoo held no magic and was purely a symbol of allegiance.

Nora ran her scrutinising gaze up and down the man before her. "What makes you think we want help from the guild? You barely look strong enough to hold yourself up against a gust of wind."

The man raised a thumb to the corner of his mouth, partially hiding his smirk. "My boss sent me."

"Who is your boss?" August queried from behind, his voice carrying an edge. "And who are you for that matter?"

"I'm Logan," the man replied, offering his hand which neither Nora nor August took. He dropped it awkwardly then stuffed it into his jacket pocket. "As for my boss, I'll take you to him and he will fill you in on all those details."

"We aren't blindly following you," Nora scoffed, rolling her eyes.

"He's at the Wandering Moon," Logan said with a shrug. "It's a gambling house in the east of the city. My offer to take you was purely a polite gesture. I know you're new to the city but if you'd prefer to make your own way there then so be it."

"We'll go with you," August stated, stepping to Nora's side, and looking down at her.

She could see his expression under the hood, his mischievous grin halting her from objecting. She knew exactly why he wanted to go with Logan. Though he was going to be extremely uncomfortable if he couldn't rationalise his actions in that head of his. If something wasn't beneficial to the king then August's shackle tattoos would definitely let him know about it. Folding her arms over her chest, Nora pouted her lips and turned away from him. She may have to agree with August because of the stupid favour but that didn't mean she had to pretend to be happy about it.

"Do you play cards?" Logan asked, leading them off the roof.

"Occasionally," August replied casually. "What's the buy in?"

"Three silvers," Logan replied, grinning.

"August," Nora warned when they reached the ground. She pointed a finger at him, jabbing his firm chest with her nail. Her wrists already began to itch in irritation, knowing her intent. "Bad idea. It's not your money."

"No idea I have today is a bad one," he teased, striding after Logan.

The man led them east as the sun made its descent, to an area of the city that buzzed with an excited energy. Loud music bled onto the street, the melodies blending and altering with each building they passed. Unsavoury sorts mixed with wide-eyed victims looking for a taste in what the night had to offer as they ventured through doors guarded by unfriendly characters or partially-dressed attractions.

"What are your names anyway?" Logan asked, inclining his head in greeting to a burly man ahead of them. He was as broad as the door he was manning, and the meaty hands clasped before him looked big enough to crush Nora's head in a single fist.

"August and she's Nora," August replied, following Logan through the doorway as the man stepped aside, sneering at them, and showing a silver tooth.

Inside the dimly lit gambling house, Nora's nose was assaulted with the scent of sweat and tobacco. Patrons packed around tables piled high with coins, either playing cards or rolling dice, whilst some waved their drinks as they cheered their winnings and added to the already sticky floor. Smoke lingered along the ceiling, the clouds constantly growing larger with every puff from those smoking below.

A trio of Lys Alvs were playing instruments in the far corner, their lively rhythm attracting dancers to congregate in the limited space before them. A woman attempting to move through the mass of people caught Nora's eye. Shoving those around her, the woman eventually gave up trying to squeeze through the bodies and shifted into a tiny grey hummingbird before flying over the heads of those in her way and straight out the door.

Nora felt someone take her hand and found August tugging her along. She hadn't realised she'd stopped moving and quickly snatched her hand free. Following him, they wove through the groups of people gathered around tables. Inquisitive gazes took in their arrival, lingering on August for the most part, before turning back to their games. Logan passed the busy bar to a closed door to the left. Knocking on the wood, he slipped inside momentarily before reappearing and opening the door wide enough for Nora and August to enter. She and August stepped into the room then Logan shut the door without following them through.

A man stood on the other side of a large desk, his hands braced on the wood as he focused on whatever was laid out before him. He wore no shirt, his scarred muscular chest on display to all, as well as the King's Guild tattoo that took up the entirety of his right pectoral.

Nora crossed her arms over her chest and narrowed her eyes in suspicion as August loomed behind her, his hood still drawn.

"You wanted to speak with us," she said by way of greeting, her smile not reaching her eyes.

The man tilted his head up, taking the cigar from between his teeth and giving Nora a full view of his face. His dark green eyes were wrinkled at the corners and his bushy brows gave him a permanent look of displeasure. At a guess, he was at least twice her age, maybe closer to triple.

"I was starting to think Logan had failed to pass on my message," he said, not wasting time with pleasantries. "Take a seat."

They didn't move an inch.

"Who are you?" she asked irritably. Who the fuck did he think he was ordering her around?

"My name is Sebastian," the man said, resting his cigar on a decorative glass ashtray. "And I believe we are both in a position to benefit one another."

Nora raised a brow. "I'm not sure what you have in mind, but I, for one, will not be getting into any positions with you."

Behind her, August's voice was as hard as steel. "Why are we here?"

Sebastian didn't flinch, his expression still fixed in what looked like a mixture of displeasure and egotism. "The King's Guild is a network. We monitor his majesty's assets."

"And what assets are we?" Nora queried, playing innocent.

Sebastian rubbed his chin. His trimmed grey beard was the same colour as the hairs that were thinning on the top of his head. "You're Alta."

"A what?" She scrunched her brows and frowned.

"Alta," Sebastian repeated gruffly.

Nora shook her head innocently. "Never heard of it."

Sebastian waved a scarred finger at her. "I have been a King's Guild member for longer than you have been alive."

"Congratulations," Nora said as though praising a child.

Sebastian growled, slamming a fist onto his desk. "Don't patronise me, girl. The King's Guild is the most devoted and prestigious of all of King Dominic's servants."

Nora raised a brow, unperturbed by his outburst. King Dominic had many layers to his defence, but it seemed Sebastian was a little confused. The King's Guild were the dogs at the bottom, happy to oblige whenever their king whistled. Basically, extremists who held no real power or responsibility. Then there were the Royal Sentries who guarded the king and his property and enforced the law. They may have not been Nora's favourite people but at least they followed commands rather than obscure interpretations of the king's word the guild members mostly believed.

Lastly, there was the Alta. Nora smirked. They were at the top.

"I know enough about my king to know an Alta when I see one," Sebastian continued. He stared her down, his gaze only flicking momentarily to August before focusing back on her. "I've been doing this a long time."

Nora sneered at him then lifted her sleeve to reveal the intricate loops that were inked on her skin like a chain wrapped around her wrist. A matching tattoo circled her other wrist, both marking her as one of King Dominic's possessions. The tattoo was darker than the one inked to Sebastian's chest; a sign of the magic preventing it from fading away. Nora had mixed feelings about the tattoos. The shackles limited her free will, but at the same time, they signified her membership to the Alta. Only a limited number of people knew of the Alta's existence, and Sebastian must have been high up in the King's Guild to be one of them.

Nora covered her wrists and took a seat opposite the man.

"And him?" Sebastian asked, nodding to August.

"He's with me," she replied simply, resting back in the chair, and folding her arms over her chest.

"If he won't show his tattoos then he can at least reveal his face," Sebastian insisted. "A show of good faith."

"Unfortunately, that can't happen as he's grotesquely disfigured," Nora replied, pursing her lips. "What do you want?"

Sebastian looked across at August, his eyes squinting to see under the hood. She knew he doubted her, but she couldn't care less. If Sebastian knew about the Alta then he also knew that she outranked him. Sebastian had to listen to her, even if he did not have faith in her lies. It was his duty.

"What do you want?" Nora repeated, picking at the dirt beneath her nails.

Sebastian dropped into the seat opposite her, leaning back and crossing his legs. "I have sworn to serve my king and, therefore, serve you. I wish to offer assistance, and in return, you will speak of my support."

"Looking to venture above your station?" Nora questioned, looking up at him through her lashes. The hidden intention in his words was not as concealed as he may have hoped.

The man scowled. "Difficult times lie ahead. I wish to demonstrate not only my devotion, but my value to the king. You are in Midskopas for a reason, and I have resources here."

Nora sighed impatiently, stuffing her hands into her cloak pockets.

"No."

"What?" he reared back as though she had slapped him.

"I said no." She stood. "We don't need nor want your assistance. We are leaving the city. If you want the king to pet you on the head like the loyal dog you are, find another way."

"If you are leaving, then you do need me," Sebastian snarled, rising to his feet as well. "You won't be able to leave the city without my help. You attacked a group of Royal Sentries. They don't know who you are to King Dominic. They will be out for your blood."

August stepped to Nora's side, his voice low and the threat clear in his tone. "I don't think you fully understand who *we* are."

"I do," Sebastian shot back angrily, yet his step away from August showed his fear. "I'm not the only one who's been watching you. The Alta may be a secret, but others are interested in your movements, even if they don't know who you truly are."

Nora was mentally kicking herself. They should have been stealthier when entering the city or avoided the place altogether. It was a careless mistake. All because of August's stupid favour. She should not have listened to him.

"You can attempt it on your own," Sebastian continued. "It won't just be the Royal Sentries you'll have to avoid. There are a lot of them, but at least they wear uniforms."

"Who else would want to stop us?" Nora shot him a glare and the image of a spotted leopard leapt into her mind.

"Who knows, but this city has become a hostile place," Sebastian sneered. "If I heard that story you gave the Royal Sentries about being here to visit an aunt and having a father with enough coin to send you with an escort, others did too."

"And you think someone would be looking to kidnap me for ransom?" Nora chuckled. "I thought you were trying to convince us that you weren't an idiot."

Sebastian scowled, gritting his teeth. "I can get you out without anyone noticing or you can do it on your own. Feel free to cause a commotion. I'm sure King Dominic will be pleased to have his secret soldiers known to the whole country."

Nora clenched her fists in her pockets. She could feel the little amount of her magic she had left rising to the tips of her fingers, wanting to escape and ignite the man before her. He was infuriating at best, but the worst part was that he had a point.

"We leave at first light and go north," August announced. "You get us out of the city without being noticed, and we will hold up our side of the deal."

"Very well," replied Sebastian, taking August's word before Nora could argue. He rose from his seat and Nora felt the urge to dive across the table and swipe the arrogant smirk right off his face. Sebastian gestured to the door, a clear dismissal. "Logan will find you accommodations and I will see you both first thing in the morning."

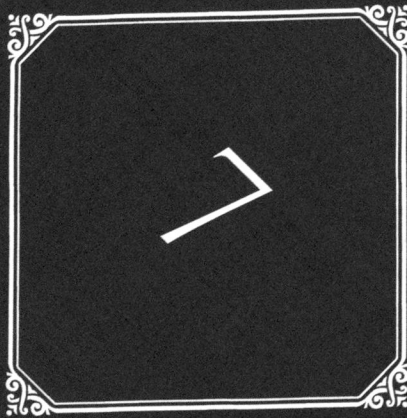

## 7

**Nora**

"So, why the hood?" Log...

lively room to a table...

They had dropped...

keeping only their coin...

"Vanity," Nora...

deserves to lay e...

Logan gri...

Augus...

aske...

"W...

Nora gestured with the glass before taking a sip of the fragrant crimson liquid and turning her gaze back to the table.

"I'm Grayson," the man with copper hair declared, shuffling a deck of cards. "Three silver buy-in, winner takes all."

Everyone at the table tossed their coins into the centre, all except Nora.

"Pay up," Grayson insisted, inclining his head to the silver pile.

"I'm not playing," Nora replied, sipping her drink, the wine not as sweet as she was used to.

"Then give back the wine and vacate the chair for someone who will," he said dismissively.

Nora spat her mouthful back into the glass and slid it towards Grayson, earning a chuckle from the stranger beside her.

"Here," August tossed three coins onto the table. "She'll play."

Nora ground her teeth. This was not what the king's money was supposed to be used for.

"Just relax and play," August whispered, angling his head to hers as the cards were dealt. "We have nothing else to do till morning."

"Fine," she grumbled, picking up her cards and eyeing her luck. She tried to ignore the prickling sensation that was growing more intense beneath her tattoos because of her disobedience. She quickly glanced at August noticing that he was either completely unaffected or was hiding his discomfort well.

A clap of thunder that rumbled through the room followed a flash of light, as Nora looked down at her hand. She chewed her bottom lip. Her cards were shit, just like the weather was about to become.

"What brings you to The Wandering Moon this evening?" asked the woman opposite Nora. She was petite with prominent cheekbones and large brown eyes that dragged over August and Nora, clearly analysing them. She wore a long-sleeved white shirt with suspenders, the buttons over her chest open to give a glimpse of the tops of her dark breasts.

"Passing through," August replied, his pointer finger tapping subtly on the table, signalling to Nora that the woman was an Anima.

Each finger on August's right hand represented one of the five races, and when he couldn't voice his deductions to Nora he would signal to her. The thumb was human, the pointer was Anima, then the last three were Elementum, Lys Alv and Mors Alv respectively. Not that they ever utilised his smallest finger.

Nora turned her gaze to Grayson, then slid her eyes to August's hand once more. His middle finger twitched slightly. With Logan at the table, that meant they were sitting with at least two Elementums. Her eyes raked over the last four people amongst them; three sat with their true expressions hidden behind composed masks as they watched the game unfold. The fourth was a handsome man sitting between her and Logan, engaged in a lively discussion with the latter, seeming to be ignoring the game completely.

"And then I woke up in a pig pen!" the man laughed at his own misfortune as he reminisced about a night that involved an absurd amount of alcohol.

"Ah, those were the good old days," Logan said fondly, his gaze unfocused as though reliving a memory. He shook his head, returning to the present. "You should have married her."

The man quirked a brow. "Who? The pig?"

"No, Roman, you idiot! Tess." Logan shook his head, taking a card dealt to him. He surveyed the ones in his hands before swapping the new card in and discarding the other onto the pile on the table. "You're pretty and all, Roman, but Tess was too good for you, and you let her slip between your fingers."

"I'm not a one-woman man though, my friend," Roman grinned cockily, puffing out his chest and sneaking a glance at Nora. "I cannot be sustained by just one woman alone."

Nora rolled her eyes. "Goddess Thyra have mercy…"

Roman faced her fully, his russet eyes sparkling. "Oh, and I suppose there is someone more appealing than me?"

"There is a long list of people who are more appealing than you," Nora deadpanned as she inspected her cards.

"Well, if you feel like moving me up your list, you may be pleasantly surprised," he winked.

"I doubt you have the technique nor the stamina for what would pleasantly surprise me," she said dryly.

Logan let out a booming laugh, slapping his thigh, and August chuckled on her other side. Even some of the other players' lips tugged up at the edges.

"Sounds like a challenge," Roman whispered, leaning in closer to her ear. His nearness sent tingles running down her spine. Nora bit her lip before shoving him away, not bothering to give him an answer.

The truth was, if she were back home in Royal Bay, she most likely would have taken Roman up on his challenge. He was extremely attractive: tanned skin, strong jaw, and tousled dark hair. Her Alta tattoos had not stopped her from noticing that. The shackles did not prevent intimacy, which helped on missions that involved a certain type of persuasion, or when she would seek out her own pleasures. She had many fond memories of times spent in the company of both men and women, but the tattoos would not let Nora's feelings go further than that. King Dominic had made sure of it in his commands during the initiation rituals when Alta received their tattoos. It was a simple command; Alta could not fall in love.

Nora took a sip of her wine and turned her attention to the game. She would not get caught up with the handsome stranger next to her. There would be no benefit for the king if she bedded him, plus she needed to keep her wits about her. The Royal Sentries would be looking for them, and even though Sebastian had promised to help, that wouldn't stop any of the people who frequented this establishment letting slip their whereabouts if asked for information. When you played on this side of the law, anyone could be bought.

Beside her, August had settled in for a long night. He had already finished his ale and was almost halfway through his second drink. Nora sent him a scowl.

"Catch up," he smirked as Grayson dealt the cards for the next game after the woman who had spoken to them had showed her winning hand.

"I don't think so," she replied, sliding her drink away.

"The sun hasn't risen yet," he teased, pointing to one of the few windows in the gambling house. Another flash of lightning lit up the sky outside and rain pattered on the glass.

"Fine," she grumbled, snatching her glass, and taking a large sip then lowering her voice so that only he could hear. "If this ends badly, and it will, it rests on your shoulders."

"It is a burden I am willing to bear," he chuckled. He raised his hand, getting the attention of a waiter and ordering them more drinks.

Nora pursed her lips at him.

"We can't leave the city without Sebastian," he added. "And even if we could it's pissing down out there. Accept it. We're stuck here so relax and have some fun."

Nora hated that he was right; they were stuck, but that didn't make the urge for her to keep pushing forward in the search for Felix disappear. She could practically feel the magic of the tattoos wrapped around her wrists burning with the need to fulfil King Dominic's commands. She sighed deeply, downing the rest of her drink, hoping it would dull her restlessness as well as the rising pain. If she was going to be bending rules, she might as well make herself as numb to the consequences as possible.

The first wine didn't take the edge off, but the subsequent ones certainly did. Much to her dismay, Nora found herself unintentionally taking August's words to heart. After six games of cards—all of which she had lost—and multiple glasses of wine, she found herself running up the stairs of the gambling house with Roman in tow.

Before she could reach the landing of the first floor, he grabbed her hand, dragging her back towards the wall and pressing her firmly against it. His broad frame kept her trapped as he crushed his lips to hers, enveloping her in his cinnamon scent. The kiss was frenzied, their mouths moving in a heated passion. She bit down on his lower lip, dragging her teeth against the sensitive skin. Roman made to rear back but she hooked her arms around his neck, pulling herself up and wrapping her legs around his waist.

Roman grabbed her thighs, his hands gripping tight enough to bruise, and shoved her harder against the wall, grinding the evidence of his arousal into her. Nora moaned, mimicking his movements with her own hips.

"Nora," Roman breathed, grinning wickedly. "Sebastian will kill me if we fuck in the stairway."

"All the more tempting," Nora replied, biting her lip.

Roman's laugh boomed as he tore them from the wall and carried her up the rest of the stairs and into one of the nearest rooms. He kicked the door shut behind them, depositing her onto the four poster bed. A girlish laugh escaped her as she landed on her back amongst the blankets. Roman stood over her, his eyes alight with desire.

"Well?" she teased, raising her brows. "Let's see then."

He shrugged off his woollen coat, dropping it to the floor without a care, then his fingers ran deftly down his shirt before it too joined his coat at his feet. Nora took in the sight of his golden muscular chest, not caring that a King's Guild tattoo marked it. Roman held her heated stare as he unbuckled his belt and dropped his dark trousers and underwear, his desire visible for all to see.

Nora licked her lips appreciatively before dragging her eyes back to his.

"Your turn," he winked devilishly.

She raised her finger, twirling it slowly in the air. "Turn around."

Roman chuckled darkly, turning his back to her.

Nora admired the lines of his powerful back and toned ass as she quickly slipped off her clothing, hating the extra time the three layers and her daggers added to the endeavour. Throwing everything but her simple black undergarments to the floor beside the bed she called for Roman to turn around.

Roman's eyes widened, hungrily taking in every inch of her as he approached like a predator. Her body sparked with the intensity of his gaze as he climbed on top of her, his biceps flexing either side of her head as he supported most of his weight. He pressed a hard kiss to her lips as she gripped his shoulders tight, digging her nails into his skin and drawing him closer. Nora's lips parted and Roman's tongue swept inside, exploring her with hungry movements. The motion had her imagining how it would feel on other parts of her body. She ground her hips against his, earning a groan she felt rumble through his chest, and he pressed her further into the mattress. She could feel his need, heat pooling between her legs at what was to come.

Nora made to reach between them, but Roman snatched her wrist away, holding it on the bed and earning a hiss to escape her lips. Her tattoos were still sensitive, even after all the alcohol she'd consumed. He lowered his mouth to her neck, slowly trailing kisses downwards.

"Very impatient," he tsked between kisses that flushed her skin.

"I'm not here just to make out," Nora teased, looking at him through her lashes.

Roman tilted his head up, smirking. "No, you're here so I can dismiss your earlier doubts."

He released her wrist and pulled back to kneel before the bed. Gripping her legs, Roman tugged her towards him, and Nora laughed as she was dragged to the edge of the mattress. She licked her lips at the sight of Roman kneeling between her thighs. His dark hair was swept messily to the side, strands slipping into his russet eyes that looked ready to devour her.

"Nice view?" he asked, pulling her underpants down her legs, and throwing the black fabric over his shoulder. There was nothing gentle about his movements and it only made her need grow. "I doubt it's as good as mine though."

"I don't know—" Nora began but was unable to finish her sentence as she felt his tongue caress up her centre.

Her head tipped back as he continued to lick her with long luxurious strokes before demonstrating his true talents whilst slipping his fingers inside her. Nora gasped, gripping the blankets in her fists as Roman went to work licking and sucking, his fingers moving in a steady rhythm, all to prove he was up to the challenge she had inadvertently set.

Roman gripped her hip with his free hand, his fingers bruising as he held her down, stopping her from grinding against his face.

"So impatient," he breathed against her thighs.

"Tease," Nora breathed, lifting a hand to her chest, and palming her breast through her bra.

Roman picked up his pace, licking and thrusting his fingers in a rising rhythm until Nora arched her back and cried out in release.

Panting, she fell back to the blankets only to feel Roman's mouth caressing its way up her body. He kissed and licked her sensitive skin, enticing welcomed shivers. She reached out for him, tangling her fingers in his dark hair, and drawing him up to her face. Capturing Roman's mouth with her own, she spread her legs further, giving him space to settle between them. He ground himself against her, her core igniting with need once more as he lined himself up and thrust inside her.

Nora cried out, revelling in the feeling of him as he withdrew slightly before slamming back in hard. There were no pleasantries—not that there had been any to begin with—and that's just how she liked it—brutally passionate. Roman braced himself with one hand beside Nora's head whilst he held her hip so he could maintain control.

"Harder," Nora panted, and Roman growled with desire, giving her exactly what she wanted.

Roman released her hip, fisting his hand in her hair and tugging to give him access to her neck. He lowered his head, sucking hard before biting down and she moaned his name as he left his mark on her. Nora curled her legs around Roman's hips as he continued to drive into her hard and fast. Her body moved to meet him with each thrust, her pleasure growing to an intensity until she gasped, her body tightening around him with her release. Roman chased her into oblivion, shuddering before collapsing on top of her.

Their heavy breathing mingled in the space between them, and Roman leaned in to press his lips to hers. Nora summoned the small amount of her wind magic she'd regenerated, using it to shove him off her before their lips could meet. Roman landed to her side, a quizzical look rippling across his handsome features.

"That was fun," Nora announced, sliding off the bed to clean herself up and dress.

"You don't want to stay and cuddle?" Roman asked, propping himself up onto an elbow. She could see the rejection in his eyes but refused to let it bother her. She owed him nothing.

"No," she replied, slipping on her shirt and trousers.

"What about round two?" he pushed, pouting his lips.

"You'll have to sort yourself out," Nora winked.

She gathered the rest of her belongings, finding her underwear on the other side of the room. Roman continued in his attempts to convince her to stay but she ignored his pleas, leaving without uttering more than a goodnight.

## 8

### Nora

"You came in late last night," August commented, wriggling his eyebrows at Nora.

"Are you keeping track of me?" she grinned. She finished tying her chocolate brown hair up in a high ponytail then grabbed her cloak and slipped it on.

"Only for safety reasons," he chuckled. "Did Roman cry when you didn't stay the entire night? I see he left his mark on your neck."

Nora smirked, not bothering to hide the red bite on her skin. "Come on, let's go find Sebastian and get the heck out of this place."

"Think we can trust him?" August asked, drawing his hood and leading Nora from their room.

"Not at all," she laughed hollowly. "But that doesn't mean we don't need his assistance."

"Agreed," he nodded. "Plus, we've always got each other's backs."

Nora smiled. "Yeah, we do."

They left the gambling house to find Sebastian waiting for them on the street outside.

"Ah, here they are," greeted Sebastian without a smile or hint of happiness; the man was all business. He gestured to his companions.

"You may remember, Grayson and Willow."

Nora nodded a greeting at the card dealer and the woman who wore a tattered jacket over a similar outfit to what she'd been wearing the previous night—trousers and shirt with suspenders.

"All right, ladies and gentlemen," declared Sebastian, rubbing his hands together. He pointed towards a side street where a horse drawn wagon waited along with Nora and August's horses. How he'd known to collect them had Nora feeling uneasy. "Into the wagon, Grayson will ride up front, and Willow and I will take your horses."

Nora threw her hands in the air. "You've got to be kidding me."

"No, I am not," replied Sebastian, pointing to the side of the wagon where a large tree and axe were painted on the wood. "You are lumberjacks travelling to The Great Northern Forest."

"Oh, that doesn't sound made up at all," commented Nora sarcastically, rolling her eyes. "The Royal Sentries are going to stop you, look inside, and see us. This is the shittest idea ever."

"The Royal Sentries trust me." Sebastian shoved two shabby tan jackets like the one Willow was wearing at August and Nora. "Here, put these on. They're your uniforms."

Nora removed her cloak and sweater and tossed them into Sebastian's hands, smirking at his frown as she pulled on the jacket. She scrunched her nose at the musty smell, then retrieved her items from Sebastian, drawing her cloak over her shoulders before stuffing her sweater into her pack. Next to her, August had expertly put on his jacket without fully removing his cloak, his head hidden the entire time.

"Shall we?" Sebastian asked, his tone as sarcastic as his movements, like a servant waiting on royalty.

"Yes, I don't know what you're standing around for," said Nora, trudging past him towards the wagon, her boots crunching on the muddy gravel with each step. August gripped her arm, halting her before she drew near to the others. He leaned in close enough that she was embraced by his scent of mint and musk. He whispered softly so only she could hear.

"That horse leading the wagon is no horse." He discreetly pointed to the chestnut stallion. "And I bet Sebastian knows it."

He released her and she climbed into the back of the wagon. August sat opposite, only to jolt back to his feet by the sound of two voices close by. Nora tensed, her fingers flexing, ready to summon her magic.

"Hope you weren't going to leave without us!" joked Roman as he appeared at the door. He smiled broadly, tossing his head to the side to flick his dark fringe from his eyes. His gaze lingered on Nora.

"Well, hello there, beautiful," he crooned.

"Get in, you're already late," grumbled Sebastian, shoving the man into the wagon, then waving Logan in as well before shutting the wooden doors.

Logan sat opposite Roman, his long limbs a tangled mess in the cramped space. Both men wore a similar jacket to the one Sebastian had given her and August.

"Isn't this cosy," commented August dryly, knocking his knee against Nora's.

She scowled before leaning back on the wagon wall, folding her arms over her chest. Logan and Roman merely grinned. *Thyra, make this quick,* she prayed silently to the Elementum Goddess as she swayed with the wagon's jostling movement over the uneven street.

Nora ignored the three annoying men she was confined to the wagon with. Instead, she let her mind drift, going over all the clues they had gathered about Felix's location, all of which led them to Kaldom. She hoped they were on the right track. She hated this feeling of uncertainty.

A knock on the wall of the wagon had them fall silent as they slowed to a stop. Nora strained her ears to the muffled voices coming from outside. She could not make out what was being said, but judging by the tone, it was not ideal. Her eyes locked onto August, and even though the upper half of his face was hidden, she could feel his dark gaze. Her mind raced with possible plans if Sebastian's fell through, but she forced herself to remain calm.

Slipping off her gloves, Nora freed her fingers and readied herself. Opposite her, August shifted in his seat. The doors to the wagon flung open, the morning light washing into the confined space. The sentry's brows creased as his eyes swept over the four of them.

"As I said, just lumberjacks," stated Sebastian from behind the grey uniformed man. "Nothing of interest."

Nora kept her face neutral, her fingers twitching at her side. After a long moment, the sentry stepped back. "Sorry, we have been commanded to check everyone leaving the city. Just protocol."

"Of course, no harm done." Sebastian patted the sentry on the back. "I have every faith you'll continue to be an upstanding member of the Royal Sentries."

"Thank you, sir." The sentry nodded.

Sebastian disappeared from view, calling out to the sentry as he walked away. "Shut those doors for me, I want to cover some ground before the day ends."

The sentry scurried forward, shutting the doors hastily. Nora let out a breath and sat back against the wood. Beside her, Roman was beaming from ear to ear.

"You shouldn't worry so much," he whispered, nudging her shoulder as the wagon once again jostled along. "Sebastian is well respected here."

"Any idea when we will be stopping?" Nora asked, rolling her shoulders.

"It's not too far," Logan answered, rubbing his left knee. "We'll reach an inn by nightfall."

"Maybe we can relive last night," Roman grinned, his heated gaze sweeping up and down her body.

Nora wrinkled her nose, shoving him back roughly and not bothering to utter a reply.

Roman winked at Logan before picking up their mundane chatter once more. She tuned them out, instead wondering how much power the King's Guild had over the Royal Sentries, or rather, how many of the Royal Sentries were either members or sympathisers of the King's Guild. There would have to be an overlap. She had always thought the King's Guild were predominantly brutes with extreme views, taking King Dominic's words as sacred, but somehow things had changed. Sebastian was exactly how she imagined a true devotee, but the others? She would never have guessed they were associated with the guild.

The light inside the wagon had begun to dim, and Nora hoped their journey with Sebastian and his companions would soon be at an end. She fidgeted with the fraying hem of the jacket Sebastian had given her, hating the lack of control she felt from being carried to an unknown destination by someone she had just met.

"What's that smell?" she asked, sniffing the air as the wagon slowed. Hopefully, they had arrived, and she would soon be rid of these people.

"Was that you, Logan?" Roman laughed from the corner of the wagon. He had moved during the journey, nestling himself in the crook. "Time and place! There's a lady in here."

Logan chuckled, but there was an odd gleam in his eyes. Nora looked to August who was slouching and rubbing the side of his hooded head with the flat of his palm.

Something was wrong.

She scrunched her nose, grimacing at the foul stench and blinking as dark smoke coiled before her eyes. She followed the trail of black to where it was entering through the small crack in the wall. "Shit!"

She flicked her fingers to summon her wind magic, but Logan was already ahead of her, his own hand moving. The smoke parted; her magic dissipating half while Logan's blew the remainder up her nose and into her mouth. It smelled of rot, and the substance left an ashy taste on her tongue. Her head lolled to the side and her eyes glistened, a tear trailing down her cheek. Logan leaned towards her, and she flicked her fingers once more, aiming for him, but the gust went wide, hitting Roman instead and shoving his head back against the wall with a thump. His eyes narrowed, his hands remaining firm over his nose and mouth, watching her.

Nora could feel her body waning as she desperately fought the urge to fall asleep. She was so very tired.

Eyelids drooping, Logan hit her head against the wooden wall with a gust of wind, and she slumped down, a dull throb radiating near her temple. He stood, hunched in the centre of the wagon with his hands splayed over her and August, holding them down with his magic. Dark smoke swirled before her eyes and her head fell to the side. August's hood had slipped, and in Nora's last moment of consciousness all she saw in her fading vision was August's calm face—as though he had simply fallen asleep. Then the world went black.

$$\diamond$$

With a soft groan, Nora awoke on her back, mind groggy and head throbbing. She gingerly turned her head to see August's shadowed face, covered by his hood. He lifted a finger to his lips, urging her to stay silent. She glanced around to see that they were alone. Outside the swaying wagon, the sounds of hooves clopping and indecipherable conversations filled the air. Slowly, Nora sat up. Ignoring the dizzy sensation, she slid quietly over to August, pressing her side against his as she sat leaned against him. The reassuring contact grounding her.

"I have a feeling we are still supposed to be unconscious," he whispered softly in her ear. "I don't think they'd be too pleased to know we are awake."

"I'm not overly happy that I was knocked out in the first place," Nora hissed through clenched teeth. "I'd very much like to let them know *exactly* how I feel about it."

August chuckled. "Of course you would."

"How long have you been awake for?" She asked, stretching out her arms and legs in front of her.

"A few minutes," he yawned.

Nora patted her hips, her daggers still attached to her belt then glanced down to find August's sword resting on the floor of the wagon. "The idiots didn't even remove our weapons."

"The Gods and Goddesses were light on the intelligence when it came to blessings for our captors. Even if they'd taken our weapons, being Guild members is proof enough of their lack of critical thinking skills," August replied.

"True, doesn't mean we should be slack. We need to get out of here before they stop again," she told him, sitting up slowly. She shook her head to clear the fogginess before removing the jacket under her cloak, giving her better range of motion. "We can use the element of surprise to our advantage and, right now, they aren't moving very quickly."

"Flee or fight?" August stood, reaching out a hand to her.

"This cannot go unpunished." Nora winked, then leapt to her feet, ignoring his hand, and flicked her wrists.

A gust of wind blew the doors of the wagon off their hinges and she and August jumped out, Nora diving left while August went right. Roman and Logan pulled hard on their reins, Nora and August's horses blowing loudly in protest as they halted abruptly. Shouts echoed all around them as Nora landed on the grass beside the dirt track, skidding to a stop before spinning around and facing her captors.

The wagon ground to a halt and Sebastian jumped from the front, storming towards them with Grayson close on his tail. Roman and Logan dismounted their horses, and all four men stopped a few paces away, displeasure etched on each of their faces.

"You are outnumbered! Lay flat on the ground with your hands on your head! No funny business and we might go easy on you!" declared Sebastian, squaring his shoulders.

"Not fucking likely!" August shouted from where he stood in the tall grass. "How about you piss off back to the little hole you crawled out of?"

"You don't scare me boy!" Sebastian bellowed, his face turning red. "I've faced your kind before!"

"You know, for a devotee of the king, you sure are going to piss him off when he finds out about this," Nora pointed out. She watched Roman and Logan's uneasy glances at each other. Maybe a few choice words would even up the numbers. "Attacking Alta and confessing to having done so before is not a good look."

"Shut up! I know you lied about being Alta. Your tattoos are a high quality fake, I'll give you that, but I saw his face, I know what he is," Sebastian spat. "King Dominic will reward us for dealing with you. Surrender, this is my last warning."

Nora raised her hand and threw a fireball, hitting Logan square in the chest. He flew back, landing at one of the horse's feet and screaming in agony as his clothing set alight. Before he could summon his wind magic to suffocate the flame, the horse threw its head in the air, eyes wide as it reared back and slammed its hooves on Logan. The Elementum went slack, his cries silenced as the water orb Grayson had thrown splashed onto his still form. Roman stormed her, his shrieks of fury turning his face a dark shade of crimson. Beside her, August shifted his stance, drawing his sword as Grayson and Sebastian converged on him.

Roman rushed forward with his sword raised in a tight grip and Nora smiled as she feinted left then spun right, dodging his blow, and sending a fireball his way. She felt alive. This was what she was trained for. Roman's pretty face and talent in the bedroom was nothing compared to the thrill of the fight. She could find another attractive body easily enough. Roman recovered quickly and sidestepped her assault. He attacked, grunting with effort, and she evaded again. He was significantly bigger than her, but Nora was quicker and stronger than she appeared. Rana had taught her to use other's weaknesses to her advantage.

*"Let them tire out and do the hard work for you," the woman would say. "Then, once they are panting away, struggling to hold their weapon, go in for the kill."*

A figure crashed into Nora, knocking her to the ground. Her head pounded violently as Willow's face twisted into view, her mouth curling with disdain. Willow wrestled with Nora, the duo rolling around in the dirt, before the Anima shifted into a greyish-brown owl with white spots and flew swiftly into the sky as quietly as she had appeared.

Nora jumped to her feet, steeling herself against Roman and Willow. The Anima raced around the campsite and came swooping down towards Nora's head, trying to distract her as she danced around Roman, avoiding his attack. She focused on dodging him while sending fireballs and gusts of wind towards Willow to keep her at bay. Instead, the woman swerved around Nora's attacks, weaving through the forest for protection. Roman, on the other hand, was gasping, sweat dripping down his face, sword lowering in his grip.

Almost there. Nora grinned smugly.

Taking advantage of Nora's distraction, Willow struck, claws digging into the side of Nora's head. Blood spilled from behind her ear, and Nora gritted her teeth, blocking out the sharp pain and forcing herself to focus on Roman. He dove towards Nora, his scream ragged, and she twisted, pulling one of the daggers from her hip and driving it home under his rib cage. She pushed up, sure to make it the killing blow.

He made no noise as his breath caught in his throat and he collapsed towards her. She withdrew her dagger—her hand crimson from his lifeblood dripping out—and stepped back, letting him slump to the floor. Now she was ready to focus her attention on the stupid bird.

Willow was circling above, seeming unsure whether to return to the fight. Breathing heavier than she would have liked, Nora threw a few fireballs at the bird, but Willow did not retaliate. With a hard jaw, Nora turned her attention to August. He was fighting with Sebastian, their swords clashing loudly as August pushed his attack while avoiding Grayson's assault. The Elementum was using a combination of fire and wind to distract August, but Nora could see that Grayson was tired. The man was winded and leaning on a tree. Nora steadied herself and called water forth, dousing Grayson before he could unleash more magic. Grayson spluttered as his head slammed back into the tree trunk, his face twisting in rage. Curling his lip in disdain, he attempted to light a fireball, but his hands were soaking wet. Uncertainty flashed briefly across his face, and Nora took advantage of his delay and tossed another ball of water at him.

A poorly executed wall of air halted most of her onslaught. Grayson wheezed behind his invisible barrier as the water that made it through the gaps in his magic dripped down his face. Nora did not wait for him to counter her; she had the upper hand and Grayson knew it. Sneering, Nora summoned fire arrows, shooting them at him fast enough to pierce the flesh and burn him from the inside out. He blocked all but one, which found its mark in his shoulder. Eyes wide, he let out a strangled cry of pain, but still launched his own haphazard attack before slumping to the ground.

Three misshapen blobs of fire hurtled towards her at the same time Willow decided to re-join the battle. In Nora's attempt to dodge the incoming fire attack she was unable to block the Anima's talons as they raked the back of her head. Wincing at the sharp pain, Nora quickly grabbed one of her daggers—Roman's blood still wet on the blade—and threw it after the owl's great tawny wings. The dagger found its mark; a clean shot through the head. Willow was dead before she hit the ground, leaving this life as an owl. The distraction of killing Willow provided enough time for Grayson to drag himself up against the tree once more and feebly throw more blobs of fire. They sputtered as they hit Nora's clothing, and she quickly used her water magic to put them out. Panting, burnt, and bleeding, Nora turned to Grayson to find August standing to his right. August's metallic sword and the crimson blood that coated it glistening in the moon. Sebastian lay still in the dirt.

"Is that all you've got?!" Nora shouted at Grayson.

A sharp pain pierced her lower back, the agony spasming up her body. She gasped, brown eyes wide as she stumbled and turned to see a young boy with narrowed eyes and teeth bared. She pulled her remaining dagger from her hip and slit his throat, crimson spilling down his neck. Mouth agape, the boy clutched at his throat instinctually, as though he could stop the flow of blood. Nora's vision clouded as she watched the boy stagger backwards, the ground coming up to meet them both.

$$\Diamond$$

Leaning into August's muscular chest, Nora's nose filled with the scent of musk and blood. She tried in vain to ignore the blinding agony that emanated from her lower back. Sweat beaded on her forehead and she cried out with every jostle of the horse beneath them. August's right arm held the reins of the mare while the other pressed against her back, stemming the flow of blood as they raced to find a Healer. Nora's knuckles where white as she gripped August, focusing on the boy who had stabbed her instead of the wound he had inflicted. It was a struggle to stay conscious, the loss of blood and pain from riding eager to drag her into the dark.

She vividly recalled the surprise in his eyes as her dagger had cut swiftly through his neck, followed by the disbelief as he grappled to slow the blood with his useless hands. He had thought he could play the hero, that he had been clever. Hiding in his horse form and only revealing himself in the pursuit of glory. Delusional, just like the others, and now he was dead. If August did not reach a village soon, then she would likely be joining him.

# 9

## Evelyn

The sun was making its descent, taking with it the light and the full strength of Evelyn's magic. Luckily, she was a powerful Lys Alv. Lys Alvs were one of the two types of Alvs, but unlike those with dark eyes that could steal health and magic, Lys Alvs had eyes like the sun and had the ability to gift what the Mors Alvs could take. Glad that she had lit the candles around the room before tending to her last patient for the day, Evelyn stood at the bedside while Margot peered over her shoulder, scrutinising her every movement. Her mentor was so close that Evelyn could feel Margot's breath on the back of her neck. One would think having to heal the broken arm of a crying child would be enough pressure without having her mentor literally breathing down her neck.

Breathe. Block them out. Breathe. It was just her and the broken arm. Breathe.

Evelyn focused her light on the bone, feeling it join back together, like melting the ends of two candles and pressing them to make one. At the same time, she could feel her bone break and muscles tear. The pain was excruciating, but she did not make a sound, did not let her face change. That was how the healing worked—the Lys Alv Healers took on the injury and then healed themselves.

Steadying her hands to make sure that the little boy's bone was mending smooth and straight, his cry turned into a whimper as his pain began to subside. Evelyn let her light move through the muscle, repairing the tears, then bringing the light to the skin's surface, fading the mauve bruises. Some Healers liked to leave surface injuries on their patients—a reminder of a lesson to be learned—and Evelyn could see the value in the practice. People needed to learn their physical boundaries, but she did not like the sense of a job incomplete, and everyone knew that strong Lys Alvs could heal injuries completely.

She removed her hands from his newly-healed arm and looked to the boy whose eyes were wide with awe. A smile spread across Evelyn's face. His reaction, like that of many before him, was one of the best things about this job. Not that she had much of a choice when it came to her occupation. Evelyn held her broken arm still, already feeling her body beginning to heal itself. It would be a couple of hours before it was done.

"Thank you! Thank you!" the little boy's mother exclaimed, then turned to her son, gripped his ear between her finger and thumb, and scolded him. "No more climbing up trees for you!" She thanked Evelyn again before leading the boy out of the room by his ear.

"How'd I do?" Evelyn asked, turning towards Margot.

"You have become an accomplished Healer, Evelyn," she replied, tapping her pencil on her notepad, and departing without another word.

"That's it?" Evelyn sighed to the empty room.

Margot had been appointed as her mentor when Evelyn was four, and the curvaceous woman with silver hair and pointed ears had always had the same steely disposition. Nurturing, but distant. They had travelled to the small village of Joyal just over three weeks ago for Evelyn's final lessons before she would become a certified Healer. The local Healer had gone on a trip to visit family, and Margot deemed this a suitable educational experience. Even though she was a Lys Alv, Evelyn still had to undergo the training as not all her kind were fit for the job. It was not uncommon for the other races to become Healers too—especially humans who were able to conjure. Humans were the only race of the five who were not born with magic, but in rare cases, some were able to learn conjuring and became powerful magic wielders in their own right.

Evelyn came from a family descended mostly of humans—especially on her father's side. The man himself had learnt to conjure and had practiced the healing arts. On her mother's side, the bloodline was a mix of humans and Lys Alvs, none of which had taken up the healing occupation; they were more into thrill seeking and pushing their magic to its limits. Evelyn's father had been so proud when she had been born a Lys Alv and had decided she was to become a Healer from day one. He had been mapping out her life ever since.

Her healing education had been extensive, as her father thought it prudent for her to know other ways to tend to the sick, not just through magic. Evelyn had spent many hours beyond practical exercises, studying texts and learning about non-magical remedies. Margot was a wealth of knowledge too, and her assessment of Evelyn's knowledge and practise had often left Evelyn feeling harshly scrutinised.

She sighed, tidying up the bed as best she could with only her left arm. Evelyn removed the dirty sheets and replaced them with fresh ones ready for tomorrow's patients. Moving to her desk, she packed her things into her leather satchel.

Before hoisting the bag over her shoulder, she pulled her grey cardigan over her butter yellow dress—the required uniform for Healers—carefully trying not to jostle her broken arm too much. There was no point bracing her arm in a sling when it would not take long to heal. The fabric snagged on her bracelet as she awkwardly pulled the sleeve down her left arm. Evelyn carefully untangled the golden metal from the grey wool and blew out the candles before walking out of the room and shutting the door. The building was small, with only two healing rooms that opened onto a cosy waiting area. The Joyal village was nestled next to a river and had a population of only a few hundred, so there was no need for a large Healing Centre. Unlike the bigger centres, whoever was stationed here dealt with all injuries and ailments.

Evelyn tapped on the door to the second room and popped her head in to see Margot had already left without saying a word. She shook her head. Typical Margot.

Shutting the door, she began extinguishing the few candles of varying sizes strategically placed around the room. Standing next to the entrance, she leant over to blow out the last one when the door was pushed open, knocking her to the side and revealing a cloaked figure carrying a body.

"Please," he panted. "Help her."

At first Evelyn just stared, shocked by what was standing before her, but the emotion swiftly disappeared, and her training kicked in.

"Quickly follow me," she directed, striding towards her room.

"I don't need to be carried," complained the person in his arms, her strained voice coming out between shallow breaths. "I can walk."

"You can stumble at best," teased the man, although there was more worry than humour in his tone. "You'd most likely collapse after a few steps. Then I'd have to carry you anyway."

Pushing open the door, Evelyn lit a few candles as the stranger lay the woman on her side on the bed. The candlelight illuminated the room and Evelyn was able to see her patient. She was short and slim, with chocolate brown hair and pallid skin, and looked as though she was on death's door.

"What happened?" Evelyn asked, moving towards the woman, ready to examine her body. From what she could see, the woman was covered in a lot of blood and had multiple wounds to her head, but other than the area above her right ear, they looked to be just scratches.

"Just an inconsequential knife wound to the lower back," replied the woman sarcastically, groaning as she rolled slowly from her side onto her front.

Evelyn's eyes drifted towards the man's hands and the handle he held against the woman's back. The man stepped back, removing a dark stained piece of bundled fabric, to reveal a large patch of blood on the woman's lower back surrounding a knife protruding from it. The wound would be difficult to heal during the day, but at night, when a Lys Alv's magic was at its weakest? Well, a challenge would be describing it nicely. Evelyn was not sure her body would be able to sustain the injury while healing the woman, but she would try.

"She was stabbed," he said, the worry palpable in his voice. "We got here as soon as we could."

"You did the right thing. Keep your hands where they are." Evelyn calmly told him. "What is your name?"

"Her name is Nora and I'm August."

She turned to the woman. "Are you an Anima?"

"No, I'm an Elementum," Nora groaned. "Is that going to be a problem?"

"No, that's fine. Animas, when seriously injured, are often prone to shifting and attempting escape during the healing," she explained, frowning. She couldn't risk healing a Nora standing. She doubted her body would be strong enough to heal a would like this and remain on her feet. "I'm going to need you to lay on your stomach on the floor."

August moved to stand beside Evelyn. He was taller, and her eyes met his stubbled chin and the blond hair that fell loose on either side. This close, his muscular build was visible beneath his charcoal cloak, yet she was unable to see past the shadows on the upper half of his face. He leant forward, scooping Nora up.

"You don't have to wear your hood inside," Evelyn offered as he gently lay Nora on the floor.

"I don't think you'll like what you see underneath," August replied, his tone resigned but with a slight edge to it.

Evelyn pursed her lips. She failed to imagine what he was hiding beneath the hood, but she would not push. If he did not want to tell her then so be it. Everyone deserved privacy, and if her profession taught her anything, it was that everyone had a right to make decisions over their own bodies.

He rose and she found herself standing close to him once more. She looked up at him and even though she couldn't see his eyes, she felt them on her. Her heart rate picked up its pace. She knew it was completely ridiculous as she had only just met this person and his face was partially hidden, but there was something about him, and she could not for the life of her get her body to listen to her brain.

"If you two are finished," Nora breathed raggedly from where she lay on the floor. "I'd like to stop dying now."

Evelyn's cheeks flushed as she sat down cross-legged on one side of Nora while August sat on the other, holding his companion's hand. Evelyn let her hands hover over Nora's wound.

"Ready?" Evelyn asked, eyebrows raised.

"Please," Nora replied, her voice barely audible.

Evelyn removed the fabric from the woman's back then tore the clothing to better reveal the wound before carefully sliding the knife out of the woman's flesh. Nora cried out as the wound oozed blood, and Evelyn quickly applied pressure with some extra bandages. Placing both hands against Nora's lower back, Evelyn's eyes fluttered closed as she concentrated.

Like the healing of the boy, she let her light move through her hands. There was no infection, and the knife had missed anything vital, though Nora was still extremely lucky to be alive. Thank the goddess! Although the healing would be painful, at least it would not be too intricate or long a process. Evelyn's light became richer, changing colour as she moved from examination to healing, pushing it further into Nora to begin repairing internally. Sharp, blinding pain exploded from her lower back, and she gasped before biting down hard on her lip, drawing blood. She tried to focus on her light, on the healing, but it was difficult to concentrate. Sweat beaded on her forehead and her breaths were quick and shallow.

Evelyn felt pressure on her lower back and opened her eyes to find August's legs bent on either side of hers. She glanced over her shoulder to see he was sitting behind her with both hands placed against her lower back, putting pressure on the area with a piece of fabric. Her cheeks warmed once again, and she did not dare look up at his face and expose her treacherous reaction.

"Can't have you bleeding out," August said humorously. "What's your name?"

"Evelyn," she told him between breaths. "How did this happen?"

"We got into a bit of a fight," he replied, his tone as though he were telling her about what he ate for breakfast.

Evelyn raised her brows in disbelief. "You stabbed her then brought her here for healing?" she asked through gritted teeth.

"No, no, no, no. I would never, could never." August replied, his voice filled with emotion. "No, we were attacked."

"Are you in trouble?" Evelyn dipped her head and closed her eyes as another wave of pain came over her. She could feel her light moving through Nora's body, knitting it back together while her own was torn apart. If not for her ability to heal herself to some degree at the same time, there would be no way she would be able to heal Nora properly without passing out in the process.

August seemed to sense her discomfort; his hands pressed firmly against her back as he waited for the wave of pain to subside before answering. "We had a run-in with the wrong sort of people, that's all."

"Will they come looking for you?"

"We got away. I don't think anyone followed us," August said reassuringly. "You're safe, no one will find us here."

"I wasn't worried about me," she replied, another smarting ache radiating through her. Blood trickled down her lower back, sticking the fabric of her dress to her skin.

After what felt like hours, Evelyn's hands dropped to her lap, revealing a smooth patch of skin free from scarring, and bruising on Nora's back. Other than the congealed blood surrounding the healed spot and the torn clothing, there would be no telling Nora was ever hurt. Evelyn, on the other hand, was not doing so well.

"Thank you," said Nora, rolling onto her side to look up at Evelyn. She grimaced. "You look like shit."

"Just part of the job," Evelyn replied, her voice strained. "I'll be fine after a good night's sleep. If you come back tomorrow, I can heal your head."

"Where are you staying? We can take you," offered August. He looped his arm under her shoulder, helping Evelyn gently to her feet.

"It's okay," Evelyn said, bracing her good arm on the bed before waving August off. "I'll be fine."

"I hate to agree with August, but you should really let us help you home. I don't want to have to stalk you through the shadows purely so he can be happy knowing you made it home safely," said Nora as she too, rose from the floor. Evelyn surveyed the woman's slow movements and breathing. The stab wound had been healed but there was a lot of blood in Nora's hair.

Evelyn purposely ignored Nora's comments about August's possible intentions, yet a faint blush crept into her cheeks. "I don't want to put you out, I'm happy to walk myself."

"We'll help, all you need to do is direct us," said August.

Evelyn nodded. "Let me just get my things and lock up."

August and Nora helped her tidy up the room and carry her bag before they left. They travelled along the deserted paths towards her lodgings, Evelyn riding their horse whilst Nora and August walked in front. She had insisted on walking—the horse ride would jostle her around just as much as being on foot—but the two ahead of her would hear none of it.

Evelyn caught snippets of their conversation, their hushed voices carrying through the night.

"—leave here…"

"—King's Guild…"

"—north…"

"—quick as possible…"

"—attack…"

"—the king…"

Evelyn tried to tune out their whispers—her Lys Alv ears made that difficult to avoid—but despite the manners she had been taught, the overheard words were far too interesting to ignore. It sounded as though they had gotten themselves into a bit of trouble with the King's Guild, and she wondered whether these two were on the run from the king.

"We're here," Evelyn called, pointing to a stone cottage at the end of a short dirt path.

August and Nora stopped, the latter leaning up against the small wooden fence that bordered the property. August reached out for Evelyn, helping her to the ground. She stifled a gasp at the movement, her healing magic working tirelessly to mend her new injuries.

"Thank you for walking me," Evelyn said, her voice breathy as she took her satchel from August.

He reached into his cloak pocket and drew out a small coin pouch. "How much do we owe you?"

"Oh, nothing," she said, putting up her hand. "Healers receive a wage from their lord or lady."

"I know, but it wasn't a simple healing," he said, untying the string of the pouch.

She placed her hand on his, halting his movements. "Please, honestly, save your money."

August's head lowered, and she mirrored his movement, her gaze locking on where their hands met. She blushed, taking her hand away.

"I should go," she said quickly.

"Would you like me to help you to the door then?" August asked before she could depart. Behind him, Nora's eyeroll was visible in the moonlight.

"I'm fine," Evelyn smiled. She made to leave but turned back, a thought playing on her mind. "I didn't mean to eavesdrop—"

"But you couldn't help yourself?" Nora smirked.

Evelyn bit her lip. "If you're in trouble with... with the king... just keep an eye out for the five squares."

August and Nora exchanged a look, but it was Nora who replied. "Five squares?"

Evelyn nodded, carefully taking her notebook and a pen from her satchel. She tore out a page, rested it on the front of the book, and drew five linked squares all sitting on their points. "If you're looking for help, just go into a building with that symbol."

"And they'll hide us from the king?" Nora raised a brow.

"Yes," Evelyn replied. She handed August the sheet of paper before turning her back to them again and slowly making her way to the cottage where she hoped Margot would be fast asleep.

# 10

## Nora

The horse slowed, the relentlessness of their travel too much to bear any longer. They had pushed the poor animal hard, and Nora felt a twinge of guilt for not allowing the stallion to rest for longer periods of time. They had been taking turns riding, sometimes riding double, so as not to stress the horse too much but to maintain a quicker pace. It was not ideal, but they needed to create enough distance between themselves and where they had left Sebastian and his companions. Someone would find them eventually, maybe even bring them back to Midskopas where she and August could possibly be identified by the guard who had questioned their departure.

Nora did not fear the Royal Sentries, but any pursuit would interfere with their plan to travel the country mostly unnoticed. Lingering with the Lys Alv may not have been the best idea, but it had felt cruel to leave the woman in such a vulnerable state after she had healed Nora. Not to mention the Lys Alv had provided them with some surprising information. The five interlinked squares all resting on their points haunted Nora's thoughts. She knew she had seen them somewhere but could not for the life of her place where.

Pulling the reins, the horse came to a halt beside a broad pine tree.

Nora handed the straps to August then climbed off, shaking out her arms and legs and cracking her neck. They had been travelling north parallel to the main road, only using the heavily-treaded pass when they crossed the west bridge of the forked river that bordered either side of Forest's Edge. This far north, a chill lingered no matter the time of day, and the breeze that caressed her face and wove its way into the gaps in her clothing sent shivers through her bones and left her exposed skin raw.

"We're not too far now," August said, tying the reins to one of the tree branches. "At this rate it will only take another day."

Nora stroked the horse's side, coming around to meet August. He cupped his bare hands before the stallion and Nora summoned her water magic, filling his hands with a drink to offer the tired animal. "If he is up for it. We have been pushing him hard for the last few days. I'd hate to kill him in the process."

"He's strong, and if we rest here until morning I'm sure he'll be fine." He countered, petting the horse's muzzle.

Nora merely nodded as she rubbed the stallion's powerful legs. She was generally not a fan of people. August was the only person that she ever felt able to be herself around. He accepted her as she was. When it came to animals—true animals— they always had a special place in her heart. She thought of her mare that they had abandoned and felt a twinge in her gut at the idea of never seeing the beautiful creature again.

"I've been thinking about that symbol the Lys Alv drew." Nora began.

"Mmm, and?" August asked, sitting down, and leaning his back against the tree.

Slowly lowering herself beside him, Nora tugged her new cloak around herself and summoned an orb of flame to keep them warm. Technically, she had stolen the cloak—a shirt, slacks, sweater, and a pair of leather gloves too—but August had not approved, leaving coin in the house she had snatched the items from. Nora's pack had been left behind in the rush, along with her coin purse. If he had taken her mare with her pack when they escaped, maybe she wouldn't have needed to steal from people.

Nora stretched out her hand and flicked her gloved fingers. "The drawing…"

"Hasn't changed since last time you looked at it," he said, retrieving the sheet of paper from his cloak pocket and passing it to her.

"I've seen the symbol before," she pondered, staring at the sketch of five interlocking squares all resting on their points. "Does it look familiar to you?"

"Not really." He shrugged.

August leant forward, dragging his pack to him from where he had dumped it on the ground. He rummaged inside his, pulling out their Alta maps of the various Valmenessian cities.

"Does it match any of the symbols on here?" He opened the map of Midskopas up and held it out between them.

Nora scanned the map, chewing the inside of her cheek as her eyes scrutinised the symbols. "Not that I can see, but that makes sense. If this is a symbol for people who fear the king and those who follow him, I doubt it'd appear on a map made for the Alta."

"Good point, but it's still worth checking," replied August, opening another map.

Again, the five squares were nowhere to be seen. After looking through all four maps, Nora sat back. She knew the symbol looked familiar, but why couldn't she recall where from? Staring off into the distance, she tried to think of where she had seen it. Was it from one of the many books she had studied? Or was it associated with someone she had been in contact with? There was something about it that nagged at her. Beside Nora, August began to pack the maps away when her eyes caught on the sketch of Felix's last known whereabouts. Snatching it from August's lap, she unfolded the paper, her eyes darting over the drawing.

"There you are," she crooned. "I knew I'd seen it somewhere!"

August peered over her shoulder, and, with one finger, she pointed to the symbol on the blacksmith's sign. Nora thought about what the Lys Alv had said—that the symbol was a sign of refuge for those fearing King Dominic and his supporters. If that was the case, then Nora would bet a hefty bag of gold that the blacksmith had been hiding something.

"Should we go back to Royal Bay?" August asked, taking the drawing from her. "Or maybe to Evelyn? Find out how this symbol connects them?"

Nora bit her tongue at August's use of the Lys Alv's first name. He was way too friendly with the woman the other night and now he was suggesting going back to see he? Nora wondered whether his motivations were solely focused on King Dominic's best interests or whether he was entertaining his own. August had always been adept in twisting things to suit him.

"I think we should keep moving, seeing as we are so close to Forest's Edge. We can search there for the symbol and see what we come up with. Heading back to Royal Bay purely to question someone who most likely won't give us any more information would be a waste of time." Nora replied, snatching the sketch back and looking at it as though it were a winning ticket. "As for the Lys Alv, even though she told us about the symbol, she's a Healer. I doubt she would have any information regarding anything of importance. Forest's Edge is our best bet at the moment, and don't forget, there's still Kaldom."

"Ah, yes, our original terrible lead." He groaned, tilting his head back against the tree trunk.

"Yes, that one, and as you always tell me, it's best to not go rushing into anything until we know more," she reminded him, folding up the paper and tucking it into her pocket.

August nudged her side with his. "Are you actually taking my advice for once?"

"Maybe," she replied, lips quirking up at the side.

"I never thought I'd see the day," he chuckled. "But I agree, no point making any rash decisions until we know more. This symbol could be coincidental and have nothing to do with Felix's disappearance."

"Correct. So, we go to Forest's Edge, search for this symbol, and if we're lucky, find out whether it has anything to do with what happened to him. If we can't find anything in a few days, we head to Kaldom like we originally intended."

August folded his arms over his chest. "Sounds like a plan to me."

Nora grinned, feeling a spark of energy jolt through her at the prospect of doing more than just following their loose lead to Kaldom. Even if the symbol was irrelevant to Felix's disappearance, it was still useful information to return to Royal Bay with. King Dominic would be pleased to have a new way to track down those who were seeking to rebel against him. Yet, she was sure the symbol and Felix were connected, something in her gut told her so.

She shuffled closer to August, resting her head on his upper arm, and closing her eyes. The warmth that radiated from the ball of flame caressed her skin, encouraging the sleepiness that was slowly clouding her senses.

"Nora," August muttered, his voice low.

"Yeah?" she asked, yawning.

He shifted slightly beneath her head. "Do you ever think about whether you would agree with the king's commands if you didn't have the tattoos?"

"Well, if that isn't a completely random change of topic... What brought about this line of thought?" she asked, sitting up a little straighter.

"It's something I've been contemplating a lot," he replied. He was tugging at the frayed edges of his cloak. "Would you agree with how he rules the people? With the new Anima laws?"

"King Dominic is trying to make Valmenessia a safe and prosperous place for all." She sighed. "The new laws are to protect the people."

"Do you actually believe that?" he asked. She could feel his dark gaze on her even though his eyes were hidden beneath the shadows of his hood. "Or do you believe his prejudices because that's what you've been commanded to think?"

"I think *you* think too much," she said, settling on a vague answer and following with another yawn. She knew it was not what August wanted to hear because he replied immediately, his thoughts spilling out.

"Don't you think the king's orders make it hard for you to know what you genuinely believe? He easily manipulates you with the power of the tattoos." He tilted his head skywards, then shook it as though accepting defeat. "I doubt you'd be able to recognise whether your beliefs are truly your own or not, whether you actually agree with the injustices he inflicts."

"The king is just and fair." Nora's brows furrowed. "And don't you mean we? Us?"

"Yeah, sorry." August shifted his body. "Whether we actually agree."

"Honestly," she let out a deep breath. "If I were you, I'd try not to dwell on it because you can't change it. I know that's not exactly an answer, but you need to let it go. Fighting is only going to hurt you in the end."

"Watch out, it almost sounds like you care about me."

Nora huffed. "Don't let it go to your head."

August fell silent, and Nora let herself be drawn back into her sleepy state. Squirming around to get comfortable against August's side, her eyelids grew heavy as the warmth from her fire dimmed.

"I think it is important to question how you feel," he whispered as Nora's eyes closed. "If you don't then you just end up accepting what the king makes you do, and then ultimately lose yourself."

*Typical August,* she thought. He could not help but question everything. She wished he would let the habit go. It was much easier to give in to the commands the king gave them. What was so bad about losing themselves to it? Without King Dominic they would be nothing. Who would want that? Being an Alta was the best thing that had ever happened to her. Still, August's misgivings about their lives left an uncomfortable feeling in her gut. She wished he would not entertain such thoughts. Nora urged her mind to still. She wanted to sleep, wanted the peace that came with it. Luckily, her body was eager to oblige, and it was not long before she drifted off.

# 11

## Evelyn

Slipping on a freshly cleaned uniform, albeit one with a spattering of stains, Evelyn buttoned up her grey cardigan as a knock sounded on her bedroom door.

"Come in," Evelyn called, finding her brush, and running it through her long black hair.

"Good morning, Evelyn," greeted Margot, eyeing her suspiciously. She was immaculate as usual, with her freshly pressed uniform and silver hair in a tight bun. "You're up early."

Evelyn knew she looked like she had just got out of bed, even if she had been up with the sun studying. Not that she had been sleeping much lately anyway.

"I was just finishing up my notes," Evelyn said, flashing her mentor a smile. "We are scheduled to return home tomorrow, and I would hate for anything to delay that."

"Mmm." Margot pursed her lips. "Only one patient today, so when you are not treating them you will continue to study your theory. I will quiz you this afternoon."

"Okay," Evelyn nodded, as her mentor left the room.

Evelyn opened the window and wooden shutters, flooding the room with sunlight and allowing the fresh air in. She wasn't sure how much more information on healing remedies and techniques she could fit into her brain, but she was determined to learn it all. The days following Nora and August's visit had been slow to the point that feelings she had managed to keep locked up tight since her arrival in Joyal were attempting their escape. Painful thoughts kept creeping into her mind uninvited and she was eager for the distraction that came with study. However, grief was a tricky fellow who wanted all her attention, no matter how many books she used to keep him at bay.

Collecting the books that were piled next to her bed, she stuffed them into her bag before finding Margot at the front door. It was a short walk to the healing rooms, yet it took longer than it should as they were stopped regularly by the towns people. Healers were well respected, especially in smaller towns, and the people in Joyal were eager to show their appreciation. Evelyn was gifted flowers and baked goods, the latter earning an appreciative growl from her stomach. At first the offers had made her feel awkward but after being in Joyal for a few weeks she had learnt that accepting the gifts graciously was the best choice, the alternative looks of rejection on the townspeople's faces having been even more uncomfortable.

Once they arrived at the Healing Centre, Evelyn spent the morning sitting at the small desk attempting to read a stack of books by the sun's glow and consuming the entirety of the baked goods she'd been gifted. The sun's rays warmed her brown skin and helped strengthen her magic, but as was becoming a usual pattern, she was finding it increasingly difficult to concentrate. Her thoughts kept drifting to her aunt and cousin; a dark place that she didn't want to visit. Evelyn rubbed at her eyes then shook her head to clear her mind before picking up from the last place she could remember.

*"The Chamomile flower is an excellent relaxant and, when used to make tea, can be prescribed to patients who suffer from stress and sleeplessness. Suitable for all ages and races, however discretion is needed when prescribing to Anima of certain shifts. For example: the brown bat."*

Arriving at the end of the sentence, she read it again, hoping that the second—or third, she was not quite sure—read through would help her retain the information. It did not, and Evelyn settled on the fact that the book would have to go with her wherever she went for the rest of her life. She leant back in her chair, closed her eyes, and pressed her neatly manicured fingers to her temples, massaging in slow circles.

"Evelyn!" Margot called from outside the door. "Your patient is walking up the path!"

Sighing, Evelyn opened her eyes and left the desk, giving the room a quick tidy, checking her schedule, and going over procedure in her mind before greeting her patient.

An older man was waiting for her at the front door. He was dressed in patchy walnut overalls over a light grey shirt, and when he saw her approach, he removed his cap to reveal short snow-white hair.

"Hello Mr Wickham, my name is Evelyn. I will be your Healer for today." She gestured towards her room. "Please follow—"

The door burst open, and two men shoved inside with a third man hanging between them. He was covered in mud and blood, his arms draped over their shoulders. Evelyn was immediately reminded of the other night—August rushing through the doors carrying Nora, his voice urgently pleading for help. Much like the men now.

"He fell off his horse," said one of the men carrying the wounded man.

"Let's get him to my room," Evelyn told them calmly as she turned to Mr Wickham. "I'm sorry, would it be too much of an inconvenience for me to treat this man first?"

"Not at all," replied Mr Wickham with a warm smile.

Evelyn led the trio to her room, where the injured man was carefully laid on the bed.

"What is his name, race and age?" Evelyn asked, looking down at her patient. He was barely conscious, his skin a grey white with blue and dark purple splotches. "And your names too, please."

"I'm Caleb and his name is Louis," replied the larger man. "He's human and twenty-four I think."

"He's twenty-seven," corrected the other man. He stood close to the bed and held the injured man's pale hand in his dark one. "And I'm James."

"Anything else I should know? How big was the horse? Where did he land? What was the ground like?" Evelyn inquired.

"We were riding through farmland just south and his horse spooked and threw him. He landed in some crops and the horse trampled him," replied James a tremor in his voice.

"Stood on his stomach and leg," added Caleb, who now stood against the wall. "Crushed a bunch of berry plants too."

Louis groaned as Evelyn placed her hands lightly over his stomach. "I'm going to use my magic now to examine his body."

James nodded and she summoned her light. It pooled just under her palms, then she shut her eyes and guided it into the man, feeling it move through his body. His right leg was broken, and his abdomen was bruised; it seemed the horse had not done as much damage as they thought.

Evelyn frowned. Louis's heart was racing. She opened her eyes and chewed her lip. Unbuttoning his shirt, she checked his skin for redness, finding a small rash on his left shoulder and neck.

"Hmmm… Louis, Louis," she called, tapping the man on the cheek to try and elicit a response. When he did not wake, her movements become more vigorous. "Can you hear me?"

"I don't want to eat the broccoli," Louis grumbled, scrunching his eyes tightly closed, then he coughed and once more passed out.

"What did the crops look like that he fell in?" Evelyn asked, turning to James and Caleb. "You said they were berries?"

"Blue, cherry-sized berries with orange leaves," replied Caleb.

Leaving one hand on his stomach, Evelyn reached out with the other and ran a finger over the berry juice on the man's cheek. She touched her finger to her tongue, tasting the sweet juice… it was an Alvish plant known as Insmor. Lys Alvs could endure a small amount of poison without any ill effects—their magic able to heal faster than it spread—but even her magic had its limits. Louis had not only fallen into the lethal berry bush, but juice had seeped into the cuts on his body, and the journey here had given the poison time to take hold of him.

Evelyn rushed to the cupboard behind her and searched through the contents for a small vial filled with a glittering green liquid. The cupboard was full of potions and elixirs made by conjurers who specialised in the healing arts. Conjurers were rare humans who could manipulate magic; they spent many years studying and perfecting their craft and dealt in potions and spells. Finding the vial near the back, she grabbed it and returned to where Louis lay.

"What is that?" asked James, eyeing the potion.

Evelyn removed the cork stopper, the strong aroma of spoiled milk wafting towards her. She lowered it to Louis's lips. "Insmor remedy. I believe he fell into an Insmor bush. The Alvish plant."

The liquid slid into Louis's throat and Evelyn placed her hands over his chest and shut her eyes. Her light flooded his body and she felt for his heart.

"Is it working?" James whispered, his eyes fixed on Louis. Evelyn held her breath, waiting for the potion to take effect and hoping she was not too late. Louis's heartbeat began to slow to a steady rhythm, and she smiled. "It's working."

Next to her, James sighed in relief, praising the human God, Frode. Evelyn opened her eyes to glimpse his delighted expression. During the times she found her job hard, reminding herself of these moments made it easier to continue. Shutting her eyes once more, Evelyn examined Louis's body. She was pleased with how fast the potion was taking effect, so she moved her light towards the man's stomach and legs. His abdomen, like the cuts all over his skin, would need minimal healing and could be left to heal on its own without any worry; his leg on the other hand, needed to be healed with magic.

"Now that the potion has eliminated the effects of the Insmor I'll heal his leg," Evelyn told James and Caleb, opening her eyes. "His stomach has some bruising, but he is lucky. It could have been a lot worse."

"Thank you," replied James with a warm smile, his eyes glistening. "Will he wake soon?"

"The potion's side effect is drowsiness, which is probably a good thing while he still has other injuries. He will wake in a few hours, a little sore and disoriented." She told him. She nodded towards her desk. "Can you pass me those scissors?"

James did as she requested. The metal was cool to the touch, and she slid the blade up the leg of Louis's pants. The thin navy fabric cut easily and soon the man's lower leg was exposed. The skin was a deep red and blue, and there was dried blood smeared down it. She dragged her chair over to the side of the bed near Louis's injured leg and sat down. Evelyn placed her hand on his leg, his skin hot to touch, and wasted no time summoning her light into the area. She loved the way her magic responded instantly and with such force when she willed it to do her bidding; it was a feeling she never grew tired of. Her light healed the man's leg as if it were a puzzle made of flesh and bone, drawing the shattered pieces together and reconnecting them.

As the man's bone healed, Evelyn's broke in a flash of blinding pain. She held back her whimper, breathing in quick gasps that she hoped were audible only to herself. She desperately ignored the sharp tear of her muscles and the heat that bloomed on her exposed leg in dark splotches, instead focusing on Louis's healing, and how her magic had worked to repair his leg.

Finally, Evelyn dropped her hands to her lap with a sigh.
"If you two could carry him and follow me," Margot directed from somewhere behind, her presence surprising Evelyn. "I'll show you to a private room where he can rest more comfortably."

James and Caleb moved around Evelyn, picking up Louis and leaving with Margot, thanking Evelyn before they left. Evelyn yawned and leaned her back against the chair, closing her golden eyes. To say she was tired would have been an understatement. Her body ached from her broken leg and the exhaustion from her study sessions that had started early in the morning and went well into late at night. She felt herself drifting off to sleep, not caring that the chair she was sitting in was not overly comfortable. If this was how she was finally going to get a good rest then so be it.

A male voice halted her from completely giving in and she reluctantly turned to see Mr Wickham standing just inside the doorway.

"Well done," he said, surprising Evelyn.
"Oh, thank you," she replied, a light blush creeping into her cheeks. She hadn't realised he'd been watching. Evelyn made to stand, resting her weight on her healthy leg. "I'm just cleaning up then I'll be with you. Thank you for waiting."

"Not a problem," he smiled. "I was happy to watch you at work, I have heard great things about you, especially given your family's history. I am also happy to say that you have passed the practical component of your Healer training."

Evelyn blinked, her body froze as her brain failed to comprehend what he was saying. Surely, she had passed out and was now dreaming. Margot appeared behind Mr Wickham and nodded.

"Surprise," she said in a tone that lacked emotion, her lips turning upwards in true Margot fashion. "Isaiah is one of the best Healers in Valmenessia."

Feeling a burst of newfound energy, Evelyn jumped in excitement only to fall back into her seat, hissing in pain. Isaiah approached and shook her hand.

"You have a fantastic bedside manner; you followed all the guidelines and were very thorough."

"That was all a test?" Evelyn asked, her voice soft as her mind attempted to process everything that was happening.

"Yes," Mr Wickham replied, "but don't worry, they have been adequately compensated... especially Louis."

"What if I hadn't known it was more than a broken leg?" She asked, her golden eyes widening.

He drew a vial from his trouser pocket, the familiar green liquid glittering in the glass. "I wouldn't have let him die from Insmor poisoning, or anything else for that matter."

"But his leg and stomach? Did a horse really trample him?" She pushed, unable to hide the incredulity in her tone.

"Our methods seem extreme, but it is crucial for Healers to be trained adequately. He would not have died, nor would he have suffered any long-term effects." Is iah stuffed his hands into his pockets and gave her a stern look. His warmth evaporated; it seemed he did not like his methods being questioned. "The end justifies the means and, as I said before, he has been generously reimbursed for his time and pain."

Evelyn bit her lip, uncomfortable with the man's methods; the situation just did not feel right to her. Now was not that time to argue though, so instead she plastered a wide grin to her face.

"Margot will assess your theory and then that's it." He congratulated her again before bidding her farewell and leaving the room with Margot.

Evelyn could not believe she had passed her practical test. It had been easier than she thought. She was one step closer to becoming a Healer. She was one step closer to fulfilling her father's dream. Her chest tightened and her breaths came in quick gasps… her father's dream. But was it her dream too? The unease she had been feeling about Isiah's methods had soured further. Frosty doubt entwined itself with her displeasure and sent an invite out to her grief. The latter was forever nestled beneath her skin, like a predator ready to pounce, but she fought it back.

Margot returned to the room and leant on the door frame. "You had no idea he was the examiner?"

Evelyn shook her head, steadying her breathing and smoothing her features to mask her emotions.

"You look in need of a lie down. I will test your theory later this afternoon. Don't look so worried. I highly doubt you will fail," Margot stated matter-of-factly. "We will be returning home tomorrow. I'm sure you've been missing your family."

Her family. The wall she had erected months ago to hide the worst of her pain crumbled, taking advantage of her current state. Thoughts rushed in, wielding sharp swords. Luckily, Margot had departed before the tears started to fall.

## 12

## Nora

Nora woke in a bed she did not recognise. The light streaming in was blinding and her body felt stiff against the hard mattress and rough blankets. She rubbed her eyes with her palms and attempted to sit up, hoping that clearer vision and an alternate angle would tell a different story.

"Wait," came August's voice from her side. She knew it was him, she could pick his low, dulcet tones anywhere. "Let me help you."

"What happened?" she croaked, bursting into a series of coughs as August aided her into a sitting position. She immediately recognised her surroundings. Once they had arrived in Fores, they had booked a room at the first safe inn according to the plan she had collapsed on her bed, giving in to the exhaustion to the on the road.

Now her surroundings were lit by the sun window and the simmering fire in the hearth glow. It was a plain room; two single be broken mirror that hung over a bucket nothing of necessity was missing.

"Here." August handed her

"How are you feeling?"

"Like sunshine and daisies," Nora said bluntly as she took a sip and slumped into her pillow, the liquid soothing her tender throat.

August smiled and ran his hand through his chin-length hair. "I'm glad you're feeling better."

"What happened?" she asked again, her brows knitting together in confusion. "I feel like I have been asleep for months."

The bed dipped as August sat by her legs.

"We're at a lovely little establishment called The Fairy's Den," he told her, shrugging his shoulders. "We're in Forest's Edge."

"I remember travelling here... I remember the Lys Alv and I remember Sebastian and his fellow delinquents." Nora's eyes grew distant as the temperature in the room rose, the flame in the fire crackling loudly within the hearth.

"I'm glad you haven't suffered any memory loss," August joked, ignoring the sudden flare of her magic. "Well, after we arrived here, you seemed pretty drained from the travel and you hadn't had much of a chance to rest properly after your injuries and using your magic, so I left you to sleep."

"You left me to sleep?" Nora's brows rose. "Why do you look so guilty then?"

"Your interpretation, not mine," August ran his hand over the blankets on her bed, finding her hand and squeezing it. "You looked like you needed the rest."

"How long have I been asleep, August?" She demanded, not trying to conceal the bite in her words as she tugged her hand free of his.

"A week," he replied calmly, ignoring her tone.

Nora's eyes narrowed. "A week?"

He dismissed her question with a wave before standing and pinching his nose. "You need a bath and I have a feeling that bucket over there is not going to be up for the task."

"Nice try, but at some point, we will discuss why you have been wasting time coddling me. Please tell me you at least looked into that symbol the Lys Alv drew..." She groaned, placing the glass a little heavy handily onto the bedside table. "You should have been following the king's commands and woken me up so we could continue looking for Felix."

"Later. You can chew my ear off later," he replied, failing to hide his resigned tone with a smirk. "Now you need to tend to your stench."

Nora frowned. "I don't smell that bad."

August took a step back, folding his arms over his chest. "You do. Trust me."

With a pout, Nora drew herself from the bed—giving August a big stinky hug on the way—and left in search of alternate bathing arrangements.

By the time she had cleaned herself up, it was mid-morning and August was lounging on the end of his bed. She walked into their room, feeling brand new after the long bath she had taken in the innkeeper's personal bathroom. The man had taken pity on Nora's state and had agreed that a bucket in her room would indeed take several years to do the job.

Nora sat on her bed and faced August. Her long brown hair was still damp but was brushed and hung below her shoulders. Her pale face was free from blood, dirt and sweat, and she had even borrowed some of the innkeeper's wife's perfume—a mild floral scent that reminded Nora of the rose garden on the grounds of the Royal Bay castle.

August raised a brow at her. "You look pleased with yourself."

"I am clean and I'm ready to get on with this job," she replied with a grin. "Now, tell me what you have been doing while I was asleep?"

"I looked for that symbol Evelyn drew, using the maps we took from the Alta quarters as a reference." He told her, holding up a map of Forest's Edge. "I figured this group would have safehouses in places like taverns, inns, that sort of thing." He tossed the map to the floor." But I couldn't find anything, and I was starting to think the five interlinked squares are either harder to spot or Forest's Edge isn't included in this group."

"Or the Lys Alv lied," Nora added disappointedly, folding her arms over her chest. "Are we leaving the city then? We should get supplies before we go to Kaldom."

"No, if you'll let me finish..." He grinned. "I was walking through one of the streets—there's some really beautiful architecture here by the way." He laughed when Nora waved her hand impatiently at him to go on. "I figured we would be leaving as soon as you awoke if I hadn't uncovered anything, so I was exploring and then what do you think I spotted? The symbol on one of the last places I would have thought to look."

"And where is this surprising location?" She raised a brow.

"A florist." He grinned triumphantly.

"A florist?" Nora stared at him incredulously. "A florist is a safehouse?"

August chuckled. "Appears so."

"Did you go inside?"

He shook his head. "I thought that'd be a better job for you. After Midskopas I've been keeping a low profile, though the weather is cooler here so I'm not the only one wandering around hooded."

"Good," she replied, standing. "I think it'd be better for me to approach these people alone. Less threatening."

"Ha! Are you trying to tell me that you come across friendly and innocent?" August laughed.

"More than you do," Nora smirked.

August rolled his eyes. "Come on, I'll take you to the florist."

Leaving the Fairy's Den, Nora stepped out onto the street and was faced with a city like nothing she had ever seen before. When they had arrived, it had been night and she hadn't been able to truly appreciate her surroundings, but now during the day... Nora's spun slowly on the spot, her mouth slightly agape. Forest's Edge was beautiful.

The city was not as large as Royal Bay, but Nora found it more appealing. The buildings were all made from wood and blended into the surrounding forest, nestling among tree trunks, or strung up high and secured to thick branches. Nora stared in awe, admiring the architecture. Each building was adorned with carvings depicting either the wares of the shop or presumably the unique personality of the owner.

August directed her to a busy flower shop, the brightly coloured floral display drawing customers from far down the street. As Nora approached, she stared at the carvings that adorned the shop front. There were flowers of every variety imaginable etched with intricate detail. Finding the symbol August had described, she traced her finger slowly over the grooves in the wood.

"Is there anything I can help you with?" asked a man with a mop of shiny jet-black hair. He was slightly taller than her, with a slim build and wearing a grey apron over charcoal slacks, a white shirt, and thick coat.

"I was just looking," Nora said, dropping her hand from the carved wall.

"They are good, aren't they?" he said, his youthful face filled with admiration. "The Royd family like their art; they have been decorating the whole city like it's one large canvas. They commissioned the carvings on all the businesses and public spaces."

Nora raised a brow, her brown eyes grazing over the shopfront once more. Did Lord Royd know the meaning of the symbols carved into the wood? Had he told the artists to incorporate them?

"Not much of a talker then," the man said playfully. "If you need anything, I'm the owner and I'm happy to help. You can even point if that suits you better."

"Actually, a woman—a Lys Alv to be exact—mentioned this symbol." Nora pointed to the five interlocking squares that were carved among the flowers. "Said if I needed help, anywhere with this symbol would be able to assist."

She turned back to face the man feeling his attention firmly on her. She could sense him weighing her up and Nora tried to keep her annoyance suppressed at the man's scrutinizing gaze. His piercing eyes seemed to measure whether she was worth helping, which was disconcerting. She straightened her back and refused to turn away.

"Did she now? Does she have a name?" He quirked an eyebrow and folded his arms over his chest. "And who, might I ask, is causing you trouble?"

Nora stepped closer to the man. He looked much too young to own a business—he could not be much older than her. She lowered her voice. "Evelyn was her name and I've had some difficulties,"—she glanced around her as though worried they would be overheard — "with the King's Guild."

His brows pinched in thought. "What is your name?"

"Nora." She said eagerly.

"Nice to meet you Nora, I'm Will." He offered his hand, and she shook it gently. "Have you got any coin on you?"

Her eyes widened in surprise. These people were taking money for their assistance? "Yes, how much will your help cost?"

"Nothing." He shook his head. "But it will help you pay for a stay at Daphne's. Wait here."

Will popped into the shop, returning swiftly with a small bouquet of flowers that looked like fine lace the colour of clouds bundled onto green stems. He handed the flowers to Nora. "Give these to Daphne, book a room, and wait for a visit from a very lovely redhead."

Nora nodded, listening intently as he gave her directions to where she needed to go.

"There's a big bush with blue flowers out the front. You can't miss it," Will finished.

"Bush with blue flowers, got it." Nora gave him a thumbs up then wished Will thanks, departing the flower shop, and heading to where August stood, partially hidden in an alcove.

"How'd it go?" August asked as she approached him. He angled his head to the bouquet she was holding. "Did you buy me flowers?"

"You wish," she said, then filled him in on her encounter with the florist as they walked.

Nearing the centre of the city, Nora stopped in her tracks. Before her, the biggest tree she had ever seen stilled her feet as well as her mind. It was taller than all the surrounding trees and buildings; its trunk as large as a house and its branches spread out wide. The rich, dark brown bark was like scales covered in contrasting speckled emerald—green moss that looked as if someone had flicked paint onto it. The bark moved up the trunk in a beautiful mosaic where it reached the lower branches. Like muscular arms, the branches spread out over the entire intersection, shadowing the area with its vibrant leaves, allowing only small glimpses of sunlight to speckle the city floor. It looked ancient and she felt mesmerised by it.

"Is this Daphne's?" August asked jokingly, elbowing her playfully. "I'm not overly keen on sleeping in a tree."

"Ha, ha, very funny," Nora rolled her eyes and gave him a shove. "No, obviously, I just wanted to stop and look… never mind." She huffed before walking down the street, following the florist's instructions. "Come on!"

"Don't get your panties in a   not," August teased at her side.

"You're such an ass." She shook her head.

"Maybe," he laughed. "But the good kind. Toned, round, sexy..."

"For the love of Goddess Thyra, please stop," Nora slapped her hands over her ears. "You are burning images of you into my brain that will give me nightmares."

August stepped in front of her, grabbing her wrists and holding her arms to her sides. "Okay, I'll stop."

"That was psychological torture," she attempted a frown, but the sides of her lips were refusing to obey.

"Whatever," he chuckled, releasing her. "I wasn't telling you anything you didn't already know."

Nora pretended to gag. "If I had eaten today, it would have been all over my shoes right now."

"You're so dramatic," he sighed. "So, when we get closer to Daphne's I'll go collect our things."

"Your things," Nora corrected him. "I'm wearing everything I own."

"Fine, I'll go collect *my* things."

"And I'll secure a room," she added. "I think it's best if nobody knows you're here with me."

August nodded and lowered his voice. "I can get my secret spy on."

"You're so embarrassingly cheesy," she replied, rolling her eyes. "But yes, you can be all secret spy."

"Fuck yeah," he whisper shouted, pumping his arms.

They made their way towards the western region of Forest's Edge. Nora had thought the main city embraced its namesake with trees and wildlife scattered around the streets, but here all the houses blended into the forest to the point that a few were almost invisible. No two buildings were the same; some were built at the base of trunks whilst others hung high up in the branches or wrapped around the trees like vines. Others even had tree branches and roots woven around or through them, becoming as much a part of the forest as the flora.

Daphne's was a two-storey oak building and was nestled between two giant tree trunks whose thick roots sat above ground, giving the impression of a fence. A plump bush with blossoming blue flowers grew amongst the left tree root, just as Will had said. Nora's boots crunched along the pebble path, edged with dark, mossy green flora that flourished in the minimal light offered by the trees. As they had drawn closer, August had left to retrieve their belongings from The Fairy's Den while she organised a room.

Nora knocked lightly on the door. Shuffling came from inside, then the door swung open to reveal a shapely woman with dark skin and tight black curls held in a brightly patterned bow. She smiled warmly at Nora, her brown eyes glowing.

"Hello there, can I help you?" she asked, one hand on her hip and the other still holding the handle.

"Yes," Nora replied, feeling instantly comfortable in the woman's presence. She held the flowers out to the woman. "Will sent me, said I could stay here."

"Found yourself in a bit of difficulty, have you?" she asked, opening the door wider and taking the bouquet. "Well, you'll be safe here. My name's Daphne, what is yours?"

"Nora," she replied, offering the woman a smile.

"Come in Nora," Daphne said, opening the door wide. "Let's find you a room and something to eat. You must be hungry."

"How'd you know?" Nora asked as she stepped over the threshold.

"Everyone who turns up on my doorstep is hungry," the woman chuckled. "Now, this isn't an inn, so there's no housekeeping, but breakfast and dinner are supplied. I think it creates a nice sort of community, don't you? Of course, it's not compulsory, you can take meals to your room if that's what you prefer."

"How many others stay here?" Nora glanced around the entry. Artworks of varying skill were hung on the walls, depicting everything from seaside locations to portraits and still life. On the right, a set of stairs ascended, and to the left was a door, much like the one she had just stepped through.

"A few. You'll eventually meet them all. Upstairs are the guests' rooms, through to the left here,"—she waved her hand towards an archway and Nora leant forward to see a long table with a collection of chairs surrounding it— "is the dining room. Through here," she pointed to the door, "is my home. My daughter and I live on the ground floor.

Come, I'll show you to your room."

Upstairs, more artworks lined the walls and fresh flowers sat on a bench under the window at the end of the hallway. Five doors stood evenly spaced on each side of the passage as Nora was led to the very last door on the right.

"Your room has a private washroom," said Daphne, handing Nora the key. "My only rule is no guests. This is a safe place, not just for you but everyone here. Ten silvers are due at the end of each week. You can give it to my daughter or myself."

"That's hardly anything," Nora commented, eyebrows high. "One night at an inn can be six silvers alone."

"This isn't a business. I'm not looking to make a profit." The woman smiled as she headed back down the hallway. "Get yourself settled and then come down and I'll make you something to eat." With that the woman left.

Beyond the door, Nora found more space than she thought she would. A double bed covered in knitted quilts and fluffy looking pillows sat in the centre of the room with oil lamps on small drawers at either side. On her right was a well-worn armchair that looked out the window to the view beyond, and to the left an empty bookcase and dresser, another door, and a fireplace that was open to not only this room but the room behind the door.

Nora opened the window and draped one of the knitted blankets over the ledge so August would know which room she was in before venturing through the unknown door to find the bathroom. Grinning, she ran her eyes over the space. There was a bathtub! As well as a tall mirror and any other creature comforts she could have hoped for. On this side of the wall, the fireplace was used not only to heat the room but to warm the water for the tub too.

Walking back into the main room feeling all too pleased with her new accommodations, she summoned a small flame amongst the wood sitting in the fireplace and draped herself on the bed. After the few weeks she'd just had since leaving Royal Bay, she could definitely get used to this new change in direction. Nora just hoped her path was pointing to Felix.

# 13

## Evelyn

A rainbow knitted blanket lay folded over the edge of Evelyn's bed, its familiar pattern, and the memories it brought to the surface, imploring an ache to invade her chest. It was her aunt's—*had* been her aunt's. The woman had been an important figure, not just in Evelyn's life but in the lives of so many in Forest's Edge. She had been stolen from them all far too soon, along with her son. Their deaths had been deemed an accident. Yet no matter the verdict, Evelyn had difficulty coming to terms with their loss over the last six months.

Over six months without them.

The blanket was not the only thing to trigger memories. Evelyn's room was filled with reminders, from the books that were arranged neatly on her desk to the artworks that adorned the walls. Reminders of her aunt and cousin were everywhere. She often wondered when she would come to terms with the finality of it all. As a Healer, she had seen what happens when Goddess Jord came to guide someone to the after, but those people had been unable to be healed. Magic was no longer an option. Her aunt and cousin had been healthy, and their deaths pushed the fleeting and unpredictable nature of life into the forefront of her mind, making her more conscious of the fragility of existence. These thoughts often brought with them overwhelming anxiety, yet some part of her desired to feel them, to keep trying to make sense of it all.

But today... today she was drained.

She had arrived back in Forest's Edge with Margot only an hour ago. She had passed all her assessments and become a fully-fledged Healer, but her eagerness over the journey home to be in her own space had dissipated. Her room now consumed her with thoughts she did not feel brave enough to bear. The uncertainty of her future on top of her grief was too much.

Evelyn needed to leave.

Although the day was on the cooler side, she decided to walk. Forcefully slamming a mental door on all that was building up, she put on her sky-blue coat and went in search of something to distract her. Usually, she would head to her friend Poppy's quarters at the Healing Centre, where they would debrief on anything new in their lives or whatever Forest's Edge gossip they had heard. Unfortunately, Poppy was working, which meant visiting was not an option until later. Evelyn considered Poppy to be her closest and dearest friend, and quite possibly her only true one. They had known each other since they were children, having both been training to become Healers.

Stepping out the front door, Evelyn breathed in the heavily pine-scented air filling her lungs and taking the edge off her worries. Venturing outside would do her good. She strode along the stone path, out the iron gate, and made her way towards the city's centre.

As she drew nearer to the crowded streets, a young boy knocked into her as he ran by, followed by an auburn coyote who leapt onto his back. They fell forward, the coyote shifting into a young girl whose hair matched the coyote's fur, both in colour and length. Flipping the boy over, she straddled him, pinning his arms at his sides, and grabbing the purse he had been holding.

"This belongs to me." She dangled the purse over his face, the coins jingling within. "Next time pick a better target."

"Dirty beast!" The boy spat at the girl's face as he struggled beneath her. "Get stuffed! Why don't you leave the coin to us civilised folk!"

Evelyn's eyes widened at the boy's remarks. She knew there had been unrest between the Anima and some of the other races, but she had not realised it had become so openly hostile, let alone warrant an attack. Forest Edge was usually one of the more accepting places to live. Often when the races did not get along, the more intolerant party would move to one of the cities heavily populated by their race. Like the Lys Alvs in Ferieton, the Elementum in Giland or the humans in Sorby. The Anima did not have an exclusive town as their shifts were so diverse, yet Midskopas and Forest's Edge were the cities most populated by them. The laws King Dominic was introducing weren't helping to bring unity to the country. If anything, by only targeting the Anima, he was increasing the divide between all of the races and making some people behave very boldly.

The Anima girl made to punch the boy on the nose but stopped, a hair's distance from his face. "You're not worth it," she snarled and shoved him into the dirt.

The commotion had drawn a small crowd of onlookers who weren't shy about watching the scene. A Lys Alv dressed in black slacks, a faded syrup-coloured coat, and a rainbow of gems adorning his pointed ears, took advantage of the influx of people.

Climbing on top of an old wine barrel, he announced: "Come one! Come all! To Mr Fritz's Fantabulous Friends Spectacular! You will be amazed! You will be mystified! You will be entertained! Shows start tomorrow, Maple Street at noon!"

Like the rest of the crowd, Evelyn halted her travel to watch as he repeated the announcement. It was a pity the show was not on today—it was just what she needed to pass the time before Poppy finished work.

The Lys Alv took in a big gulp of air, readying himself to repeat the announcement, but Evelyn did not stay for another run through. Instead, she continued on her way, pondering what she would do with her time that would be a sufficient distraction. Get a coffee and cake? Buy a new dress? Visit her sister at work? She was busy making a mental list of possibilities when a low voice spoke from beside her.

"Fancy seeing you here," he drawled.

Caught off guard, Evelyn stumbled, tripping over her feet, and careening straight for the dirt. She shut her eyes, bracing for the impact that never came. Instead, a muscular arm wrapped around her middle, spinning her around and drawing her to a firm chest. Evelyn stared at the stubbled chin, her breaths coming in short bursts as her heart galloped within her chest.

"Sorry, I didn't mean to frighten you," he said, releasing her and taking a small step back.

Evelyn flattened her hands down her coat as though trying to wipe away any wrinkles. "It's okay, August," she spluttered. She knew it was him—there was no way she would ever forget his voice.

His shadowed mouth quirked up at the side. "You remembered my name."

"Ah," she stuttered then forced a smile. She was certain it looked more pained than anything as a blush crept onto her cheeks. "What brings you to Forest's Edge?"

"Thought I'd visit." He said. She could feel his gaze fixed on her even without seeing his eyes. "How about yourself?"

"I live here," she replied, noticing how those that passed by reacted to August's presence. Curiously, people gave the man a wide berth and eyed him warily. She looked up at him through her lashes. "Will you be staying long then?"

"No decision has been made," August said, reaching out and twirling his fingers through her black hair. "Though seeing you has been quite the temptation to extend my stay. What are you up to on this fine day?"

Evelyn swallowed hard. "I needed to get out of the house, so I thought I'd go for a stroll. I was hoping something would pique my interest as I walked."

"I think I may need you to heal me after that burn!" August laughed, snatching his hand away and placing it on his chest. "Am I not interesting?"

"I-I—" she slapped a hand over her mouth, her golden eyes wide.

"To be fair, Nora would probably agree with you on that."

Evelyn dropped her hand, frowning. "I didn't mean it like that."

"So, you *do* find me interesting then?" His tone was playful.

Her cheeks reddened, and she bit her lip, unsure of what to say. How did he have this effect on her when this was only their second meeting? She needed to get a grip!

August's head snapped to the side. "Did you see that?"

"What?" she asked, following his gaze to a side alley.

"I thought I just saw…" he shook his head. "I better be going, but it was nice seeing you."

"You too," she replied, a little disappointed that he was leaving. She did find him intriguing and felt drawn to his presence. Whatever that meant.

She turned to leave but was stopped by August's hand on her wrist. "Before I go, I'd be kicking myself later if I didn't ask, but I heard someone shouting about a show tomorrow at noon. Would you like to go watch it with me?"

Evelyn smiled as butterflies danced in her stomach. "Yes, I'd like that very much."

August smiled broadly, releasing her hand, and backing away. "Great! Fantastic! I think he said Maple Street at noon, so I'll meet you there?"

"Okay, I'll be there," she nodded.

"Great!" he called over his shoulder as he jogged down the street. "Fantastic!"

"You already said that!" she shouted after him.

"Ha! I did!" He laughed.

Then August was gone, and Evelyn was left with the disbelief that she had actually said yes to plans with him. She stepped into the nearest store and found herself in a stationary shop with no need for any new writing materials. She walked amongst the shelves, admiring the designs of the letter paper, and tried to sort through her thoughts. She was not a people person. Yes, she was a Healer and that meant her job involved interacting with a lot of people, but when it came to her personal life, she was very selective in who she spent time with. She had one friend, Poppy, and that was it. And now she had agreed to meet up with August.

At least her mind now had no room for other thoughts.

After completing three full laps of the store and receiving suspicious glances from the owner, Evelyn purchased some paper she didn't need and stepped out into the street. She needed to speak her mind, so there was only one place she could go. She turned and walked towards the Healing Centre to wait for Poppy to finish work.

The Forest's Edge Healing Centre was located just north of the main city in an area known as the Manor Grounds. As well as the Healing Centre, the Manor Grounds also housed the City Guard—which was inaccessible to the public—and five small temples, each dedicated to the five Gods of Valmenessia.

At the entrance of each temple, a marble statue of the God or Goddess it was dedicated to stood in the centre of a pool of clear water. Frode, the human God, was a powerfully built man; he held a book in one hand and long sword in the other, his face set to appear as though he was thinking. The statue of Thyra was a tall woman with her palms upturned, holding a flame in one and water spilling out of the other, and her hair billowed around her as though caught in a gust of wind. Aren was in his eagle form, his large wings spread wide as though in mid-flight. And the twins, Jord and Nyssa, were almost identical. Two women with long flowing hair, their pointed ears visible through the strands, were dressed in gowns that were elegant in their simplicity, their only difference being their eyes. Golden gems lit the Lys Alv's eyes, sparkling in the sunlight, whereas obsidian with inlaid emeralds were used for the Mors Alv's eyes, giving the impression they were absorbing the sunlight.

The pools beneath the statues were tiled with mosaics depicting stories of their lives and what they stood for, and when the sun hit the water, the coloured ceramic shimmered. Evelyn thought the statues and their accompanying mosaics were beautiful and had visited each on many occasions. She had only seen the inside of the temples for the Lys Alv Goddess, Nyssa, and the human God, Frode. Her parents had never taken her to the others, and she had never thought to visit them on her own. All the temples were in immaculate condition, even the Mors Alv temple for Goddess Jord. The Mors Alvs may have been eradicated by King Dominic many years ago, but their temple was still being cared for.

The Healing Centre, City Guard, and temples created a grand avenue that led to an extravagant manor which sat behind an ornately designed towering iron gate. Unlike most buildings in Forest's Edge, those on the Manor Grounds were made of blue stone and surrounding them were trees that stretched far into the sky. The Grounds held a variety of colourful flora and commissioned artworks, portraying not only the city's natural allure but also the beauty created by its inhabitants.

Leaving the main path, Evelyn strode towards the entrance to her workplace. The Healing Centre was an architectural masterpiece. Shaped like a wheel, it had been constructed around an ancient tree. Thick branches hung over the centre, hiding the roof tiles with its leaves so that only the fireplace chimneys peaked through the rich green canopy.

Evelyn only had to wait an hour for Poppy to finish up and luckily, as an employee, Evelyn was able to wait in the Healers' communal room. She sat in a heavily cushioned armchair that embraced her so snuggly that she dreaded the moment she would have to get up. She liked this spot in the corner of the narrow room as it was furthest from the door and closest to the fireplace.

She had been staring into the fire, going over her encounter with August in her head when Poppy flopped herself down on the chair opposite, the flames warming further at the presence of the Elementum. Poppy's blonde hair was tied neatly into two buns on either side of her head, a few plaited strands at the front framing her ivory face like a headband. Evelyn had always liked Poppy's hairstyles and had admired her friend for doing them, especially when Evelyn could rarely be bothered brushing her hair, let alone styling it.

"What happened?" Poppy asked by way of greeting.

Evelyn frowned. "Why do you think anything happened?"

"You have that look about you, the 'I'm over-thinking' look." Her friend eyed her knowingly.

"I think I need to move out," Evelyn said, snuggling further into her seat.

Poppy sat up a little straighter. "I wasn't expecting that."

"I need my own space," Evelyn added, her fingers twisting in her lap.

"Evelyn... your home is massive," Poppy groaned. "You could be in there with one hundred people and never see any of them."

"I know, but it would be good to have my own place." Evelyn tilted her head back and stared up at the ceiling.

"Why do you need more privacy? What do you plan on doing?" her friend asked suspiciously. "Becoming a toxin dealer? Or having a different man over every night?"

Evelyn had no desire to be anywhere near toxins, let alone become a dealer. She had no interest in what one would call the wilder forms of entertainment. Forest's Edge, like most cities, had its night life, and there were areas in which people could visit less reputable establishments for products and services that certainly weren't legal, but Evelyn steered clear of those. Training and working as a Healer had shown her what happened when toxins went wrong, or those providing certain services became unfriendly, and she did not want to be involved in that any more than healing the unlucky soul who'd fallen prey. Toxins were bad news, and as for those services... well, she had only ever shared her body with those she felt comfortable with.

"No," she sighed, dropping her gaze to her friend. "I just want to feel like my space is my own. You know?"

Poppy wrinkled her brow. "I guess... but memories will follow you everywhere. You can't escape your own brain."

"I don't know what memories you're talking about," Evelyn said flippantly, waving Poppy off.

"I think you know exactly what I'm talking about." Poppy replied with a tsk. "And can we move past the part where you pretend like you don't want to talk about what's on your mind and skip to where you just tell me?"

"I'm not sure this career is for me," Evelyn sighed, picking the simplest topic that plagued her mind.

Poppy's mouth dropped open. "You just became a certified Healer, and you want a career change already?"

"I don't know... maybe?" Evelyn mused.

Poppy jumped up so she could rest the back of her hand on Evelyn's forehead, her tone full of concern. "Are you sleeping alright? Eating well?"

Evelyn swatted her friend's hand away. "I'm fine!"

"Maybe we should go out and have fun, meet some new people." Poppy sat on the arm of Evelyn's chair.

"I've met plenty of new people," Evelyn replied, picking at the lint on her dress and avoiding Poppy's eye contact.

"Like whom?" Poppy nudged Evelyn with a finger.

"August." Evelyn glanced up at her friend and regretted saying his name as soon as it left her lips.

Poppy raised an eyebrow and a coy smile spread over her face. "Who's August?"

"Just someone I met," she said, fidgeting with her clothing.

"A friend?"

"No," Evelyn said, drawing out the word.

Poppy giggled. "More than a friend then?"

"No, definitely not."

"Why not?" Poppy asked, gripping Evelyn's shoulder. "Is he ugly?"

Evelyn rolled her eyes. "No... I mean I don't think so, not that it matters."

Poppy didn't say anything, wiggling her eyebrows and grinning mischievously instead.

Evelyn chuckled. "He asked me to go see a street show with him tomorrow."

"Ooo," Poppy crooned, dropping into Evelyn's lap, and throwing her arms around her friend's neck. "You're going on a date!"

"No! We are going as friends," Evelyn laughed, untwining her friend's arms.

"Did he say that? That he wanted to go as friends?" Poppy prodded, her lips quirking up at the side.

Evelyn paused, thinking about her interaction with August. He never mentioned going as friends but the word "date" or anything that would suggest the sort had not spilled from his lips either.

"He didn't!" Poppy exclaimed, jumping up and clapping her hands, interpreting Evelyn's silence. She stared at Evelyn, smiling from ear to ear in triumph. "You're going on a date!"

"How can you be so sure?" asked Evelyn. She tried to keep a straight face but was failing terribly at hiding her amusement.

"I just am! And this is perfect because you clearly want a change in your life, or at least some distraction from the grief, so why not let this be it," Poppy said. "It's much cheaper and easier than moving to a new house or changing occupation."

As much as Evelyn wanted to disagree, Poppy had a point.

"It's not like you're marrying the man," Poppy continued. "It's just a date. Have fun, and if you don't like him just leave. Simple."

"Simple?" Evelyn raised a brow.

Poppy nodded, her smile broad. "Simple."

# 14

## Nora

Levitating the tray off food out of the dining room with her wind magic, Nora halted to see she wasn't alone in the entryway.

"You're new here," observed the woman who looked strikingly similar to Daphne, albeit a younger version. She was wearing golden spectacles that were too large for her small, round face, making it appear as though they were going to slip off at any moment. Along with her bright outfit, they gave her an air of eccentricity.

"I only arrived about an hour ago," Nora replied. "Are you Daphne's daughter?"

The woman nodded. "I'm Sage. And you are?"

"Nora." She said, feeling as though she'd said her name more times in the last few hours than she had her entire life.

Sage lifted a brow, her big brown eyes scrutinizing, and Nora held her stare, except for when her eyes occasionally drifted to Sage's full lips. Nora found them rather difficult to ignore.

"Where are you from?" Sage asked, leaning her back against the front door. The warmth Nora had felt with Daphne was absent in Sage, replaced by a clinical assessment that left Nora feeling uneasy and completely bare.

"Rovton," Nora lied, naming the city that sat on the most eastern coast. "I arrived in Forest's Edge this morning."

"How'd you know to come here?" Sage inquired, raising a brow.

"Forest's Edge seemed like a good place to start anew." Nora said, turning away from Sage to walk up the stairs, her tray following along diligently. "As for here specifically, I ran into a Lys Alv in a little village on the way. She told me how to find somewhere to stay where I'd be safe."

No reply came from Sage and Nora assumed her words were being assessed, weighted against some criteria.

"Your mother is such a good person to let me stay here," Nora said, as she reached the top of the stairs.

"She is," Sage agreed, easing herself away from the door. "Don't take advantage of her desire to help people." And with that, she departed, leaving Nora bristling from the warning.

Nora strode into her room, a frown creasing her brow. She flicked her wrist to place the tray of food on the table but accidently released her hold on it completely. Luckily, August sensed her mood and caught the two bowls before they hit the floor with the tray and bread rolls.

"You're in a mood," August said, placing the bowls down carefully. "Daphne's daughter Sage could be a problem," Nora replied, chewing her lip. "She's suspicious and nosey."

He chuckled. "Sounds like someone else I know."

She stuck her tongue out at him then picked up her bowl and a roll, and sat on her bed. Breathing in the aromatic warm soup that sat on her lap, Nora's mouth began to water at the scent of stewed vegetables. She could not identify what was in it from sight—it was mostly a brown sludge—but at least it smelled delicious. She tore off a piece of bread, dipped it into the bowl and tasted the mystery liquid.

"Sage appears to be very distrustful of newcomers," continued Nora around her mouthful. "Which is strange don't you think? Considering the sort of establishment her mother runs. I would have thought she would be more inclined to welcome people with open arms, but the bitch basically threatened me."

"Sounds like she's a good judge of character to me," August joked. He had taken his food to the armchair, devouring it quickly. "She's gotten under your skin already, that's for sure."

Ignoring his comment, Nora tapped her spoon against the side of the bowl, the metal clanging as it hit the porcelain. "I'm going to have to get her to trust me if I want to investigate this possible link between these people and Felix. Either that or annoy her so much she avoids me completely."

"I'm going to put my money on the latter," he replied, scarping the last of his meal from the bowl before placing it precariously on the arm of his chair.

"You have no money so that counts for nothing," she said, scooping a big spoonful of soup into her mouth. "What are your plans with the Lys Alv?"

"As I already told you," he said. "I'm taking *Evelyn* to a show."

"So you're seducing her then." Nora nodded. "What makes you think she knows anything worthwhile anyway? We're looking into the symbol and these people as possible links to Felix. Other than knowing what the symbol was, what more value can she possibly have?"

August shrugged. He had taken out his sketch pad and was now moving a thin piece of charcoal lightly over the paper. "I'm spying on these people too remember? Evelyn said yes to hanging out with me, so I already have a better in than you do."

"Seduce away then," Nora waved her hand at him. "But don't tell her you're with me. For my plan to work I need to be alone... And don't get too attached, if she's a dead end—"

"Nora," he sighed, lifting his gaze, the charcoal stilling in his hand. "I know what I'm doing."

She spooned more soup into her mouth. She knew he did, but that did little to halt the unease twisting in her stomach.

Three quick knocks startled Nora from her meal, and August stilled in his armchair. She reluctantly placed her bowl down and walked over to the door as August drew his hood and crept into the bathroom on silent feet, his empty dinner bowl and sketch book in hand. Taking a deep breath, Nora opened the door to find the back of a tall woman.

The caller turned around and grinned, emphasising the freckles that were scattered on her cheeks. Her long, blood red hair was loosely braided to one side with her fringe sweeping across her pale forehead.

"Hi Nora, I'm Florence," she said, offering her hand. "Will said you'd be expecting me."

Nora accepted Florence's hand, offering her own smile. "Thanks for coming to meet with me. Would you like to come in?"

"That'd be great," Florence replied, following Nora into the room, and taking a seat on the newly vacated armchair. "You're probably wondering why I've come to meet with you. I help liaise with the newcomers; see what your needs are, like if you need a job or more permanent housing. Or whether there is an immediate threat needing to be dealt with. That sort of thing."

Nora sat on the edge of the bed. "What do you mean by threats?"

"If an individual or an organisation is still looking to hurt you, I am able to intervene and hopefully make it go away." Florence explained, tapping her fingers on the arm rest.

Nora leant forward. "You mean the king and those who follow him? You have the power to do that?"

Florence smiled, her azure eyes blazing, neither confirming nor denying Nora's question. "First tell me a bit about yourself. Who are you? Where are you from? Why are you seeking refuge?"

Nora thought back to the story she and August had concocted after he had slipped in through the window with their belongings. His belongings. She only had the stolen clothes that she was currently wearing.

"You already know my name," Nora started, playing with the knitted blanket by her thigh. "I'm from Rovton but have been travelling for a while. I got caught up with the King's Guild. I said some things about the king a little too loudly in a tavern and they weren't completely happy about it."

"I can imagine." Florence leant back, crossing one leg over the other, looking completely at ease.

"I don't think they're still after me," Nora chewed the inside of her cheek. "But I'd rather be safe than sorry."

"I understand." Florence nodded. "The King's Guild are like dogs with a bone."

Nora smiled. Even if she weren't pretending, she would have agreed with that. "Are there many of you?" she asked. "What I mean is, the symbol the Lys Alv told me about—does it mean something all over Valmenessia?"

"If you look hard enough," Florence's blue eyes sparkled. "You will always find someone to help you."

"That's rather vague." Nora replied with a chuckle.

Florence grinned foxily. "Do you have any coin?"

"Not much," she replied, deciding not to push Florence's lack of answer yet again.

"So you'll need work." Florence tapped her finger on her chin. "Do you have an skills?"

*Not many that would be appropriate mentioning,* Nora thought, stifling her smirk. "I'm pretty good with my Elementum magic and a quick learner when it comes to most things."

"Pretty broad but I can work with that," Florence replied, her lips pursed and eyes focused on the ceiling.

They sat in silence and Nora took in the woman before her. Florence had an air of confidence that was comforting rather than arrogant—like she could take on any situation and everything would work out. Her attire only added to her aura. She was dressed in tight charcoal slacks with knee-high leather boots and what looked to be a very warm and expensive thick coat. Her occupation as a liason clearly paid well.

Nora couldn't help but wonder what Florence thought of her.

After what felt like an eternity, Florence returned her gaze to Nora's. "How do you feel about flowers?"

Draping the blankets neatly over the bed, Nora gathered her boots and sat on the soft mattress. The morning light was creating patterns with the glow that snuck in between the trees.

"First day!" August grinned, walking out of the bathroom and towel drying his hair. He wore only dark grey slacks, his scarred and muscular chest on display. "Remember to play nice with others."

Nora wanted nothing more than to smack August's stupid face, with his stupid chiselled jaw and stupid sculpted nose. She shoved her foot into her boot then threw one of the pillows. He caught it with ease, dropping both the pillow and his towel on the armchair, his smile growing wider.

"You're not funny," she grumbled. She had woken feeling barely rested and the sight of him looking so chirpy irritated her.

August placed a hand on his chest. "Oh, but I am."

She rolled her eyes. "When are you meeting Evelyn?"

"Noon." He said, rummaging through his pack.

"Have you given any more thought to your plan? You were light on the details last night." Nora stood with her hands on her hips, narrowing her brown eyes.

"The only plan I need is to be my charming self," he replied simply, shrugging on a shirt.

"That is the worst plan you've ever come up with," she scoffed, grabbing her cloak. "You'll be back here, waiting around for me by twelve thirty."

His fingers paused on a button as he looked up at her. "Such little faith in your best friend."

"Yep," she smirked, hand on the doorknob. "Best friends don't lie to each other."

"Apparently not," August chuckled as she shut the door.

Nora trudged down the stairs, her mind going over the implications of what Florence had said and hinted at the night before. Once she had left, Nora and August had discussed the woman's words at length and had surmised that, whoever these people were, they had connections and resources available to them. Whether they had used them to kidnap Felix, well, that was something Nora was determined to find out. August had also told her that Florence was an Anima. What her shift was, however, was still a mystery, which meant they needed to be even more careful. Looking up as she reached the bottom step, she came face to face with Sage.

They collided, almost tumbling to the floor with the stack of books the woman was holding. "Goddess!" Nora exclaimed, holding onto Sage's forearms as they steadied themselves. "Shit!"

"You need to look where you're going," Sage accused, crouching to retrieve her belongings.

"You mustn't have been either if you didn't move out of the way," Nora retorted, dropping to her knees to help. She picked up one of the books, turning it on its side to read the spine. "*Mystical Energies and other vibrations.*" Nora quirked a brow. "Interesting."

Sage snatched the book. "That's none of your business."

Nora picked up another, reading the title. "*Powerful Crystals: A Beginners—*"

"Again"—Sage grabbed the book—"none of your business."

"Oh, this one, I like this one way more than the others," Nora said, purposely trying to antagonise Sage. She was planning on trying to get along with Sage, but it was clear the woman wasn't interested. So Nora would annoy Sage until the woman steered well clear of her. "*Stormy Nights on the Maiden Voyage.*"

Sage made for the volume, but Nora moved quickly, darting out of the woman's reach, and rising to her feet. "Can I borrow this? I promise to return it."

Before words could fall from Sage's mouth, Nora slipped into the dining room and hastily grabbed a plain slice of toast and an apple, then headed straight for the front door. Sage stood nearby, her remaining books once again piled in her arms and her brown eyes burning.

"Give it back," Sage demanded through gritted teeth.

"I will when I'm finished," Nora winked. "I really appreciate the loan!"

And with that, Nora darted out the front door. She could feel Sage's frustration pressing into her back, and even though it was incredibly tempting to turn around, she restrained herself. Annoying Sage was going to be an enjoyable pastime.

# 15

## Evelyn

Mr Fritz's Fantabulous Friends was a travelling showcase of talents, and Evelyn was excited to see the acts. At least, that's what she told herself was causing the buzzing in her stomach. She stood at the end of Maple Street, her golden eyes snagging on each hooded individual that wove through the mass of people.

Evelyn jumped as a firm hand gripped her shoulder.

"Hello there," drawled a low voice. August's warm breath caressed her cheek as he leaned in from behind.

Evelyn angled her head to see him, conscious of how close her lips were to his. August wore his usual hood, hiding the upper half of his face, but she was still able to see his strong, stubbled jaw that led to a playful smile. It made her want to giggle shyly.

"Hi," she squeaked, then coughed, trying to get a hold of herself. She stepped forward, spun around, and smiled. "Hi—"

A woman bumped into Evelyn's back with a grumble, pushing Evelyn into August's muscular chest. He caught her, strong hands gripping her upper arms as Evelyn breathed in August's scent of mint and musk.

August chuckled, hands on either side of Evelyn to brace her. "That was fucking rude."

"Oh," she stepped back, releasing herself from his hold and trying to shove down her thoughts on how good he smelled. "I'm sorry, I didn't mean to bump you."

"Huh?" he tilted his head. "I meant the woman. You are more than welcome to bump into me whenever you like."

Evelyn felt her face heat. How did he have this effect on her? "Should we find somewhere to stand for the show?"

"I don't think we'll be able to see from the street," he replied, glancing around before tilting his head towards the sky. "I think I know where we can get a good view." He took her hand, leading her away from the crowd.

There were other people in the side street as they entered, and Evelyn noticed they were climbing up the branches of a nearby tree and onto the building's roof. It was three storeys high, and the branches did not appear overly secure. She hesitated and felt August squeeze her hand.

"You're a Lys Alv," August said, squeezing her hand at her hesitation. "If you fall, you'll heal."

"It will still hurt," she countered with a pout.

"Your choice," he shrugged, letting go of her hand. "But it'd be a shame for you to miss it... not to mention I'll be all alone."

She groaned but could not help the small smile that spread over her face. Watching him climb the tree, she tried not to stare at the way his muscular body was visible even under his cloak. She shook her head, clearing her thoughts and praying to the Goddess Nyssa to watch over her. Taking a deep breath, she followed him up the branches.

On the rooftop, people were perched along the far side overlooking Maple Street. August led her to a spot on the roof's edge and sat, his legs dangling over the side while Evelyn stood, refusing to join him.

"You should sit," he patted the spot next to him. "There's a lovely seat here for you."

"No thank you," she replied, crossing her arms over her chest as the butterflies in her stomach threw a wild party. "As I made it clear before, I'm not interested in falling today."

"But as I said before, you're a Lys Alv," he reminded her, his tone teasing.

"As you keep reminding me," she pouted. "But again, it will hurt if I fall."

"I won't let you fall. I promise," he said, drawing a cross over his chest with a finger. "Swear it on the Gods and Goddesses. All five. Heck, I'll even swear it on the Makers too."

Evelyn bit her lip, then slowly crept towards the edge before cautiously sitting and balling her shaking hands on her lap, trying to focus on the stage instead of the drop below. August reached over and squeezed her hands in one of his. Her stomach did a flip, but she didn't pull away. She liked the way his strong calloused hands felt against hers. Plus, if she fell, she could pull him down with her, which would serve him right seeing as it was his idea to sit on the edge of the roof in the first place. Evelyn worried her lip; Poppy was going to love hearing all about this.

"Doesn't the rush make you feel alive?" he asked wistfully.

Evelyn grumbled. "Painfully alive, and I'd really like to keep it that way."

August laughed and Evelyn could not help grinning at him. His joy was infectious.

"Tell me something about you." He said, running his thumb along her hand. "Do you have any siblings?"

"I have a sister," Evelyn replied, her voice a little higher than it usually was. She cleared her throat. "Her name is Jasmine and she's older than me."

"Is she a Healer like you?" He asked, leaning forward to peer out over the edge.

"No," she said, leaning back to counter his movement as her heart thundered in her chest. If he leant forward any further he was going to fall and pull her with him. "She works at The Humble Tart Bakehouse as a pastry chef."

"I like the name," August replied, sitting back up straight, his shoulders shaking with amusement.

"Yeah, the owner has a wicked sense of humour," she added with a chuckle of her own. "Jasmine makes most of the cakes and pastries there. Many are her recipes too; she gets that from our father."

"Your father is a chef too?" He tilted his head to the side.

"No, he's a Healer." Evelyn shook her head, remembering to correct herself. That was not his job anymore. *"Was* a Healer."

"Shit, I'm sorry." August frowned and squeezed her hands.

"Oh no," Evelyn shook her head again, her golden eyes wide at his misinterpretation. "He's not dead. He just has a different job now… What I meant is he's a Conjurer and Jasmine is one too. The only difference is my father uses his conjuring talents for healing and she uses hers to make delicious sweets."

Evelyn sometimes wondered whether her father would have planned for Jasmine to be a Healer too if he had known that she would eventually be able to conjure like him. Multiple Conjurers in one family was almost unheard of.

"Your father and sister are human?" August asked. It sounded more like a statement than a question.

"Yes," she nodded. "And my mother and I are Lys Alvs."

There were many ideas as to why children of mixed races were born like one parent or the other. Evelyn had heard lots of theories; some believed it had to do with whether one parent was stronger, which God or Goddess was watching over the child, or even the position of the parents during conception, but what Evelyn had come to understand was that it was random. The only way to know for certain which race your child would be was to conceive it with someone of the same race.

"Is your mother a Healer too?" August asked, his thumb moving back and forth over her fingers again, making them tingle.

"No, she's an artist," she smiled proudly. "Have you seen the carvings on the buildings?"

"Yeah, they're amazing." His shadowy grin had her heart doing somersaults.

"She does them… well, not all of them," she told him. "But she's done a few."

"Any I should look out for?"

"Umm," she bit her lip. "She's done quite a few but I think my favourites are; The Forest's Edge Library, a café called the Otter's Retreat and Will's Florist."

"I'll have to check them out," August replied. "Or maybe you could show me them yourself. Give me a little tour?"

"Sure," she nodded, a grin tugging at her lips. "So, what's your family like?"

August's head tilted down. "My parents died soon after I was born, and I have no siblings."

"I'm sorry." Her heart sank at the thought of August growing up without a family. She adored her own and felt a pang of remorse for what he had missed out on.

"Don't be, I don't have any memories of them and was never told so much as one of their names or what they looked like." He said nonchalantly, yet his slumped shoulders stated otherwise.

"Do you wish you knew something about them?" She asked gently.

"Of course, but I have no one to ask." August shrugged. "Sometimes I think not knowing may not be such a bad thing. Some people are better off not having their parents around at all."

"They could have been good people," She offered with a small smile. "Your parents I mean…"

"They could have been good, or they could have been horrible," he confided, turning away from her. "It doesn't really matter because they are dead. That much I know for certain." He sat up a little straighter. "Look, it's not all doom and gloom for me. I have Nora and if I had the choice, I'd choose her over them any day."

Evelyn smiled. "It's nice that you have such a good friendship."

August let out a deep breath. "She knows me—every little detail— and still loves me. We have been through a lot together, things that others wouldn't understand. She's family. The family I chose."

Evelyn tilted her head to the side. "Why isn't she in Forest's Edge with you?"

"Ladies and gentlemen!" came a booming voice from the street below, interrupting their conversation before August could reply.

Evelyn turned her attention to the stage where a short man with slick black hair and dressed in a charcoal suit stood at its centre. Even though she could not see them, she could feel August's eyes on her and felt the butterflies fluttering once again in her stomach.

"Introducing… Marvellous Mateo!" the man roared, and August too, turned to watch the show.

The crowd cheered loudly as a chubby man walked onto the stage and raised his arm out in front of him, his palms facing the audience. Fire appeared in the shape of three large snakes chasing their tails to create circles. The flames snapped and flashed as the front row of the crowd stepped back from the heat. With a flick of his fingers a small fireball separated from each snake and shot into the sky where they exploded into bright orange and yellow sparks, just out of reach of the canopy of trees. He repeated the magic, faster and faster and with orbs of varying size. The larger balls created explosions so loud and bright Evelyn had to shut her eyes. The people below were cheering and applauding, delighted by the show of power. Even though this part of Maple Street had less tree coverage, Evelyn was surprised the Elementum had not lit anything on fire.

The Elementum waved his hands and the circles of flame replicated multiple times before rising higher into the air above the crowd. Three magpies flew overhead then double-backed and wove through the rings of fire. The circles then changed shape, some becoming squares and stars of flame whereas others merely changed in size. Again, the birds flew through the floating fire as the crowd "oohed" and "ahhed" below. As the magpies turned in the sky, the Elementum transformed the floating fire into one long flaming tube with many twists, turns and loops. The black and white birds flew in a sharp line and entered the tube. The audience went silent and all that could be heard was the flames as they crackled and sparked intensely. Evelyn held her breath and glanced at August, the visible part of his face-tinged orange from the fire. She turned back to the spectacle to see the magpies fly out the other end of the flaming tube and transform into three identical young girls. They each did a tumble turn and fell gracefully towards the ground where two Elementums slowed their fall and caught them in their wind magic. The crowd erupted and Evelyn was sure the cheers and applause would be heard miles away.

"That was amazing!" August exclaimed.

"I don't think I took a single breath the whole time they were in that fire tube," said Evelyn, unable to hide her grin. "Those girls are braver than I am."

"You're brave," he replied earnestly.

She laughed humourlessly. "Maybe in a very loose sense of the word."

"You are. You are sitting on the edge of a roof." He waved his unoccupied hand before them.

"Don't remind me," she groaned.

"And you were brave the night I met you," he said, his voice sending a tingle dancing along her skin.

"That's not bravery," she looked to her hands. "That's just my job."

He took her chin in his hand, raising her face to his hooded one. "You spend your day freely receiving painful injuries for the benefit of others. If that's not brave, I don't know what is."

She frowned half-heartedly. "I guess."

Below, a magician dressed in the most ostentatious glitter suit walked onto the stage followed by a petite woman who wore a matching glitter leotard. As the magician spoke to the crowd, his assistant waved her hands over a colourfully painted box before climbing inside, and popping her head, hands, and feet out of holes in the wood. The assistant smiled unnaturally wide as the magician locked her inside. Then, with a wink, he produced a serrated saw and cut the box in half. The crowd cheered as the assistant waved her hands and feet from the two separate halves. The magician then returned the two boxes together and after shouting some supposedly magical words, the assistant emerged intact, followed by deafening applause from the crowd. The duo continued to perform more illusions for the eager crowd; sleight of hand and tricks of the eye spurred on by the audience.

Following the magician was a pair Lys Alvs who stepped onto the stage wearing tight leather pants and vests that accentuated their muscles and curves. Drawing their glistening swords, they demonstrated the blades" deadly edges by slicing through apples that were thrown at them by their fellow performers. The crowd grew restless at what seemed dull compared to the previous acts, but then the Lys Alvs lifted their swords above their heads and swallowed the blades to their hilts.

Gasps rang out, eyes wide in horror, yet this was only the beginning. The Lys Alvs removed the blades and proceeded to consume more sharp objects as well as various poisons. Once it was clear that neither Lys Alv was going to bleed from their orifices, pass out, or die, the audience cheered and shouted for more.

"Does that stuff bother you?" inquired August.

"Not really," Evelyn replied as she watched the show below. "My mother's family are travelling performers, kind of like these people. When they come to the city my mother always takes us to see their show. My uncle's act is similar to this."

"Did your mother ever perform?" he asked curiously.

"No, she would make the flyers and stand around with an upturned hat to collect coins from the audience." She told him, smiling warmly at the story her mother had recounted to her. "Then one day she met my father and fell in love. She moved here and the rest is history."

Evelyn could not believe how much she had told him about her life, especially when she knew so little about him. Every question he asked she could not help but reply and if she was honest with herself, she was really enjoying his interest in her life.

The show ended, but August and Evelyn did not move from their spot straight away. The crowd on the rooftop and on the thoroughfare below dispersed into the nearby streets, and Evelyn felt mindful of the fact that they were now alone. She was keenly aware of the dull murmur of those that lingered below, of the sounds of the show being packed away, and of August sitting so close when they now had plenty of space around them.

"I should go," she said, biting the inside of her cheek.

"So eager to get rid of me again," he joked, a hand pressed over his heart. "You wound me."

"I didn't mean it like that," she said softly.

August rose from the roof's edge and offered Evelyn his hand. She took it hurriedly, telling herself that the rush to grasp it had been purely because she did not want to accidentally fall over the edge. She followed him down the tree, glad that she had chosen pants rather than a dress, and as she stepped onto the last branch, she turned to drop to the ground, but he gripped her hips and lifted her. The movement brought her so close that she came face to face with August and was given a full view under his hood. His eyes glowed and reminded her of the sky, both at night and during the day. The contrast was beautiful.

Her voice was barely audible as her words left her lips. "You're a Mors Alv."

August laughed, his shocked expression disappearing within seconds, causing Evelyn to believe she had imagined it. "You have an odd sense of humour."

"I wasn't being funny," Evelyn scrunched her nose. "I saw your eyes. At least I thought I saw... Now I feel stupid."

"You're not stupid." He waved the thought off.

"Well, I must be if I'm imagining things," she said, hands on her hips.

"It was just a trick of the light," he said, shrugging. "Or lack thereof."

Frowning, Evelyn looked up at his hooded face. He had taken a step back after her declaration, so she was unable to sneak a second glance to determine whether she had imagined those dark eyes—black orbs like coal with bright blue irises.

Before she was born there had been a royal decree commanding the eradication of Mors Alvs from the continent after Queen Helen had been murdered by a trusted Mors Alv advisor. Soldiers had been dispatched and rewards had been offered, and the population of Mors Alvs had disappeared. Her tutors had called it "The Eradication of Death" and had painted a picture of the Mors Alvs as evil beings who killed for pleasure. Evelyn's parents had sought to teach her an alternate account. They had emphasised the importance of not judging a race by the actions of a few and to always think critically, especially when a narrative like that conveniently fits with the leader's objective. To say that her parents did not think highly of King Dominic would have been an understatement.

"I could have sworn..." she shook her head. There were no more Mors Alvs, King Dominic had made sure of that. "Never mind."

"Want to get something to eat?" he asked, happily changing the subject.

"I do, but I have to get ready for work," she pouted. "I'm on the night shift."

August stuffed his hands into his pockets. "You don't sound too happy about that."

"I just prefer working during the day. There's more of a routine. The night shift usually alternates between eerily silent to chaos," she explained, rubbing her neck. "Even though I constantly ask, I don't get rostered on to tend to patients with conditions that have no need for my magical interventions, like aging and circumstances that they're born with or are predisposed to. So, unless someone comes in injured there is little I can do but paperwork and odd jobs."

"Tomorrow then?" he asked hopefully.

"Sleeping." A small smile tugged at her lips. "Then work."

"Is this your way of getting rid of me without having to say you're not interested?" he teased.

"No!" In her mind she imagine slapping herself. "I genuinely have work."

August grinned, the shadows making the lines of his smile appear villainous. "I'm glad to hear that you want to spend time with me."

Heat crept up her neck.

A clatter came from the opposite end of the side street. August angled his head toward the noise as Evelyn scrunched her brows, trying to see who or what had made the sound. As far as she could tell, there was no-one else in the passageway.

"I think it's time to say goodbye. I wouldn't want to make you late for work," August said, taking her hand and drawing her attention back to him. He lifted her hand to his mouth and kissed her knuckles, his lips soft against her skin. "But I will see you again soon, I promise."

# 16

## Nora

"Did you hear about Lord Akedale?" asked the elderly woman who stood on the other side of the counter, watching Nora intently. Her snowy hair was tied in a neat bun atop her head and her hands were clasped before her as if holding herself back from assisting Nora.

"No," Nora replied, trying to hide her frustration at her poor attempt at a bouquet. The bundle of flowers lying before her looked nothing like one of Will's beautiful arrangements. When Nora had arrived at the florist that morning, Will had given her a rundown of her tasks, but no further direction. The rest she was apparently supposed to figure out on her own. "What happened?"

"My grandson just returned from Midskopas," the woman continued, "said Lord Akedale was executed for treason! He and the loyal members of his court were strung up outside his estate for all to see."

"What?" Nora's brows rose and she pulled the ribbon too tight, ruining the bow. If this were true, it would have happened just after she and August had left. "Did he tell you what the crime was specifically?"

"He wasn't enforcing registrations, but why would he have? The man was an Anima." The woman said, waving her hand dismissively. "He wouldn't have been happy to push such horrible laws on his race."

"Seems a bit extreme for him to be executed," Nora commented, pouting her lips.

"Exactly!" The woman threw her hands into the air. "If you ask me, King Dominic was just looking for an excuse to remove Lord Akedale from his position of power."

Nora raised an eyebrow. Turns out the florist was a hive of gossip. People did not just buy flowers for their loved ones or for their homes to look pretty. Customers came to see Will because he offered more. Bouquets for love, grief, apologies and friendship, plants for potions, ointments and toxins, and flowers for decoration and art. There were literally blooms for everything imaginable, which meant Will's clientele was diverse too.

"Mark my words," the woman continued, gathering the ribbon scrunched around the bouquet and tying it in a perfect bow. "The king will place an Elementum in Midskopas any day now. Just like in the other cities." She dropped her coins onto the counter before collecting her flowers. "You'll see."

Nora chewed her lip, watching the woman leave.
"Mable sharing her wisdom?" Will asked, appearing beside Nora, a bushy potted plant in his hands.

"She thinks King Dominic is replacing the lords and ladies who aren't following his laws with Elementum," Nora said, putting away the roll of ribbon.

"And you believe he isn't? Or do you think he's justified in his actions?" Will queried, placing the plant down on the counter.

"Which other cities has he removed the lords and ladies and put in Elementum?" she asked, avoiding his questions.

"Dostvet Harbour, Rovton, Crestoy, and Midskopas will be the fourth." He told her, pruning a leaf with each mention of a city. "We won't know for certain for another few days at least, but once it's announced, King Dominic will have all the major southern cities under Elementum rule."

Nora scratched her chin. "What about Sorby and Ferieton? Their lords and ladies aren't Elementum."

"The Lys Alvs in Ferieton and the humans in Sorby wouldn't be seen as a threat to him… yet." Will picked up the plant, its foliage now perfectly trimmed. "Enough politics, I'm sure there are more customers you can serve."

Staring after Will, Nora thought about what the man had said. Like Mable, Will was certain the king was putting Elementum in positions of power instead of the other races. If King Dominic was removing lords and ladies who were not following the laws, then he had good intentions driving his actions and maybe replacing them with Elementum was just a coincidence. These people were most likely twisting the situation to appear sinister.

"Hey, Nora!" came a female voice, drawing Nora from her thoughts.

She looked over to see Florence walking towards the counter. She was dressed in a turquoise sweater emphasising the braided red hair that fell over one shoulder, and strode with one hand on her hip. Behind her, Sage had her arms folded over her chest as though she were already irritated by Nora's presence.

"Hey Florence," Nora smiled. "Hey Sage. Is there something I can help you with?"

Florence glanced around at the display of greenery. "Just checking up on you."

"Ha!" Nora opened her arms wide. "Feel free to check me out all you want." She shot Sage a wink.

"Check up on, not check out," Sage groaned.

Florence chuckled. "I'm actually here to pick up an order."

"Okay," Nora hesitated, trying to remember what Will had taught her. She retrieved a large book from underneath the counter and dropped it down onto the wooden top with a thud. She flipped it open to the page that listed current orders. "Is it under your name?"

"Yeah, it should be a box of dried thorn apple," Florence clarified. Thorn apple was from the Nightshade family if Nora remembered correctly. What was the woman needing a whole box for?

Peering up between her lashes, Nora glimpsed Sage watching her. Sage's eyes were narrowed in Nora's direction. Hopefully, her public animosity would not affect Nora's plans.

"I'm really enjoying the book you leant me," Nora said casually, returning her gaze to the order list.

"You mean the one you stole," Sage seethed.

Nora shrugged. "That's your perception."

"That's the fact." Sage's words came out coated in frustration.

Florence laughed, watching the interaction with amusement. "Have I read this book before?"

"No, and Nora did not borrow it." Sage insisted, fisting her hands at her sides. "She took it without asking after knocking—"

"Found it!" Nora declared, a little pleased with herself for doing her job successfully. Sage fell silent but Nora could tell the woman was biting her tongue. "I'll just go get that for you. Won't be a moment."

Nora went into the back of the store to where Will had shown her the orders were kept. She hugged her arms to her chest as she entered the cold, poorly lit room. To the left, buckets of water housed flower arrangements and potted plants, and to the right was a shelf filled with boxes, vials, and smaller parcels. She made her way to the shelf and searched for the box labelled with Florence's name and contents. To Nora's relief, it did not take long for her to find it. With teeth threatening to chatter, she slipped the box from its place on the shelf, her eyes growing wide. For a box of dried thorn apple, it was surprisingly heavy and made a metallic clinking noise when she moved it. Nora was tempted to open it, curious to see what Florence had *actually* purchased, but was interrupted by Will.

"I'd thought you'd gone to pick, dry, and box the thorn apple yourself with how long you're taking," he remarked, ushering her out of the room with a wave of his hands. "There are other customers and tasks."

"Do you want the job done fast or done right?" she asked, striding past him and back to where Florence was waiting.

"Both," he replied with a close-lipped smile.

"My order?" Florence asked, pointing at the box as Nora returned to the main store with Will. Sage was wandering around, stopping to feel and smell the wide variety of plants. How the florist was able to obtain such a wide selection of flora amazed Nora. Clearly this man had contacts.

"Here you go," Nora handed it over. "It's rather heavy and noisy for a box of thorn apple."

Florence's eyes widened for the briefest of moments before her face became unreadable, and the woman tilted her head to the side. "So, do you think you'll be staying in Forest's Edge for a while?"

"I'd like to," Nora smiled hopefully, her lies falling easily from her tongue. "With any luck this job will go well, and I can get somewhere more permanent to live."

*And you trust me enough to let me in on your secrets,* she thought.

"You seem like you're fitting in well here," offered Florence with a wink. "You've made an impression on Sage."

Nora grinned genuinely now and rested her hip against the counter, watching the two women leave the store. If Florence thought she was fitting in, then that was a good sign. And Sage, well, she was enjoying antagonising the woman.

"I didn't realise it was break time," said Will sarcastically, tugging Nora away from her thoughts.

"I was watering the ferns," replied Nora, keeping her cool as she hastily summoned a fine mist over the potted plants. "See?"

"I see," Will smirked. "I do indeed see."

◇

A figure caught Nora's eye from where she was sitting beneath a towering pine tree with a small ball of flame illuminating the page before her. It wasn't big enough to warm her but provided ample light to read by in the otherwise dark night. She watched as the figure drew closer and her shoulders relaxed, recognising August. He prowled towards her, his dark figure like a demon lurking in the shadows.

Nora remained where she was, returning her gaze to the book she was reading. "How was your day with Evelyn? Find out anything interesting?"

"As a matter of fact, I did." He snatched the book from her, the little ball of flame following so he could read the page she was on. "This is not appropriate for a young lady."

"And I'm only a few pages in," Nora said, standing and taking the book back. She wiggled her eyebrows at him. "So, I can only imagine how inappropriate it's going to get. Sage has great taste in books, but that's beside the point. Tell me what you learnt."

He moved to lean against the tree. "You know how Lord Royd commissioned the engravings on the buildings? Well Evelyn's mother has done a lot of them, including the florist."

"Really?" Nora replied. "That *is* interesting. Maybe the little Lys Alv is useful after all."

"She's taller than you," August pointed out, dropping his hood, and running a hand through his dirty blond hair. "Did you find out any more about who these people are?"

Nora sighed. "Unfortunately, no, but there has to be more than just Florence, Will, Daphne, Sage, Evelyn, and now her mother." She used her fingers to keep track of the names as she spoke. "There must be more than six people. Plus, a woman came into the store today and spoke so openly about her views of King Dominic, and let me tell you, she wasn't confessing her love."

"Anything of note?"

"She accused King Dominic of replacing the southern lords and ladies with Elementum." Nora told him. "As though he has some vendetta against the other races."

"There's definitely a pattern." August shrugged.

"You sound just like them," she retorted, rolling her eyes. "Coincidence doesn't mean there is a vendetta. The Elementum he's promoted are clearly the best for the job. You and I both know he has no issue with the other races. There are Anima, humans, Alvs and Elementum in the Alta as well as the Royal Sentries. Surely that wouldn't be the case if he had some sinister plan."

August sent her an annoyed glare. "All that proves is he's happy to use anyone, but if you look at the people in charge—King Dominic, his advisors, Rana…"

"They're all skilled and have merit to hold their jobs." Nora argued. "Are you telling me that he shouldn't hire people based on merit? That he should choose people based on some sort of quota? The hard workers will no longer reap the benefits if that's the case!"

"So Elementum are the only race that works hard?" He quirked a brow.

"Don't twist my words," Nora grumbled, folding her arms over her chest. With a heavy sigh she decided to change the subject. There was no point arguing with August; King Dominic's way was the right one, even if August refused to see it. "Florence and Sage came to the shop today too."

"Did they see how terrible you are at being a florist?" August teased.

"No." She stuck her tongue out. "Florence came to pick up a package. Dried thorn apple."

"What would she need with a box full of Nightshade?" He looked at her curiously.

Nora shrugged. "That's not the most interesting part. When I moved the box, it made a clanging noise like there was something metal in there. Something is definitely going on in this city."

August stepped towards her. "Do you still think any of this is linked with Felix's disappearance?"

"I honestly don't know," she pouted. "But it's valuable information, nonetheless. I haven't been able to ask any more about the symbol, but I will soon. Felix is our number one priority, no matter how interesting these people are."

"I'll continue pursuing Evelyn, find out more about her family and what their role is in all this. If Lord Royd commissioned the engravings like the florist told you, then maybe whoever these people are have a more powerful backing than we realise."

"Would make sense with how confident Florence was about making problems disappear," Nora agreed. "Okay, I will ask Will next time I get a chance. I just don't want him to think I'm prying."

"Even though you are," he chuckled.

"You say that like it's a bad thing," she smirked. "I definitely think my way in is through Florence or Will. They seem to like me."

"Should I be worried?" August joked. "Are you going to get a new best friend?"

"Maybe." She tapped her lip. "I *am* due for an upgrade. Jealous?"

August threw his head back. "Ha! Not at all! I know you love me most even if the idea of saying it aloud is worse than death for you."

Nora wriggled her shoulders as though agitated by a tense muscle. The tattoos that encircled her wrist would not let her fall for anyone romantically, but they did not stop her from feeling other kinds of love—the ones people felt for their family and friends. King Dominic had not commanded that kind of love away. Nora wasn't sure why, but then again, most Alta did not have families. On the rare occasion they did, they were estranged for some reason or another.

August was her family. King Dominic commanded her love through the shackle tattoos, but August was the only person she felt it for willingly. She was not sure whether she would feel the same about the king without her tattoos, but it was something she refused to think about. King Dominic had taken her in. He saw that she was special, and she owed him everything.

"Let's head back to our room," August said, drawing his hood and setting off towards Daphne's.

Nora stuffed the book into her cloak pocket as she walked at his side. "We agreed to take a couple of days to look into this symbol. If we can't find a connection to Felix in that time we will move on."

"Do you think a few days is enough time?" August asked.

"I hope so," she replied. "We'll have to make it work. The king wants us to find Felix and we can't waste any more time."

"I wouldn't call our trip so far a waste of time," he scoffed.

"We'll have to agree to disagree then," Nora said. "Either way, his command to find Felix feels like talons tearing into my chest. Each day the claws go deeper and deeper. Doesn't it bother you?"

"I try not to think about it," he replied dismissively, draping an arm over her shoulder. "If you were as powerful as me, you'd be able to block it out too."

"I think you're confusing stupidity for power," she quipped, slipping out from under his arm and grinning.

They made their way through dark, trekking over roots and fallen branches, and wove their way towards Daphne's, the air around them chilling Nora to the bone. Homes were nestled amongst the shadowy trees, the warm light trickling from their windows making little impression on the eerie dark. Nora kept her fireball burning, lighting the way at her feet to stop herself from tripping, but as they drew closer, she extinguished her flame.

"I'll meet you inside," she said, stepping towards the front of the building.

August snatched her cloak in his fingers, halting her movement. "Give me a boost with your magic first."

"Lazy ass," Nora chuckled, following him around the back.

As they neared, voices emerged from an open window on the ground flower. Nora and August exchanged a quick glance then tiptoed closer on silent feet.

"Who else is coming?" a smooth, high voice asked inside the room. If Nora had her bearings right, these people were inside Daphne and Sage's part of the house.

"Just Florence," replied a husky male voice. "Speaking of which…"

"Sorry I'm late," apologised a female, her tone confident. *Florence,* Nora thought, sitting down next to the open window, and leaning her head against the wall. August slid down beside her, and she welcomed the warmth of his body pressed to hers.

"Any news from Gemma?" questioned a melodic voice. This voice was familiar, but Nora had difficulty placing it.

"She said from what her contacts have told her, the king is expanding his armies," replied Florence.

"Damn!" snarled the husky male voice. "We should be expanding our numbers too. We are running out of time."

"Keep your voice down," scolded the first woman.

Nora resisted popping her head up and sneaking a look through the window at who was speaking with Florence.

"We are doing the best we can, it's not like you're recruiting high numbers." Came the melodic voice. "And I don't know about you, but I want loyal members. I'm not interested in recruiting people who cannot be trusted. Gemma wants us to be smart."

Sage. The melodic voice belonged to Sage. Nora must not have recognised it at first because the woman was not annoyed like she was now. Nora grinned. Seems she was not the only person Sage reprimanded.

"Let's not bicker amongst ourselves," chided Will. Nora easily recognised his voice after spending the day listening to him order her around. "What else did she have to say?"

"She is going to tally our members and supplies; looks like the faction leaders are readying for a big push," explained Florence.

"Does she think that's safe?" Sage asked.

"It's never going to be safe," said Will. "All factions working together to make a big push is precisely what we need. We can't keep letting him target the Anima population. Registrations, arrests, harassment… The strong Anima he captures are either murdered or sent to the mines. Royal Sentries and the King's Guild are taking these laws as an opportunity to flout their prejudices."

"It's the Mors Alvs all over again," said the unknown woman.

"Exactly! So rather than exterminate the Anima outright because their population is much larger than the Mors Alvs ever were, he's taking his time. Weakening them," added Florence. "And ultimately the result will be the same if we do nothing. Word is he's taken Midskopas, and I'm not eager to wait around and see if he comes for Forest's Edge."

There was a long pause. Nora glanced at August, his shadowed lips were in a firm line.

Could they be right? Was King Dominic trying to eradicate the Anima like he'd executed the Mors Alvs twenty years ago? Nora shook her head. King Dominic was a just and fair ruler. They were doing what August had done before; twisting the narrative to suit themselves.

"Gemma also said," began Florence, breaking the silence, "that something is amiss with the king's personal soldiers."

That piqued Nora's interest and she felt August tense beside her.

"What does that mean? It hasn't been confirmed that the Alta are even real. For all we know someone is feeding us false information to keep us busy," said the man with the husky voice. "We could be freaking out over a fairy-tale for all we know."

"Fairy-tale or not, from the intelligence Gemma's getting, there looks to be reason to stay alert," Will said. "If the Alta are real, would any of you know how to spot one?"

# 17

## Evelyn

The sun slowly rose giving the sky a ginger glow that filtered through the trees. As Evelyn left a patient's house after dropping off some healing supplies, she buttoned up her floral print jacket and wrapped a scarf around her neck to ward of the morning chill. Setting off in the direction that took her along the outskirts of the bustling city towards her home, she tread carefully as the path was slick with morning dew and an icy fog lingered among the trees. Yawning, she covered her mouth with a gloved hand, the fatigue from working the nightshift trying to take hold.

Evelyn continued onto the path that ran between the houses and thick forest. It was not the most direct route, but she liked to stroll this way as it helped to clear her mind. The stillness and scent of the pine trees had a calming effect, not that it was working very effectively right now. Withdrawing the piece of paper from her pocket, she unfolded it to have another look at the sketch August had left in her room at work. The picture was of them sitting on a rooftop surrounded by trees. Evelyn's heart gave a little flutter and smiled at the memory of being with August and the romantic gesture of capturing the moment with charcoal on paper. How could she like him so much already?

Carefully folding up the paper, she placed it back into her pocket and continued to make her way through the trees before spotting a young boy sitting on a cluster of rocks at the path's edge. She was not sure whether to approach, but she had been trained to care for others and leaving him alone felt wrong. As Evelyn drew closer to the boy, she noticed that he looked dishevelled; his ash blond hair was a tangled mess with dirt and twigs entwined in it, and his clothing was not much better. His face was downcast, yet she could still see that one of his eyes was looking like a tomato and that his bottom lip was bleeding.

"Hello there, my name is Evelyn," she said softly, crouching down so that she was at his eye level. "Are you okay?"

The boy sniffed. "They ripped my jumper."

"I'm sure it can be mended," she said gently, looking to where he was sticking his finger through a hole in the hem of his sweater. "The people who did that to your jumper, did they also hurt your face?"

"Yes," he whimpered, a tear rolling down his freckled cheek. "They chased me and shouted mean things, then punched me."

"I'm sorry they did that to you. I can't do much about your jumper, but I can heal your face. Would you like me to heal you?"

The boy looked up and saw who he had been speaking to. His brown eyes widened as he nodded eagerly. "Yes, please."

Evelyn knelt on the dirt path in front of him. Removing her gloves, she placed her hands gently on his face. The healing took a matter of moments, and when she sat back, the boy looked at her with concern.

"I don't like it when it does that," he said, pointing to the cut on her lip.

"It's okay, she reassured him. "It will be gone soon."

The boy's features soften, his mouth tugging up at one side, and she knew the injuries on her face had already begun to fade.

"Would you like me to walk you home?" she asked, getting to her feet, and dusting the dirt from her knees. She slipped her gloves on then offered him her hand.

"Yes!" He smiled from ear to ear, wrapping his fingers around hers.

"What is your name?"

"Franklin."

"It's lovely to meet you, Franklin," she smiled warmly.

Franklin led her away from the path they were on and into the makeshift trails between the houses. As they wove through the trees and buildings, climbing over the occasional root, branch, or boulder, he told her about his family and the things he was learning at school. Evelyn listened intently, enjoying his take on the world. They arrived at his home and as they walked up the path a woman came rushing out of the house.

"There you are!" the woman exclaimed, followed by a burly looking man. She scooped Franklin up and squeezed him tight.

"I was out looking everywhere for you," sighed the man, his features softening.

"This nice lady walked me home, Mama," Franklin told them as his mother put him down.

The boy's parents startled, as if only noticing Evelyn was there.

"I found him on the outer path," she explained.

"And she healed me," Franklin added, grinning broadly.

His father crouched so that he was eye level with the boy. "Your tutor sent a messenger Anima to say you hadn't turned up for classes."

Franklin looked down at his hands. "I didn't mean to run away," he sniffled, "they were hitting me and ripped my jumper."

His mother tugged him close to her side and wrapped an arm around his shoulders. She turned to Evelyn. "Some other kids have got it in their heads that they can pick on my boy."

"Little shits," Franklin's father swore. "They pick on him because he's an Anima."

"I'm sorry to hear that," replied Evelyn sincerely.

"It's those damned laws the king has been passing. Encouraging this sort of behaviour," continued the man. "If he—"

"Not now," interrupted Franklin's mother, prodding the man's shoulder and dismissing him back towards the house with a stern look.

Evelyn took that as her cue to leave. "I'd better get home. It was nice meeting you Franklin."

She smiled at the boy, and he replied with his own toothy version.

"Thank you for helping my son," said the woman, squeezing Franklin a little tighter.

"My pleasure."

Waving at the mother and child, Evelyn departed. Rather than making her way back to the path she'd originally been travelling, she decided to take the shorter route. Her shoulders drooped and her shoes were scuffing against the dirt as she dragged her feet along. Finally arriving home, she slipped into her room with a sigh of relief and removed her jacket and scarf, dropping onto her bed without changing.

"Knock, knock!" came her father's voice along with the sound of his knuckles on wood.

"What are you doing here?" Evelyn asked, sitting up on her elbows. Her father stood in the doorway, dressed in rich brown trousers and fine grey shirt, a broad smile on his face that created creases at the outer edges of his eyes.

"I live here?" he quirked a brow.

"You know what I mean," she groaned, a small smile tugging at her lips. "I'd have thought you'd be busy with more important things."

"Nothing is more important than my children," he said earnestly, walking towards her and drawing her up of the bed for a tight hug. He pulled back, hands gripping her upper arms. "Also, I haven't seen you since you returned, which one would think to be odd seeing as we just clarified, you live with me."

"Sorry, I've had a lot on my mind and my shifts here started straight away."

"It's okay, your mother and I understand, but you should join us for dinner tonight. We would love to hear all about your trip and celebrate you becoming an accredited Healer."

"I'm on night shift tonight and it's not that big of a deal," Evelyn groaned. "We don't need to celebrate."

"Am I not allowed to be proud?"

"Yes, but can you be low-key proud? No celebration necessary."

Her father raised a hand as though about to declare an oath. "Low-key proud it is. We'd still like to see you. Breakfast tomorrow?"

"Okay, breakfast," she said, giving in. "Busy day full of meetings ahead?"

"Unfortunately, no," he sighed, running a hand through his greying chocolate-coloured hair. His warm smile was gone, replaced with a tired expression that seemed to suck the usual glow from his brown skin.

"I'm off to the Healing Centre to be debriefed on more of these strange attacks. These murders and the Makers' Marks… Forest's Edge has always been a safe place… I need to get on top of it."

"Isn't it the job of the City Guard or the Royal Sentries?"

"Yes, but they report to me, and I need to keep the people calm and feeling safe," her father replied. "The last thing I need is for people to be panicking about being killed and having the Makers' Mark drawn on their foreheads in blood."

Evelyn grimaced.

He frowned, massaging his chin. "Any chance you would promise to never walk the streets alone until the murders are solved?"

"Is there any reason I would be targeted?" she asked, a chill running down her spine.

"Not specifically," he sighed, "but it would give your mother and I peace of mind."

Evelyn shook her head.

"Didn't think so," her father said. "I spoke to Gemma this morning, she wanted to meet with you."

"What about?"

"I'll let her explain when she sees you," he replied, hugging her before drawing back. "I better go hear those reports."

"Thanks for stopping by."

He paused in the doorway, a hand on the wooden door frame. "I'll see you at breakfast?"

"Yes," she said, dragging out the word and rolling her eyes playfully. "I'll be there."

## 18

## Nora

Forest's Edge was not the most orderly of cities. As well as being immersed in the forest, there were luscious bushes and garden beds scattered throughout the streets, and vines hung from overhead branches, making the thoroughfares difficult to manoeuvre when filled with people. Even though it was past midday, the chill Nora had felt that morning still lingered in the air, the leafy canopy inhibiting the sun's rays from heating the city below. The locals did not seem as bothered by the cool weather as Nora, who had her arms crossed tightly to her chest as she walked.

Will had sent Nora to the library, which turned out to be only a few streets away. The double storey building stood beneath two towering trees, their leafy green branches hanging low, embracing the library. Like many of the other buildings, the frontage was covered in carvings. Stacks of books were etched like a border along the ground and around the sides of entrance, and a large tome rested atop the door frame. Spilling out of the book were words that formed a story of the five Gods and Goddesses: Frode, Thyra, Aren, and the twins; Jord and Nyssa. Nora looked up; the story was engraved all the way up the building.

*Father Sun and Mother Moon watched over the world for many eons. Father loved the mountains, valleys and rivers, and Mother loved the flowers, trees, and creatures. Together they cared for the world. As time passed, Mother came to find herself with child. Frode—the first son—was born on a stormy night and grew to value knowledge, dedication, and perseverance. Two cycles of the seasons passed, and Mother gave birth to another son, Aren. He was strong, loyal, and had a love for all living creatures.*

*One warm summer day Mother gave birth to a daughter and called her Thyra. She was strong-willed, ambitious, and fearless. Nyssa and Jord were born soon after on the night of a full moon. Twins of balance; Nyssa strengthened by Father Sun, Jord by Mother Moon. Both felt all things deeply.*

Nora frowned; the beginning of the tale was more simplified than she remembered. Pushing open the heavy, dark-stained door, Nora stepped into a brightly lit room filled with lines of tall wooden tables and stools for reading and studying. To the left were rows and rows of floor-to-ceiling shelves that appeared to house thousands of books and scrolls. Behind the tables was an ornate staircase that led to the second floor which overlooked the first and, from what she could see, it too looked to contain more rows of shelves stacked to the roof.

As she approached a large mahogany desk on the ground floor, the air became thick with the scent of parchment, ink, and coffee beans. Behind the desk sat an older man with thinning white hair and a rather large nose.

"Excuse me?"

The man continued reading his thick, ancient book—it looked just as old as him—surrounded by a dozen cups of coffee of varying degrees of consumption. He ignored her entirely.

She cleared her throat and tried again. "Excuse me?" she said, louder this time, hoping that maybe he was hard of hearing rather than rude. Again, the man continued to ignore her, and she grew increasingly frustrated.

"Can I help you?" a voice asked from Nora's left.

She turned to see the woman she had been looking for weaving her way through the tables. Sage was dressed in a short maroon dress with a patterned trim; navy-blue tights; knee high leather boots; and a matching belt that accentuated her hips. Her thick dark hair was parted and tied on either side of her head, the ribbons failing in their attempt to restrain the tight curls. This close, Nora was able to appreciate the woman's beauty—especially her curvaceous body, which was emphasised by the way she strode with one hand on her hip.

"Yes," Nora replied, sincerely grateful. She had been just about ready to shake the old man at the desk.

"Scratch that," Sage said, halting a few steps away and folding her arms over her chest. "No one can help you."

"Sounds about right," Nora laughed and tried keep her eyes on Sage's face rather than the woman's chest that was currently being accentuated by the way Sage was standing. "Will sent me to give this to you." She handed over a wooden box—this one with yellow and orange petals on the lid. She had tried to pick the lock on the walk over, but to no avail. "What's inside?"

"That's a bit rude," Sage pointed out.

Nora shrugged. "Can you help me find books on floristry?"

"That I *can* help you with." Sage tapped her plump lips; an action that drew Nora's gaze. "Give me a second while I look up the aisle number."

She left Nora with the ignorant man for a few minutes before returning, a piece of paper in her hand.

"They're upstairs. Follow me, I'll show you."

"Thanks!" Nora followed Sage through the bookshelves and up the stairs, trying to focus on the task at hand rather than the view before her.

Nora shook her head. Why was this woman so distracting?

"What do you do here?" Nora asked, trailing her hand along the polished wood of the banister, and trying to clear her mind of other thoughts.

"I'm a research assistant." Sage replied over her shoulder.

Nora quirked a brow. "What are you researching?"

"Stuff."

"Sounds not at all broad and lacking any detail." Nora said sarcastically, rolling her eyes.

On the second floor, Nora observed the contents of the bookshelves as she was led through them. From what she could see, the library contained a large catalogue in a variety of genres and languages. It was not as big as the library in Royal Bay, but the collection here was beyond substantial.

"Here we are." Sage ran her fingers over the spines of the books, reading their titles before pulling out a few and handing them to Nora. "This should get you started."

Nora held her arms out in front of her so that Sage could pile the volumes atop them. "I don't think I'll be needing all of these."

"You never know," replied Sage without turning her head from where she read the titles on the shelf. "Take them home and maybe you could return the book you stole from me now that you have alternate reading material."

"But your book is just getting good." Nora teased, grinning wickedly.

"I'm sure it is." Sage rolled her eyes.

"It's absolutely filthy," Nora chuckled. "There are definitely no maidens on the voyage anymore."

Sage laughed, the sound surprising Nora and causing her heart to skip a beat. "I've heard it's got a good storyline."

"Who's paying attention to the storyline?" Nora's eyes widened. "Wait, haven't you read it?"

"No, some rude person stole it from me before I could get a chance to start," Sage said with a sly smile, dropping another book on Nora's growing pile. "I'll leave you to it."

"One more thing," Nora said, halting Sage's steps.

"Yes?" Sage asked. She folder her arms over her chest.

"The story engraved on the front of the library…"

"It's an abbreviated version of how The Makers created the races," said Sage. "If they tried to fit the whole thing, no one could read it."

"But that version is so boring." Nora groaned. "I know it's only the introduction but… where's the flare? Adventure? Violence? Heartache?"

"It's not like everyone doesn't already know the story," Sage sighed dramatically, walking away.

With her arms full of books, Nora went to find somewhere to sit. There was no way she was going to bring all these books home with her.

She had no interest in learning flower arrangement or care.

At the far end of the second floor of the library, she found a sitting area near the balcony that overlooked the first floor. Leather couches were placed uniformly in the open space and, even though it was the afternoon, the area was illuminated by filtered sunlight, oil lamps along the walls, and candles on small tables next to the seats.

Placing her stack of books on one of the tables, Nora dropped into the couch next to it, wriggling around to get comfortable. Choosing the book on top of her stack, she scanned the pages before dropping it on the floor and retrieving the next in the pile. She repeated the process for the following three books that turned out to be just as useless as the first. Grumbling to herself, she picked up another. It was a well-worn book, the title barely legible, and she carefully turned the pages only to find exactly what she had been hoping for.

Flicking through the book—the paper crinkled and yellowing with age at the edges—Nora found a drawing of the flowers Will had asked her to give Daphne. She ran her fingers over the pale lace-like flowers that had been painted in watercolours, the green stems vibrant against the aged paper. She scanned the accompanying text. *Wild Carrot is a white, flowering plant with a stiff stem...* She ran her eyes further down the page. *The Wild Carrot symbolises a safe haven or sanctuary.*

Nora grinned like a child who received dessert for dinner. Just as she suspected; the flowers had meanings and they were communicating through them. She could not wait to show August her discovery and get his thoughts. Nora stuffed the book into her cloak pocket and stood, stretching her arms. Will expected her prompt return and she had already lingered far too long. If she was going to get him to like her and ultimately trust her, she had better not annoy him too much.

She practically skipped down the stairs, slipped out the front door and into the tawny glow of the setting sun, hopeful that the book she had tucked in her cloak would answer some of her burning questions.

$$\diamond$$

Sticking to the shadows, Nora trailed Florence as she strode through the street. Heavy rain soaked Nora's clothes, the fabric clinging to her skin and weighing her down. She swept aside the hair plastered to her face and prowled into the night. The tree canopy did little to hinder the downpour. Florence ducked into an alleyway before slipping under the eaves of a single doorway. She knocked three times, then a warm light spilled into the drenched alley. Nora summoned her water magic and used it to manipulate the rain to form steps. She raced up the floating puddles and onto the roof—her body moving swiftly—and crept along the rooftop until she had a clear view of who had answered the door. She may have been unable to hear their conversation over the pouring rain, but at least she now had a visual.

A tall, dark-skinned man with cropped black hair and an amused expression stood in the doorway. His brown eyes glanced around the alley as he leant on the doorframe, crossing his muscular arms over his chest. Florence spoke, the man's shoulders shifting in reply as he tilted his head back. Nora may not have been able to hear them, but the two in the doorway were very clearly enjoying themselves.

Shivering, Nora started to regret her decision to follow Florence. She had spotted the woman on her way home from working at the flower shop and had made the quick decision to trail Florence. She hadn't wanted to miss the opportunity to learn more, but now… now she wondered if Florence was merely catching up with a friend.

Beneath her, Florence retrieved a flat wooden box from her cloak, similar to the one Nora had brought Sage. The top was painted with white flowers and little navy-blue orbs, and Florence handed it to the man. His eyebrows drew in and he nodded stiffly. A few inaudible words passed between the pair and then Florence stepped back into the rain.

Maybe this little endeavour had not been a waste after all. What was in the box Florence had given the man? And what had they been discussing to make the conversation turn serious? With so many questions running through her mind, Nora had forgotten about Florence. The woman was heading back the way she had come, the rain easing to a patter as it fell around her. Nora caught up, treading with care on the rooftops and using her wind and water magic to steady herself and stay close to her target.

Florence stopped abruptly, her gaze flickering upwards, and Nora quickly grabbed hold of one of the branches above, pulling herself up into the tree canopy. Florence's eyes narrowed, searching the leaves. Nora stilled, holding her breath as she watched the woman below. Scowling, Florence stepped closer to the building, disappearing from Nora's line of sight. The rain poured with a vengeance and Nora's feet felt slick against the branch on which she crouched. Her eyes darted around her.

Fuck! Where had Florence gone?

Movement to Nora's left caught her eye and she hoisted herself further up into the trees, hiding in the thick clusters of leaves and branches. Azure eyes glowed as they scanned the soaking tree canopy. Rain trickled from the leaves onto the fiery coat of the fox, each drop glistening in its fur. So, this was Florence's Anima shift.

Nora watched as Florence searched for her, water dripping from the tip of her shiny black nose. Teeth bared, Florence growled, the sound cutting through the pattering of rain. Florence leapt from the rooftop, hopping from branch to branch before landing on the muddy ground and continuing down the road. Nora did not follow, instead she made her way back tiher room at Daphne's, speculating the whole time about what was really happening in Forest's Edge. There were too many unanswered questions swirling in Nora's mind. The symbol, the overheard conversation about not only the Alta, but the supposed factions. And now these mysterious boxes tied to Florence...

Nora sighed. As much as all these breadcrumbs fed her curiosity, she needed to focus on the command King Dominic had set: finding Felix. There may be more going on in Forest's Edge than meets the eye, but it only mattered if it led her to him. He was the priority.

There was no point in using her magic to attempt to dry herself as Nora trudged home to Daphne's, the rain continuing to pour with the vigour of a crying child. Boots caked in mud, she scraped one of the heels on a root near the front door.

"What happened to you?" Sage asked, lowering her umbrella as she stepped under the eaves.

"Went for a swim," replied Nora with a casual shrug. "Thought it'd be fun to be fully clothed."

Sage sighed. "Do you have to do that?"

"Do what?"

"Be obnoxiously sarcastic."

"You bring it out in me," Nora grinned, taking a step. Her boots slipped on the root that was now slick with mud, and she fell backwards, landing on her ass. "Shit!"

Not only was she soaking wet, now she was filthy too.

"Here," Sage rolled her eyes, reaching out a hand.

Nora took it, grinning wickedly, and pulled the other woman to the ground. Sage failed to brace herself, falling right into Nora's lap.

Eyes wide, she scrabbled away, slipping into a muddy puddle. "I was helping you!"

"It was an accident!" Nora lied, neglecting to hide her mischievous smile.

"There is something seriously wrong with you!" Sage exclaimed, using her umbrella as a cane to help her stand. The umbrella wobbled, unable to find a secure footing, and she fell back into the sludge.

Nora gripped her stomach, the laughter escaping her in a torrent.

"It's not funny!" Sage shrieked, eyeing Nora through her mud flecked glasses.

"You'd think it was if you could see what I see," Nora teased.

"For a second there today at the library I was starting to believe you were normal!" Sage growled. "I see that I was clearly mistaken!"

Sage ran a muddy hand over her tight black curls, then screamed, launching herself closer to Nora. "There's something in my hair! It's moving!"

Nora rose to her knees as Sage moved closer.

"Get it out!" Sage waved her hands; panic dancing in her captivating brown eyes.

"Calm down," Nora shushed, rising onto her knees. She looked down at the other woman's hair and carefully picked an insect from Sage's locks. "It's only a bug."

Sage shivered. "Gross."

"Your hair always looks so nice, it must have thought it would make a good home," Nora said, gently placing the insect on the ground. Brows creasing, Sage looked up at Nora. "Did you just compliment me?"

Nora scrunched her brows. "I complimented the bug in its choice of accommodation."

"To think for a second there, I almost thought you were being nice," Sage groaned.

"I did just remove a bug from your hair." Nora stood, offering her hand to Sage, but the other woman shook her head, rising on her own. "Don't you trust me?"

"Not a chance," Sage replied, opening the front door.

"What happened to you two?" Daphne asked, her eyes dragging up and down the two of them as she strode down the stairs, quilts in hand.

"We fell," Sage said.

Her mother quirked a brow.

Nora nodded, smiling as innocently as she could muster. "Yeah, what she said." Sage stared at her incredulously. "See you in the morning!"

Leaving the mother and daughter in the entry, Nora climbed the stairs to her room and wondered whether August would be inside. When she opened the door, however, the room was dark and cold. She summoned fire, the flames crackling into existence among the sticks in the hearth as she strode straight into the bathroom.

Summoning water into the tub, she used her fire magic to heat the liquid as it slowly filled. Nora shucked off her filthy clothing, then slipped into the warm water, her muscles relaxing at the touch. She grabbed the book on flower meanings that she'd managed to keep dry, and flicked through the pages. She planned to investigate the decorations on the boxes she'd seen today, but all her mind would focus on was Sage and how beautiful the woman looked sitting in the mud.

## 19

**Evelyn**

Yawning, Evelyn stretched her arms wide as she left the Healing Centre and made her way home. The sun had only just started to rise, and a thin mist lingered in the air. Tugging her jacket tighter, she was glad home was only a short walk away.

What she'd presumed would be an easy and somewhat boring night had turned into quite the opposite. She had been run off her feet, healing patients, filling out paperwork and assisting other Healers. During the last hour of work, she could barely concentrate on anything, her mind drifting to thoughts of her warm, comfy bed.

Nearing home, she decided to stroll through the gardens instead of sticking to the main street; it was a quicker and more scenic route. She only had to walk for a short time before reaching an archway made from flowering trees in full bloom, forming a tunnel of intertwining branches and snowy blossoms. She passed through the floral archway, stepping over tree roots that grew beyond the boundaries of the forest and split the gravel path. Her knowledge of the twists and turns were her only safeguard from falling. Beyond the archway, the amber lights shining through the distant windows of her home created a magical atmosphere in the morning light.

As much as her home had become a bittersweet place in the last few months, she would hate to never see its stone walls or walk its many hallways again. It was her family home—it had been for many generations—and even though her aunt and cousin no longer resided within, there were still so many happy memories that lingered in the rooms. She just needed to remind herself of that more often and focus on the good rather than the hurt.

Evelyn was sidestepping a fallen branch when an arm snaked around her waist at the same time a calloused hand covered her mouth, dragging her into a darkened corner of the garden. Evelyn's heart thundered in her chest; her body frozen in fright. She was roughly spun around and shoved against a tree trunk, an icy blade pressed against her exposed throat.

"Don't move," growled the man who held her, his grip on her arm bruising her flesh. He licked his broken yellow teeth, a foul acidic stench wafting between them.

Tears streamed down Evelyn's face and her lower lip trembled. "Please…"

"You have been chosen by the Makers," the man continued, ignoring her appeal and the trembles that were rattling through her. "Embrace their greatness."

Before another plea could leave her lips, he sliced the blade across her throat, warm blood instantly pouring from the wound. Her knees buckled and the man let her fall. Evelyn gasped, wide eyed, and pressed her hand against her neck to stifle the flow of blood. Using all her strength, she summoned her healing magic to her neck, determined to close the wound.

The man pushed her onto her back and straddled her body, tucking away the crimson-stained blade. Evelyn let out a gargled scream, her mouth filling with blood as the man dug his fingers into the gash in her neck. Her golden eyes rolled back into her head, the excruciating pain causing her vision to spot as the world flashed in and out of focus. The man pressed his fingers to her forehead and began to draw. She convulsed beneath him, digging the nails of her free hand into his thigh. He barely noticed as he continued his work.

Evelyn struggled to stay conscious as her magic used up her energy to keep her alive. Once she passed out she would die. Whether or not she could heal herself did not matter. He would simply cut her neck again.

Adding more blood to his fingers, the man placed them against her skin once more. He spoke, but all she heard was the rapid beat of her heart pounding in her ears.

Suddenly he was shoved to the side, his head hitting the nearby tree trunk, causing leaves to fall from above like emerald snow. The man shook his head, blinking rapidly as a boot connected with his face, knocking him out cold. Evelyn blinked up at the woman who stood above her.

"Evelyn!" the woman cried, golden eyes wide. She sunk to her knees and placed her hands over Evelyn's.

Tears burned in Evelyn's vision at the sight of the Lys Alv. She had never been so glad to see Gemma in her whole life.

"It's going to be okay, I'm here now. You're safe," Gemma said, her voice calm and assertive.

Evelyn failed to hold back her sobs. Her mind felt cloudy as her magic drew the last of her energy, and blood continued to seep through her fingers from the wound at her neck. Like a friendly embrace, she felt Gemma's magic entwine with her own.

"Everything is going to be okay," Gemma reassured as Evelyn struggled to stay conscious. "Everything is going to be okay."

## 20

**Nora**

Nora shoved August against the wall. "You did not let me win!"

"Didn't I?" he laughed. "How can you be sure?"

"You're an ass." She turned up her nose and strode down the narrow hallway to the room they shared.

"Here comes trouble," teased Felix, blocking her path with his body and placing his powerful arms on either side of the wall. He was not as tall as August, but he still towered over Nora.

"Move," she slapped her hands onto his hard chest, curling her fingers so that her nails dug into his flesh beneath his shirt. "Or I'll make you."

He barely flinched, his eyes glistening wickedly as he smirked. "Such fighting spirit for someone so small."

Nora lifted her hands to Felix's throat, her fast movement catching him off guard as she held it mere inches from his brown skin and summoned her wind magic, the air around his neck tightening.

Felix's breathing quickened, yet he flashed her a toothy smile. "You play mean."

"Says the asshole who's blocking my way." She dropped her hand, releasing him. Felix was only a few years older than her and August, yet *in the short time since he had joined the Alta, they had not developed a friendship. He was solitary, but not unfriendly. Regardless, Nora had little time for his teasing.*

*"Maybe I like mean," he drawled, leaning in closer to her.*

*Nora curled her lip and gave him a heated looked aimed to melt the skin from his bones. Felix laughed, stepping to the side, and running a hand through his cropped black hair.*

*"Didn't want to come to her aid?" He looked over her shoulder, the intricate swirls of his shackle tattoos dark against his wrist.*

*"Between the two of you, she wasn't the one who would have needed my help," August replied dryly.*

*"I'd love to stay and chat all day," Nora announced, inspecting her finger nails. "But you bore me."*

*"I have somewhere to be anyway," Felix replied, stepping past Nora. "The king wants me to check out something."*

*"That's lovely." She rolled her eyes. "And you think we care because...?"*

*"Just making small talk," Felix shrugged innocently.*

*"Try two levels up," August suggested. "Hyde was in the training room. He might be interested in your chit chat."*

*Nora snickered. Hyde was one of the cruellest of the Alta, the man taking pleasure in inventing new ways to inflict pain on anyone who dared bother him. She would know; she had an ugly scar on the bottom of her heel curtesy of the guy.*

*"Maybe I'll go find him," Felix continued down the hallway, stopping at the stairs to face them. For a moment, he appeared almost regal, his tone that of a ruler from a story book. "He who travels the skies is never alone."*

*A chill crept along her skin like a caress, the sensation vanishing just as quickly as Felix's noble demeanour. Felix departed without another word and Nora stared after him, unsure of whether she had imagined the whole thing.*

$$\diamondsuit$$

"Norrraaa!" August sang, shutting the window, and shrugging off his cloak. He moved to sit by her side.

Rubbing her eyes, she stared up at August from where she lay on the bed, though not truly seeing him. Her mind was still trying to grasp the remnants of her memory.

"Nora," he nudged her playfully, "what's going on in that brain of yours?" He tapped a finger to her temple. "Good daydream?"

She looked up at him. "What comes to mind when I say, 'He who travels the skies is never alone'?"

August stroked his stubbled chin, lips pursed in thought, "I'm not sure, but it sounds like something one of the Gods or Goddesses would say."

"Any ideas which one?" Nora frowned trying to recollect the many tales of the five Gods. She had never paid much attention to the stories of the Gods and Goddesses other than Thyra, and she couldn't remember hearing any stories where Thyra said anything about the sky.

"No, why?" August asked, his head tilted to the side causing strands of his dirty blond hair to fall over his dark eyes.

"I'm certain that's what Felix said the last time we saw him," Nora said, as she sorted through her memory.

"So—" he began, swiping the hair from his face.

"Why would he quote the Gods and Goddesses randomly," she continued, cutting him off. "I can't ever remember him doing it before."

"Maybe he spoke like a philosophical asshole to the others," August suggested with a shrug.

"Hmmm" she tapped her lower lip.

"Do you think he was trying to tell you something? Like a secret message for your eyes only? Ooo a sexy love letter?" he teased, wiggling his brows.

"You're a giant child," she sighed, shaking her head. "Never mind. Forget that I mentioned it."

Felix's last words left uncertainty lingering in Nora's gut. She had originally passed it off as nonsense but if the symbol Evelyn had provided them had taught her anything, it was that every detail could mean something.

"Where have you been this early in the morning? Or should I say, *all* last night?" Nora asked, deciding to look into Felix's last words later.

"Think I wouldn't notice your absence? How's Evelyn?"

"Are you finished?" He gave her a pointed look. "I've been doing the same as you. Trying to find Felix."

"And did your all-night adventures prove fruitful?" she pushed.

"You could assume that," August said, and Nora fought the urge to push at his frustratingly vague answer. He had never kept anything from her before so there was no reason for her to think he was hiding something. He must be embarrassed at his lack of progress and trying to hide it with ambiguous answers.

Nora brushed his remark off, sitting up and grabbing the book that lay beside her. She shuffled closer to August, bumping her side with his. "I found this at the library yesterday. It has all the meanings of flowers and other plants."

August took the book from her, flipping through the pages. "My favourite flowers are daisies; I wonder what that says about me?"

"Probably that you're a big fool," she ribbed.

"Close," his lips quirked up at the side as he tilted the page towards her. A bunch of pastel daisies were painted above a section of text. August tapped on one line. "Yellow daisies represent innocence and hope."

"Same thing," Nora laughed. "Anyway, remember the flowers Will gave me to gift to Daphne when I first came here? They mean sanctuary, and last night I followed Florence, and she was given a box decorated with blackthorns, which symbolise protection and hope against adversity. Oh, and yesterday Will gave me a box for Sage, but the petals on it weren't distinct enough to know what flower they belonged to."

"Interesting," he said, flicking through the pages.

"Indeed, but not exactly helpful." Nora sighed. "I need to find this Gemma person they mentioned. Their information comes from her so she's our real target. The rest are just stepping stones."

"Then keep doing what you're doing," August replied. "Keep immersing yourself into their lives and hopefully soon you'll meet her. Getting access to Gemma is the crossroads. Either she knows about Felix, or she doesn't. Whichever way we will have a clearer direction moving forward."

"You're right," she said, shoulders slumping. "I just feel like I'm finding all the edge pieces of a puzzle, and nothing makes sense or is useful at all. I want the fucking pieces that show me what the actual picture is—the ones that tell me how to find him."

"We have time," said August, draping his arm around her and tugging her close. "The king told us to find Felix and we are trying. Just because it isn't happening as quickly as we want doesn't mean we are failing. Sometimes things just take time."

"I don't want to regret switching tactics," she sighed, dragging her legs up and resting her chin on her knees. "What if delaying Kaldom was a mistake?"

"What if going to Kaldom and not following your gut had been a mistake?" he countered.

She glanced at him sidelong. "Since when are you so wise?"

"I've always been this way." He grinned. "You choose to ignore it."

"What do you think we should be doing?" she asked, biting her lip. "Have you learnt anything more from Evelyn?"

"I'm working on it, she opens up more and more each time I see her. I think we should extend our stay here though. We shouldn't rush things especially if our goal is to gather information from this Gemma person," he said then gave her arm a good squeeze. "Also, we should train at some point today. Your arms are too thin."

"They are not!" she shrieked, pinching her arms, and inspecting herself.

He was winding her up purely to take her mind off the investigation, but knowing his intention did not stop her from getting annoyed.

"Little twig arms," he chuckled.

"I hate you." She stuck out her tongue. "Anyway I have to work today so you'll have to train by yourself. Maybe you can train your own arm muscles!"

She made a vulgar gesture and August roared with laughter. The sound was contagious, and Nora could help but join in. For a moment it felt like they were back in Royal Bay, and she yearned to return home to normality. She had known finding Felix would be hard, but it sometimes seemed near impossible.

"I can hear you talking to someone in there!" came a voice from outside her room.

Nora's head snapped towards the pounding that echoed on the wooden door. Jumping up, she marched over to the commotion whilst August disappeared, slipping out the window like a ghost. Grabbing hold of the door handle, Nora pulled and stared at the accuser, fire burning in her eyes.

"What the fuck do you want?" Nora demanded, not bothering to restrain her anger.

"You're not allowed to have guests in your room," Sage rebuked, her hands gripping tightly on her hips.

"I'm alone in here." Nora swung the door open, the wood hitting the wall with a loud thud and exposing her room. "See?"

Sage marched in, reminding Nora of the canine Anima she had once seen in Dostvet Harbour, sniffing among the crates on the ships, looking for imported contraband.

"I heard you talking and laughing." Sage stated firmly.

"I was reading aloud," Nora smirked, pointing to the book of flower meanings on the floor. "Helps me retain what I'm studying better, and I laughed because I thought it was funny. Some people have a sense of humour, I know that might be strange to you."

"You're lying," Sage said, sliding her golden glasses up the bridge of her nose.

"You're obsessed." Nora smirked.

Sage's eyes grew wide. "I am not!"

"I don't blame you," Nora shrugged nonchalantly. "I would be obsessed with me too."

"You are the most obnoxious person I have ever met!" Sage yelled, storming closer to Nora. "You're up to something."

Nora took a step, bringing them so close that, if she breathed in deeply, her chest would brush Sage's. "Am I?" she whispered, gazing up at Sage's chocolate brown eyes. If she were to look straight ahead, she would have been staring at Sage's plump lips instead. Which would have been a terrible idea for Nora's self-control.

"Y-y—" Sage jumped back. "Yes! And don't do that!"

"Do what?" Nora pouted her lips innocently.

"You know exactly what you're doing," Sage breathed out as she rushed towards the door, her hands fidgeting at her sides. "I'll be watching you."

"Good," Nora winked. "I wouldn't have it any other way."

Sage's mouth opened and closed like a fish out of water before she shut it firmly, pressing her lips—the ones Nora was doing her best to ignore—into a hard line as she slammed the door shut.

Grinning, Nora fell back onto the bed. She loved messing with Sage, not only because the woman was extremely suspicious of her, but as she loved seeing all the different expressions she could elicit. Alta were commanded not to fall in love, but that did not rule out attraction. Nora definitely found Sage attractive. August had suggested staying a little longer and Nora felt in her gut that he was right. They were on to something, and giving themselves more time to uncover the secrets Forest's Edge held was the smart move. They would leave the city eventually once they'd exhausted all avenues of their investigation, so why couldn't she have a little fun with Sage in the meantime?

# 21

## Evelyn

Curled up under the warm blankets, Evelyn stared out her bedroom window. The morning mist had made the forest glimmer and shine, illuminating the greenery. Long vines curled invitingly around the trees, kissed by blossoms of pink and white, and fury plants housed woodland animals, all seeking refuge from the cold. She urged herself to embrace the fairy-tale-like atmosphere beyond the glass that she had often read about in her favourite novels rather than the nightmare that kept forcing itself into her mind.

She'd spent the last two days in her room, feigning terrible menstrual cramps—something a Lys Alv couldn't even escape—as an excuse to avoid leaving her bed. Gemma had helped her to her room after the attack, but she hadn't seen the woman since, and Evelyn assumed her family hadn't been told. If they had, Evelyn would not have been able to escape their fussing. Gemma concealing the attack had surprised Evelyn and had left her feeling both relieved and curious.

"You will get up." Evelyn sternly told herself. "You will not let that man ruin your life."

She was working up the courage to leave the cosy confines of her room. At least that's what she'd been telling herself. Her heart hammered in her chest, her body frozen with indecision.

"You can do this, you can do this," she chanted, squeezing her eyes closed. "You can do this."

With a heavy exhale she forced her golden eyes open and quickly extracted herself from her blanket cocoon before her mind could change. Standing next to her bed, she stared down at her safe place and shook her head. No, she would not spend another day hiding.

Washing and dressing for the day, Evelyn decided she'd go and purchase a new outfit from her favourite dressmaker. Now that she received her own Healer's wage, she thought it would be nice to spend it on something special. It's not that she had ever gone without—her parents were more than comfortable when it came to coin—but there was something exciting about spending the money she had earned. Hopefully the endeavour would help keep her intrusive thoughts at bay.

Walking down the hallway to the front door, Evelyn found Gemma in her path. The sight of the Lys Alv wasn't unusual. The woman often visited regularly to speak with Evelyn's parents about all manner of things, and after what had happened, Evelyn felt a surge of warmth towards her saviour. Gemma's long pale fingers lightly gripped Evelyn's tensed arm, halting Evelyn from passing by.

"Evelyn," Gemma greeted, her smile not quite reaching her golden monolid eyes. She looked immaculate as usual, her chin length wavy hair neatly brushed, and forest green matching trousers and coat neatly pressed. "I'm glad I caught you."

Literally, Evelyn thought, trying not to look down at the hand that still held her. Whatever warmth she had felt disappeared. "Thank you again for saving me, Gemma."

"You're welcome. I always take care of my own," Gemma replied. "We didn't get to talk much afterwards. I hear you're a certified Healer now."

"Yes," Evelyn replied, nodding. She'd always known Gemma wasn't the soft nurturing type, but it still surprised her a little that the woman hadn't asked after her wellbeing. She'd almost died...

"I know you have only started working at the Healing Centre," Gemma said matter-of-factly, "but I assume you're settled in by now and I wonder whether you'd like a little extra work."

That piqued Evelyn's interest. "What kind of work?"

"As you know, I run the Forest's Edge faction, and my last Healer has found other employment." Stated Gemma, her gaze assessing. "I was hoping you would be their replacement."

Evelyn's brows rose in surprise. "Isn't there a Healer you know better that is more experienced than me? I'm only just certified."

"There are others, but I want you. You are far more talented from what I hear, and your family has a long history of working side-by-side with the faction," Gemma said, letting go of Evelyn's arm. She tucked her white blonde hair behind her pointed ear, showing the numerous silver hoops pierced through it. "I trust you, Evelyn, and I hope that you trust me too. Now that your studies are over, I think you should be more involved."

Evelyn lingered in the hallway, watching Gemma walk away, her mind deliberating the Lys Alv's offer. It was tempting, especially when the uncertainty about the direction her life was talking still lingered. Working with Gemma wouldn't just be a step out of her comfort zone— it would be a leap. Maybe a drastic change was exactly what she needed? It is not like it was a cause she did not wholeheartedly agree with. Plus, if she kept busy, she would have less time for the long line of intrusive thoughts she was eager to keep at bay. Yes, maybe having an official role in the faction was just what she needed.

Stepping out the front door, Evelyn embraced the cool moss and woodsy-scented breeze that caressed her exposed skin. She strode down the main path towards the city centre, her shoulders tense and moon shapes marked into her palms. What would usually have been a pleasant experience now had Evelyn on edge. She did not want to feel like this shaken version of herself, yet she could not help constantly looking over her shoulder or jumping at every sound. Evelyn tried to focus on the positives, on the purpose Gemma's offer would give her and the new dress she would be purchasing today.

Her favourite dressmaker was located on the eastern edge of the city, and the streets Evelyn walked were filled with the sounds of laughter, chatter, and the many other expressions of life. The bustle of people eased some of her nerves, the numerous people around making her feel somewhat safe. Evelyn was two streets away from the dressmaker when she was plucked into a side alley.

There was no way she would be a victim again.

Spinning around and adrenaline flooding through her, Evelyn forced her knee up, making contact with the hooded figure's groin.

The man swore as he bent over, his hands over his private area. "Fuck! It's only me!"

"Oh, my Goddess!" Evelyn cried, a shaky hand covering her mouth as her golden eyes went wide, recognising August's voice. Her heart was pounding rapidly in her chest, threatening to break free of her ribcage. "What made you think that was a good way to greet me?!"

"I wanted to surprise you," he groaned, stumbling over to a wall, and grunting as he hit the dirt. "It seems you are not the only one surprised."

"Let me help you," Evelyn said, biting her lip to stop her tears from falling, and knelt beside August.

He dropped his head back against the wall, features scrunched as he hissed. She was close enough to see under his hood, and when he opened his eyes, his dark black and blue eyes found hers.

August was a Mors Alv.

There was no denying it; she had seen his eyes. Black orbs with sapphire blue rings. Her tears dried up, but her heart continued to thunder in her chest. If she were not able to heal herself with magic, she would have thought her body unable to undergo any more stress as uncertainty swirled in her stomach. She had never seen a Mors Alv in person before, only having seen pictures in the books she studied.

Leaning closer, her eyes snapped to his as he peeked through his eyelashes. She recoiled slightly; her body subconsciously aware of his magic. Of his race. Hurt flashed across his features, different to that of the physical pain he was experiencing, and she immediately felt guilty for her reaction.

"Sorry," she apologised, reaching out to him. "I didn't mean to…"

"It's fine," August breathed, making space between them.

"No, it's not," she said seriously, her voice still a little shaky from the fright. "I shouldn't have reacted that way."

"I shouldn't have grabbed you like that," he replied with a groan.

"Kicking you isn't what I'm apologising for," she sighed, shuffling closer. "Although I do feel a little bad about it.

"Only a little?"

"It was a reflex after the other day," she said defensively.

August scrunched his brow. "What happened the other day?"

"Nothing," Evelyn dismissed hastily. "What I *was* apologising for was my reaction when I saw your eyes. That too was a knee-jerk. I know what your race is August, and, before you deny it, just know that it doesn't bother me."

"It should," he replied, his tone matter of fact. "I'm dangerous."

"Why?" she asked, tilting her head to the side. "What could make you more dangerous than anyone else in this city?"

"You've read the history books," he said, the final "s" coming out as a hiss as he breathed in sharply.

"I have, and I can tell you that race has nothing to do with how dangerous someone can be. Elementums, humans, Anima, Alvs, they've all featured in history doing villainous things. Should I fear everyone?"

August attempted a grin.

"I can heal you," she offered, returning his smile with one of her own. "I think it would make us both feel better."

"Look at you, trying to find an excuse to feel me up," August teased, his voice strained. "I've only met you a couple of times."

"Oh!" Evelyn's eyebrows rose. "No... I won't have to touch you... I... ah—I can hover over the area."

August winked, "Sure... hover over the area."

"Fine," she exhaled loudly. She leant her side on the wall and crossed her arms, hoping to appear more confident than she was. "But if a certain part of you falls off don't come crying to me."

August frowned and glanced down at his groin quickly before looking back at her, his eyes narrowed in concern. "It can't fall off."

"Who knows?" She picked at her clothing, feigning indifference even though her heart pounded in her chest. "Guess you'll have to wait and see."

"Okay, heal me."

"I don't want to anymore," she replied, rising to her feet. "I have somewhere to be."

"Eve!" he begged, reaching out and taking her hand. Butterflies swirled in her stomach at the use of her nickname. It was so familiar and felt right when he said it. "Please."

She sat back down, her golden eyes twinkling. "Fine! But I've a better idea."

"I'm all ears," he grinned, indicating with a long finger to where one of his pointed ears was concealed under his hood.

She lifted her hand, the one that he still held in his larger scarred one. "Just take the magic from me and heal yourself."

August dropped her hand and shook his head. "No."

"Why not?" she asked. "You can't hurt me; I heal almost instantly."

"I don't want to steal your magic, it's wrong."

Evelyn leaned closer, looking deep into his eyes. "It's not stealing, I am giving it to you."

August stared back, his gaze searching, and she could see him warring over what to do. She smiled reassuringly, hoping to convince him that it was okay. As crazy as it seemed, Evelyn wanted to gift him her magic. She may have only met him recently and there was still so much she had to learn about him, but she didn't care; she trusted him. Besides, she had healed strangers before. Was gifting her magic really all that different?

"I want you to do it," she said, not taking her golden eyes off his. "I trust you."

August sighed. "If you're sure…"

"I'm sure," Evelyn replied, offering her hand once more.

His hand almost completely covered her own as he took hold of her palm and she watched as he shut his eyes. Her hand began to tingle as though she had sat on it for a long time. Evelyn fought the urge to shake it, and instead summoned her light and directed it towards August. It felt like healing someone; her magic was draining and yet she was not taking on any injury. Before she knew it, August opened his eyes, his mouth slightly opened in awe.

"That's it?" she asked, her hand no longer feeling tingly.

"All done," August replied hesitantly. "How do you feel? Did I hurt you?"

"I'm fine!" Evelyn laughed, surprised. "That was easier than healing someone."

He got to his feet, pulling her up with him. "Thank you."

"You're very welcome," she beamed.

Even though it had been a few days since she had seen August, the idea of him had started to grow on her, especially as he'd been leaving sketches in her healing rooms to find. Now that he was here, she realised she had been looking forward to seeing him again. Somehow, in the slight amount of time that she had known him, he had managed to squeeze himself into the little group of people who she felt able to be herself around. She was glad Poppy had encouraged her to give him a chance.

# 22

**Evelyn**

"What are your plans for the rest of the day?" August asked as Evelyn led him out of the alley now that he was healed. "Mind if I join?"

"You may," she said, glancing at him briefly. The idea of spending more time with him made her want to grin like an idiot.

"Where are we going?" August asked as they ventured down the street.

He walked with a confident sort of swagger and the fact he still held her hand made Evelyn almost skip along beside him… almost. He made her feel confident and safe, two things she desperately wanted after the other day. She had had her throat slit, and yet, here she was strolling down the street hand in hand with August as if nothing had ever happened. She knew she still had to go through the motions of her feelings but right now, all she wanted to do was stuff them in a corner and enjoy her time with August.

"Here," she declared, pushing open the wooden door to one of her favourite stores and leading him inside.

The dressmaker's shop was filled with an array of fabrics of varying colours and textures that lined the walls and occupied all other available spaces. In the centre of the room, boxes of buttons, threads and jewels sat on a round table, overflowing onto the wooden surface. The sunlight shining through the shop window caused the colourful gems to sparkle and, above them, silk and lace ribbons hung from the rafters. To the left there was a messy workstation and mannequin dressed in a glamourous pink silk gown.

The dressmaker popped his head out from behind the mannequin and asked through the pins held tightly between his lips: "Can I help you with anything?"

"Just browsing, thank you," replied Evelyn. She noticed the man's attention move to August, his stare scrutinising, as they wandered through the store.

"He thinks I'm going to steal something," commented August as he ran his fingers over a rainbow of silks.

"Maybe you should take your hood off?" she proposed.

"I think that would make it worse, don't you?"

"Oh yeah," she frowned. "Is it like this everywhere you go?"

"Mostly… but the alternative is they see who I really am. Not everyone is as kind-hearted as you," he said. "The hood isn't ideal, but it is the easiest way."

"I don't think I'll ever get used to the way people look at you," Evelyn frowned.

August stepped closer. "You say that like you're planning on spending more time with me."

"If you're free," Evelyn replied, her lips tugging up at one side. "I don't know how pressing your other mysterious duties are."

"I think they can wait." He replied coyly.

Evelyn lifted a bundle of red velvet, the colour similar to the blush she felt on her cheeks, and caressed the soft fabric. "I love this fabric. What do you think of the colour?"

He moved even closer, reaching out and touching the crimson fabric in her hands. She caught a glimpse of his handsome face under the hood: a strong jaw, sculpted nose, and his striking black and sky-blue eyes. She knew she was staring but she couldn't help herself. August held her stare and smiled, and her heart threatened to beat out of her chest.

"It's nice but I think this colour would be better." He picked up a roll of royal blue fabric and draped the silk over her.

Evelyn turned to look at herself in the mirror. The colour complimented her brown skin and had her golden eyes glowing.

"But you could pick anything, and you'd look beautiful," August whispered into her ear.

"Ahh, thank you," she stumbled over the words, his closeness making her feel hot all over.

Evelyn turned, taking the roll of fabric from his grasp and went to find the dressmaker.

"Would you be able to make a dress for me in this fabric please?" she asked the man, slinging the excess fabric from her shoulders and rolling it up.

He looked up at her from where he knelt, pinning the hem of the mannequin's dress. "What style are you after?"

"Something simple and comfortable for Frost Season," she replied.

The dressmaker went to his workstation and rummaged around, lifting papers, ribbons, and scraps of fabrics until he found a notebook. He used a thin ribbon to open the book, before turning it in Evelyn's direction and sliding it towards her. The page had a list of names with dates, fabrics, and measurements alongside them.

"Fill in your details and I can do your measurements in two days." He told her. "If you have a sketch or another dress in the same style, bring it with you."

Evelyn found a pencil and wrote in the book as he instructed. When she was finished, she bid the man farewell and left, August in tow.

"So what have you been up to the last few days, other than sketching pretty pictures for me?" Evelyn asked, biting her lip as a grin spread across her face.

"Well," he began, playfully drawing out the word. "When I'm not covered in charcoal or sneaking into the Healing Centre, I've been exploring the city. Seeing as you have been working and... what else did you say? Ah, sleeping, that's right." He chuckled. "I didn't want to disturb you."

"Sleep is very important," she teased.

"Apparently," he replied with a nod. "At least I get to see you now.

Even if it did cost me a kick to the—"

"Only because you snuck up on me!"

"Fair point!" August laughed, raising his hands in defeat. "Where to next?"

"We could get something to eat," she suggested. "Are you hungry?"

"I'm always hungry," he replied with a chuckle.

They went to the heart of Forest's Edge to a busy store selling baked goods. A line spilled out the door, all customers waiting to make their purchases.

"The Humble Tart Bakehouse," recited August, reading the sign that hung above the store's front window, showcasing a display of cakes. "If I remember correctly, your sister works here."

"Yes, so don't worry, I won't have to line up. Wait here," she told him.

Evelyn left him on the main street as she made her way to the back entrance and let herself in. As soon as she opened the door she was embraced with the stuffy heat of the huge oven and the sweet smell of poached fruits and chocolate. Standing at the work bench in the middle of the room was her sister, spooning stewed apples onto squares of pastry.

"Hey Jasmine," Evelyn greeted her sister as she approached the table.

"Hey," her sister replied without looking up from her work. "What's up?"

Evelyn had always been told that Jasmine and she looked almost identical—other than the fact that she was a Lys Alv and Jasmine was human—yet Evelyn could never understand how others could possibly think that. Jasmine had long, straight black hair, a stunning smile, and rich dark brown eyes. Evelyn had no idea how anyone could say they looked the same, when she was shorter, curvier, and her hair was harder to tame.

"Can I have some pastries?" Evelyn asked sweetly.

"Take whatever you like." Jasmine nodded. "But first… tell me who you will be sharing them with."

"No one," replied Evelyn as she picked up a small basket and started making her selections.

"Really?" Jasmine raised a brow.

"You know I made a friend," Evelyn sighed.

"Yes," her sister grinned. "But you haven't told me anything else. At least tell me their name."

"August."

"Oh, good, strong name." Jasmine nodded approvingly. "And?"

"And that's all you need to know for now," Evelyn said simply. Usually she would have told her sister more, but it did not feel right to talk too much about August. She wasn't worried that Jasmine would not like him, it was more that she wanted to avoid getting him into any unnecessary trouble.

Luckily, Jasmine did not push her further for information. Instead, she pointed to a tray of tarts filled with swirls of shiny purple and teal jam. "Don't take those unless you are the only one eating them or your friend is an Alv too. I don't want to hear anyone complaining about my baking making them hallucinate or wind up at the Healing Centre because they've accidentally eaten Alv berries."

Evelyn nodded, placing a couple in the basket. "Thanks for these."

"You're welcome. I'll see you at home," Jasmine replied, already refocused on her work as Evelyn slipped back out the door.

"That was quick," commented August as she approached him. "What did you get?"

"You'll have to wait and see," she teased, hiding the basket of pastries from view. "Come on."

Evelyn led him to one of her favourite spots in Forest's Edge. It was a bit of a trek to get there, and August kept pestering her the whole walk, but she thought the surprise would be worth it. She pushed aside the spindly branches that blocked the path—the person responsible for its upkeep long gone—and led August through the archway formed by the entwined trees. The passage opened onto a modest clearing with a stone slab at its centre that was under threat of being completely overtaken by the grass that surrounded it. There had been no sign of maintenance for many years, yet Evelyn still saw its natural beauty and felt that the wildness made it even more so. They sat on the cool stone, and she placed the basket of pastries between them.

"Interesting choice of location," August said, choosing a small blueberry cake.

"I like it here. It's peaceful," she replied with a shrug, "and no one ever comes here."

"I can tell," he said, consuming the cake in two bites whilst looking around the clearing.

There were weeds sprouting in the grass and patches of flowers and bushes that had probably once grown in rigid locations or patterns now spread freely.

Evelyn pouted as she picked up a chocolate pastry twist. "I thought it was a good spot, especially because you wouldn't have to wear your hood here."

"I'm sorry, it's great," he said, sounding genuinely concerned that he had upset her.

They sat in silence for a moment, and she noticed that he had his hands splayed out in front of him with his palms facing the grass, then he dropped his hood. It was strange to see his face without the charcoal fabric obscuring it in some way, and even though he was the first Mors Alv she had ever met, the darkness of his eyes was not as eerie as she expected it to be, especially as his blue irises glowed in the sunlight.

"What were you doing with your hands?" she asked between mouthfuls.

"Checking to see if there was anyone around, and you were right, there's no one," he explained. "At least, no one with magic."

"I didn't know you could do that," she commented, eyes wide. "I was only ever taught that you could take magic when you touched people."

August lay back on the stone, placing his arm under his head so that it rested on his wrist. "I'm not surprised. Information on Mors Alvs is limited in many areas and over-exaggerated in others."

"My father would agree with you on that," Evelyn said, looking down at him. "He supplemented my formal lessons with his own as he found the king's education lacking. Those are my words; his were a little more colourful."

"I like your family already," he replied.

"You say that like you plan on meeting them."

"I don't plan, I *know* I will meet them." He winked.

Evelyn scrunched her nose. "That's very presumptuous. What makes you think I'm going to introduce them to you?"

"Who said anything about you introducing them to me?" He smiled cockily, tugging on Evelyn's sleeve so that she lay down next to him. "But if you insist, I guess I can let you do the honours."

Evelyn stared up at the clear blue sky. Even though there were no clouds to hide the sun, the day was crisp. The clearing was one of the very few places in Forest's Edge where the trees did not inhibit the view of the sky, and Evelyn loved coming to the area during both the day and night to watch the clouds or stargaze. She could feel the warmth of August at her side and gently leaned into him. Unlike when she'd healed him in the alley, here they were truly alone.

"So, how's work?" August asked, his voice husky.

"Exactly what you'd expect," she told him, glad that he spoke first. "Healing people, paperwork, more healing people, more paperwork."

"You don't sound happy about it," he commented. "Isn't there are part of your job you like?"

"I do like the feeling I get after healing someone," she said. "But mostly it's just…" she shrugged.

"Is that because you would rather be spending all your time with my handsome self?" He teased.

Evelyn laughed half-heartedly.

"Ever feel like you're living your life for someone else?" she asked, not expecting him to understand. He hadn't mentioned anyone other than Nora, and from all he'd told her of his life, other than hiding his race, he was free to do as he pleased.

"More than I'd like," August admitted.

Evelyn looked at him, surprised by his answer. He did not elaborate, shrugging it off instead, but she didn't care that he hadn't elaborated. Her mind had already drifted elsewhere as she realised how close they were laying. They were so close that she could see the subtle differences in the colours of the hairs that grew along his jaw, and when August faced her, their eyes locked. Her body felt alive, conscious of every place it touched his.

"I was attacked the other day," Evelyn blurted, suddenly embarrassed by the way her words came out. They shattered the moment, but she couldn't hold them back as they tumbled from her lips. It was as if the part of her that was hurting was trying to sabotage the other part that was desperately trying to forget.

August's brows raised. "What?"

"That's why I freaked out when you grabbed me before. The other morning… a man—" she swallowed, the words stuck in her throat.

"Eve." He rolled onto his side, his front now flush with her side.

She took a deep breath. "He grabbed me on my way home from work, and he," a tear ran down her cheek. An icy chill enveloped her as memories of her attack came crashing in.

"Fuck." August swore, placing an arm around her waist and drawing her close. "You don't have to tell me this if you don't want to."

Evelyn nodded, taking comfort in his embrace, as her tears continued to fall. Maybe talking about it would help. She needed to tell him, to tell someone. Gemma hadn't mentioned anything to her family and Evelyn wasn't sure she wanted to tell them either, but she had to speak about what happened to someone. She'd tell Poppy the next time she saw her friend, but it felt right to confide in August too.

"I think I'd like to."

August waited patiently, as Evelyn composed herself, and then she explained what had happened as best she could.

"He cut my throat," she sniffed, her hands trembling. "A friend of the family, Gemma, found me before he… before he…"

"What did Gemma do with him?" August asked when she'd finished, his eyes alight with violence.

The intense look on his face caused Evelyn to shudder so she turned her golden eyes to the sky. "I don't know."

He gripped her chin, turning her head so that she was looking at him. She'd meant it when she'd said Mors Alvs weren't any more dangerous than the other races, but right now, August made her previous convictions waver.

"If she doesn't kill him, I will," he vowed.

Evelyn didn't know how to reply to his declaration and knew she was glimpsing the man beneath the playful arrogance. The man who scared those he passed in the streets and appeared late at night with a severely wounded friend after a bloody fight.

"Eve," his face softened, his hand on her chin gently cupping her face. "I'm not going to let anyone hurt you ever again."

Evelyn nodded, biting her bottom lip. Part of her swelled at his words but there was a voice in the back of her mind, shouting a warning that pierced right through her.

## 23

## Nora

Moonlight created a soft glow, emphasised by a light fog that dulled the sparkling diamonds in the night sky. Nora stared out the shopfront windows from where she sat on the floor next to an open display cabinet. She had stayed back to help Will restock after an unexpectedly busy afternoon where she had been run off her feet assisting customers and fetching orders. Much to her annoyance, there had not been time to delve further into her investigations.

Turning back to the task at hand, she summoned her wind magic, levitating one of the many small bottles of dried plants from the box in front of her onto the shelves. She had no idea whether they were going into their right spots, but she didn't really care.

"Will?" Nora inquired, her eyes momentarily flicking to her boss.

"Mmm," he replied, adjusting a large bouquet of pastel flowers.

"What does the symbol mean?" Nora asked. "The one with all the squares carved into your shopfront?"

"That help can be found here," he replied simply.

"I know that part." She rolled her eyes. "What does it mean though?"

"Each square represents one of the five Gods and Goddesses of Valmenessia," he explained. "And they're linked to show that they're equals. None is greater or lesser than the other."

She frowned, mentally kicking herself. That was an obvious conclusion now that he'd explained it. At least... the squares representing the five Gods and Goddesses, that is.

"Is it used in places other than Forest's Edge?" She knew it was, but still wanted the confirmation. Florence had been rather vague on the topic.

"It is used all over the country."

"To let people know of safehouses from the king?" She pushed.

Will looked up at her, his gaze assessing. "You have a lot of questions tonight."

"I'm curious," Nora shrugged. "And maybe I want to know if there's more to what you're doing here because I want to be involved. Does the symbol represent something other than refuge? I get the impression Florence's job involves more than helping people settle at Daphne's?"

Will didn't reply, instead his attention returned to adjusting the flowers before him, and Nora was left wondering whether to push the subject or ask again another day. She would need to work harder to gain his trust—Daphne and Florence's too, if she wanted to meet Gemma anytime soon. Nora might have to join Daphne for breakfast the next morning, see if the woman would be more open to answering her growing list of questions.

"Florence seems to like you," Will said casually, though it was blatantly obvious he was changing the topic. "Sage on the other hand... her feelings could go either way."

Nora turned to face him, one eyebrow raised. The bottle of sunflower seeds she had been shelving halted mid-air. "How would you know how they feel about me?"

"I have ears and you all talk rather loudly. Also, other people tell me things," he replied, glancing sideways at her, but not stopping his work. "Back to Sage."

"You tell me," she replied, returning to her task. "Do you know her well?"

"I know a little about everyone."

"That's not creepy at all…" Nora said wryly.

Will laughed. "I know she's a friendly and intelligent woman."

"Beautiful too," Nora added, floating the sunflower seeds the rest of the way onto the shelf. "But I doubt she cares what I think in that regard."

"She is," he agreed with a nod. "Though there are more important things than looks."

"Yeah, but it's still nice. Especially if you don't want a relationship and just want to… you know." She winked at him.

"Not everyone wants to do that," he rolled his eyes.

Nora quirked a brow. "Have you never?"

"I have," he huffed. "Not that it matters, but I have no interest in seeking it out."

"Was it that bad?" she chuckled.

"It's not about it being good or bad. I'm not oblivious to how physical intimacy feels," he replied dryly. "I'm just not interested."

"But don't you want to fall in love one day?" she asked, her brows furrowed.

"Love and sex are not the same thing, Nora," Will groaned, explaining it as though she were more than a couple years his junior.

"I know, but when you fall in love…" she rolled her wrist, motioning with her hand.

"Who says I'm not in love with someone?"

"Don't you want to be intimate with that person then?" she asked, then her brown eyes went wide. "Wait… who is it? Have I met them?"

"You can be intimate in other ways," he replied, ignoring her other questions.

Nora shook her head. "I don't know if I could live without it."

"Luckily, the world doesn't revolve around you," he pointed out. "They are my choices and I'm happy with them."

"Wait… the world doesn't revolve around me?" she teased, grinning playfully.

Will threw his hands in the air. "I don't know why I hired you."

"Because I am marvellous company?" Nora grinned. "I can only imagine how bored you must have been before I started working here.

Life must have been dull."

Nora floated the last bottle onto the shelf, then stretched her arms and legs and cracked her neck. She hadn't used much of her magic today, and yet she felt more drained than usual. It could have been her restlessness that was consuming her power, though she'd never heard or experienced anything like that happening before. The days since King Dominic made his commands to find Felix continued to pass her by with little progress. She wanted answers to her questions, and she wanted to find Felix. Every moment spent completing tasks unrelated to her search was another moment wasted.

Glancing around, Nora was still bewildered by the range of plants Will had on sale. She was not well-versed in botany, but even she knew it should have been impossible to have such a wide variety of living cacti. Will himself was an oddity. He was surprisingly young to own a store. If she guessed his age correctly, he had to be under thirty. She stared at her boss; his mop of black hair was swept back from his emerald eyes. Nora had been known to be a sucker for the dark hair, fair eyes, and tall types—at least taller than her, which was not hard.

"You're staring at me," Will pointed out. "I'll start charging if you keep it up."

"You'll have to dock my pay," Nora replied, with a grin. "How did you come to own a flower shop?"

"It used to be my mother's," he began. "I didn't have the heart to sell it when she died, and I find being here helps me feel closer to her."

Nora's brows rose, she hadn't expected that answer. "That's sweet."

"Don't be sarcastic," he scolded.

"I'm not," Nora pouted. For once in her life, she was being sincere. "What did you want to be when you were younger?"

"You say that like I'm really old," Will laughed. "I'm twenty-six, just so you know. And I never had a plan, except to travel. I still want that." He paused. "Speaking of travel, you're done. Go home."

Nora stood, dusting off her pants. "Are you sure you don't want me to help you with anything else?"

"No, go! You're no real help anyway." He smiled, waving her away. "I'm going to have to fix up those bottles once you've gone. Plus, you're distracting me."

Nora chuckled, retrieving her cloak from the cupboard behind the counter. Buttoning it up, she braced herself for the cold weather outside. She turned to Will, halting at the front door, her hand on the brass handle. "Don't miss me too much!" she blew him a kiss.

"Go already," he laughed, "or I'll change my mind and find something else for you to make a mess of!"

She waved and stepped out into the cold night, the icy wind whipping through the streets. Nora shivered, pulling her cloak tighter around herself. There were minimal people out at this hour and most had their head down as they walked, eager to get to their destination.

Thoughts of searching for Felix invaded her mind. She and August had been in Forest's Edge for over a week now and, even though they had more clues, it felt like they were no closer to finding Felix. Nora worried her bottom lip; she needed to meet Gemma soon. Gaining Will and Florence's trust was taking longer than she liked, and she had a feeling it could take a while longer yet.

Nora spun to her left, the sound of whispers nearby snapping her attention to the present. She scanned her surroundings but there was nothing of note. The people that walked the street with her had not showed any sign of having heard the noise. Looking to the trees and rooftops, she tried to see whether there was anyone hiding. She glimpsed spotted grey fur darting away… at least she thought she did. The movement was so quick she could have all but imagined it. She strained her eyes, squinting in the darkness, but there was nothing. Luckily, this part of Forest's Edge had limited tree coverage, so there were less places for people to conceal themselves if they were hiding, not that it made her feel less on edge. Resolving that maybe she had imagined the noise, she summoned a flame to her gloved palms to warm them as she walked.

As she travelled back to Daphne's, Nora continued to scan the streets for any signs of unwanted followers, reminding her of the many nights she had been sent out to monitor or assassinate people as per the king's request. She had not been alone on those occasions. August had been with her, and his company had made it enjoyable, helping the time to pass quicker. They would make up stories about the lives of the Royal Bay citizens who came into view, or sometimes Nora would do tricks with her magic. Thinking about it now made her chest ache to be back there.

Again, the sound of hushed whispers drew Nora's attention and as she turned, she was knocked to the ground, her flame extinguishing in a puff of smoke. Her head spun and vision blurred as warm blood oozed from her hairline where she had been struck, running down her forehead and into her eyebrow. Pressing her hand against her wound, she attempted to stand up as the hazy street slowly came back into focus.

"Look what we have here!" growled a male voice.

"I'd love to, but I think you got blood in my eyes," she drawled to the best of her ability. Even injured she couldn't help being a smart ass. "Probably best to not hit people on the head if you want to begin with that line."

"Still have that rude mouth!"

"Yeah," Nora replied. "I'm kind of attached to it."

Her heart was racing as her body readied itself for fight or flight. Her vision cleared and the pain of her wound dulled as she looked into her attacker's green eyes, narrowed, and burning with hatred.

An eery silence enveloped the now deserted streets. Where the other people who had been nearby moments ago had gone, she did not know. Instead, Sebastian stood before her, his broad chest puffed out and sword in hand. The moonlight reflected off his thinning grey hair and silver beard. Behind, Grayson's large hands twitched at his sides, embers flicking from his fingertips. His wide shoulders blocked her path, and his cracked smile danced with revenge.

August had said these two were no longer a concern and she'd assumed he had killed them. Clearly he had hoped they would have scurried on home with their tails between their legs. Unfortunately for them, that was not the case. She would have to have words with August as to why these two men were alive, but for now, it was time to send Sebastian and Grayson into the arms of Goddess Jord.

"Where's your friend?" Sebastian barked, rolling his shoulders, and adjusting his stance.

"Who knows?" Nora shrugged. "I didn't think you liked him much anyway."

"Let's just deal with her and worry about him later," Grayson told

Sebastian, eyes wide as he inclined his head towards Nora. "She's the one who killed them all anyway."

"So eager to join them?" She dragged the back of her hand over her eye, wiping the blood away. "Two against one is not exactly a fair fight, but I'll go easy on you."

Sebastian's laugh was cold and hollow as it echoed in the night. He lunged, swinging his sword ferociously as Nora jumped back. His blow missed by mere inches, and she immediately summoned her wind magic. It hit him in the chest, throwing him backwards and knocking him to the ground with a groan, his sword slipping from his grip and clattering beside him. Fire flew erratically from Grayson's hands, some finding their mark and hissing as they singed Nora's clothing.

"This cloak is new!" she shouted, scrunching her nose at the odour of burning material as she summoned water to douse the sparks.

Drawing her hands to her chest, she channelled her magic, then threw her hands out forcefully towards Grayson, a jet of water hurtling at his chest. The burly man leaned into it, his feet sliding backwards ever so slightly, but he held his ground. Sebastian rose, snatching his sword and raising it once more. With a snarl, he pounced. Nora did her best to counter their assaults, but the men were prepared, working together to block Nora's assaults.

She threw water and fire at them in relentless attacks, but each summons of magic took more energy from her than the last.

"What the fuck?" Nora hissed to herself. Her magic was waning quicker than usual, and her attacks were soon becoming defensive manoeuvres. If she did not end them quickly, they would overcome her.

Nora ducked into an alley, sidestepping another of Grayson's orbs of fire. However, Sebastian was on her heels, refusing to let her gain any ground or advantage. Ducking, she dodged another of his blows, her head spinning from the quick movement. Even though it had slowed, blood still oozed from her forehead. If she didn't act now, either they would kill her, or she would throw up... or both. Her heart hammered in her chest as she pushed down the rising panic. Now was not the time to let fear take root.

A searing pain burst through Nora's shoulder as Sebastian struck her. She cried out, staggering back, and gripping her shoulder where his sword had sliced through the layers of fabric and into her flesh. She pressed her hand into the wound as hard as she could, but the blood seeped through her fingers, drenching her clothing.

Grimacing with pain, she moved farther into the alley, drawing them in with her as she summoned a gust of wind with her good hand and gave them a quick, hard shove. Nora yelped as the movement jostled her injury, the action having the desired effect on the two men. As her attackers steadied themselves, Nora didn't hesitate. Summoning her water magic, she used the cold night's air and turned them into ice arrows, sending them flying into the men before they could counter. The arrows hit their targets, and Sebastian cried out as dark red bloomed on his exposed white shirt. Grayson snarled and, baring his teeth, he threw another orb of fire. It landed at Nora's feet, but she didn't pay it any attention, instead focusing on summoning the air from their lungs and stifling Sebastian's cries—her own breathing a mess of gasps. This kind of magic was a last resort as it would drain everything she had—not that she had much left—but if she did not kill them now, they would surely murder her.

Grayson clawed at his throat, his face turning blue as Sebastian fell on his side, his eyes wide as he succumbed to death. Nora held on, grasping at whatever magic she had remaining. Every last drop. Finally, Grayson too crumpled to the ground, and she staggered over to him. Staring down, she watched the light leave his eyes as a small smile spread on her face.

No one—*no one*—got the better of her.

Nora unclenched her fist, releasing her magic and letting her legs buckle beneath her. She rolled onto her back, a strangled cry escaping her lips. Her shoulder was in agony, the pain sending shockwaves through her body. Her injuries were bad—she did not need to be a Lys Alv to know that. Eyelids drooping, she thought of how easy it would be to fall asleep on the street, how she barely noticed the hard ground or the cold night air.

Nora bit her lip as a blurred figure appeared above her and pressed on her shoulder wound, forcing a cry to escape her lips. Heat continued to leak into her clothing, slick and oozing.

"Sage?" Nora gasped, her eyes slowly coming back into focus. She stared up at the woman; a ring of bright light glowed around her head. Sage was a goddess.

"It's okay," Sage said, brown eyes wide as they darted over Nora's face. "You're going to be okay. Florence has gone to get help."

"What are you doing here?" Nora asked between breaths.

"Saving you from bleeding out all over the place."

"But you don't like me," Nora rasped, her head swimming from the pain.

Sage opened her mouth before snapping it shut just as quickly. "You're going to be okay. Florence is really fast in her fox form, she'll be back any minute."

"You didn't answer my question."

"It wasn't a question though, was it?"

Footsteps thumped nearby and suddenly Florence was on Nora's other side.

"Will is getting a horse," Florence declared. "Evelyn's on night shift so we're taking you to the Healing Centre. Hold on for a bit longer."

"I guess I can stay, I don't have any other plans," Nora groaned, earning a chuckle from Florence.

"Surely there's a Healer that's closer!" Sage exclaimed, revealing the moon that glowed eerily brilliant behind her head. "The bleeding is slowing but she could lose the arm if we wait any longer. Evelyn can't grow Nora's arm back if it dies."

Nora grimaced at the image that flashed in her mind. "It's not that deep a wound… is it?"

Florence peered at Nora's shoulder, raising her eyebrows, and jutting out her pink lower lip. "You wouldn't be awake if it were that bad."

"There's a lot of blood!" Sage chided.

"Don't be so dramatic," Florence chuckled. "I can hear Will, let's get you up."

Hauled to her feet, Nora groaned as a sharp pain radiated through her back and down her arm, but that was nothing compared to what came next. Standing was easy compared to being lifted onto a horse.

"Son of a bitch!" Nora cried out, sweat dripping from her forehead as an arm gripped her around the middle and pressed her close. Florence and Sage had somehow managed to boost her onto the horse's back and into Will's arms.

"Always with something to say," Will commented from behind her. "This is not going to be pleasant, so I'll be expecting something a little more colourful."

Bracing herself, Nora gripped the pommel with her bloodied hands and prayed to the Goddess Thyra that Will had a strong hold on her. The horse took off and Will received what he asked from her and more.

# 24

**Evelyn**

E velyn had thought she had some free time between her paperwork and random patients, but she had been wrong. She sat at her desk—her scribbled notes and patient records stacked neatly to the side, while Poppy skipped around the room. There was not much to her workspace; a thin bed against the far wall; a simple wooden desk next to the bedhead; and, on the adjacent wall, cupboards filled with a variety of books, ointments, salves, tonics, herbs, and other healing necessities.

"I'm dating someone." Poppy blurted, her random statement surprising Evelyn.

Evelyn's eyes grew wide. "Does this person have a name?"

"Zaim," Poppy giggled.

"Who is Zaim and since when?" Evelyn exclaimed.

"Only recently." Her friend bit her lip.

"Why are you only telling me this now?"

"You've had a lot going on," Poppy waved her hand flippantly. "Plus, it's only been a few months, I guess I didn't want anything to spoil it."

"A few months!"

"He's so handsome," Poppy placed both hands over her heart, her dress swinging around her feet, and ignored Evelyn's outburst. "And romantic too."

"You really like him, huh?" Evelyn asked, toying with the pin on her cardigan. She wore the same uniform as Poppy: yellow dress and grey cardigan, a bright amber sun indicating to all that she was a fully certified Healer pinned to the wool. "So much that you kept him a secret for months?"

"I didn't want to ruin the little world we had created together. I think he's the one!" her friend squealed, planting her hands on the edge of the desk. "I know we haven't been dating very long, but if you know, you know... right?"

"That's what I've heard," Evelyn replied, her smile not quite meeting her eyes. She was happy for her friend, she really was, but if Poppy truly loved him, why was Evelyn only hearing of him now? Maybe Evelyn was unable to truly understand because love had never graced her before. Evelyn liked August. She liked him a lot, but love? That wasn't even on her mind yet.

"You're not happy for me?" Poppy pouted.

"No, no, I am," Evelyn stammered, standing and taking her friend"s hands in her own. "I really am. It's just, I wish you'd confided in me earlier." She squeezed Poppy"s hand. "Ultimately, if you're happy, then I'm happy."

"Are you sure?" Poppy batted her lashes.

Evelyn nodded. "Yes. Although I would like to meet this mystery person that has stolen your heart."

"Yes!" Poppy threw herself into Evelyn's arms. "He has stolen my heart like a thief in the night! And I will definitely introduce you two! You will be fast friends, I—"

The door burst open and a woman Evelyn never thought she would see again was carried into her room.

"Uh, hi," Nora panted in Will"s arms, a greyish sheen to her complexion. "Fancy seeing you here, though you look busy. Should we come back later?"

Eyes wide, Evelyn stepped out of Poppy's embrace and rushed over to where Will was placing Nora on the bed. "What happened to you?"

"She was attacked," Will answered for Nora. "But she handled herself surprisingly well."

"She looks like she's ready to meet Goddess Jord!" Evelyn retorted, hands already hovering over the shoulder wound.

"You should see the other two," Will smirked. "I'm going wait for Florence and Sage outside." He faced Poppy. "Care to join me?"

"Evelyn might need my assistance," Poppy replied, folding her arms over her chest.

"Oh, well," Evelyn started, golden eyes darting between Will and Poppy. The former raised his eyebrows pointedly and Evelyn suddenly understood. Nora had not been attacked by just anybody. "I'm fine, you should go."

"Evelyn?" Poppy pushed, concern clear in her blue eyes. She had her secrets and it turned out Evelyn had her own too.

"Go. It's okay." She waved Poppy and Will away, the latter shutting the door behind them. Evelyn did not bother wasting time by preparing bandages as she turned her attention to Nora.

"That was awkward," Nora commented, the tension in the room all but evaporated since the others' departure. "It's pretty, isn't it?" The woman glanced down at her wound before paling and quickly averting her gaze.

"Not as good as your back wound," Evelyn replied flatly, her tone demonstrating none of the sarcasm of what she had said. "I can't believe this is the second time someone has carried you into my healing rooms bleeding, and I've only met you twice."

"I'm trying to be consistent," Nora said sarcastically.

Evelyn groaned, fighting back an eye roll. "Are you ready?"

Nora gripped the edge of the bed, bracing herself, which Evelyn thought was odd considering the process would bring only relief for the woman.

Breathing in deeply, Evelyn placed her hands over Nora's shoulder—half an inch from touching flesh—and summoned her light. Nora's arm would heal with little trouble, though it would be painful for Evelyn. Evelyn's light moved through the wound; the cut was deep but nothing major had been hit. Urging her magic forward, it took on the role of a skilled seamstress, carefully knitting the muscle and flesh back together with a glowing thread that mended and revitalised with each stitch. Searing pain burst from her own shoulder as invisible nails dug in deep, slicing through the skin and tearing the tissue apart.

Like Nora, she focused her eyes on the wall of her healing room. If anyone had walked in at that moment, they would have been bewildered by what could have been so terribly interesting about a plain, pastel yellow wall. Evelyn's mouth was firmly closed, fighting a battle against the cry that so desperately tried to escape. She refused, determined to hide her anguish, and keep her expression as neutral as possible.

"Does it hurt a lot?" Nora asked, her voice thick.

"It doesn't tickle," Evelyn replied through gritted teeth, glancing down at the woman. Nora watched her, brown eyes disconcerting, and after a moment's reflection, Evelyn added, "It's fine. It's only a momentary pain, a few hours at most, and then my magic heals the wound and it's like it never happened."

"Until someone else comes in to be healed..." Nora added.

Evelyn attempted a shrug but was gifted a sharp jolt of pain that radiated up her shoulder instead. "It's my job."

"Yeah, don't get me wrong because I'm happy that you're healing me, but don't you ever feel like you've had enough of feeling other people's pain?" Nora prodded, her voice steadying with each passing minute. "I mean, I got injured because someone attacked me, but you're getting hurt willingly."

Evelyn bit her lip, surprised by Nora's comments. It sounded strange when put like that, as though she was happily being injured repeatedly every day and would spend the rest of her life in this room doing just that. While others lived their lives, she would be here feeling and healing the repercussions of it. Gemma may have offered her a greater purpose for her skills, but it was still more of the same, and after her own attack... The desire to uproot her whole life was becoming stronger and stronger by the day. She wanted to live a little herself, not just heal those who do.

"When you say it like that, it does sound awful." Evelyn pressed her lips together to stifle a yelp.

"I wouldn't want to do it," Nora admitted, her breathing returning to a stable rhythm and pink blossoming into her complexion once more.

"But I think that has more to do with me being utterly selfish than anything else."

"That's not true," Evelyn replied, removing her hands from Nora's shoulder, and staggering backwards towards her supplies. She grabbed a bandage and pressed it to her shoulder before slumping into her chair. "At least August doesn't think that."

Nora's eyes narrowed and she cocked her head. "Please tell me he has other things to talk about than me all day?"

Evelyn chuckled, leaning back against the hard wood. "We talk about other things but when it comes to you... he doesn't tell me outright, but he doesn't have to. When he speaks of you, he doesn't give me the impression of you being that way."

Nora tapped a dirt and blood-crusted fingernail to her chin. Her newly healed arm still lay limp at her side. "Interesting."

"How so?" Evelyn asked, her skin flushing from more than just the injury. She had thought August was overly confident, cocky, and secretive, but Nora was worse—and slightly infuriating too.

"It just is," Nora said simply.

"August didn't tell me you were in Forest's Edge though." Evelyn said, frowning. Why hadn't he? They'd shared so many other things...she'd shared so many things...

Nora shrugged, turning her head to the door as Sage walked in. Sage took three steps towards Nora, then quickly stepped back, halting with her arms hanging awkwardly at her sides. Evelyn watched in fascination as Nora merely smirked at Sage.

"How are you doing?" Sage asked, then hastily added, "Both of you?"

"I'm much better," Nora said, sitting up and wiggling her arm about. "As you can probably tell, Evelyn has seen better days though."

"It won't be long until I'm completely healed," Evelyn said. "It would have been better if you had come in during the day when my magic is strongest, but nothing was broken so it shouldn't take too long for my magic to work. I'll be able to heal your head wound in a few minutes."

"No need," Nora waved her off, sliding off the bed and practically gliding towards Sage. "I'm consistent, remember Evie?"

*Nora hadn't let Evelyn heal her head last time either…* Evelyn watched as Nora edged shamelessly close to Sage.

"Plus, scars are a turn-on, right?" Nora drawled.

Evelyn could have sworn the temperature in the room rose, as Nora stepped to the side, twirling around like a dancer. Evelyn was faced with a full view of Sage's wide brown eyes and rosy cheeks.

"Thanks for healing me," Nora said as she stepped towards the door. "I guess I'll see you around."

Sage blinked slowly. "What just happened?" she asked after Nora had left.

Evelyn stifled a giggle. "I would say that she'd bewitched you with a hidden potion, but she's an Elementum, not a Conjurer."

Sage frowned, pushing her golden glasses up the bridge of her nose.

"I thought you were seeing Ashe?" Evelyn asked, an eyebrow raised.

"We were never exclusive, and as you know, he left the city for a while." Sage shook her head. "But that has nothing to do with Nora because I'm not interested in her that way."

"Mmmhhmmm, okay," Evelyn smiled knowingly.

"You're right, I'm not convinced either," Sage sighed. "What have I gotten myself into?"

"I don't think you're to blame. If anything, you may have been… for want of a better word"—the giggle Evelyn had been holding escaped her lips—"ensnared."

◇

Evelyn walked through the corridor of the Forest's Edge Healing Centre, the windows overlooking the tree on her left and Poppy keeping pace on her right. Outside, the moon shone brightly, except for under the ancient tree where the light was hindered by the thick canopy.

"That was a little bit of excitement for the night!" Poppy giggled after Evelyn explained briefly what had happened to Nora.

Evelyn chuckled, nudging her friend with her good arm. She held her other arm firmly at her side so that her shoulder was able to heal without being jostled too much. "She was seriously injured."

"And now she's not," Poppy declared. "So it's interesting gossip."
Evelyn rolled her eyes.

"How are you doing anyway?" Poppy asked, her eyes filled with concern. She had changed her hairstyle whilst Evelyn had been treating Nora, and now her blonde hair was plaited and coiled into a single bun atop Poppy's head. Her hair pulled into the style so tightly it made her ears stick out.

"I'm fine," replied Evelyn simply.

"I mean after the attack the other day. You were almost killed," her friend pointed out. "There is no way you're fine, hearing that that woman was attacked must have affected you."

Evelyn shrugged. Poppy was right; she wasn't, but she also did not want to talk about it. She wanted to move on. Gemma had informed her that the man who attempted to murder her was now sitting in a prison cell and unable to hurt anyone anymore. All Evelyn wanted to do now was to forget what had happened.

"If you want to talk," Poppy said sadly, placing a comforting hand on Evelyn's wrist, "I'll be here for whenever you're ready."

"Thanks," Evelyn smiled. "But let's talk about something else… anything else."

"I can tell you about the date I had with Zaim the other day?" Poppy suggested.

"Why not?" she giggled.

Poppy beamed and recounted her story for Evelyn. It would almost have been somewhat of a stereotypical date if it weren't for the overly romantic aspects that Evelyn was sure Poppy was exaggerating.

"It's definitely love," Poppy sighed once she'd finished. She wrapped her arms around herself, giving herself a tight hug, and grinned broadly. "Speaking of love, how are things going with you and your lover boy?"

"Please don't call him that," groaned Evelyn. "And I don't know… I thought things were going well but then…"

"What?"

"The other day he was really intense, like "I'll kill whoever looks at you" intense," she began.

"That's hot," Poppy replied, fanning herself.

"And I feel like he's keeping secrets," Evelyn finished, pursing her lips.

"You haven't known each other that long, it makes sense that he doesn't tell you everything," her friend said.

"Then why is he so protective? We aren't close enough for him to act that way."

"You told him about the attack, that's why," Poppy rolled her eyes. "He sounds so hot, I don't know why you're over thinking it."

"I am not overthinking anything," Evelyn rebuked.

"You are." Poppy wiggled her brows up and down, grinning. "You make a face."

"I do not!"

"You do! It looks like this," Poppy replied, looking off into the distance, a small smile touching her lips before frowning. "Your mouth shows the progression of your thoughts. First you're happy and then you're overthinking it."

Evelyn could not help but laugh. "Fine, I make a face."

Poppy smirked. "I love being right."

# 25

## Nora

Back in Royal Bay, Nora had spent most of her time with August, and even though there were other members of the Alta, Nora had paid them little attention. The other Alta were older, meaner, and were mostly just pains in the ass. Even when Nora and August were small children, the Alta were unkind, some having gone so far as to enjoy opportunities to physically train or punish them. Whether it was August and Nora's young age, the power of their magical abilities or a combination of both, the older Alta did not hide their disdain for the duo—especially when she or August showed them up during a group training session. She had learnt from early on that the only person she could rely on was August.

So when she arrived back to her room at Daphne's, she fought every instinct not to shout the roof down.

"You told me that you dealt with Sebastian and Grayson!" she hissed, jabbing her finger at August's chest. "And yet, I had to visit your little girlfriend to heal me because they attacked me in the fucking street!"

"Nora—" August began, his hand wrapping around the one she had at his chest.

"Don't *Nora* me!" She pulled herself from his grip, but he held strong. "You lied, and your lies could have gotten me killed. They ambushed me for Thyra's sake! I was stupidly under the impression they had already been taken care of! And now Evelyn could be a problem too!"

August frowned, his dark eyes filled with concern. "Were you hurt that badly?"

She shot him a glare. "I shouldn't have been hurt at all. Why didn't you kill them in the first place?"

"I was a little preoccupied saving your life at the time," he ground out. "You're welcome by the way."

"Something is going on with you," she said, her brown eyes searching his face as if she could find the answer written there. "I don't know what it is, but something has been changing in you for a while. You think I haven't noticed, but I have. I know you August, and something is different."

His distinctive Mors Alv eyes were fixed on her, the blue rings within the black lacking their usual glow. Nora thought they were his most striking feature, even though they instilled fear in most people. Nora had never seen August as a threat, even after he nearly killed her on the first day they met. She trusted him more than anyone else in the world. At least she had, but this new August? Their bond... something had shifted.

August shrugged. "So what if something has changed? Change is not a bad thing, you know."

"It is when you are straying further and further from King Dominic's commands!" she accused him, struggling to keep her voice low.

"I still follow his commands," his jaw twitched.

Nora threw her hands in the air. "Loosely."

"That's your interpretation," he narrowed his eyes. "I see it differently."

"You shouldn't be able to." She could feel the presence of her shackle tattoos as if they were iron braced around her skin; their imagined weight providing comfort, but also burning with every strayed step. "It's the king's way, there *is* no interpretation."

August turned away from her, striding over to the armchair. "Why is Evelyn going to be a problem?"

"She knows I'm not here alone," Nora told him, sitting on the floor in front of the fire. "If she tells the others they'll have no reason to trust me."

"I'll talk to her."

Nora stared into the fire, the flames crackling as they devoured the log in their clutches. "You better hope she hasn't said anything already or this whole investigation could be royally fucked before we've found out anything useful."

Weaving through the ancient trees, Nora followed Daphne into the depths of the forest. A cloudy mist twirled among the fallen leaves with each step that she took towards the amber glow. A group, larger than she had expected, gathered around the flame; some sitting on rocks and fallen branches. Embers flittered from the blaze like butterflies setting off towards the night sky after twirling around the flickering orange petals.

"The celebration will begin soon," Daphne said. The older woman was dressed in a thick coat, a grey wool scarf and matching headband at the edge of her forehead, holding back the thick black curls.

"What are they celebrating?" Nora asked.

"When an Anima turns five, a member of the community with a similar shift will step up as a mentor," Daphne explained.

"A mentor? What about the parents?"

"No one will ever replace the child's parents, but a mentor gives an alternate perspective. Amina are very community orientated." Daphne smiled warmly. "Is it not like this where you're from?"

Nora shrugged. "I wouldn't know."

It wasn't a lie. She had never been invited to anything like this before, nor had she been close enough with an Anima to have heard about it. Rana may not have seen it as important if she had left it out of her lessons.

"That's a shame," the older woman said. "It is an ancient Anima celebration still cherished in the other northern cities too, so I have been told."

Daphne sat and children scurried from all over, crowding around her and finding places to sit at her feet. Nora stuffed her gloved hands into the pockets of her newly repaired cloak and stood awkwardly nearby, suddenly left alone.

"In a time long ago, when the sun and moon watched over their children from high in the sky, the Gods and Goddesses roamed the land, protecting this world from terrors that wished to wreak havoc," Daphne began, leaning forward and dropping her voice. "Some forces still make attempts, even to this day!"

Numerous eyes widened as the children huddled closer.

"One creature, who dwells in the darkest depths of land, is known as the Morken. It never tires of its thirst for all that is good in this world and searches every waking moment for a way to get out of its cage."

"Who put it in the cage?" piped up a young boy, his arms tangled with the companion next to him.

"Aren, of course!" Daphne declared as though the Anima God was the obvious answer. She threw her hands in the air and the children all beamed up at her.

"The Morken had lived under the land for many eons, biding its time and growing in strength, until one day it broke through to the surface. A being of pure evil"—Daphne curled her fingers and flashed her teeth—"it used its long, sharp claws and fangs that were stained with the blood of its enemies to climb out of the depths. Then it was unleashed! Its darkness spread all over, killing all manner of creatures and turning the land and rivers to dust. The sky turned grey, emitting the foul stench of decay."

A few of the children whimpered, clinging to one another. Nora was not entirely sure this was an appropriate story for the young ones, but then again, who was she to say anything?

Daphne continued, seemingly unworried about the scared faces before her. "Aren saw the destruction and shifted into his mighty eagle form." She stretched her arms out wide. "He flew into the darkness and fought the Morken, forcing it into a cage made of bones and hurling it back under the land it had feasted upon."

"Then, opening his enormous golden wings once more, he flapped with his mighty strength and blew the darkness that had plagued the land away with a fearsome gust of wind!"

From behind the children, someone waved a hand in the direction of the storyteller and a puff of wind blew towards them, whirling through their clothes and hair. The children cheered, their worried expressions replaced with toothy smiles and excited wiggling.

"Thanks to Aren, the land was able to heal; the sky returned to its calm blue, and the water flowed once more to the parched land. The plants and trees grew luscious and green, and the creatures were able to return to their homes."

"I wonder what the other Gods and Goddesses were doing while Aren was saving the world on his own?" commented Will in a low voice.

Nora turned around to see Florence, Will, Sage, and another man she had never seen before approach. He was tall, with a muscular build and a swagger August would be envious of.

"Sitting on their asses whilst Aren did all the heavy lifting, of course," Florence said with a grin.

"More like Thyra wouldn't have bothered herself with something so easy to rein in as the Morken," quipped Nora, nudging Florence.

The unfamiliar man laughed. "I second that."

Florence scowled half-heartedly at the man.

"I didn't know you'd be here," Nora commented, turning to Will.

"Do I look like the kind of person to miss a party?" her boss said, holding up a bottle. "This is Omari, by the way."

"And you must be Nora," Omari smiled, dimples and all. "Should we find somewhere to sit?"

The small group found an unoccupied fallen tree trunk on the opposite side of the fire. Will passed around his bottle, and Nora took a swig of the bitter liquid.

"That's strong," Nora grimaced, holding the bottle near the fire to get a better look at the amber liquid within.

Will chuckled. "I would have gone with smooth and well-balanced."

"Had you never heard the story of Aren and the Morken?" Florence

217

asked. "You seemed captivated by Daphne's retelling."

Nora shook her head. "I don't know much about the Gods and Goddesses, other than Thyra of course."

Sage rolled her eyes, yet a surprising smile graced her lips. "Of course."

"How well do you all know the old stories of the Gods and Goddesses?" Nora asked the group.

"Any story in particular?" Will requested. He sat close to Florence, one pale hand resting on her thigh.

"Actually, have any of the Gods been known to say something about not being alone in the sky?" Nora picked at the sleeve of her cloak. "Something along the lines of 'he who travels the skies is never alone'?"

"I thought you didn't know any of Aren's stories?" Florence's grinned, eyebrows raised.

"I don't," Nora replied, shrugging her shoulders. "I overheard it and thought it was interesting that's all."

"Well, the line is from Aren's final tale," Florence said, gazing into the flames, the amber glow giving her far-away expression a dramatic flair. "After many generations ruling over the Anima, Aren decided his time among the mortals was over. Of course, the Anima were all heartbroken, not wanting their God who had protected and provided for them for so long to leave, but he knew that he needed to go for them to grow as a people. Gods cannot rule forever, and eventually the people had to learn to govern themselves. Aren waited for a new leader to be chosen: King Yosef—the Gods' blessed."

Nora had heard of King Yosef; he was the first king of the Animas, dating back thousands of years to when Valmenessia was split into four kingdoms. Back then, none of the races—except for the Alvs—had mixed, instead warring over territory and power. The rulers did not get along, or so the stories said. From what Nora had read, the Gods and Goddesses all came from the same parents—the Makers—but after a time the siblings" loyalties moved from their family to their races, and that's when the kingdoms were created, and the fighting started. The merging of races into one kingdom had only come about in the last few hundred years and, even then, there were still communities that were exclusively one race.

"On the day of the coronation," Florence continued, "Aren performed the ceremony in front of the entire Anima empire, crowning King Yosef for all to see. But before the festivities could begin, Aren said to the people: 'He who walks the land is at home, he who swims in the sea is among kin, and he who travels the skies is never alone.' Then he shifted into his giant eagle form and flew into the clouds."

"So, it's a farewell before he dies?" Nora wondered, slumping her shoulders. Did Felix know he was going to die? That would certainly make their search that much more difficult. Dead people weren't as easy to find, especially if they'd had time to decay.

"Yes and no," Florence mused. "It's a farewell, but he doesn't die— Gods and Goddesses are immortal, remember."

"Where does he go then?" Nora asked.

"To live amongst the other Gods and Goddesses and, from there, he watches over the Anima, guiding and protecting us," Florence smiled.

"Is it common for Anima to quote the phrase?"

Florence scratched her head. "Not really, but I wouldn't say it's unheard of."

Nora tapped her chin. Was Felix trying to tell her and August that he had willingly left the Alta? Or was she reading too far into it? She wished August were around to bounce ideas off, if only he wasn't so tied up with Evelyn all the time.

"Welcome everyone!" called a man in a maroon cloak and coffee brown boots. "Thank you for joining us tonight as we celebrate Hali becoming a mentor for my daughter Vivian!"

Cheers and applause broke out amongst those gathered as two figures next to the man hugged. Someone added powders to the fire, turning the flames into sparkling rainbow tongues that crackled as they greedily licked the night sky. Sweet pastries and cakes were passed around, as well as glass bottles and overfilled cups.

"Is that it?" Nora asked, taking a sip from a bottle that had been handed to her. It was filled with liquid much sweeter than the one Will had brought with him. "Isn't there a ritual or more talking?"

"Does there need to be?" Will asked, a grin tugging at his lips.

"I think I like Anima celebrations," Nora said, taking a piece of chocolate cake from a tray and stuffing it into her mouth.

Florence laughed. "That's because us Anima know how to have a good time."

"Where's Jasmine tonight?" Sage asked Omari.

"With Evelyn," he replied, biting into a square pastry dusted with icing sugar that clung to his dark fingers.

"Nora met Evelyn the other night," Florence said. "It was a rather eventful introduction."

Omari raised his eyebrows. "Is that so?"

"Yes, and I've actually met her before," Nora added. There was no point in hiding the fact seeing as she had mentioned to Will that Evelyn was the one who had told her about the symbol. The issue, however, was that Evelyn could easily let slip that Nora wasn't in Forest's Edge alone. August had better speak to Evelyn and sort it out.

"When?" Sage's words tumbled out of her mouth. "Has she healed you before?"

"A little while ago," Nora shrugged, dusting cake crumbs from her lap. "And why do you assume she was healing me? I could have met her on the street or at a tavern or many other places."

"But you didn't meet her at any of those other places," Will deduced with a grin, his bottle halfway to his lips.

"The other day wasn't the first time I had a run-in with the King's Guild. Hence why I came here for help," said Nora in a low voice, aiming for a hint of fear. "I already told Florence that was the case. It's not like it was a secret or anything."

"You were attacked by them twice?" Sage asked, her eyes wide in bewilderment. She looked Nora up and down as if bloodied evidence would suddenly appear out of nowhere.

"Yes," Nora said simply.

"How did you survive two attacks?" Sage demanded. "And why didn't you mention more attacks the other day?"

"Lucky I guess," she said, averting her gaze. "And I was kind of preoccupied with all the bleeding and stuff."

"And... any more details?" insisted Sage, ignoring Nora's comment about her injuries. She clearly couldn't help her inquisitive side; Sage was constantly searching for answers. "How many times have you been targeted? Are you sure they were the same group? Are more looking for you? Why do they keep coming after you?"

"Sage, I'm sure Nora will provide us with all the details, but now is not the time or place," Florence said, turning to Nora. "Gemma wants to meet you."

"Who's Gemma?" Nora scrunched her brow. She knew exactly who Gemma was, or at least that Gemma was someone she wanted to talk to. Nora had overheard enough of their conversation the other day to know that Gemma knew things that could answer a lot of her questions.

"Gemma is someone who can help you and, quite possibly, change your life if you let her," Omari offered.

"Why does she want to meet me?" Nora asked.

"That you will find out tomorrow. I'll collect you at nightfall," Florence said.

"Sounds mysterious," Nora replied dryly.

Will chuckled. "I'm sure Gemma would be thrilled to hear that."

# 26

## Evelyn

Standing in one of the many rooms in the manor, Evelyn faced Jasmine and grimaced. They had moved the furniture, giving them plenty of space. The air felt stuffy from the fire that crackled in the hearth, and Evelyn took a deep breath, concentrating on Jasmine's movements. Her sister wore navy blue trousers and a white shirt, and stood with her legs shoulder-width apart. A stark contrast to the usual pastel dresses with embroidered floral designs that she usually wore. The clothing change, however, did not alter Jasmine's impeccable posture and graceful movements.

Evelyn always felt plain next to her sister. They both had their mother's plump lips and delicate nose, and their father's brown skin, but her sister was taller with long black hair that could be easily styled. Evelyn was shorter, with golden eyes and pointed Lys Alv ears that peeked through her often unruly dark waves. Jasmine was made for the future that was now laid out before her, even if her passions lay in baking and pastries.

Jasmine had been teaching Evelyn self defence for the last hour or so. Evelyn had finally told her sister about the attack and had begged her not to tell their parents. She didn't want to be trailed by guards everywhere she went. Jasmine had agreed, but insisted she teach Evelyn how to defend herself. Jasmine had always loved to train when they were younger—unlike Evelyn who preferred being curled up with her books or some wool and knitting needles.

They had been focusing on key areas of the body to strike if violence was the only option for escape. Jasmine guided Evelyn's movements and adjusted her technique. They had just finished up with the eyes and had now moved onto the knees.

"Remember, you want to do a low kick, kind of like a stomping kick down," Jasmine instructed. "If you think you won't be able to hit your attacker's knees, then a good stomp down on their toes won't go astray." She lifted her foot then slammed it down onto the floor." Now, let's add the movements we have gone through tonight and I'll pretend to attack you."

Jasmine did not hesitate, lunging swiftly. Evelyn tried to use the techniques she had just learnt but her sister was so fast, she found herself on the floor with Jasmine on top of her within in a matter of seconds.

"Again," Jasmine said, letting go of Evelyn and standing up.

Jasmine pounced on Evelyn repeatedly, shoving Evelyn onto the floor so many times she could feel her magic tingling through her, healing the bruises as she panted heavily. She had not thought herself unfit, but she was not used to this sort of activity.

"We'll keep going until you get this," Jasmine told Evelyn as she offered the Lys Alv a delicate hand up.

Evelyn adjusted her stance and when Jasmine lunged for her, Evelyn fought back, her foot slamming into her sister's knee. Jasmine collapsed to the ground, her face twisting in pain as she groaned.

"Oh my Goddess!" Evelyn exclaimed, leaning over Jasmine. "I'm so sorry! I'm so sorry!"

Jasmine rolled onto her side, her leg curled up and her hands clasped over her knee. "It's fine, I'm fine. I didn't expect you to make contact so hard."

"I'm sorry! I wasn't thinking, and I just kicked." Evelyn knelt over Jasmine's knee, carefully prying her sister's hands away. "You're not fine. Just let me have a look."

"I'm okay," Jasmine groaned. "I just need a minute."

Jasmine took a couple of breaths then let Evelyn help her to her feet. The woman tentatively took a few steps, waving Evelyn away when she tried to help.

"Please, let me help," begged Evelyn. "I feel terrible."

"This is all part of the training," Jasmine replied through a strained smile, lowering herself onto a chair. Evelyn worried at her lip and Jasmine sighed. "Okay, you can check my knee if it will stop you looking at me like that."

"I don't want to force you…"

Jasmine leaned forward, dragging up the fabric of her trousers, revealing bronzed skin that already showed signs of bruising. "See, nothing's broken."

"The bruising is pretty bad." Evelyn sat in front of Jasmine and leaned in, observing the deep, reddish blush that was spreading over her sister's knee. "I can heal that in no time."

Placing her hands just over the injury, Evelyn summoned her light, guiding it through the damaged flesh. She drew in a sharp breath as she took on the hurt. The bruising faded within moments, and she could feel her magic healing her at the same time, cooling the burning sensation that radiated from her own knee.

Nora's honest comments about Evelyn's occupation the other night crept into her mind. Why was she spending her life continuing to hurt herself for the benefit of others? She still believed in healing those in need, but was it necessary to inflict pain on herself every day? Is that what her life was going to be? Is that what she wanted? Healing her sister was her choice, but healing others purely because she was born with magic… where was the choice in that?

"Thank you," Jasmine said, covering her leg once more. "You did really well tonight, but before we go to bed, remind me of my first rule again.

Evelyn shuffled backwards, stretching her leg out before her, and leaning back on her hands. "Prevention is the best defence. Don't put yourself in a dangerous situation in the first place."

"Good," Jasmine nodded. "And what if danger finds you like it did the other night?"

"Hit hard and fast because my attacker will most likely be stronger than me. Any lenience or delay will give them more of an advantage. Go for the eyes, throat, solar plexus, groin, or knees," she told Jasmine, repeating the words her sister had told her at the start of their training.

"Next time I'm going to bring Florence so she can shift, and we'll see whether you can defend her assault." Jasmine stood, picking up her cloak from where it lay draped over the back of another chair.

"That's impossible," Evelyn giggled, "she's so cute as a fox."

"Don't let her hear you say that," Jasmine laughed. "Come on, it's late."

"I suppose it is," Evelyn yawned, getting up and following her sister from the room.

She was not overly keen on learning to hurt others. It went against everything she had ever been taught, but if it meant she could continue having her independence, and prevented her from being a target yet again, well… she would learn to get used to the idea. It would be no good leaving herself vulnerable again.

"Good night," Jasmine said, reaching the top of the landing.

"Night," Evelyn replied, climbing up the last few steps and turning in the opposite direction to Jasmine. "Don't let the bed bugs bite! I won't heal you!"

Jasmine's melodic laugh echoed as Evelyn made her way to her room. It had been nice to spend some quality time with Jasmine. It had felt like too long had passed since they had spent more than five minutes alone together. Part of her wished they could stay up all night and talk, especially since there was a lot on her mind. Evelyn wanted to get Jasmine's advice about August, to tell her all about Poppy's mysterious romance and about Gemma's offer to join the faction. She sighed. She would have to make time soon.

Shuffling closer to August the next day, Evelyn peered at the page he was reading. They were curled up on the floor, nestled in a deserted area of the library between two of the many rows of books, Evelyn listening as August read one of the novels he had randomly picked from the shelves. She had chosen the book from the small selection he had procured, discarding many dubious options such as *King Orion and His Menagerie of Wives,* a novel about an eclectic king who had a multitude of anima wives—all a different species. August had laughed and pouted in false disappointment when she had flung it over her shoulder.

"It can't possibly say that!" Evelyn exclaimed, her voice carrying throughout the hushed library as her eyes darted over the text he was reading. "You have to be making that up!"

"I'm not!" chuckled August, leaning back so Evelyn could get a better look. "I swear!"

"Let me have it." Evelyn took the book so she could see for herself. "This was supposed to be a sweet tale."

"You could describe it that way," he grinned.

Evelyn could feel the warmth of August as he leaned over her shoulder. She tried to focus on the novel in her hand but could not help smiling at his closeness. It was moments like these that made Evelyn briefly forget about all her worries. She was enjoying August's company more than she would like to admit.

"See," August said, leaning back against the shelves. "I told you I was reading exactly what's written."

Evelyn tossed the book onto the floor and rested her back next to August. "I don't think I'm ever going to get that description of him eating a peach out of my mind."

"You didn't like the description of the mouth-watering fuzzy peach?" he teased.

"I don't think I will ever look at a peach the same way," she replied, heat climbing her neck.

August took her hand and squeezed. He had dropped his hood after they had found this secluded section of the library and had done the hand gesture thing, deeming no one with magical abilities was around. Now, she had a full view of his distinctive features; his strong nose, chiselled jaw covered in stubble, and those dark eyes. Blue rings within black pools. Goddess, he was handsome.

"I can think of one way to clear your thoughts," August said, his voice thick.

He leaned in, one hand moving to rest on her thigh, the skin beneath tingling with the touch as he drew idle circles with his thumb.

"I'm listening," she said, sounding so unlike herself but relishing in it. Evelyn edged closer, her heart pounding in her chest and tongue running slowly over her upper lip as his eyes tracked the movement.

August slid his free hand into her hair, gripping the back of her neck before slipping it higher to cup her head. Evelyn closed her eyes, her heart beating rapidly as she crept closer to his lips. She wanted to kiss him; her body buzzing with the possibility of what she desired.

"This is not a brothel!"

Evelyn's eyes snapped open, heat flushing her cheeks as she jolted backwards and out of August's reach.

"Loitering is not allowed in the library," said the scholar, Phillip, as he approached them. His chin and nose were as sharp and pointed as his tone. Evelyn had only met the man a handful of times, and each was as unpleasant as the last. She had no idea how Sage put up with him as a boss.

"Well, aren't you fucking rude," August replied, drawing his hood before turning to face the man. "And we are not loitering, we were reading. Isn't that what a library is for? Not that what we are doing is any of your business anyway."

"I work here so it is my business," Phillip huffed. "I have eyes and what you were doing was *definitely* not reading."

"Jealous?" August asked, resting back on the shelf, and folding his arms over his chest.

"Evelyn!" Phillip exclaimed in outrage. "You know better than to behave in this disgusting manner. To associate yourself with such a disgraceful character."

"Don't you dare speak to her that way!" August growled, the threat clear as he rose to his feet.

"August." She placed a hand on his arm as she too, stood. "Please, let's just go."

"This is a place of work and study," Phillip snapped, staring down at them—an odd phenomenon considering August towered over the man. "Leave."

August pounced, gripping Phillip's shirt in his fists, and shoving him hard against the shelves. Books tumbled to the floor around them, landing with their pages splayed open. "By all means go do those fucking things, but if you ever speak to Evelyn that way again I will cut you open ever so slowly and hide your organs amongst the shelves."

Phillip paled, his eyes darting from Evelyn to August.

"Let's just go," Evelyn pleaded again, tugging on August's arm. His threat was like ice in her gut. "Please, August."

August gave Phillip another hard shove before releasing him, a feral growl escaping his lips, and turned to Evelyn. She took his hand, leading him away through the rows of books.

"Sorry," August sighed once they'd stepped out onto the street. "I shouldn't have gotten so angry."

"No, you shouldn't have," Evelyn agreed, crossing her arms. "He was rude, but there are better ways to handle things."

"You think I should have ignored him?" August huffed. "Let him speak to you that way?"

"I didn't say that." She dropped her arms, her shoulders sagging. "You can call people out, but there's no need to get aggressive. That's all. Tell him he's rude and his behaviour is inappropriate, then walk away."

"Sorry," August repeated, taking her hand, and pulling her close.

"It's not okay, but I accept your apology," she smiled, looking up at him. "Let's get something to eat. I'm starving."

"Me too," he grinned.

She glanced around the street, biting her lip. "I know just where to go. There's a café nearby."

"I don't know about a cafe," he said, pointing to his hood.

"This one is perfect." She tugged his hand. "I'll show you."

The café was located near the centre of Forest's Edge and was partially built into a tree's exceptionally large trunk. They pushed through the crowded interior and made their way up the stairs to the rooftop dining area where they found a free, round wooden table near the railing made of interlocking branches. Vines hung from the upper branches, suspending violet flowers and green leaves over the tables, and emitting a sweet floral scent.

"Nice spot," whistled August, looking out at the bustling street below.

Frost Season was only a week away, its coming arrival evident in the clouded skies that could be glimpsed through patches in the tree coverage. A light breeze swirled around the open dining area, blowing the few loose strands of her black hair over her face.

"It is a favourite of mine," said Evelyn as August reached over the table and slipped the loose hairs behind one of her pointed ears. "Plus, you can easily get away with what you're wearing because we're outside and many of the other patrons have their hoods drawn or are wearing woollen hats."

"Why haven't you brought me here before then?" he asked. "Or were you keeping it up your sleeve?"

Evelyn's eyes sparkled. "It's always good to keep some of your cards a secret."

"I look forward to uncovering more then," he mischievous grin visible beneath the shadow of his hood. Her mind instantly returned to their near kiss in the library.

"I hope they are worth the wait," she replied a little breathlessly.

August chuckled.

Her brows rose. "What?"

"Sometimes you are so confident and then at other times you're the complete opposite," he said, shaking his head.

"What can I say," she shrugged. "I'm inconsistent."

"I like it. Keeps me on my toes," He replied then reached over and took her hand in his. "And anything you offer me is worth the wait."

Evelyn bit the side of her cheek. She had no idea how to answer that, let alone unpack all that his words could imply.

A waiter approached the table, his misty blue eyes looking bored, and August sat back, her hand cold in the absence of his touch. How anyone could think a Mors Alv was akin to death was beyond her.

"Ready to order?" the waiter asked, holding a small notepad in one hand, and twirling a pencil between the fingers of his other.

"Yes," replied August. "I'll have the vegetable pie and an ale."

The waiter nodded, scribbling the order onto his notepad before raising an eyebrow at Evelyn. "And you?"

"I'll have the pumpkin soup and…" she looked to the bottom of the menu and quickly scanned the available drinks. "A pear cider."

"Great, won't be long" he replied, taking their menus, and leaving to serve another table.

"How's work been treating you?" August asked her once they were alone again.

"The same as always, although Nora came in the other night," Evelyn said. "How come you didn't tell me she was in Forest's Edge? When did she get here?"

August leant his forearms on the table. "Only recently, but we're not staying together."

"Why not?" she asked, surprised at his comment. "Did you know she was attacked again?"

"She mentioned it." He shrugged, appearing to be neither here nor there in caring about Nora's wellbeing. It was odd considering how he usually spoke of his friend.

"She gets into quite a bit of trouble doesn't she." Evelyn replied, then fixed him with a concerned stare. "Are you in trouble too? Is that why you have been separated?"

"I'm fine." He said stiffly. "Can we not talk about this? And can you promise not to tell anyone that Nora knows me?"

"I didn't mean to pry. You two are so close I, I—" she shook her head. "Why don't you want people knowing that you're friends?"

"Please," he leant forward. "Just trust me and keep this secret."

Evelyn chewed the inside of her cheek. Why did August want to keep his relationship with Nora a secret?

"Sorry," he said, with a heavy sigh. "Eve, I don't mean to put you in an uncomfortable position, but I need you to do this for me. I trust you, can't you trust me too?"

Evelyn fidgeted with her hands beneath the table. Did she trust him?

"I won't tell anyone," she told him softly then pushed on, her voice strengthening with each word. "But you need to explain to me why you want me to keep this a secret."

"Alright, I promise, just not today." August nodded. "Let's talk about something else. I'm here with you, not Nora."

"Okay." Evelyn agreed reluctantly.

She was finding August increasingly hard to read, sort of like a choose your own adventure novel but the storylines weren't remotely related, and she wasn't the one turning the pages.

"What have you been doing when you're not with me? Sightseeing?" she asked, plastering a smile to her face.

"This city has plenty to keep me occupied," he replied, sounding relieved that she had moved the conversation along. "There's always something to see and do."

"What's one of your favourite things you've seen so far?"

"You," he said without missing a beat.

Evelyn felt her cheeks flush and was grateful his eyes were hidden by his hood, unsure if she could handle the full effect of his gaze.

"Are there any places you'd recommend that I visit?" he asked.

"Umm, the Manor Grounds would be a good place to start. There's some really cool art around the gardens and the five temples are located there too." She told him, sorting through her mental map of the city. "Oh, and the market district is always fun, especially near the end of the week. There's usually singing and dancing, and plenty of good food."

"We should go together," August suggested. "You could be my tour guide."

"Sure," she smiled. "I think I can manage that. I used to go there all the time with Poppy when we were younger. It's a lot of fun."

"Why don't you go there anymore?"

"I don't know," Evelyn shrugged. "Just busy I guess."

"Tell me more about Poppy." He said. "I don't think you've mentioned her before."

A smile spread over Evelyn's face. "She's my best friend and I've known her my whole life. Poppy is great. Smart, kind, loyal, and completely hilarious. She's everything you could ever want from a friend. I don't know what I'd do without her."

"You're lucky to have such a good friend," he said as their lunches floated over to them. The Elementum waitress standing near the staircase moved her arms, gently placing the plates and drinks onto the table. She then focused her attention on another table's order.

"Sort of like the one you don't want anyone to know you have?" Evelyn asked, blowing on her spoon to cool her pumpkin soup before tasting the amber liquid. It was creamy with a hint of spice, just as she liked.

"Yeah," he replied, voice husky. "Like her."

## 27

## Nora

Number four Emerald Lane was a barely noticeable door in the middle of two storefronts and if it were not for Florence, Nora would have easily missed it. After Florence knocked three times, it opened to reveal a tall man with tanned skin, an elegant jawline, long, thick eyelashes and a wide smile. He was ridiculously intimidating—the smile making it that much worse—and all was compounded by the leather armour that emphasised his muscular build. Shiny daggers and throwing stars glistened from where they were strapped to his body, and the handle of a sword peeked over his right shoulder. Nora's eyes flicked up and down as subtly as she could, weighing her possible opponent.

"Florence," he said, inclining his head in greeting, his spikey brown hair glistening in the lamp light. "How's things?"

"The usual," she replied, stepping into the hallway as the man backed up to give them room. "This is Nora."

The man turned his smile on Nora. "Nice to meet you. I have heard a lot about you. I'm Aeolus."

"Good to meet you too," she said. "I have heard absolutely nothing about you."

"I've been told you have a way with words," Aeolus laughed, leading them down the long, narrow hallway lit by oil lamps that were hung along the length of the walls.

"Aeolus is Gemma's second," explained Florence.

Nora nodded, studying her surroundings as they moved deeper inside. The musty-smelling hallway sliced through the building before they turned a corner and ascended a stairwell. A surprisingly spacious room opened before her, a collection of mismatched furniture scattered throughout. Well-worn couches, tables in need of staining, and shelves that leaned on odd angles filled the space. Nora followed, taking note of the maps, weapons, clothing, and various other supplies that lay on the tables and sat on the shelves as Aeolus guided them towards a door at the far wall. There was a lot to take in and Nora wondered what secrets and plans were nestled amongst it all.

"It's not much," Florence commented, noticing Nora's gaze darting around the room. "But you'd be surprised how much you can achieve with a few supplies and a group of people who believe in a cause."

*You have no idea,* Nora thought, taking in the possible entry and exit points. There was the door they entered from, as well as three arched windows and a blazing fireplace.

She was ushered through a door and inside, the walls were covered in annotated maps of Valmenessia and its major cities, as well as drawings of buildings and their internal layouts. Diagrams of strange objects were also pinned beside the locations. Nora assumed some were recent inventions whilst others she recalled from history books. A round table surrounded by an assortment of chairs, varying from stiff practicality to overly luxurious, filled most of the space. Omari and Gemma sat next to each other, eyeing the newcomers. The white-blonde Lys Alv radiated authority, her golden eyes fixed on Nora and sent chills twirling beneath her skin.

"Come, take a seat," ordered Gemma, gesturing with long fingers to the seat opposite her. "I assume Aeolus introduced himself at the door and, of course, you know Omari."

"Nice place you have here," Nora replied, sitting in a high-backed wooden chair with a velvet cushioned seat. "It's very… eclectic."

"That's a nice way to put it," Florence chuckled as she sat next to

Nora on what looked like a bar stool whose legs had been shortened. Aeolus took his place at Gemma's side, the Lys Alv now flanked by the two men.

"I've asked you here because Florence and Will believe you would be an asset to our faction," Gemma began, leaning forward and resting her forearms on the table, directing all her attention on Nora. "You've come up against the King's Guild twice and managed to escape their grasp."

Nora's lip tugged at one side but refused to let her pride show fully. "I did what I had to do to survive."

"I'm sure you did." Gemma's golden eyes were a mix of amusement and shrewdness. "Tell me, why were the King's Guild pursing you?"

"Didn't Florence tell you?" Nora asked, raising a brow. When Gemma didn't reply, Nora pushed on. "Does there really even need to be a reason? They're brutes. For all I know, they overheard me saying something about the king and decided I needed to die. It doesn't take much to set them on a murdering rampage. Their devotion is the stuff of cults."

"You're not wrong," Aeolus laughed bitterly, placing his hands on the back of his neck, and stretching his arms, his muscles flexing beneath the tight leather.

"And the way you fought?" Gemma's brows pinched together as Nora felt the scrutiny of the woman's gaze. "Florence was fairly impressed."

"I've learnt what I can to survive." Nora shrugged, wondering how much of the fight Florence had witnessed. She took a deep breath and spoke the truth in the hopes of adding some credibility to her lies. "I don't have a family; they passed away when I was a child, so I've had to adapt."

Thoughts of flames and smoke, of her mother's cries and an ashy field, thundered at the bolted door she had put in place in her mind to keep the memories at bay. She refused to open it; some things were best kept behind locked doors.

"We could help you," Omari said earnestly, sensing her discomfort. "You're not alone."

"You, Nora, are just another example of why what we are doing is so important." Gemma pushed her shoulders back and held her chin high. "King Dominic doesn't care for the people of Valmenessia—the fact he lets his guild run wild is proof of that. You're not the only one to be victimised due to the king's actions, either through his direct orders or from his unwillingness to punish those they terrorise in his name. We want to put a stop to that."

Nora leant back, sitting up straighter and folding her arms over her chest. "I'm in."

"You have made the right choice," Aeolus said. "Working with us, helping us rise against the king... There's lots to do. Paperwork, supplies—"

"I want to be actively involved, not just work on the sides," Nora said, glancing between the three people in front of her, conviction dancing in her eyes. "I've already shown how I fight, that I can do more than gather supplies."

She didn't have time to waste with petty tasks, she wanted to be where the action was, around those making the plans and privy to all the information the faction had.

"I told you she's not one for idle work," Florence smirked. "Her magical skills were way too honed for someone who has practised using them."

Nora restrained her smug grin. "It's been a necessity to learn how to protect myself."

"And now I'm going to give you an opportunity to protect others too," Gemma said. "I have a job for you."

"What do I have to do?" Nora asked curiously.

"There is someone in Forest's Edge who shouldn't be," Gemma replied, tapping her fingers on the wooden table. "I believe King Dominic has stationed someone here to spy."

Was this some sort of trap? Nora kept her face neutral, her mind racing with ways she could get out of there alive. It would be five against one, Omari and Aeolus the draw cards as she didn't know whether they were Elementum or human, but she could manage it. It would be messy, but she'd get out.

"Do you know who this person is?" Nora asked, keeping her

breathing steady.

Gemma nodded to Omari, and he slid a piece of paper towards her. Nora stared down at the familiar charcoal portrait before her.

"We think he already knows that we are not loyal to the king," Aeolus said, drawing her attention away from the picture. "So we need someone capable of killing him that he wouldn't expect coming. Someone who could get close without causing suspicion. After the way you handled those men who attacked you, it should be a simple task."

Nora chewed her lip. Out of all the people in the country, why did it have to be him?

"Okay," she agreed, holding back a resigned sigh. "I'll do it."

Gemma was the key to finding the answers Nora wanted about Felix, and she was going to have to prove to Gemma that she was a valuable asset that was trustworthy beyond a doubt. King Dominic had commanded Nora to find Felix and if participating in the plans of the faction brought her closer to Gemma's secrets, then she would play along. Even if that did involve a little blood on her hands.

◇

Lowering herself onto the windowsill, Nora prayed to Thyra that the thin strip of wood would hold her weight. Thankfully, it did, and using her wind magic for extra support, she peered through the dusty window. Inside, the darkened room was deserted. The candles and fireplace were now extinguished and, as far as she could see, there were no signs of life. She had waited until it was the dead of night before returning, hoping that Gemma and the others were long gone after their meeting earlier.

Carefully, Nora attempted to slide the cold glass window upwards, but to no avail. She tried again, but again it would not budge. Swearing, she dug her nails into the grooves of the wooden walls and summoned her wind magic once more, solidifying steps of air for her to reach the adjacent window. With her body pressed against the wall, Nora edged herself towards the next window. Once on another thin ledge she placed her hands on the glass, grateful when the pane slid upwards.

Soundlessly slipping inside the uprising's base, Nora lit a small orb of fire and began her search. Moving from table to table, she hunted for anything that could point her towards Felix. She ignored the weapons and other supplies, focusing on the paperwork scattered on a few of the tabletops. Scanning lists of names and locations, as well as coded messages, Nora found no mention of Felix or the Alta. Deciding that whatever was in the communal area was a waste of her time, she let herself into the back room, smirking when she found the door unlocked.

Inside, she flicked through the papers on the table and ran her eyes over the diagrams and maps pinned to the walls. Again, there was no sign of Felix. However, the sketches of weapons nailed around the room drew her attention. They all depicted either legendary gear Nora had seen in books, or new designs thought up by the artist. There was the ruby infused Blade of Flames, the obsidian steel twin daggers known as Manu Mortem, and Aren's Arrows, the feathers of the diamond-tipped arrows said to have been gifted by the God himself. Then there were the new inventions; complex mechanical weapons and armour that infused both clever craftmanship with magical objects. Unlike the legendary weapons, these sketches appeared to favour power over appearance.

Moving towards a set of shelves, Nora noticed a familiar wooden box painted with white flowers and little navy blue berries on top. Unlatching the lid, she lifted it to find a collection of clear stones, like small egg-shaped pieces of ice. Scrunching her brow, Nora wondered what they could possibly be used for and about a thousand questions sprung to her mind.

Footsteps sounded in the next room, and she quickly extinguished her flame, softly lowering the lid of the box, and moving to silently conceal herself under the table. Nora cursed under her breath. It was almost three in the morning. Who in their right mind was awake at this hour? Narrowing her eyes, she stared at the flickering candlelight as it drew closer. Boots and thick legs appeared at Nora's eyeline, and she held her breath as the intruder stepped around the table, stopping only to rummage through the papers on top of it. After a few excruciating moments, the boots made to retreat from the room and Nora sighed.

The intruder halted abruptly, and a male voice filled the air. "Who's there?"

*Shit!* Nora clenched her fists.

Staying low, she slipped out from under the opposite side of the table. Before the man could move to identify her, she summoned her fire magic and extinguished the candle. On lightning-fast feet, she bolted past him, using her wind magic to throw him across the room. The man called out as he hit the shelves with a loud crash.

Nora did not wait for him to recover, running as fast as she could into the larger room and down the hallway. Shouts came from behind, the intruder in pursuit as Nora swung the door open and continued into the street without looking back.

The cold air whipped at her exposed face as she raced through the city, darting through alleys, and leaping from trees. She felt alive, her heart racing as fast as she was moving. There was no way he would be able to keep up.

Nora managed to lose her pursuer. She grinned broadly before heading in the direction of Daphne's. Slipping through her bedroom window, she silently thanked the Goddess Thyra for watching over her.

Losing her grip on the window, it closed with a loud bang, the sound causing Nora to flinch and curse herself. Nora waited a few moments, her heart beat and breathing the only noise in the room as she listened for any movements of people having been woken up. With a sigh of relief, she flicked her wrist, lighting the fire within the hearth.

The lack of annoyed grumbling or lump in the bed meant August was still out, presumably with Evelyn. He had been spending a lot of time with the Lys Alv and Nora hoped August would have something valuable to add to their investigation into Felix's disappearance. Other than mentioning Evelyn's mother as one of the people who engraved the wooden storefronts, he hadn't offered anything else, which utterly pissed her off. She hated the pressure of their investigation resting on her shoulders.

Stripping off her black uniform, Nora slipped on her nightshirt and snapped her fingers; the candles lighting and adding to the hearth's warm glow.

Soft footsteps sounded from the hallway and Nora chewed her lip, deciding whether to pretend she was sleeping or seek out whoever was beyond her door. Curiosity getting the better of her, Nora padded over to the door, easing it open with a subdued groan. Sage stood outside, her hands fidgeting in front of her.

"Did you hear it too?," Sage asked, moving closer to Nora's room. "I was up and heard a bang. I thought I'd check it out."

"It was me," Nora replied with a shrug. "I knocked something over in the dark."

"Oh," Sage said, her lips forming a plump circle.

"You're either up very late or way too early," Nora commented.

"Early," Sage sighed. "My boss, Phillip, has something he wants me to look into that can only be done at this ungodly hour."

"Sounds like the beginning of a murder mystery," Nora chuckled.

"Yeah, it does, and Phillip is one of the most unpleasant people to have ever walked the land so you may just be looking at the assailant." Sage smiled. "I should go back down stairs."

"Actually," Nora opened the door further, revealing not only the room within, but herself in little more than a shirt that failed to cover much of her pale legs. "Come in, I'll give you your book back."

"Okay, sure," Sage nodded. Nora's lips quirked to one side as Sage swallowed hard before stepping into the room.

Nora moved to her side of the bed and carefully slipped the book from beneath the one about flowers she'd borrowed from the library. Turning around, she found Sage had shut the door and was now standing by the fire.

"Did you like it?" Sage asked, her tone failing at casual.

"It was filthy," Nora chuckled, moving to stand between Sage and the door. "So, I loved it."

Sage laughed, the sound like a warm embrace that had Nora grinning broadly. "How's your head? I know Evelyn healed your shoulder, but you left before she could help with your other injuries."

Nora entwined her fingers through her hair near her forehead, moving her chocolate brown locks aside to show her the cut, the action lifting the hem of the shirt higher up her thighs. "My sexy scar is coming along nicely."

"I see." Sage's brown eyes emulated the flames crackling within the fireplace as she took a step closer.

"You're staring," Nora said without taking her eyes off the other woman. "Although, you're more than welcome to."

"I should go." Sage breathed.

Nora held the book out to Sage. "What about this?"

"Right, my book," Sage nodded, taking hold of it.

"You don't have to rush off," Nora replied, not letting go.

Nora tugged on the book, stepping back until she felt the wood against her back. Sage never broke eye contact, continuing to follow until Nora was trapped between Sage and the door. Nora's stomach clenched, and shivers moved in waves up and down her skin. Sage was beautiful, but in the firelight, she was devasting. Her intense gaze, full lips, and curves in all the right places had Nora wanting to see what lay beneath the fabric of Sage's clothing.

And right now, Sage was close, close enough that when she took a final step, their bodies pressed, provoking a moan to escape Nora.

"I should go," Sage said once more, her voice thick, yet she had not drawn away from where their bodies met, nor had she dropped her hold on the book they both clasped.

"You can leave whenever you like," Nora whispered, restraining herself from reaching out and running her hands all over Sage in a desperate attempt to explore and see what sounds she could elicit from Sage's lips.

"And if I want to stay?" Sage asked.

"Then stay," Nora said, giving in and closing the distance, capturing Sage's mouth with her own.

Sage's lips parted instantly, her tongue brushing against Nora's as she pressed Nora further onto the door. Nora let out a moan, letting go of the book so that one hand could entwine in Sage's hair, gripping the base of the woman's head while the other was free to clutch Sage's waist, pulling her closer. There was no holding back, just a pure explosion of passion.

Every teasing moment that had passed between the two had built to this, and Nora revelled in it, letting her body take the lead, her desire more powerful than the words of protest that tried to force themselves into her mind. August skewed the king's commands all the time so why couldn't she? Surely kissing Sage was just another way for Nora to gain access to the faction's secrets. Yes, that's exactly why she was doing this. At least that was what she was trying to convince herself. Nora slid her hand lower, grabbing Sage's ass.

Fire sparked beneath her skin as Sage dropped the book to the floor with a thud and her hand moved to Nora's thigh. She caressed the skin gently as her hand slowly ventured higher and higher until Sage's fingers were touching the skin beneath Nora's shirt. Nora gasped as Sage reached her breast, the woman's hand hot as it cupped, a thumb circling ever so gently around Nora's nipple.

"I've wanted to touch you since the first moment I saw you," Sage admitted, her breath hot against Nora's lips.

Nora grinned slyly. "Touch or throttle me?"

"A bit of both," Sage laughed, tilting her head back.

Nora took the opportunity, planting soft luxurious kisses along the woman's silky neck; taking her time to savour every taste. Sage shivered beneath Nora's touch, her hand on Nora's breast squeezing with each kiss. Nora's lips slowly ventured upwards, her kisses becoming feather-light as she crept along Sage's jawline before Sage impatiently captured Nora's mouth once more. Nora could do this all day; lose herself in Sage until there was nothing left.

Nora released Sage as though she'd been hit by lightning and turned her head, breaking the kiss. The shackles tattoos around her wrists felt as though they were biting into her skin, and she expected to see angry red sores next time she lifted her sleeves.

Sage pulled back slightly and looked down at Nora, her lips red and concern evident in her eyes. "Is everything okay?

"You should go," Nora breathed, dropping her gaze.

"Oh," Sage whispered, stepping back.

Nora felt the absence of Sage's warmth immediately, but forced herself to move. She turned the door handle, opening it for Sage.

Sage paused in the threshold. "Did I—"

Nora cut her off, her words sounding hollow as they left her lips. "Just go,"

Sage opened her mouth, but Nora shut the door in her face, unable to stand the sudden change in atmosphere that she'd created herself. Her tattoos were scalding her wrists, the magic punishing her for her traitorous thoughts. Drawing her sleeves up, she found her inked arms unharmed, no blood or marks to be seen.

Nora sighed, pressing her back to the door before sliding down to sit against it. She eyed Sage's book nearby and kicked out her leg. The book skid along the floor, stopping mere inches from the fireplace. "Fuck," she groaned, leaning her head back against the door and looking up at the ceiling. "Fuck, fuck, fuck."

# 28

## Evelyn

"What do you think?" Evelyn held the royal blue dress with her fingertips and swirled, the skirt fluttering through the air.

She surveyed her reflection in the three tall mirrors that surrounded her. It was very glamorous, not exactly the sort of dress she would usually have had ordered, but the dressmaker had done a wonderful job. He had matched the fabric she had chosen with a fine lace, the royal blue material complementing the lighter shade.

"You look beautiful," August replied, his hooded head sweeping up and down, taking her in. "Absolutely stunning."

Evelyn felt her cheeks flush and turned away from him. She thanked the Goddess Nyssa that the dressmaker had gone to serve another customer. "I don't even know when I'd wear it. I think it's a little too opulent for me." She hoped her voice sounded casual as she pushed on. "I probably look completely ridiculous."

A hand gripped her upper arm and she jolted, turning to come face to face with August. How he had managed to reach her so quickly and without a sound was beyond her. The old stories used to talk of Alvs that could move swiftly on quiet feet, but she had just thought that was a tall tale. She was an Alv and practically stomped everywhere she went. And even if the stories were true, shouldn't she have been able to hear him? She did have Alv ears after all. Surely, they should have picked up on the slightest of sounds.

"Do you think I would lie to you?" His voice was scarcely a whisper. They stood, barely an inch apart, and she felt the urge to reach out and close the tiny gap between them. Angling his head downwards, his lips drawing closer to hers. "You are magnificent Evelyn; whatever you wear, you will always be the most beautiful person in the room."

Staring into his eyes, she slipped her hand beneath his hood, placing it on the back of his neck. She pushed up onto her toes as his arm wrapped around her waist, pressing her close. Running her tongue over her lower lip, she closed her eyes, ready to close the distance between them.

A bark had Evelyn's eyes springing open and she turned her head to see a large charcoal and caramel dog with droopy ears and a prominent black nose sitting expectantly to her right. In a blink of an eye, the dog shifted, revealing a young woman with a letter in hand, a familiar green wax seal visible on the paper.

"A note for Ms Evelyn Ro-" The Anima began.

"That's me!" Evelyn sprang out of August's hold, her cheeks flushed as she accepted the envelope from the woman's hand. "Thank you."

The woman pursed her lips, but made no comment as Evelyn rummaged through her coat that hung on the back of a nearby chair, finally finding a couple of copper coins in one of the pockets.

"Here," Evelyn dropped the coins into the woman's open hand. "Thanks again!"

"You're welcome," the woman replied, then shifted back into the bloodhound, the Anima messenger padding out the door. Evelyn tore open the letter, eyes scanning over the elegant scrawl. Her eyebrows rose and she chewed her lip as she read.

"Everything okay?" August asked, coming to stand beside her.

She pressed the letter to her chest. "My father wants to see me," she replied, hurrying into the change room.

"Did something happen?" he pushed, concern lacing his words.

"I don't know!" she called from behind the curtain. Slipping the exquisite dress off, Evelyn carefully hung it on a hook before shoving on her trousers, shirt, and sweater.

Hopping out of the change room with one boot on and the other in hand, Evelyn slumped onto the chair that held her coat. "Can you tell the dressmaker that I'm happy with the dress and to send word when he wants me to pick it up?"

"Why are you hurrying off?" August asked, kneeling before her to help her tie her laces. "Is there some kind of emergency?"

"Honestly, I have no idea." She jumped up from her seat, stepping around August. Grabbing her coat, she shoved her arms into it as she spoke. "He didn't say so it could go either way."

"Slow down," he said, placing a hand on her shoulder.

"Can you tell the dressmaker about my dress?"

August nodded.

"Thanks," she smiled, backing towards the door. "I'll see you later, I promise!"

Even though August's upper face was hidden beneath his hood, she could have sworn he was looking at her like she was some strange creature as she practically ran from the store. Her father's letter had erupted an array of possible reasons why he had called for her, most of them leaving an uneasy sensation in the pit of her stomach. He did not usually ask for help and not having written the reason troubled her.

It did not take long to arrive at the Healing Centre, and after popping her head into a few potential places he could be—receiving annoyed glares from those she disturbed—she found him in the morgue. Shivering as she entered the dark stone room, Evelyn approached her father. He stood over a naked body, a thin sheet all that hid the person's dignity from the chest down.

"You got here very quickly," he said, turning towards her, his face grim.

"You said you needed my help, but other than that your letter was very vague. How was I supposed to know not to rush here?" she replied, still trying to catch her breath.

"It's nice to know I can count on you, and I want you to know if I felt I could ask someone else for help with this I would have." He turned back to the body. "I had thought that we'd apprehended the person responsible for the recent spout of killings, but it looks like another has taken his place. We had three more murders last night. All with the Makers' Mark drawn on their foreheads. I called you because there are no signs of any wounds."

Evelyn fought back the fear rising like acid in her throat. The man who'd made an attempt on her life was behind bars thanks to Gemma, but now there was someone else murdering people? Her father didn't know that she'd almost become a victim; there was no way he would have asked her here if he had. "Are you sure the man hasn't escaped?"

Her father shook his head. "No, he was found dead in his cell yesterday morning, tortured beyond recognition and left to bleed out. It was one of the most gruesome scenes I have ever seen, and I have no witnesses or suspects."

Relief that her attacker could no longer harm anyone rushed through Evelyn like a torrent. She'd never been glad for someone's death before but there was a first time for everything. She took three deep breaths and focused her eyes on the pallid skin of the corpse before them. "These three people, could it have been poison?"

"I thought so at first, but I tested their blood and found nothing." He said. "I'm curious to know what you think."

"Isn't there someone else who would be better to examine the bodies? Someone more experienced?" She asked, her words coming out weaker than she would have liked.

Her father placed a comforting hand on her shoulder. "If I could have asked anyone else, I would have. This is a delicate situation; people are already afraid and if word gets out that the murders are increasing, not only in quantity but in strangeness, especially after we were so sure we had apprehended the person responsible…" He sighed, his sentence trailing off as he ran a hand through his hair, the black strands falling across his brow. Her father looked tired, and she was worried things were worse than he was letting on. "I know I'm asking a lot, but you are talented and strong. I trust you to help me with this, and Gemma told me you'd be working with her soon, so it is important for someone in the faction to be aware of what is happening too."

"Alright," Evelyn nodded, hoping she sounded tougher than she felt.

Now that she was going to play a bigger part in the faction, it made sense for her to be more involved in the mysteries that occurred in Forest's Edge. She would have to put her own personal feelings aside.

Placing her hands over the man's chest, she summoned her light. She had only ever examined the deceased less than a handful of times, and only ever in training. Lys Alv magic was often used when the cause of someone's death was obscure, but it was an aspect of her job she had hoped to avoid. There was something wrong about letting her magic move through the dead. It felt invasive; the deceased was at rest, and it felt like trespassing.

Evelyn shivered at the stillness of the man who lay before her. His blood no longer pumped, and his muscles were at rest; the spark that usually flowed through all living things had been extinguished. Evelyn searched with her light for a cause of death. Her father was right, there was no sign of poisoning, nor did the man have any physical wounds. She checked his lungs, but they too appeared unharmed. "No poison, nor was it suffocation."

"Hmmm, what about his brain?" Her father asked, watching her as she worked.

Evelyn let her light flow towards the man's head, saddened by the lack of energy that usually danced there. A fly buzzed nearby before landing on the man's left eye, his vacant gaze unperturbed by the presence.

Her spine tingled and she snatched her hands away. "All appears fine. His body is—was—healthy. It is almost as though his life force was sucked out of him."

"Let's examine the other two," her father suggested, leading her to another table where an elderly woman lay.

Evelyn let her light move through the woman, and although the elderly woman was further along in age than the man, she had otherwise been healthy. They moved on to another deceased woman, this one much younger than the previous. Her eerily pale skin was firm, her face full of youth. She could not have been much older than Evelyn. Examining the body, Evelyn tried not to think about the woman's age, the life that was cut short. She wondered what kind of life the woman had led. What were her dreams?

Dropping her hands, Evelyn turned to her father. "They're all the same. I can't find any reason for them to have passed."

"Notice anything about her skin?" Her father gently raised the woman's hand, turning it slowly and revealing a subtle shimmer as the light danced along the flesh.

Evelyn frowned. "You already have an idea as to what caused their deaths."

"I was hoping you would prove me wrong. I haven't seen a death like this for many years," her father said, brow furrowed. "There is only one race that could possibly do this, and many believed King Dominic had killed them all."

Mors Alvs.

Evelyn thought of August. He was the only Mors Alv she had ever seen. Could he be the one murdering these people? It couldn't be true. August wouldn't do this... would he? The blood drained from her face as a chill crept down her spine. Bracing her hand on the table, she felt lightheaded, her heart swelling with fear. She and August mostly spoke about her when they were together, and when she had asked him questions, he was often vague, especially when it came to speaking about what occupied most of his time. Not to mention how quickly his anger rose to the surface or that he didn't want anyone to know he was in Forest's Edge.

How well did she really know August?

"Good morning sunshine," Nora drawled, leaning her hip against the banister. She wore a burgundy knit jumper over grey slacks and brown boots, and her chocolate brown hair was pulled back in a high ponytail, fastened with a black bow.

"Good morning Nora," Evelyn groaned from where she sat on the bottom step, resting her elbows on her knees and her head on the palms of her hands.

"You know, usually people sleep at night," Nora said as she stuffed the last bit of toast into her mouth.

"I tried; trust me I did." Evelyn replied with a pout.

Evelyn's shoulders sagged and her golden eyes were unfocused, staring off into the distance as she worried her bottom lip. Sleep had evaded her last night, thoughts of August murdering people keeping her wide awake.

"Lying awake dreaming of a certain Alv, about this high"—Nora raised her hand above her head—"with a dopey face and asshole attitude?"

Evelyn's cheeks flushed and Nora's smile broadened. "Are you working today?"

"I was just on my way out," Nora replied, turning her head away, before a smirk split her face. "Good morning, Sage."

"Nora," Sage replied flatly, and Nora's smirk disappeared instantly.

"Hi Sage," Evelyn grumbled.

"Oh, you're here too!" Sage exclaimed, coming around Nora to stand before the staircase. Her hair was tied atop her head, fixed with a magenta headband, and she was dressed in an olive-green knee length dress over dark tights, with leather boots and a fur lined grey cloak. "Perfect! Are you ready to go?"

"Mmmhhmmm," Evelyn stood, placing a hand over her mouth to stifle her yawn. "Lead the way."

"Where are you two off to?" Nora asked, following them out the door.

"None of your business," Sage replied, looping her arm with Evelyn's.

"Evie looks thrilled to be joining you," Nora grinned, her brown eyes glistening with delight.

Evelyn ignored the nickname, the display before her consuming her attention. She knew she should look away, but she could not tear her gaze from the duo. The way Nora purposely phrased everything she said to elicit a fire to burn brightly in Sage's eyes. There was a tension there, a passion even Evelyn could feel was all-consuming. Whatever was going on between these two, it was intense.

"Go away, Nora. I don't have time for your shit today." Sage shot back, dragging Evelyn with her.

Evelyn glanced behind her to see that Nora was watching them walk away, a frown on her face.

"What?" Sage asked.

"Your dynamic is an interesting one," Evelyn noted innocently.

Sage groaned. "She is the most infuriatingly confusing person I have ever met."

Evelyn's lips tugged to one side. "She totally is."

Laughing, they made their way towards the denser forest, the inhabited areas no longer in sight. Sage wove through the trees, stepping deftly over fallen branches and tree roots as Evelyn treaded close behind, glad for the extra training she had been doing with Jasmine. Sage had asked Evelyn to assist her with some sort of research, but the woman had not been forthcoming with specifics.

"Not much further," Sage called over her shoulder.

"Be honest, are you planning to murder me and bury me deep in the forest where no one will know to look?" Evelyn teased, picking up her pace so that she now walked beside Sage. "It's already been tried once before."

Sage spun to face Evelyn; her face crestfallen. "Evelyn..."

"Bad joke?" Evelyn stuffed her hands into her pockets. Jasmine must had told her friends, which meant that Florence, Omari, and Will probably knew what happened too.

Sage shook her head. "If it makes you feel better about what happened then no."

"I don't think I'll ever feel better about it, but I might get used to it..." she shrugged. "The fact that it happened, that is."

"It's okay to feel anxious or scared," Sage offered Evelyn a warm smile. "Time will help you heal. Take each day at your own pace."

"Thanks."

"I didn't do anything," Sage replied, taking off once more.

"But you did," Evelyn said, her boots crunching the leaf litter. "As usual, you are full of wise words."

A cool breeze whirled between the pines as the sun struggled to creep through the upper canopy. The forest grew denser with every step they took.

"Much farther?" Evelyn called to Sage who had disappeared ahead.

"No!" Sage declared, her head popping out from between a cluster of trees. "We're here!"

As Evelyn drew nearer, she could see where Sage had been waiting near a hollow formed by two large trees.

"Is this what I think it is?" Evelyn asked, climbing through the hollow to find the sun's rays sparkling through the emerald leaves, illuminating a ring of rainbow stones and bright red toadstools. Birds sung happy tunes and a family of miniature snowy rabbits hopped past her legs, disappearing as she turned in a circle. "This is like something out of an old book."

Sage smiled warmly. "It's an ancient Alv ceremonial site from Frode knows when. I've been searching for one for months and then a Lys Alvs from the city told me about it. Apparently not many people know it's here; that's why it's in such good condition."

"I always thought the stories exaggerated this kind of stuff." Evelyn said, twirling around in awe. "I can't picture myself or any of the Alvs I know dancing around here on a full moon."

Sage giggled, and Evelyn wondered if she, too, was picturing Gemma skipping around the stones. Evelyn burst out laughing when she imagined August joining in.

"I know you haven't been to Ferieton, but have you heard much about it?" Sage asked, and when Evelyn shook her head, the woman continued. "Go there and you might change your mind. The Alvs that live in the city are a lot more into their traditions."

"Thank you for sharing this with me," Evelyn said, sitting on the ground outside the circle of stones. The moss was strangely soft, like sitting on a fluffy cushion, and she breathed in a sweet woodsy scent.

"I had an ulterior motive," Sage admitted.

Evelyn raised her brows. "Oh?"

"I was hoping you could help me analyse the stones." Sage gestured to the rainbow stones that made up the circle. "I should be able to feel their magic, but only an Alv can free me from their effects once I've touched them."

Evelyn raised a brow. "Really? What kind of effects?"

"You'll see," Sage smiled mischievously. "The stones shouldn't affect you in the same way as me. At least, not when they're in a circle like this. This is an Alv ceremonial site after all."

Evelyn nodded. "Where do we start?"

"I'm not one hundred per cent sure," Sage replied, retrieving a notepad and tin from her bag. She opened the metal lid and withdrew her drawing materials. "I'll sketch them, and then touch the stones. I just need you to make sure nothing bad happens to me. Let's start with that cobalt one."

Evelyn looked at the translucent light blue stone that was sparkling in the sunlight. It was nestled in the grass between two others of contrasting colours. She watched as Sage hastily drew on her page before edging towards the stone, her arm outstretched. Palm hovering over the stone, Sage closed her eyes.

"Anything?" Evelyn asked, biting her lower lip.

"Not yet." Sage gently placed her hand onto the stone. When her fingers touched the rock, she breathed out a hearty sigh, her shoulders sagging. "I want to travel the country, I hate spinach and I like Nora."

"What?" Evelyn coughed, grabbing Sage's hand from the stone.

Cheeks reddening, Sage pushed her golden glasses up the bridge of her nose. "Wow, that was weird. It was like my mind cleared and I saw my truths laid out before me, as if a heavy fog had lifted." Sage clapped her hands. "Oh, I think this stone's magic is to help you see what you want. Like one minute I was in a noisy bar and trying to listen to a friend talk, then the next everyone had left, and I was able to finally hear what they were saying. I felt in control and confident in what I want."

The stone sounded exactly like what Evelyn needed right now. She placed her hand on the smooth, cool surface, yet she felt nothing. Her mind and future were still as indecisive as ever.

"Helps you see your desires," Sage said, making a note on the page. "Self-confidence and possibly self-reflection."

"I wish it would work for me," Evelyn frowned.

"I'm sure there would be a way for Alvs to use them. I can do some research for you if you like?" Sage offered.

"Oh, no, it's fine." Evelyn sat back. "Should we do the next one?"

Nodding, Sage moved on to the next stone in the circle, a reddish brown one. Again, she placed her hand on the stone and shut her eyes. The effect was almost instant as Sage began to sway as though mesmerised by music that only she could hear. Her free hand tapped a beat on her thigh, and she started to hum. Evelyn watched as Sage sat back, kicking her legs out in front of her as her movements became more vigorous, her free arm waving wildly in the air.

"Sage," Evelyn drew out her name, snatching Sage's hand from the stone.

Blinking, Sage looked to where Evelyn had taken her hand, her fingers no longer touching the red stone. "That one made me feel like dancing, like I had just eaten a bag of sweets and needed to move to use up all the extra energy."

"That sounds a lot like what I've read from the old tales about these circles."

"I'm going to say… boosts your energy levels, encourages dancing and connection to your body." Sage noted down on her page.

"Is there a reason why we are here or is this a hobby?" Evelyn asked, resting back on her hands as Sage wrote down her findings.

"It's all to do with Phillip's research. He's studying the effects of crystals and other lost magical arts." Sage explained. "I'm gathering data for him, and for Gemma too. She is interested in this stuff, but for different reasons than Phillip."

"Gemma is interested in crystals?" Evelyn tilted her head. The idea of Gemma being interested in something often considered a whimsical form of magic surprised Evelyn.

"Yeah, anything to get an advantage." Sage shrugged. "I'm helping her with naturally occurring and made magical objects."

"So, things Conjurers make?" Evelyn asked.

"Yes, like swords and jewellery. That sort of thing," Sage said. "They are combined with magical objects that you can find in nature, like crystals, gems, and parts of powerful creatures."

Evelyn leaned forward, finding the topic fascinating. "Have you found or made anything?"

"There are a couple of items of interest," Sage told her. "But I think Gemma wants to keep them a secret for now."

"Fair enough," Evelyn replied, pointing to another stone; this one a charcoal colour with a squiggle of bright yellow running through it. "Should we do the next stone?"

Evelyn spent the next hour or so helping Sage test and document the stones of the Alv circle. It was interesting work, and she was enjoying having another distraction from her worries. If she could just find something like this every few hours, she'd never have to think about her troubles again.

## 29

**Nora**

Scrunching her nose, Nora moved to stand by the small fire that flickered in the hearth. With her back to the flame, she summoned her magic to increase its heat, embracing the warmth as it melted the chill she felt deep in her bones.

"Why are you sitting here in the cold?" she asked, rubbing her gloved hands together.

"It's not that cold," August replied from where he lay spread out on the bed and holding a novel over his head.

Nora quirked a brow, "Is Sage's book keeping you toastie?" She tried to sound light hearted but any mention of Sage made her teeth grind and tattoos sting.

"It's not cooling down the room, that's for sure," he chuckled, then sniffed loudly. "Did you bring back anything to eat?"

"You know I did." She pointed near her feet to where she had sat the basket.

"Thank you," August sung, darting towards her. He lifted an embroidered napkin to reveal a crusty bread roll and clay pot. The aroma of roasted meats and vegetables seeped through a tiny crack in the pot's lid. "How'd your meeting with Gemma go?"

"There was a lot of valuable information." She told him. "But there's nothing that points to Felix's whereabouts, which is our main priority."

"Think it's time to move on?" He asked.

"Not yet." Nora trudged over to the armchair and collapsed into its embrace, kicking off her boots and resting her feet on the windowsill. "Gemma has given me a job and once I've done it, hopefully I will be trusted enough to be able to find out whether she knows anything about Felix. I haven't quite worked out how I'll ask, but I'm sure I'll think of something."

"You always do." August looked up from his meal. He had moved to sit on the floor at the base of the bed, leaning back against the mattress.

"I am the brains after all," she teased, tugging her gloves off and resting them on the arms of the chair. "Oh, do you remember when I asked you about the last time we saw Felix? What he said?"

"He was going to deal with an Anima disturbance." August replied between mouthfuls. "What about it?"

"Yeah, but right before he left. After he told us about Rana's orders."

He scrunched his brows. "How he said something about flying through the sky?"

"He who travels the skies is never alone," Nora quoted. "Do you remember me telling you?"

"Yeah," he said, drawing out the word. "I don't really remember him saying it though."

"You really need to pay more attention. Rana always said your weakness lay in missing the finer details. No wonder she has us working together all the time." Nora shot him a wicked grin. "Anyway, I've been doing some research and apparently Aren said that after King Yosef's coronation, just before he shifted into his eagle form and flew away."

"Are you trying to tell me that Felix is a God?" August chuckled. "I know his shift is an eagle…"

"No, don't be ridiculous," she pouted, waving off his comment. "A lot of people shift into eagles, and besides, the Gods and Goddesses are no longer among us. What I'm saying is that Felix may have been planning to disappear. Aren had planned to leave and then said that line right before he departed, and Felix did the same. His leaving could have been a choice."

"Okay, say I believe you," August said, his eyes glimmering as he ran a hand through his now shoulder-length dirty blond hair. "He's an Alta, you can't just up and leave whenever you like, the tattoos don't allow it."

"You desperately need a haircut," she turned her nose up at him. "And as for leaving the Alta, you have a point, but what if he found a way to skew the king's commands? You do it all the time."

"I have been known to interpret his commands differently, but I don't skew anything, and what you're suggesting is not distorting." He rebuked. "To be able to disappear would be outright disobeying commands. Alta aren't allowed to leave Royal Bay without permission, and we searched the city. He wasn't there."

"So, you think he's dead?" she scoffed. "And what? We were sent on a wild goose chase to retrieve his body?"

August sighed deeply. "No, I think—"

"Look, even if I'm wrong it doesn't change the fact that we still need Gemma's intel. All this theory does is require us to be cautious; if we do find him, he might not be keen on us rescuing him if he left of his own accord."

"Okay," he conceded. "We'll be careful."

"Good. I should be finished with the job Gemma gave me by tonight if all goes to plan," Nora continued. "Hopefully, that will gain me some trust and therefore insight into their plans."

"And if it doesn't? Or say you do succeed but there are no more leads on the Alta or Felix?" August asked, stuffing the last bit of bread into his mouth.

"Well, I still have my first meeting tomorrow night," she said. "But if that's a bust too… It looks like we may have to go to Kaldom after all. Irrespective of how badly I want to know what they're up to."

"Feel free to elaborate on the last part."

"I'm yet to see what Florence has been ordering in with her thorn apple, but I found the box engraved with the blackthorn at their headquarters, and it was filled with clear stones. I haven't had a chance to research what they are used for." She told him, picking at her nails. "And then there were the sketches of powerful objects I recognised from old tales like the Blade of Flames. There were drawings of other strange objects I didn't recognise all over the walls too. I think they're not only looking for weapons to aid their cause, but making them as well."

"I wonder whether they have found any of the legendary weapons… and it would be interesting to see if any of the sketches you saw of new inventions have been successful," August pondered, scraping the pot clean with his spoon. "Anything else?"

Nora narrowed her eyes at his tone. "What about you? What have you brought to this investigation lately? You ask a lot of questions, and I'm doing all the fucking work."

"I have been looking for Felix too." He countered adamantly. "Don't be a bitch."

"Have you been looking for him under Evelyn's bed? You've been spending an awful lot of time with her." Nora argued, the flames in the hearth growing with her anger. "The fact that I have only now been able to tell you something that happened days ago speaks volumes. You're never here and have nothing to show for your absence."

"If I remember correctly, it was your idea for you to pretend you were here alone." August growled. "You wanted to take control of the investigation. Don't blame me if you're doing the bulk of the fucking work."

"You're a real dick you know that? I can't believe you're turning your lack of anything useful to offer on me?" She hissed, leaning forward in her seat. "As if I'm forcing you to sit on your fucking ass all day and twiddle your thumbs among other favoured body parts?"

He gritted his teeth. "I told you, I'm chasing a few leads."

Nora rolled her eyes. "And? Care to share?"

"Not right now, no," he said, folding his arms over his chest. "I'll let you know when it's all coming together."

"Excuse me?" She jumped from her seat, her hands forcefully grasping her hips. "Since when do you hide things from me? We don't keep secrets from each other."

"I'm not hiding anything. I'm waiting, that's all," he said, drawing a cross with his finger over his heart. "No secret keeping. I promise."

"Your interpretation of secret keeping is clearly different to mine," she said, narrowing her eyes.

"Speaking of interpretation," August said, changing the subject, "I know you think you're in top shape but you're looking a little on the skinny side. Slacking off on your workouts?"

"Nice try asshole, but we have not finished talking about your shady behaviour!" She all but shouted. "And I am not skinny!"

"Keep telling yourself that," he chuckled, standing, and stretching his arms over his head. "Come on, let's go train."

"And where do you suppose we go, smarty pants?" Nora rested her weight on one hip. "Or do you plan to show everyone you're a Mors Alv and then we have to fight the public? Is that your idea of training?"

"No," he sighed. "Don't be an idiot."

"Fuck you."

"Come on, I know a place," he winked, walking out of the room.

"This discussion isn't over." Sighing in frustration, she shoved her feet into her boots, her curiosity getting the better of her and quelling her anger. It didn't disappear completely, just lingered below the surface, ready to strike.

He took her to a small clearing where there was plenty of room to practise non-magical combat in private. Nora glanced around at the unkempt garden that looked to have been neglected for years.

"How did you find this place?" Nora asked, removing her travelling cloak before stretching her muscles.

"Eve—Evelyn," he replied, copying her movements. She noted him correcting himself, but didn't comment. It would only start another argument that would get them nowhere.

"Is it safe to do that?" she asked, gesturing to where he dropped his cloak.

"There's no one around," he said, jumping to warm his body up. "That's why I brought you here."

Without waiting for August to be ready, Nora lunged, striking low and hard with her first blow, the movement fuelled by the anger she still held. Caught off guard, August was unable to dodge her right fist fast enough as it connected with his ribs, just missing his gut. He stumbled backwards, gasping, and catching himself before Nora's left punch followed. August sidestepped and deflected the strike, grabbing Nora's arm with both hands and flinging her to the side. Nora skidded a few metres, her boots tearing at the grass before she dug her feet into the ground and slid to a stop.

"Did you just throw me?" she laughed. "I hit you and your first response was to throw me? Really?"

"I like to think of it more like swatting," he replied nonchalantly, shrugging a shoulder. "Like what you would do to a fly."

Nora grinned and took off, closing the distance between them before leaping towards him and extending her right boot to kick August in the head. Sailing through the air, the cool breeze caressing her face, she missed her mark by a fraction. August slipped her guard and landed several punches to her gut in quick succession. She grunted as she steeled her stomach, but the pain never came—he was clearly holding back. Gritting her teeth, she blocked his last few strikes as anger reddened her cheeks, then sidestepped August and grabbed his arm, stomping down on the back of his knee. He thudded to the grass, hissing in pain, his face contorted as she pulled back on his arm. Shoving him roughly onto his face, August groaned from the movement, and she knelt on his back, curling his arm, and earning another grumble from him.

"What the fuck was that?" she demanded. "You pulled your punches."

"We are training," he panted, spitting dirt from his mouth. "I don't want to hurt you."

"Who said anything about hurting me?" She shoved him as she hopped off his back. "Give me some credit, August, what's the point of training if you go easy on me?"

He stood, dusting the dirt and grass from his clothing, and rubbing his shoulder. "You're right. I'm sorry."

She rolled her eyes. "You've changed."

"Or maybe you've just become more of an ass," he growled.

"Possibly," she smirked. "But either way, you need to sort yourself out. This new August is not going to last in the Alta."

Nora stalked through the trees that bordered the path, watching the familiar hooded figure before her. She'd been following him for the last hour, monitoring his movements as he went about his business in the city. Now they were alone, however, and she needed to act. There was no point putting it off any longer. Gemma wanted him dead, and she had yet to fail at a task put before her.

Stepping out of the bushes, she stood in the centre of the path and called out. "Zaim. We need to talk."

The man turned around, lowering his hood at the same time to reveal his curly brown hair. "Hello little Nora."

"Hey jerk face," she replied with a tight lipped smile full of attitude. "Fancy seeing you here."

"I go where my king commands," he replied, stepping closer to her. "Just like you."

She folded her arms over her chest and jutted her hip. "What are you doing here?"

He tsked at her. "I can't tell you that. King's orders."

Nora rolled her eyes. "Fine, don't tell me, but you have to leave."

Zaim scoffed. "Again, I can't."

"Can't or won't?" she pushed. She tapped her foot on the gravel as her irritation grew with each passing moment.

"A bit of both." He smiled like a hunter eyeing his prey. "Why do you want me to?"

Nora sighed. She would have to tell him the truth or there was no chance he'd even consider helping her. "I've been sent to kill you."

Zaim chuckled. "Good luck with that."

"You know I could," she narrowed her eyes. "If these tattoos weren't holding me back I'd have done it and been on my merry way already."

"Luckily King Dominic only wants us to kill other people then isn't it?" he replied. "No matter how deep the desire to do otherwise."

If the king hadn't commanded Alta from killing each other, Zaim would have been dead years ago. The man was sadistic, and he'd made Nora's childhood a living hell every moment he got. He was an Elementum like her, and even though she had more power, his skills had surpassed hers, at least that is, until she'd turned fourteen. He hadn't been able to touch her since.

"Obviously I can't kill you right now," Nora grumbled, "but we can fake it, and you can get out of the city."

"I told you I can't leave."

"Fine, lay low then," she huffed, throwing her hands in the air. "I don't care what you do. I just need some people to believe that you are dead."

Zaim smirked at her. "Why would I help you?"

"King Dominic sent me to find Felix and to do that I need to gain someone's trust." Nora told him. "This is apparently how I do that."

"Sounds like your problem, not mine," he dismissed her with a wave.

"It's King Dominic's problem so it is yours," Nora hissed through gritted teeth. "He may not have commanded you outright to find Felix, but you have to do what's in his best interest. Helping me is what the king wants."

Zaim eyed her for a long moment, and she fought the urge to lunge at him and break his stupid nose.

"Get on your knees and we have a deal," he said finally.

"I'm not sucking your dick if that's what you're hoping for," Nora sneered, standing her ground. "I'll bite if I have to go anywhere near you like that."

"If that's supposed to turn me off, then you don't know me at all," he replied before pointing to the ground before him. "Kneel. I want you to beg me."

Nora felt her anger building inside her. It was always a power play with the older Alta, and Zaim was no different. He knew she was stronger than him magically, but he loved any opportunity to make her appear weaker.

"Fuck you," she growled, dropping to the dirt before him.

"That's not how you beg," he scolded, grabbing her ponytail, and pulling her head back. She clenched her fists, refusing to give in to the temptation to fight him as she looked up into his eyes. "Try: please master Zaim, will you help me with this task that I am so fucking hopeless at completing on my own. I am an embarrassment to the name Alta and desperately need your help."

Nora stared daggers at Zaim before repeating his words, forcing the vile words from her lips. She would kill him, maybe not today, but she would find a way.

Zaim shoved her back with a laugh. "I liked that," he licked his lips. "I might get you to repeat it when we return to Royal Bay. It will be just like when you were a little girl."

"Not a fucking chance," Nora hissed, rising to her feet. "It's time for you to die now."

# 30

**Evelyn**

Breaths coming in quick succession, Evelyn knocked on the door before her. An icy breeze whipped at her cheeks, adding to their flushed appearance, as she waited for August to answer. She had told Poppy where she was meeting him, just in case. Evelyn wanted to believe he wasn't a threat, but she couldn't help the small voice that told her to be careful all the same. She tried to focus her mind on why August had asked her to meet him here, refusing to let the fear of being alone with him overcome her.

The door creaked open, and August stood before her, backlit by a warm glow. "Hey Eve," he smiled, opening the door wider. "Come in."

Evelyn hesitated, her heart pounding in her chest as she suddenly second guessed herself. Was coming here a bad idea? Sleep had failed her over the past couple of nights. She'd been too busy tossing and turning, plagued by images of the bodies from the morgue. During the day she'd been able to keep her mind busy, but at night… the night held no such protection. As much as she hoped August was not involved, suspicion kept creeping into her thoughts. Those poor people had been killed by a Mors Alv, and the only one Evelyn had ever known to exist was standing right in front of her. Blood drained from her cheeks as icy fingers crept along her spine.

"Is everything okay?" he asked, scrunching his brow, and reaching out for her.

She flinched away, her nerves making her jittery. August frowned at the movement.

"Eve—"

"Sorry," she said, straining to smile. She knew it was not believable, but she didn't know what else to do. "Long couple of days."

Evelyn stepped passed August and was immediately enveloped by the heat emitted by the stone fireplace in the corner. The room was sparse, a two seater table and a plump sofa that sat before the flames were all that the space contained.

"You weren't wearing your hood when you opened the door," she pointed out.

August moved to sit on the sofa, and she followed, noting the closed door on the back wall, and wondering what was hidden behind it.

"I sensed you," he explained, sitting down.

"You sensed me?" she asked, torn between being fascinated and disturbed. She shuffled to the edge of her seat, keeping her distance, and sitting up against the armrest on the opposite end to August.

"I can feel your magic, kind of like a magical fingerprint." He told her, glancing down at the gap she'd left. "It sounds creepier than it is, and I can only do it with people I know well or who have strong magic." His voice became light. "Mostly I use it to annoy Nora; she's never been able to sneak up on me."

Evelyn's attempt at a laugh came out more like a strangled cough.

"Are you sure you're okay?" He inquired, sounding genuinely concerned for her wellbeing.

"Yeah, I'm just tired." She tried to keep still as he adjusted himself in his seat. Her shoulders were tense, and her hands fidgeted in her lap.

"Have I done something to offend you?" He asked, his voice low. "You seem like you don't want to be anywhere near me."

Evelyn immediately felt terrible. Her fear was purely because of something she was not even sure he was guilty of. He may not have murdered those people. It was a possibility… wasn't it?

"No, umm, you haven't done anything wrong." She sighed, "I have a meeting later and it's been a big week. My father asked me to examine some bodies the other day as well. It left me a little shaken."

"Oh Eve, that's shit." His hand reached out and he gave her arm what should have been a comforting squeeze. It took all her willpower not to flinch away. She needed to give him the benefit of the doubt. Wasn't that the right thing to do?

"Have you heard anything about them?" She asked him., swallowing hard. "They had the Makers' Marks on their foreheads… the man who attacked me…" She shook her head. "He's dead now, but there have been other victims after his death. These people I saw had the marks."

August frowned. "Yeah, I figured there were others involved. Murders like that have been happening in other cities I've been to."

Evelyn shivered. "How do you think the victims are chosen? Randomly?"

"From what I've heard they're random." August shuffled to her side, gently draping an arm around her shoulder, and pulling her to his chest. "Don't be afraid, I'll protect you."

She sat stiffly pressed against him. Protect her from a murderer or from himself? Evelyn bit her lip; she should just tell him what was on her mind. Clear the air. It would be awkward but at least she would know for sure.

"August—" she began, a tremor creeping into her voice.

"Yeah?" he asked curiously, his dark gaze searching hers.

Evelyn took in a deep breath, bracing herself. "Have you been killing people?"

"What?" He released his grip as though stung and stood abruptly. His incredulous expression looked back at her, the hurt clear on his face.

Eyes wide in horror, she stared back at him. The words had tumbled out of her mouth as though they had a mind of their own. She had wanted to ask, but hadn't meant to be so abrupt. She wanted to slap herself. Where was her tact?

"What I meant was, umm…" she sighed, shoulders slumping. Her gaze dropped to her hands, unable to look at him. "Well, as you know, I went to examine some deceased people. Three to be exact. They had been murdered but there was no sign of physical trauma. No poison and it wasn't suffocation. If they weren't dead, I would have thought they were completely healthy."

"So, you think I killed them?" He demanded.

She bit her lip to stop it from trembling as she glanced up at him. "No, umm, I don't know. I hope not."

"For someone who's not sure whether or not I'm a fucking murderer, you've been awfully brave coming here alone." He spat furiously, making her jump. The anger he directed at her twisted like a knife in her gut.

"August," she breathed. She was torn between keeping her distance and reaching out to comfort him. "I honestly don't know what to think. I desperately want to believe it's not you, but these people were killed by a Mors Alv."

"And I'm the only Mors Alv in Valmenessia?" he growled crossing his arms and turning towards the fire. "The likelihood of that is fucking ridiculous!"

"Maybe, but you never answer my questions about what you do with your spare time." She added. "Nora can't possibly be with you all the time because the others talk about being with her too."

"I didn't kill those people." He breathed heavily. "I can't believe I have to even say that to you."

"But you did kill someone didn't you," she said, voice strained. She thought back to what her father had said about the man that had attacked her. How he'd been tortured before being left to die.

"He couldn't live after what he did to you," August growled, his hands moving into fists at his sides. His reply had sparked a fire in her stomach, and she felt her earlier fears melting away. Was it wrong that her heart raced at his words?

Evelyn stood and placed a gentle hand on his arm. He turned slowly to face her, his dark gaze capturing her immediately. "So you can see then... from my perspective? What was I supposed to think when..."

"When all arrows point to me?" He shrugged out of her grip and stepped back. He had created a space that felt like miles between them, especially after his declaration had drawn her to him, as though he tugged on a piece of string tied to her very being. "I guess I shouldn't be angry. You barely know me, no wonder you could so easily believe I would be responsible."

"So let me in," she said, a tear slipping down her cheeks. "Stop hiding from me."

They stood in silence, August watching her as she stared right back, holding his gaze. She hated that she'd let her fears take root and tangle with her insecurities. She believed him when he said he didn't kill those people, but that didn't let him off the hook for keeping secrets.

"Eve," August whispered finally, coming to stand before her once again with sagging shoulders.

"I'm sorry I accused you," she said, wiping her eyes. "It came out all wrong, but I want you to talk to me. Tell me things so my mind doesn't conjure up its own conclusions. I already have enough going on up there that I don't need to add you to my anxieties."

"You're right. I'm sorry too," he took her hands, tugging her towards the sofa and dropping to the cushions with her on his lap. "I should have told you sooner. How can you possibly trust me if I don't let you in?"

She angled her head, her breath catching at the proximity of his face to hers. Evelyn felt like she was on a boat travelling down a winding river of emotions. First rowing throwing fear, then safety in August's arms, and now… now she was about to go over a waterfall.

Time seemed to slow, and she wondered whether he was going to kiss her. Goddess, she hoped he would. Running her tongue over her lips, she could feel herself aching to close the gap between them, to feel his lips against her own. Evelyn used all her resolve to not move towards him, sure he could feel her body trembling.

August's dark gaze flickered from her lips to her golden eyes. He was looking at her so intensely, as though captivated, and she felt her cheeks warm. She took a deep breath, praying to the Goddess Nyssa that she was not imagining things.

August paused and his eyes searched her face before he sighed deeply, as though coming to a decision. "I want to kiss you. Fuck, that's all I've thought about since the moment I saw you, but I want you to know all there is about me. My history. My life. I want you to know who I am."

"I want that too," she replied breathlessly, earning a warm smile from August.

He tucked a strand of her black hair behind her pointed ear. "I'm going to tell you everything about me, but first, I asked you here for a reason. There's something you need to know."

# 31

## Nora

It was a clear night and the waxing crescent moon had long set, leaving only the stars to light the dark sky. This part of the city, or so Nora had been told, was split into two distinct halves. The northeast was known for its night revelry and venues that offered a certain kind of entertainment: be it substances, fighting, or flesh. The southeast was bustling during the day with the comings and goings of school children and professional businesspeople. The only feature the two halves had in common were their similarities in architecture; the streets were home to terraced buildings that were wedged side by side as though squashed together between the trees, the force stretching them up and out, creating long, thin dwellings.

Tonight was the eve of the Feast Day of Jord, Goddess of Balance, Truth and Passing, so there were very few people about. The Mors Alv Goddess was rarely celebrated in public these days, yet people were still superstitious, noting the day on the calendar and not leaving their houses on the eve and day dedicated to Jord. There were five feast days throughout the year in Valmenessia. Each designed to give thanks to one of the Gods or Goddesses. Nora's favourite was Thyra, Goddess of Nature and the Elements, but she may have been biased as Thyra *was* the Goddess of Elementums.

Since the persecution of Mors Alvs, celebrating Goddess Jord was not encouraged. However, Nora and August had always celebrated. Their festivities usually involved stealing a bottle or two of ale and a few pastries from the royal kitchens and having a secret night-time feast of their own. Walking through the cold, shadowy night with Sage, Nora longed for those days and hoped that she and August would find Felix soon. Sage had not spoken to Nora the entire walk, not that Nora had said anything herself. She didn't know what to say and it didn't feel right to antagonise Sage like she usually would.

After the other night, everything had backtracked between them to the point that they were further back than they were when they first met. Nora's attempt to act normal the morning after had done nothing to help the situation. Now, they just sort of existed and whenever Nora thought about it too much, her tattoos burned with a vengeance.

Nora stifled a yawn. She and August had stayed up late the last two nights, and she'd awoken each morning feeling exhausted. Her magic drained too. She hadn't felt at her strongest since Giland. Nora thought she must have caught some illness and was resigned to seek Evelyn out the next day.

Reaching the familiar door on Emerald Lane, Nora and Sage stepped into the hallway and made their way to Nora's first faction meeting. Excitement coursed through her at the possibility of not only learning more about the faction's plans, but hopefully uncovering further clues as to Felix's whereabouts.

Unlike when Nora previously visited number four Emerald Lane, this time, when she stepped foot into the surprisingly expansive room, it was filled with people gathered in groups around tables and seating areas.

"Hey," smiled Omari as he noticed Sage and Nora's approach. He was leaning his back against the wall, his arms around a beautiful woman who was resting on his chest. "How was your day?"

"The usual," replied Sage. "How about you two?"

"Busy," the woman frowned, turning to face them. Nora was taken aback by how similar she looked to Evelyn. "Omari came to help out today. It was quiet for a few days there, but then we got all those customers in the last two."

"Turns out I am completely useless when it comes to baking, but am excellent at customer service," Omari grinned, giving the woman a squeeze. She looked up to him with her brown hooded eyes and he kissed her on the nose. "Jasmine, this is Nora, by the way."

"Hey," Nora inclined her head, stuffing her hands into her pockets. "I'm going out on a limb and guessing you're related to Evelyn?"

"She's my sister," Jasmine confirmed. "How are you finding Forest's Edge?"

"Good, the people have been mostly welcoming." Nora said, glancing sidelong at Sage before she could stop herself, the joke falling from her lips.

"Maybe some people can see that you have an attitude problem," Sage shot back, clearly not happy about Nora's teasing.

"Ooo," Omari sang, "play nice you two."

Jasmine elbow him in the ribs. "Stay out of it."

Nora turned away from the little group as Sage dove into conversation with Jasmine. Instead Nora took in those gathered around her. She wished August was here with her; as far as she could tell there were Lys Alvs—their pointed ears and golden eyes distinguishing them from the other races—and presumably humans, Elementum, and Anima, but without August's magic she could not be certain. At the front of the room stood Gemma, her white-blonde hair and height making her stand out. She wore tight fitting leather pants and a corset over a navy-blue shirt, accentuating her curves. A variety of glistening weaponry was strapped to her person, from daggers to a sword sheathed at her hip.

A moment later Aeolus appeared at Gemma's side, whispering in her ear before she stepped in front of the awaiting crowd. Like his leader, he too was dressed ready for a fight.

"Thank you all for coming tonight," she said, her voice loud and clear, silencing the gathered groups. "It is inspiring to see our numbers growing yet again."

Florence appeared at Nora's left, slightly out of breath, with Will close behind. "Right on time," she whispered, turning to Will. "Told you we weren't late."

Will rolled his eyes and Nora turned her attention back to Gemma.

"We have made excellent progress over the last few months to undermine the king, and other factions are also reporting successes in their cities, but there is still more to do. Factions in Fellbun, Kaldom, and Ferieton are all reporting an increase in numbers. Royal Bay, Giland, Sorby, and Rovton's numbers are holding steady, but are proving difficult to grow, obviously benefitting from King Dominic's rule. As for Midskopas, scouts have been sent, but the city is in upheaval and now, with the new Elementum ruler, Lady Ignisto, we fear whatever remains of the faction there may need to abandon the city."

Clenching and unclenching her hand in her pocket, Nora kept her face as neutral as possible. Factions in every city. This was bigger than Nora had thought. Why hadn't Rana said anything? Surely rebellions in every city were more important than finding Felix?

"The Northern Wolf Pack has been taking on more Anima—not exclusively wolves—as they attempt to aid those fleeing the cities," Gemma continued. "The remaining members of the Southern Wolf Pack have also fled to their northern kin. We believe those who were unable to escape have been imprisoned in the mines. Luckily for those living here in Forest's Edge, Lord Royd has already confirmed that he will not be punishing anyone who disobeys the king's new laws. However, the Royal Sentries are still present in the city and Lord Royd cannot stop them from doing so. If we want to prevent King Dominic from removing Lord Royd as he did Lord Akedale in Midskopas, then we all must play our part.

"Reports also show the King's Guild is growing in numbers almost as fast as we are, with many of our members having been targeted by the bigoted group. The king is yet to condemn their actions. In fact, Lord Royd passed on King Dominic's most recent communication which I'll read to you now." Aeolus handed Gemma a folded piece of paper. She held it out before her, her golden eyes narrowed.

*"Many centuries ago, a regime was founded to form a great union between all races that would establish justice, ensure peace, and promote prosperity for all Valmenessians. Yet, a radical movement is attempting to demolish all that we have built, and we can't let that happen. Wild Anima want to tear apart all that we hold dear, aided by*

*misguided and powerful individuals who seek control and foster unrest. We cannot let them win.*

"*It is your duty to find and eradicate any individual or group who fights to ruin our precious country. Royal Sentries in your cities will be recruiting loyal citizens to bolster numbers. We will never submit to anarchy.*"

Murmurs filled the room, some even shouting their anger towards King Dominic. The tension was palpable; those around Nora were like dark clouds rumbling on the horizon. She wondered how long it would take for the lightning to strike.

"One man sits on a throne and spouts hate, sowing the seeds of conflict. He first wiped Mors Alvs from the land and now has eyes on the Anima. The southern half of the continent is ruled mostly by Elementum, with Sorby and Ferieton the only cities left untouched as they are not deemed threats. However, who knows when the king will begin targeting the other races?"

"We must continue to make a stand; we must continue to fight. This country belongs to all people, not just the king and those he deems worthy. We must continue to push for the rights of all." Gemma's blazing gaze scanned the crowd. "Although we are making progress, there is still more work to be done. I need you all to continue to grow our numbers. The best chance we have in overthrowing King Dominic is through the power of the people. By standing together, we are stronger than he could ever dream to be."

"You all have your talents and know your duties," Gemma grinned broadly. "Now, let's get to work."

The crowd cheered before returning to their smaller groups, the room abuzz with chatter, but Nora was left feeling perplexed. Couldn't these people see that King Dominic's laws were for everyone's benefit? He was replacing lords and ladies because they were not enforcing laws. The Anima do not have to flee their homes. There were no laws requiring them to leave, they just needed to follow the law. It was that simple! Nora ground her teeth. Why couldn't these people understand what was so obvious to her?

"What is everyone doing?" Nora asked, glancing around the faction headquarters. Gemma was still standing at the front of the room, talking to Aeolus.

"They all have jobs to do," Florence replied, pointing to the different groups of people. "Weapons, maps, strategy, communication, recruitment, housing, supplies... there's a lot to do."

Nora looked to each group as Florence pointed. "How does Gemma keep everything under control with so many people involved?"

"Not everyone is here to work," Will chimed in. "I'm purely here to socialise."

Florence rolled her eyes as a wide grin spread on her face. Will wrapped his arm around her waist, pulling her close. He gave her a swift kiss on the forehead before linking arms with Sage and departing towards a group laughing in the far corner.

"He's kidding right?" Nora blinked.

"No," Jasmine smiled. "Some people are here for exactly that reason. These sorts of meetings aren't scheduled often. Usually it's only about fifteen of us that attend, and we discuss plans and things like that. From there we delegate if needed. Most people want change in this country but don't actively want or know how to step out of their comfort zone unless called upon. Gemma likes to have everyone here now and again  to strengthen the community spirit, and update everyone as a whole, hence the big speech."

"So, are we here to socialise like Will and Sage or actually do something?" Nora asked as a scrap of paper flew over to them.

She'd assumed Gemma would want to speak to her about the job she'd been given. Zaim had been mostly cooperative after she'd begged him, much to her disdain, and the two of them had created a believable murder scene. Minus the body of course.

"Gemma wants us," Omari said, folding the paper and nodding at Aeolus' serious expression across the room. "And to answer your question, everyone is doing something in their own way. Gemma gave you that job to see where you'd fit and how badly you wanted a seat at the table."

"And did I get one?" She followed him and Jasmine, weaving through the tables and huddled groups, with Florence by her side.

"I heard you sorted out that little issue without too much trouble," Florence grinned at her as they neared the back room. "So I'd say it's all yours, but that's only my vote."

Nora returned the woman's smile. "I hope everyone else feels the same as you."

"After you ladies," Omari said, opening the door to the back room.

Nora followed Jasmine and Florence through, closely followed by Omari who shut the door with an audible click behind her. Gemma and Aeolus stood shoulder to shoulder before Nora's view was instantly obstructed. A torrent of water forcefully shoved her against the wall, the back of her head cracking against the wood and black spots dancing before her eyes. Gasping, she fought to regain control, summoning her water magic to halt the flow that was assaulting her.

Aeolus was instantly on top of her as she slid down the wall. She thrashed out but he moved quickly, easily defending her attacks and matching her magic with his own. She felt her power fighting the onslaught, but it was draining faster than usual again. Another jet hit her, as though someone had thrown a large bucket of water at her face.

"Behave or we will force you to," commanded Gemma, her voice coming from the other side of the room.

"Fuck you," Nora wheezed, struggling to breathe, her magic failing to rise at her call.

Panic coursed through her as she tried in vain to summon any drop of magic she could. She'd felt weaker over the past few days, and even moments ago like her magic was draining quicker, but she should still have had something left. She should still have been able to sense her power.

Nora glanced down at her wrists to see heavy pearlescent white shackles encircled them, covering her tattoos. "What the fuck did you do to me?"

"They are something we have been working on," Gemma replied, her tone like ice. "They have been designed to inhibit the wearer's magic. Made by a very talented blacksmith Conjurer here in Forest's Edge."

"How barbaric," Nora growled, glaring at her wrists. Her shackle tattoos were like art. Intricate designs in black ink that, when looked at closely, were made up of words that were like a song. Even though they were more permanent and binding, their weightlessness and beauty were a stark contrast to the shackles that now covered them.

"Compared to your king using potions to inhibit magic or are you referring to your tattoos beneath them? I'd say my shackles are more like jewellery fit for royalty," Gemma replied mockingly. "Which is almost comical because I'd love nothing more than for the royal family of Valmenessia to wear them."

"Like that's ever going to happen," Nora hissed through gritted teeth. She imagined she looked like a drenched feral cat to them; baring her teeth whilst sitting in a puddle.

"What was your reason for coming to Forest's Edge?" Gemma asked, ignoring Nora's comment. "Why did the king send you here?"

Water dripped down Nora's face as she smiled sweetly, her lips pressing together firmly.

"What does the king know of our plans?" Gemma demanded, crossing her arms over her chest.

She could feel the others' eyes on her but refused to let her attention sway from Gemma. It was a bad idea to take your eyes of the person in charge of your future, and as much as Nora hated it, Gemma had all the power. When Nora refused to reply she was hit with another torrent of water. Her lungs burned as she struggled to protect her face.

"Feel like talking yet?" Gemma asked, once the cruelty relented.

Blood trickled from Nora's nose, and she spat crimson onto the ground beside her. She clenched her hands to stop them from shaking as Aeolus crouched beside her. Their eyes met and she could see no emotion in his features. His muscled figure, dressed in leather, loomed over her, yet she refused to feel the threat even though she was in a very vulnerable state.

Nora flicked her eyes to the side of the room where Florence, Omari and Jasmine stood, watching the scene with anger in their eyes. How quickly they had switched to seeing her as the villain. She clenched her lips shut turning her gaze back to Aeolus. He raised his hand over her chest and her lungs began to burn. She coughed, water spilling from her mouth, forcing her lips open as her body convulsed.

He dropped his hand and she gasped, tears falling from her eyes. "What does King Dominic know about the Forest's Edge faction?" he asked, looking bored.

She remained silent and braced herself as Aeolus' hand hovered over her chest, but this time his magic trickled through her chest. She coughed uncontrollably, the action grating in her throat as he continued to speak. "Little Nora, just a tool for King Dominic to wield. Or should I say… a puppet?"

Panting as he lowered his hand, she narrowed her eyes as her chest heaved. Her voice came out in short rasping bursts. "Fuck. You."

"What do you know of King Dominic's advisors?" He questioned without emotion. "Are you privy to his plans for Valmenessia?"

Nora stared him down.

Aeolus drew one of the many blades strapped to his person and sliced it through the fabric of one of her trouser legs, the metal glistening in the light. He slid the cool blade along the exposed skin of her calf. "Why do you let your pride get you into such difficult situations? Just answer the questions."

Nora refused to take her eyes from his as he cut, the blade slicing through her skin as if it were a soft piece of fruit. She bit back her scream, swallowing the noise, as blood trickled down her leg, dripping into the puddled water on the wooden floor.

"Feel like answering our question yet?" he asked, holding the bloodied blade between them.

Aeolus shrugged when she kept her tongue still, then pressed the blade to her open wound, the cut going deeper. Nora cried out, unable to hold it back as spots appeared before her eyes.

He drew back once more, watching her closely. "If you just answer our questions, we could have a Healer in here within minutes. You wouldn't even be left with a scar."

Nora didn't utter a word and Aeolus sighed. He turned his head to Gemma who nodded stiffly. Aeolus tore Nora's trousers, revealing her thigh underneath, and she trembled as the metal of his dagger caressed her flesh.

"Let's try some different questions, shall we?" He said. "Tell us about the Alta. How many of you are there? Who is the leader?"

Nora's breath hitched as the blade made a long shallow cut, but her lips remained a tight thin line.

Aeolus tsked, then repeated his questions. "How many of you are there? Who is your leader?"

"Just me," she uttered, attempting a smirk. "I'm the only Alta and I'm the leader."

He dropped the blade and, with one swift movement, punched her in the gut. Nora gasped, her knees curling up instinctively. Aeolus shoved her legs down and hit her again and again, the impact shuddering through her entire body.

"For all the sass and overconfidence I've been told you are over flowing with, you're not what I anticipated," Gemma said, her voice coming from somewhere above.

Nora looked up at Gemma, glaring as best she could, her words coming out clipped and strained. "Next time, you can be the one shackled on the floor and I'll inflict the pain. See how long you last."

"Aeolus." Gemma commanded.

Before Aeolus made a move Nora began to laugh, the sound husky. "You must be even stupider than you look if you think torture is going to get me to tell you anything. Do you honestly believe King Dominic would have made it that easy? There is nothing you can do to me that hasn't already been done. And on top of that, do you really think that I would have the ability to tell you anything if I wanted to? Which I don't." Nora smirked, blood spattering her lips. "You are in way over your head."

Gemma glared at Nora; her stare as sharp as a blade. Utter silence filled the room. Nora must have been a pathetic sight, slouched against the wall, drenched to the bone in water and blood. Aeolus still crouched by her side, monitoring every breath, every movement Nora made.

A knock on the door cut through the silence like a jagged knife. Nora's hands flexed instinctively, grasping for the magic that would not answer her call.

"I hear we have a little problem on our hands," came an authoritative voice. Nora looked up to see a tall man with brown skin and black curly hair standing in the doorway. He looked oddly familiar, yet she could not place him. She was sure she had never seen the man before...

The sound of people talking and going about their jobs carried through the open door, and Nora wondered why no one had bothered to check on what was happening in the back room. Were they used to their leader torturing people?

"Lord Royd," Gemma said as the man moved farther into the room.

Lord Royd took a seat at the table, adjusting his pine green jacket with gold trim, before crossing one leg over the other. He tapped his fingers on the wooden arms of the chair as though the scene before him was a regular occurrence. "Is this the woman Eve told me about?"

Eve? Nora's brows rose. Lord Royd was Evelyn's father!

Gemma grinned. "Yes, she is the woman your daughter told you about. Unfortunately, Nora hasn't said a single word of value, so you haven't missed anything."

"Maybe we need a different sort of persuasion," he mused, tilting his head at Nora as though she were a riddle.

"What do you have in mind?" Gemma asked.

It was a strange exchange. Lord Royd clearly held authority, but the tone in which he spoke to Gemma was not as a leader should. He was speaking to her as his equal.

"Occasionally you need to break something in order to unravel what's inside." The man inclined his head to Aeolus and the latter left the room. "The mind is complex and brute force can solidify the barrier."

No one spoke as they waited in a tense anticipation, then Aeolus reappeared with Evelyn and a hooded figure Nora would recognised anywhere.

Nora's heart stopped. Either that, or it beat so fast she could not tell one thump from the next. Her world spun; her compass no longer able to find north.

What.

The.

Fuck.

Why was he here?

# 32

## Evelyn

The scene before her made Evelyn shiver. Nora looked as though she had been hauled from a raging river after having fought a legendary beast. Her face was red raw, blood dripped from her nose and mouth, and there were oozing gashes on her calf and thigh. Nora appeared not to care, too busy eyeing August with disdain from where she sat on the floor.

"Look who we have here," Gemma sang, her words obviously meant to taunt Nora. "You must be August."

Next to her, August dropped his hood to reveal his dark eyes that never strayed from Nora's. Evelyn couldn't imagine what he was going through. Nora was not only his friend, but she was his family. Evelyn knew he was racked with guilt for both confiding in her and asking her to tell the faction about Nora. She had tried to reassure him that it was a kindness and what he hoped to do was in Nora's best interest, but Evelyn could tell that her words had not sunk in and August was still beating himself up about it.

"What have you done?" hissed Nora through clenched teeth.

"It's for your own good," August replied, his voice thick with emotion. "I'm trying to help you."

"By having these people lock me up against my will and torture me?" She thrust her shackled wrists into the air, the pearlescent chains glimmering in the light.

"I didn't know they were going to hurt you," he sighed, running a hand through his hair. "But this isn't you. Everything you do? It's the will of the king. You can't possibly know what you want with his commands controlling you."

"Really?" she sneered. "You seem to know what you want."

"I no longer have the tattoos," he said, standing up taller. "King Dominic doesn't control me anymore."

Nora reeled back as if slapped. "That's not possible."

August rolled his sleeves, revealing his bare wrists. "I think my magic eroded the tattoos. The way I can take magic from others, turns out I could take it from my tattoos too. They had been fading over the last year and the further we got from King Dominic the easier it was for my magic to eat away at them. They had completely disappeared by the time we reached Midskopas."

"When you called in your favour," Nora whispered.

"Yeah, I wanted to test out my new found freedom," he replied with a shrug. "King Dominic has no control over me now. You may not have realised that I didn't have the tattoos, but you've known for a while that I've been able to do what I want."

The room was silent, and like Evelyn, everyone was frozen, watching the lies between Nora and August unravel. It was as if a fuse had been lit and they were all waiting for the bomb to explode.

"Why did you stay?" Nora's voice was strained. "Why did you bother staying with me?"

"You're my best friend and my family. I'd never abandon you." August stepped farther into the room, but Nora's glare kept him at a distance. Evelyn placed a hand on his back, and his shoulders sagged.

"So, what was your plan? Pretend to be Alta until you could find someone to lock me up?" Nora shouted at him, whatever vulnerability she'd just shown dissolving in an instant. "Is this my life now? Will you visit me regularly in my cell in between their bouts of torture?"

August shook his head. "Lord Royd has agreed to help remove your tattoos."

"Has he now? What's in it for him?" Nora scoffed. "If your magic removed your tattoos, why haven't you tried to remove mine?"

"I did." His voice was soft and plagued with pain. "I took the opportunity when we first arrived in Forest's Edge. You had passed out from exhaustion, and I knew you couldn't put up a fight if you weren't happy about what I was attempting. I tried using my magic on the tattoos, but it didn't work. I don't know why I could remove mine but not yours. You didn't wake up for days when I attempted it."

Nora narrowed her eyes. "You could have killed me…"

"I know," August replied softly causing Evelyn's heart to ache for him.

"I will arrange for your tattoos to be removed," Lord Royd declared, his voice cutting through the sombre atmosphere. "But there are conditions. You will be kept under strict guard and will be questioned for information once the tattoos are removed. If you are not cooperative, we will use other methods to extract answers. You have not come to us willingly like August and you have given us no reason to trust you."

August tensed at Evelyn's side, and she spoke before he could say anything he would regret.

"If she shows herself to be remorseful, surely you'll give her the benefit of the doubt?" she asked her father. "Isn't that what we're trying to do? Fight for a world that is equal for all? And if that's the case, shouldn't we be acting in the way we wish the world to be?"

"She has committed terrible crimes," Gemma stated, drawing Evelyn's attention.

"Under the magical command of the king," defended Evelyn. "She had no choice, and unlike August, she hasn't had an opportunity to be free. We should at least try to be open-minded so that Nora has the chance to make her own choices and show her true character. Torturing her like this isn't going to help her see our side."

There was a long silence as though they were all part of a stand-off, waiting to see who would move. Evelyn decided she would be the one to take the first step. Crouching next to Nora, she placed her hand over the woman's leg, summoning her light to heal one of the bloodied gashes. It was only a flesh wound, and other than the initial pain, Evelyn

287

had little discomfort. She moved her light up Nora's body, feeling for other injuries and healing them just as swiftly.

"Thanks," Nora whispered as the cut on her lip sewed itself shut.

"At least this time you let me heal your head," Evelyn offered Nora a small smile before returning to August's side.

"Eve has a point," her father sighed, pride glistening in his eyes. "We cannot condemn Nora for actions that are out of her control. However, if she continues to follow the king once she is free to make her own choices, then our hands will be tied." He turned to face Nora, looking down at her as though she were a puzzle to solve. "Let's see who you truly are."

The fire flickered against the fireplace, blackening it as its warmth and crackling created a cosy atmosphere. Evelyn sat on the well-worn sofa underneath a pastel blue blanket she had knitted, re-reading her favourite book. Poppy had called it "a predictable tale of love and evil" but that didn't make Evelyn love it any less. There was something about it that just drew her in and it was the perfect escape. Yes, another distraction to keep her from her ever growing pile of unpleasant thoughts in her mind. She was nearing the end of the novel when August sunk into the opposite end on the sofa and draped his muscular arm over the back. Evelyn glanced at him briefly, hoping he couldn't tell that she did indeed notice his presence.

"Saw that," he stated.

"Hmmm?" she murmured, trying hard to concentrate on what she was reading and wishing she had the ability to be stealthy.

"I saw you checking me out," he said, and she looked over at him to see him staring into the fire, his eyes aglow and a grin on his face.

"I'm not saying that you're right," she said, marking her page and closing the book, "but what made you think that I was looking at you?"

"Because you do this," he chuckled, turning his head, and staring at her. She waited for him to turn away, but he did not, his gaze set on her face. She couldn't help but admire his strong jaw that was covered in stubble, and the way his lips quirked more to the left when he smiled.

"I do not stare that obviously!" she exclaimed, scrunching her brow.

He held up a hand. "Wait, I'm not finished."

She crossed her arms and pouted, and still he did not take his eyes off her. She was more subtle with her glances than he was being. "Are you finished making fun of me?"

His smile was broad. "But you make it so easy... also you're cute when you pout."

Evelyn felt her cheeks warm. "It's good to see you smiling."

"Is it bad that I feel relieved?" August sighed. "Maybe even happy too?"

"Not at all." She said, shuffling closer to him. "You did the right thing and Nora will come to understand that soon."

"She'll never forgive me," he groaned, wrapping his arm around her, and tucking her into his side. "She's going to see this as a betrayal for the rest of her life. Even if it is a free one that she can control."

"You don't know that she won't see your side," Evelyn replied. "As you said before, she's your family. She'll see that you have her best interests at heart, and she'll forgive you. I'm sure of it."

"It's kind of you to say," he said. "But you don't know Nora like I do. The woman likes to hold a grudge."

"And if she does, you won't have to endure it alone." She smiled at him. "I'll be right by your side."

"Thanks." He replied, squeezing her gently. "Your father was not what I expected."

"In what way?" Evelyn laughed.

August shrugged. "It could be that he listened and appeared to trust me, or maybe it's because he's the *lord* of Forest's Edge." He raised a brow. "How did that never come up in the many times we spoke about your family?"

"I don't know," she said, twisting her fingers. "Him being in the role is new-ish, and before him my aunt was lady of the city so it's sort of normal and I just presume everyone knows. It's not that big of a deal."

"It kind of is," he chuckled. "But I don't want you to feel bad for not telling me. I kept a lot from you."

She nodded. "But no more secrets now."

"Exactly, no more secrets."

August looked deep into her golden eyes. She gently touched his jaw; the stubble was rough against her skin as she slid her hand towards the back of his head. Their eyes locked and she pulled him towards her at the same time his arm lowered to her waist and drew her to him. Their mouths pressed together in an urgency she had not expected, his soft lips searching hers passionately. Her free hand scrunched in the fabric of his shirt, pulling him closer, her heart beating rapidly as the world around her slipped away and all that remained was her and August. Evelyn had been kissed before, but the way August held her and the feel of his lips against her own was like nothing she had ever felt before.

They had been so close to kissing last night—August's revelations postponing the moment—but Evelyn now felt it was worth the wait. She had never felt so confident, so at ease, her worries a distant thought as he invaded her every sense. Evelyn embraced this newfound confidence, wanting to lose herself in the way August made her feel. She felt her magic rise to the surface, her light dancing just beneath her skin, as their kiss heated.

Unclasping a few buttons of his shirt, she slipped her hand under the fabric and dragged her nails down his muscular chest; smothering his moan with her lips. They drew apart, breathless, the taste of mint lingering on her lips. August grinned broadly, the bright blue of his eyes sparkling in the morning light.

From all the recent loss and uncertainty in Evelyn's life, she relished in having someone who made her forget. She hoped this was a sign of more good things to come.

## 33

**Nora**

Resting her back against the stone wall, Nora embraced the cool chill that seeped through her clothing. The morning light crept in through the three small glass windows that lined the upper wall, allowing her to see her surroundings. They had moved her last night to a cell made of thick black stone with a heavy wooden door that took up most of the wall opposite her poor excuse for a bed. The lingering smell of human waste and hopelessness was thick in the stale air, making her eyes water with each breath she took.

Nora had tried sleeping after failing to find some way to escape her cell, but her dreams provided her little escape, instead bombarding her with a familiar nightmare. Standing alone in her soaking nightgown, the field around her blackened as embers drifted around her and the scent of ash suffocated her lungs. Nora didn't welcome the dream, but dwelling on her reality wasn't much better.

Analysing every memory she had of her time in Forest's Edge, Nora strived to find the moment it had all gone wrong. Then she remembered that August had betrayed her. The thought pierced sharply through her heart, more painful than any torture she'd ever endured.

Cocking her head to the side, she looked up at the wooden door expectantly, the sound of footsteps outside her cell piquing her interest. The jingling of keys was followed by a loud click and the door groaned open to reveal Zaim and a green uniformed guard.

"You have ten minutes," stated the guard in a no-nonsense tone. "We will be just outside."

The door slammed shut behind Zaim and his nose crinkled at the unpleasant smell caused by the cell's previous inhabitants. He looked completely out of place in his immaculate fur-lined jacket, charcoal slacks, and leather boots.

"Hello little Nora," he said casually, dropping a bunch of pastel blue flowers at her feet. "Looks like you got yourself into a bit of a bind."

"Always such a pleasure to see you," Nora drawled, ignoring the flowers, and staring up at her fellow Alta member. His curly mouse brown hair was styled to look as though he had only just woken up. "How many times did you have to get on your knees for that guard to be let in here?"

Zaim glowered at her. "I see you woke up on the wrong side of the," his face twisted with disgust. "foul pile you're using as a bed."

"What are you doing here?" Nora snapped impatiently. "I hope it wasn't just to bring me flowers."

"No, and it's certainly not freeing you either, so you can go back to sulking. You're stuck here, princess." Zaim winked.

"Then fuck off and leave me alone," she scowled.

"I don't think so," he replied, stuffing his hands into the pockets of his jacket. "I have come to say goodbye."

Nora rolled her eyes. "Are you under the impression that I'll miss you?"

"Once I collect the key to the north, I'll be returning to Royal Bay." He said, ignoring her snarky comment.

"That's lovely," she replied sarcastically. "You should go then, I'd hate to delay your departure any longer."

Zaim chuckled, the hollow sound sending chills up her spine. "It's pathetic how useless you have become. You're tattoos will be gone soon and then King Dominic won't want you. You're defective, and the Alta only keep the best."

"And I suppose that's you?" Nora laughed, the hollow sound reverberating around the room. "You've always been full of yourself. Pity your skill has never been able to live up to your ego."

"Says the little girl who got herself caught by the enemy." His brown eyes narrowed as he bared his teeth. "I'm going to have so much fun with you."

"Oh really? How so?" she said, sounding bored. She picked at her nails, refusing to look him in the eye. "I thought you said you're leaving?."

"You're still an Alta, which means I can't kill you now."

She rolled her eyes. "Obviously."

"But once Lord Royd removes your tattoos, King Dominic will want you dead. You'll be fair game, and I will come for you." He told her, his words like ice coursing through her veins. "It will be just like when you were little though you won't live long enough to reminisce over the time we spend together."

Nora held his glare, refusing to show anything but pure hatred on her face.

Zaim knocked on the door, and it swung open before he spoke his parting words that left ice in her veins. "Remember how much fun we had?"

◇

Nora awoke to a kick to her stomach. Groaning, she snapped her eyes open, and was roughly lifted from where she had been curled up under a thin blanket on the floor, awakening her from her restless sleep. Images of a blackened field faded as she recognised her attacker in the morning light.

"Rise and shine," Aeolus sang mockingly, his hand gripping her upper arm firmly as she steadied herself on her feet. "It's the big day."

"I can't believe they're doing it," Nora yawned, yanking her arm away from him, the movement causing her to stumble. She stretched her shackled arms awkwardly above her head, attempting to cover up her imbalance. "I told them it wasn't nice to throw a party in honour of your stupidity, but I guess they've decided to go through with it anyway."

"You think you're so funny," he snarled, shoving her in the back towards the open door where Omari stood, his face showing no emotion. "We'll see who's laughing when your tattoos are removed."

A shiver ran down Nora's spine, her face paling as she was ushered out the door. Her feet were like lead, reluctant to carry her, but Aeolus pushed her onwards whenever she hesitated. Omari led her down the hallway of cells and up a flight of stairs. Unlike Nora's cell, the prisoners on the upper level were visible through bars, and her eyes flickered over the captives. They were in varying states, from unkempt to immaculate, sobbing to deranged. Nora wondered where she fit on the spectrum.

A man sitting on a pile of hay caught her attention, his black eyes like pits of darkness boring into her. Her mouth dropped and Aeolus shoved her in the back as her feet slowed.

"Turns out August isn't the only Mors Alv in Forest's Edge," Aeolus growled, giving her another shove.

Outside the prison, the air was like ice and a light snow fell from the gaps between the canopies. The first snow of Frost Season. Shivering, Nora was put into another cell, however this one had wheels and was pulled along by two black horses. She sat on the floor of the cramped space, her mind reeling at the thought of being separated from King Dominic's bond. Without the connection, she would lose her purpose and, not only that, she would also feel *everything*. Would she still see the world in the same light, or would she be lost without the king to guide her?

"Welcome to Lord and Lady Royd's Manor," declared Omari in mock welcome as he opened the door and tugged her out by her shackles.

"And what a welcome," Nora replied sarcastically, stumbling. "Do they give all their guests this royal treatment?"

"Only the best for you, Nora." Aeolus sang, appearing beside her.

Nora stared up at the stone manor, surprised by how much the building was at odds with the rest of Forest's Edge's woodsy architecture. The place was like a fortress. Stumbling through the expansive entryway, she was faced with an open foyer with two grand staircases that wrapped around the walls on either side, leading to the second floor. Large portraits hung from the dark stone walls, and Nora shivered, feeling their eyes scrutinizing her as she climbed the stairs.

On the second floor, Aeolus once again knocked her forward, but this time she lost her footing and tripped, her arms catching her before her face could collide with the tiled floor. Crying out as her cheek knocked into the pearlescent shackles, Nora wondered whether it would have hurt more to have hit the ceramic squares.

"Was that really necessary?" Omari grumbled as he helped Nora to her feet. He held her firmly, his hand lingering on her elbow as they turned down the left hallway.

Stopping at one of the many doors that lined the passageway, Aeolus knocked three times before opening it, revealing what appeared to be a guest room within. Omari directed her towards a four-poster bed that sat in the centre of the room. Big enough for two, it had pastel pink sheets and white gossamer with embroidered flowers hanging from its frame. The black iron chains sitting on the covers were a stark contrast to what would have been a pretty scene.

Along with the elaborate bed, the room had a stone fireplace and a bay window with seating that overlooked a quaint snow-speckled garden. It was also filled with a rather large number of people, considering the room's size, ultimately making it feel extremely cramped. Hunched over a small table next to the bed was Lord Royd, checking vials of a wide range of colours and flicking the pages of a large tome.

Nora planted her feet firmly to the spot, refusing to get any closer to the bed. She ignored her stinging cheek from where it had grazed the shackles. "I'm flattered you have invited me, but restraints and this many people isn't really my style. I'm more of a one person, maybe two... three if I've had a bit to drink, kind of girl."

"Everything that has come out of your mouth today has been utterly ridiculous," Aeolus sneered, grabbing her free arm, and dragging her forward.

"Consent is not ridiculous." Nora feebly tried to step backwards and wriggle out of his grip.

"No, it is not," replied Lord Royd, his tone authoritative as he turned to face her. Wrinkles kissed the edges of his weary eyes, but she could see the determination in them. "This is for your own good, as well as for the good of my people. As a matter of fact, the tattoos restrict you from providing true consent. Under the king's command you are forced to choose what is best for him, hence your free will is already hindered. The removal of the tattoos will fix that, providing you with the opportunity to truly choose what is best for you." He gestured towards the bed. "Now, let's get this over and done with."

Aeolus and Omari lifted Nora off the ground as though she weighed no more than a chair and dropped her onto the soft mattress, the wooden frame squeaking in protest. She rolled but was caught by Omari who pushed her onto her back, holding her shoulders firmly in place as the other two men chained her legs to the bed posts. Nora tried to kick but it was no use, they were too strong.

The pearlescent shackles were removed from Nora's wrists as Aeolus slipped a thick leather strap underneath her back before threading it through a brass buckle over her chest. Pulling the leather tight, her arms were trapped against her sides, the strap inhibiting their movement not only away from her body but also from bending at the elbow. Nora attempted to summon her magic, but nothing came; not a spark, drop of water, or caress of wind against her palms. It was like walking a familiar path with a friend, silent in the comfort of one another's presence, only to turn and find them no longer there, as though they had turned onto another street without bidding farewell. She pushed down the feelings of panic as Lord Royd leaned over her, his eyes flicking up and down her body.

"It won't come." His brown eyes filled with pity as he traced a finger over the tattoos on her wrist. "It takes a while for your magic to recover from the effects of the restraints."

"You'll pay for this," Nora hissed, hoping she sounded more confident than she felt. She doubted she could do much in her current state, but Goddess Thyra help her she would make them suffer for this, one way or another.

The man smiled humourlessly. "You know, one day you might actually thank me."

Lord Royd retrieved a vial of shimmering gold liquid from the table next to the bed. Pouring it over Nora's right wrist, he used his fingers to rub it in. At first Nora felt only the gritty liquid being massaged into her skin, but then the man's fingers began to make swirling motions and trace patterns whilst he muttered words Nora did not recognise. Suddenly, her skin felt as though it were burning from the inside out, the flames lapping at her flesh to consume her. Her body jerked, something deep down inside her fighting to keep hold, its determination becoming frantic as Lord Royd's conjuring magic flowed through Nora. Vision blurring and sweat beading on her forehead, Nora found her breath difficult to catch. Two kinds of magic were at war, and she was merely the battleground, her body spasming with each attack.

The king's shackles held fast, tightening around her wrist like barbed wire and refusing to be pried away easily, but Lord Royd was determined, and his conjuring magic was strong. Nora felt as though she were being torn apart, her very essence being tugged in opposite directions. A guttural scream escaped her lips, the agony of the king's shackles clinging tightly to her soul. Waves of nausea whirled within her stomach, and white spots flashed erratically in her vision. She barely noticed as the hold on her shoulders tightened or when a hand clamped down over her mouth, muffling the screams she could not control. She didn't care. She just wanted the pain to stop. Thankfully, the Goddess Thyra must have been watching over her because it was not long before the world turned to black.

## 34

## Nora

Heart pounding, Nora stood before the altar, excitement flooding through her as if she were a firework and someone had lit the spark. This was the ceremony that would solidify her purpose in life. It was everything she had worked so hard for.

The Makers' Temple was a marble structure situated on the castle grounds, reserved purely for the use of those with royal blood and for special ceremonies. The general public was banned from entering. Nora had never stepped foot in the temple until today, but she doubted the feelings of awe would ever lessen with an increase in visits. The interior was like stepping into the afterlife, the stories of old come to life before her. A rainbow of light shone through the floor-to-ceiling stained glass windows that overlooked the altar; the dazzling colours flickering over the shiny white marble of the pillars, walls, and pews. The five Gods and Goddesses, ethereal in the morning light, observed those who dwelled within the temple. Incense burned, tickling Nora's nose. She stifled a sneeze and looked to King Dominic, his strong presence unwavering.

August had been marked with his tattoos a year prior, a fact that grated at her. She was just as skilled as him, just as knowledgeable and loyal—maybe even more so—but she had been made to wait. Now, on *her thirteenth birthday, she would receive the gift she so desperately wanted.*

*The conjurer stepped forward, her frail body at odds with the power that resided within her. Reaching out with a spindly hand, the woman beckoned for Nora to approach. Nora offered her wrist and the conjurer's bony fingers dug into her soft skin as she took a deep breath. This was it.*

*Grey eyes found hers, probing deep into Nora's soul. "Are you ready?"*

*"I am," Nora replied, her voice steady.*

*The conjurer nodded, and with a flick of an elongated finger on her free hand, a child appeared with long golden hair and skin as pale as snow. Dressed all in white, she carried a glass bowl filled with an obsidian liquid, flashes of silver swirling through it like smoke twirling in the air. Nora watched as the child placed the bowl on the altar, then waited as the Conjurer drew out her knife and plunged it into her own palm. Bright red blood blossomed like a rose from the wound as the woman barely gasped. The Conjurer held her hand above the bowl and let her blood drip into the swirls, merging with the silver and black.*

*Slipping a thin glass tube with a metallic nail at its point from her pocket, the conjurer dipped the tip into the bowl, the liquid turning the clear pencil-like instrument black. Placing it to Nora's skin, she winced as it carved her flesh. Like long papercuts that entwined her wrist, the obsidian fluid spilled into the sliced skin as the conjurer muttered incomprehensibly. Nora bit her lip, refusing to cry out, and did her best to endure the pain that was now building, thankful for Rana's training.*

*Keeping her wrist as still as possible, she tried to ignore the burning sensation. The slick liquid moved through her body, clawing at her very essence. Nora felt the need to fight it, to push back whatever it was that was attempting to hold her in its clutches, panic threatening to take hold. She looked to her king for strength; his shoulders back and chin held high, regal, and authoritative, his scrutinising eyes focused on her. He had known from the day they met that she was special, and he did not shy away from it. He had kept her, trained her, had given her purpose. She would not let her fear betray him.*

*After what felt like an eternity, the conjurer beckoned for Nora's other wrist, and once again Nora braved the pain and the invisible tendrils that curled around her, taking hold from the inside out. Finally, wrists marked and held before her, King Dominic stepped close, raising his arm above hers. The conjurer's chanting turned rhythmic like the deep beating of drums as the king retrieved a dagger from his hip and made a quick slice of his exposed wrist. The crimson blood rained onto Nora's arms, seeping into the cuts, and causing them to bubble and fizz. Nora fell to her knees. Whatever had been striving to take hold of her now had a steel grip, resolute as it clamped down.*

*Nora was not sure how long she had been on the floor—it could have been seconds or hours—her chest rising and falling rapidly as she raised her head and looked to her king. Although her wrists were aching, red rimming the inky black tattoos that now entwined like a vine around a tree trunk, the pain was dulling, and her mind was beginning to settle.*

*Was it over? Was she an Alta?*

*King Dominic stroked her hair, bejewelled fingers running through the strands. He gazed down at her, "Now, it is time for my commands."*

$$\diamondsuit$$

Forty-two, forty-three, forty-four...

Nora counted her heartbeats, taking slow breaths as the swell of emotion threatened to devour her. The inky design of the shackle tattoos were gone, her wrist now frighteningly bare. She was no longer bound to the king's will—a fact that caused panic to rise like ice in her veins as she struggled to maintain her composure. Everything used to be tied to him. Every action, every decision; it was all for King Dominic. But now... now it all rested on her shoulders. The damage she had caused was hers and hers alone, and it was a heavy burden to bear.

Forty-five, forty-six...

Sitting up, Nora glanced around the room. They had not moved her, and she was no longer chained to the large fourposter bed. Instead, the pastel pink sheets cocooned her, protecting her from the morning chill, the fireplace containing nothing but ash.

The curtains of the bay window were open, letting in the pale light and providing a glimpse of the garden beyond. Nora would have contemplated her escape, if it were not for the redhead sitting on a chair next to the bed, watching Nora intently.

"Good morning," Florence grinned. Her crimson hair was plaited to the side in her usual style, and she wore the same outfit Nora had seen her in on the night they met. "Have a nice nap?"

"What are you doing here?" Nora croaked, the words scratching her dry throat.

"I asked her to come," came August's voice and Nora angled her head to see him standing near her feet; his broad shoulders slumped. He looked dishevelled, his shirt askew and eyes tormented. "How are you feeling?"

The sight of him twisted her stomach. "I don't want you here."

"Nora—"

"You betrayed me." Tears slipped from her treacherous eyes. "You were all I had, and you gave me up the first chance you got."

"I did this because you are my family." He said with a heavy sigh. "You *are* all I have. I love you and want to help you. I did it for you."

"Liar!" She shouted at him. "You betrayed me because it was what *you* wanted. You didn't think about me, about what I wanted. I was happy! And now… now…" a sob escaped her. Now she was just as Zaim had said. Defective. King Dominic wouldn't want her anymore.

"How can you be happy when you don't have control of your own mind?" He asked, the frustration clear in his tone.

"Easily!" She snapped.

"Because you didn't have to feel the guilt for your actions?" August's voice was low, his dark eyes watching her sadly.

"Shut up." Nora growled.

"It hurts, doesn't it? Knowing what you've done," he said. She hated the way he was looking at her, as though she were some injured animal in need of coddling. "The people you have killed for him. The injustices you have ignored or inflicted on others in his name."

"I said shut the fuck up!" She knew she sounded childish, but she didn't care.

"You need to feel it!" He shouted at her as though raising his voice would force his will on her. "That's what life is. You can't walk around blind to what is happening around you, pretending everything is fine when it isn't."

"He's right, Nora," Florence said beside her. "You can't change what the king made you do, but you can do something about it."

Nora shrugged her tense shoulders, the movement coming across nothing like the unruffled action she intended. She refused to acknowledge the tears that pooled in her eyes. "What if I agree with the king? What if I like how the world works?"

Truth was, she didn't know what she believed anymore. Yes, she felt guilt, but she wasn't entirely sure why. Her head was a confused mess. She felt like she was fighting multiple opponents without any magic or skill, unable to attack, let alone defend herself.

August sighed. "You don't. Otherwise, you wouldn't be so upset. You know what he has been doing is wrong, not just to the Alta but to the Mors Alvs, the Anima, and anyone else who stands in the way of what he wants."

"Why did you agree to come here?" Nora sniffled, looking at Florence through her wet lashes. August brought out too much emotion in her and she needed a reprieve from his onslaught, as well as the one that was already taking place in her head.

"I hoped that he was right," Florence replied, her blue eyes searching Nora's as though looking for an answer. "That you are a good person who was forced to do bad things. I don't forgive you for using me or my friends—I don't know if I ever will—but I'd like to get to know you without the king's control, and Will would too."

"I'm probably still a sarcastic antagonising asshole." Nora pouted.

August laughed. "Fingers crossed."

Nora shot him a half-hearted glare then turned back to Florence who was smiling warmly.

"You're not an asshole," Florence offered. "Just feisty and perhaps a tad on the arrogant side, but Will and I like that about you."

"Seeing as you two are okay, can we be okay too?" August asked. Dark eyes found Nora's and she felt a surge of emotion in her chest, causing her to falter. Guilt, anger, and affection rushed through her like a tangled current through an already uncertain sea. He offered her a small smile, but she refused to return it; he had betrayed her and there was no way she'd forgive him for it.

"Where's Evelyn?" Nora asked as August's smile dropped into a frown. "Didn't she want to join the welcoming committee?"

"She's with her mother and Jasmine," he replied sombrely, sitting down on the foot of the bed.

"Lord Royd died," Florence said quietly. "After removing your tattoos, he was a little tired, but the Healers examined him and deemed him healthy. They told him to rest, but in the morning... he never woke up."

Lord Royd was dead.

The words reverberated through her. Nora's face paled as she fought back the tears. Why should she feel guilty? It was not her fault. She did not ask for the tattoos to be removed, and she definitely wouldn't take responsibility. The added weight would crush her.

"No one blames you," Florence said as though sensing Nora's thoughts. She tried to take Nora's hand, but Nora pulled away, tugging it to her chest.

"If anything, it's my fault," August said, facing the window. "I asked him to do it."

"No, you asked for help, and he chose to do it," Florence insisted, looking between August and Nora. "This is not on either of you. Evelyn and her family don't blame you, so you shouldn't blame yourselves. The fault lies with King Dominic and only him."

"Oh, you're awake," interrupted Will as he entered and shut the door behind him. He brushed his dark locks out of his bright, green eyes, taking in her appearance. "Judging by the tears, I assume you're either murderous or remorseful. I hope the latter. How are you feeling?"

"Wonderful," Nora groaned. "Absolutely wonderful."

"I have to say, I was shocked to hear that you were an Alta." He said, smiling warmly at her scowl. "Part of me had hoped Alta were only a terrible rumour, but alas."

"Will, maybe now's not the best time?" August sighed irritably. "She's already—"

"It's fine," Nora said, cutting August off and gesturing with her hand for Will to continue. "Get it off your chest. Everyone else is, you might as well say what's on your mind too."

"I'll be quick." Will sat on the bed, and she now had someone looking at her from every direction. "From what I've heard, and as you probably know there's limited knowledge of the Alta, but I've been told that they are evil people who take pleasure in violence and other people's pain. I thought you were better than that."

Nora pouted like a scolded child, but she didn't speak, letting him continue. What could she say to that? She and August may not have been that way inclined, but she would bet a thousand golden coins that most of the other Alta members were. She only had to look back on memories of her childhood to confirm their cruelty.

"Your life choices when it comes to your occupation—other than working for me"—he winked—"are poor, but I hope you decide to change that. You're young and strong. This doesn't have to be your life, nor can you stand by when the treatment of others is becoming more and more unjust. There is more at stake here than just following the king's orders without thought. The country is changing and if something isn't done, a lot of people are going to be either displaced, enslaved, or killed. You have the power to change things. As an Elementum, you have greater power than most. Use it for good."

"That was some speech," she sighed, her shoulders sagging. "Did you practise in front of the mirror before you came here?"

Will's emerald eyes were full of hope as they watched her. She did not know what she could possibly do. She was twenty years old without family or connection, not some lord or royal, and she may have been strong in her Elementum magic, but she doubted that was the power Will was alluding to. Whatever power he thought she had, it was clearly evading her.

"I really hope you choose to do the right thing. I was rather enjoying your company," Will chuckled, running a hand through his dark hair. "Oddly enough, I do like you."

"Don't sound so surprised," Nora said dryly, her lips tugging to the side. She was over the heaviness of the conversation.

"I told her as much," Florence grinned, coming around and placing a hand on Will's shoulder.

"Aren't you a bit old for Florence?" Nora teased.

"You keep saying that! I'm twenty-six and Florence is twenty-three. I'm going to have to look into broadening my imports on medicinal plants if you keep talking like that!" Will laughed, rising, and following Florence to the door. "Now, get some rest and think about your next move. We're hoping it's the right one."

Nora couldn't make any promises. She no longer knew what was right or wrong anymore.

"Nora," August began after Will and Florence had left, breaking the heavy silence between them. He came around the bed and sat down, the mattress dipping as he sat close by. "I—"

Nora dove forward, crashing into his solid form and gripping his shirt tightly as though holding on for dear life. At first, August appeared to be shocked by her affection, losing whatever he intended to say. However, the surprise was brief and she felt his arms wrap around her, pulling her closer, cocooning her in the safety of his embrace.

"We are family, Nora," he whispered. He placed his chin on her head and sighed deeply. "No matter what happens, no matter where we go or who we meet, we'll have each other. You and I will always be family."

She ignored his words. August had betrayed her, and she hated him for it. Their embrace was a goodbye, whether he realised it or not. She was going to escape this place and he would not be the reason she failed. Her heart broke at the loss of August, but she was used to losing family members. What was another name on the list?

He may have been holding her, but Nora never felt more alone. She would have to get used to the feeling. After all, without August, she had no one.

# 35

## Evelyn

An ocean of grief took hold of her, pulling Evelyn down, wave after wave after wave. The current's grasp was tight against her body, like a child's grip on a beloved teddy bear. Her thoughts swam upwards, reaching for an understanding she wasn't sure existed. How could her father be dead? Months' worth of feelings that she'd been trying to keep at bay were like weights tied to her feet, making it hard to navigate through the waves of grief.

For all she knew, this pain and uncertainty was all that there was. Her chest ached, longing for a breath, a single gasp of air. If only for a slight relief, and yet she didn't know whether she had the desire to oblige her body or whether it was better to go without and continue drowning in it all.

"Evelyn," Margot's words were dull, like shouting underwater. "Evelyn."

"Yes," she mumbled, turning her head. Her mentor stood before her with a downcast expression and sympathy clear in her golden eyes.

"Evelyn?" She asked softly. Odd, coming from a woman who showed little to no emotion for the entire time Evelyn had ever known her. "I came to offer my condolences and check in on you."

"Thank you," Evelyn nodded stiffly.

"I also saw Poppy on my way over and she asked me to give you this." She held up a cream-coloured envelope.

"Oh." Evelyn took it, breaking the wax seal and retrieving the letter within. Her golden eyes scanned the cursive script; Poppy's handwriting was a familiar sight that had a tear fall down her cheek. Wiping it away with the back of her hand, she folded the paper and faced Margot again.

She tilted his head to the side, her silver hair partially slipping from behind one of her pointed ears. "I better go see your mother, but I meant what I said. I may not officially be your mentor anymore, but I am still here for you."

"I appreciate it," Evelyn said, rising and was surprised when Margot pulled her into a tight embrace. Tears fell from her eyes as Margot held her close and she let herself be comforted.

"Come visit whenever you like," Margot said, releasing Evelyn and stepping back. "Or send for me, which ever works for you."

"I will," she replied, wiping her eyes as Margot left.

Blowing out a breath, Evelyn grasped the letter tightly in her hand; the distraction Poppy had sent her was a lifeboat that could stop Evelyn from drowning. And she so desperately wanted to escape the flood. If she could hold everything back for just a few hours, minutes even, then maybe she could face it all when she was more prepared.

She had sent a note to Poppy by Anima messenger as soon as she had found out about her father. In less than a year she had lost her aunt, cousin, and now her father. She swallowed hard; another family member lost. No, she had to push it back, push it all back. Leaving the house would be a good thing, all the reminders would only try to drag her down.

Evelyn left the living room, hurrying away to change into a comfortable dress and jacket before heading off to meet Poppy. The Healing Centre was on the Manor Grounds, so it was only a short walk through the gardens. The first snow of Frost Season had fallen the night before; a light dusting that had covered the grounds like icing on one of Jasmine's pastries. An icy breeze swirled through the air, capturing her hair, and encouraging the strands to take flight. Evelyn wrapped her arms around herself, dropping her chin into her scarf as she picked up the pace, praying to the Goddess Nyssa that her boots would not slip on the slick stone path.

Stepping through the entrance of the Healing Centre and striding towards the hallway of the living quarters, Evelyn kept her head down. News would have spread already, nothing was kept secret for very long when your family ruled the city. Evelyn was not interested in looking into sympathetic eyes or stopping to hear condolences.

Knocking on Poppy's door, she took three deep breaths, readying herself to see her best friend.

"Oh Eve!" Poppy cried, launching herself at Evelyn as soon as the door was wide enough to fit through. She wrapped her arms around Evelyn, squeezing tightly. "I'm so sorry!"

Evelyn buried her head between Poppy's neck and shoulder, allowing the tears to flow. She was glad she had chosen to see her friend. Poppy made calming noises as she stroked Evelyn's hair, each touch unravelling the ache in Evelyn's heart.

A cough sounded from inside Poppy's room and Evelyn looked up, her face puffy and wet, to see a man lounging on the loveseat by the window. His arms were draped over the back with his legs spread out wide as though he owned the place.

"Oh, this is Zaim!" Poppy declared, pulling Evelyn farther into the room. "I wanted you to meet under better circumstances."

Wiping her eyes with the sleeves of her jacket, Evelyn sat on Poppy's bed and tried her best to smile at Zaim.

"Nice to finally meet you," he said, running a hand through his curly mouse brown hair. It looked unkempt, but in a way that suggested he had spent a fair amount of time in front of the mirror to achieve the effect. "I've heard so much about you."

"Poppy has told me a lot about you too," Evelyn replied as her friend propped herself on the man's lap. There was something about Zaim that had Evelyn feeling as though spiders were crawling up her spine and she fought the urge to shiver.

"I know you're going to be great friends," Poppy said. She gestured to the coffee table where a teapot, cups, and a tray of pastries sat. "Would you like something to eat or drink?"

Evelyn shook her head. "I'm okay."

Her friend leaned forward, picking up two bite-sized slices of cake before straightening and popping one of the desserts into Zaim's open mouth. His eyes stayed focused on Evelyn as he chewed, causing her to swallow the bile that rose in her throat. She hid her grimace as Poppy wiped the corner of Zaim's mouth with a napkin.

"How are you coping?" Poppy asked, "I wanted to be with you after I got your note with the terrible news, but Zaim suggested I invite you here instead. We will have more privacy and the manor must feel suffocating with all those memories. Not to mention how worried I was for you not to have anyone there to take care of you while you mourn."

"I wanted to see if you were okay," Poppy replied, tearing her eyes from Zaim to look at Evelyn. "I was worried about you, with no one to take care of you."

"My mother and Jasmine have been with me." Evelyn told her. "August too."

Zaim laughed, earning a reprimanding slap on his shoulder from Poppy. Or tap, rather—her hand made no sound when hit him nor did he flinch.

"Why is that funny?" Evelyn narrowed her eyes.

"It's not," Poppy said quickly, frowning at her boyfriend. "Zaim just has a terrible sense of humour sometimes. He didn't—"

Poppy never finished her sentence. Her blue eyes rolled back into her head, and she dropped like a heavy sack. Zaim made no move to catch her as Poppy's head hit the table top with a sickening crack.

Evelyn was on her feet, golden eyes wide, and stared down at her friend who had landed with a thud on the floor between the loveseat and the coffee table. "What in Nyssa's name did you do to her?"

"I was wondering when the tonic would kick in," Zaim said, leaning back and propping his feet on the coffee table, Poppy unconscious beneath his legs. "Relax, she's only sleeping. Sit, Evelyn, we have a lot to discuss."

"I'm not going to sit here with you while Poppy's head is bleeding on the floor! You have got to be kidding me!" She took a step towards her friend, but Zaim was fast. He sprang to his feet and grabbed Evelyn, shoving her back against the bed.

"Listen to me very carefully." He hissed, his voice dripping with venom. "Unlike pathetic little Nora and August, I am very good at my job. King Dominic has sent me here to do something, and I will fulfil his commands."

"You're an Alta?" Evelyn whispered, stuck between Zaim and the bed. She locked her knees, holding her ground even though she felt ready to collapse into a puddle on the floor.

"I am." He grinned wickedly, towering over her. "And you're about to find out what the Alta are really made of. Not that weak-minded bullshit the other two have led you to believe."

"What do you want?" Evelyn asked, lip trembling. She felt like a child compared to this man who dominated the room.

"Nothing." Zaim sniggered. "King Dominic, however, wants Forest's Edge, and you will give it to him."

"I don't have that power." She quivered, her tears falling once more.

"But you will," he said, caressing her cheek, then licking the tears from his finger. "I killed your aunt and cousin and had planned to get rid of your father too, but luck was on my side it seems."

Evelyn felt like she'd just been hit by lightning at his matter of fact tone. There was no emotion, just cold hard facts, as though he were telling her about the weather. "I knew my aunt and cousin's deaths weren't an accident."

"Of course they weren't," he said simply as though it were the most obvious thing in the world. "But I'm an Alta, not some sloppy assassin so I can see why it was undetected."

Rage boiled inside Evelyn, fuelled by her grief. She lashed out, putting everything Jasmine had taught her into practise. Shoving herself into his chest, her hands raised to claw at his face. Zaim stumbled back in surprise, her nails making contact and digging into the soft skin below his eye. Blood rushed from the wound and down her fingers as he roared, swinging his arm around and knocking her in the head. A crack echoed throughout her skull, bright stars flickering before her eyes as she collapsed to the floor, gripping the sides of her head in her hands.

"You stupid fucking bitch!" He bellowed, kicking her in the stomach

Evelyn screamed, the guttural sound tearing from her throat as she fell to her side. She could feel her magic rising in her trying to heal her injuries but what use was healing magic in a fight, especially when she had barely any training. Crying out, her head was tugged towards Zaim's snarling face. Blood seeped from beneath his eye as he held her by the hair inches from his face.

"Listen to me very carefully," he sneered, his breath hot on her cheek. "Consider this a token of good faith."

He twisted his hand, and a whimper escaped her lips at the sharp pain. "You can either come to Royal Bay of your own free will, or I'll drag you there and send pieces of Poppy back to her friends and family along the way." Evelyn let out a whimper as he shook her head. "What will it be?"

There was no real choice. Evelyn would not let him hurt Poppy, so if that meant going to Royal Bay to keep her friend alive, that was what she would do. She was not ready to lose anyone else she loved.

"I'll go," she breathed, her heart racing. "I'll go willingly if you leave Poppy here."

Zaim spat in her face. "That's not part of the deal."

Evelyn held back the urge to vomit. "Please don't hurt her."

He leaned in closer so that they were an inch apart. The look in his eyes had her trembling on the floor. "Then come with me quietly."

Heart cracking in two, Evelyn looked to where her friend lay motionless on the floor. Her voice was barely a whisper when she answered. "Okay, I'll go to Royal Bay with you."

# 36

## Nora

Fumbling with the lock on the window, Nora swore under her breath then slammed her shackled wrist on the metal. Before August had left the day before, a guard had come to put the pearlescent shackles back around her wrists. So much for giving her the benefit of the doubt… She hated the shackles, their presence a reminder of what should have been bound there.

The padlock fell from the window frame along with the metal loops and bits of wood. Wrists bleeding around the pearlescent restraints, Nora slunk back towards the bed and hid the broken lock and fragments of window frame underneath.

The guard stationed at her door popped his head in, his shiny black hair sticking up at all angles. He narrowed his eyes at where she sat on the floor.

"What are you doing?" he asked as she slammed her wrists into one of the bed's feet. The wood made a cracking noise, nothing like the sound of her shackles on metal but loud enough to have the desired effect. The guard scowled. "Stop that!"

Nora pouted, dropping her bloodied hands. "You're no fun."

"Those shackles aren't going to break that easily and now I'm going to have to get a fucking Healer," he grumbled, shutting the door with a loud thud.

The lock gave a resounding click, and once again she was alone. Nora waited a few minutes before returning to the window. She opened it, the scent of pine wafting into the room, and shivered against the chill as she looked around the garden beyond. It was picturesque; the bright green grass was sprinkled with delicate snow just outside the canopies of three evenly spaced towering trees. A wooden swing hung from the thick branch of the leftmost tree—it too, speckled with white. Beyond the trees, rows of garden beds that looked like piles of fluffy white pillows bordered a tall fence ensnarled in vines—the last obstacle in Nora's way, if all else went to plan. She pictured herself slipping out the window and dropping to the ground below where she would sprint through the icy grass towards the snow-covered garden beds, then leap onto the fence and vanish over it.

*Soon,* she told herself. *She would run soon.*

Nora shut the window and crept back to her bed. The only faces she'd seen since August, Florence and Will were unknown guards dressed in forest green that checked in on her, and brought her meal last night whilst scowling. Even though the desire to eat had evaded her, she had forced herself to consume the entirety of what she had been given. She needed to keep her strength if she was going to escape.

The guilt for those Nora had hurt in the past had thrown her into a restless sleep as it attempted to devour her alive. She didn't know what she believed anymore. The only thing she understood was that she felt like shit. She could not stay in Forest's Edge, but returning to King Dominic in Royal Bay was out of the question as well. She had thought about going to Kaldom; the freezing weather would be miserable, but at least no one would think to look for her there, not even August.

August. She didn't want to think about him. She'd said her goodbye yesterday and slammed the door to that part of her life. There was no going back.

Looking over her shoulder, the door to her room opened to reveal a man dressed head to toe in Lord Royd's guard uniform, carrying a tray with her morning meal. Without a word, he dropped the metal tray onto the end of her bed, before grabbing her wrists, his golden eyes scrutinizing her wounds. Nora inspected her food whilst he healed her; an apple and a piece of bread with what looked like strawberry jam spread over it.

A few minutes past and the guard stood, her wrists no longer bleeding, and made to leave. Nora hopped up too, following the man on silent feet as she walked around the bed. Picking up the tray of food, she let the apple and bread fall onto the bed sheets.

"Hey," she called to the man's back. "What about my water?"

He spun around, eyes wide at her nearness, and she wasted no time, swinging the metal tray at him. A sickening crunch announced his broken nose mixed with his anguished scream. She drew back and gawked as blood gushed from his face, guilt rising like bile in her throat. The guard hunched over, clutching his long nose in a failed attempt to stem the bleeding.

"Fucking bitch!" He swore, his voice sounding wet.

"I'm sorry. I really am," she replied earnestly, before slamming the tray down over his head.

The guard dropped to the floor where he lay motionless. Nora crouched beside him, refusing to look at his face as she began to pull off his jacket. She needed weapons, shoes, and a coat if she were to have any chance of surviving an escape and this was the only way she could get them.

"Wilson! Is everything alright in there?" shouted the guard who'd brought her breakfast  and Nora's head snapped to the door just as the man swung it open. His brown eyes bulged as he saw the other man lying unconscious on the floor and Nora trying to undress him. "What the fuck?"

Nora sprung to her feet, grabbing the metal tray, and lunging for the guard. She swung the tray towards his gut, but all she met was air. He threw his fist, hitting Nora in the shoulder and Nora stumbled backwards, groaning from the strike.

"You can't keep me here!" Nora shouted, using the tray as a shield as the guard started wielding a dagger.

Her fingers gripped the edge of the metal, her hold not as strong as she'd like. Unlike the guard, however, she was fighting for her survival, which made all the difference. At least she prayed to the Goddess Thyra it did. The guard ignored her words, thrusting the blade in the air. Nora matched each attack, the loud clang of steel on metal pounding in her ears as the brutal onslaught reverberated through her shackled arms. Her fingers were slick, her hold on the tray waning but she kept on fighting, determined to leave this place.

The dagger pierced the centre of the tray and Nora twisted her arms, the guard screaming as his wrist bent at an odd angle. He released the dagger and Nora took the advantage, swinging the tray into his gut. He cried out clutching his stomach and staggering backwards. Nora followed, punching the guard, and knocking him back into the door. Gripping the man's black hair in her restrained hands, Nora breathed heavily as she forcefully knocked his head against the door frame. She tried not to think about the pain she was causing, focusing on her freedom that was so close she could almost taste it.

A large hand gripped Nora's shackles, stopping her from inflicting another blow. She gasped as her hands were painfully flung above her head, the skin around her wrists tearing once more. With a grunt she kicked out, her foot flying as the man she'd thought she'd knocked unconscious stepped aside and took advantage of the movement, pushing her backwards. She fell through the doorway, her head hitting the wooden floor with a crack. Stars flashed in her eyes; her body screaming.

He dove on her, sweat dripping from his hair as he fought against Nora's flailing limbs. She growled in frustration, her desperation keeping her from giving up. He held her down, a mixture of sweat and blood dripping from his scowling face onto her own. Nora needed to escape; she could not face being stuck in Forest's Edge, crushed by the emotions that haunted her.

Aeolus appeared by the guard's shoulder. "Calm down or I'll make you."

Nora glared, hiding the rising panic at her failed attempt of an escape. She reluctantly stilled beneath the man. He released her and she gasped, each panting breath sending pain shooting through her body. Aeolus reached down and she could not help flinching away from him as he gripped her elbows and lifted her to her feet.

"What the fuck are you doing?" Aeolus tugged her shackles

towards the door, her wrists smarting as the pearlescent metal rubbed against the newly opened wounds.

The guards did not follow, and she did not look back as she was led down the hallway. The rush of her attempted escape dwindled, and she stumbled, trembling with the guilt that now plagued her. She had hurt those guards. They were only doing their jobs and she had hurt them. She could no longer hide behind the king's commands; their pain was all her fault.

"I can't stay here," she said, the words sounding pathetic even to her own ears.

"Eager to get back to your king?" Aeolus asked, dragging her along.

Nora took a deep breath, her lip trembling. "No, but I can't remain in this city either."

Aeolus glanced over his shoulder. "Is the scary Alta crying?"

"No," she sniffed, turning her head. "Allergies."

He laughed, tugging at her shackled wrists. Nora winced, cursing her new-found conscience. As they approached large wooden doors, Nora instantly felt the heat of the inner space, her body drawn to its source.

Led farther into the modest reception room, a fire sizzled on the far wall, the auburn flames licking the stone hearth opposite a round table, the wood polished to a high sheen. Around the table sat Jasmine, Omari, Florence, Will, Gemma, August, and Sage.

"That took longer than expected," said Gemma, an eyebrow raised.

"Nora attempted an escape," Aeolus replied, coming to stand by the table and dragging Nora with him. "Two of the guards are injured, but they'll survive."

"Nora…" August began.

"I wasn't going back to *him*, if that's what you're thinking," she said, her gaze flickering over everyone seated before her. She hated seeing the anger or pity in any of their eyes. "I just don't want to be here either."

"Why don't you both sit down so we can begin," Jasmine said, gesturing to the two empty seats.

Nora slumped into the seat next to August, pissed that she was now wedged between him and Aeolus. She could feel August's gaze on her, but she refused to look in his direction.

"Now," Jasmine began, sitting up straighter with her shoulders back. "I asked you all here because it's time to put a stop to King Dominic's tyranny. We can no longer hide in the shadows. We need action."

Realisation dawned on Nora. Jasmine was now Lady of Forest's Edge, and what she was declaring… it would mean war. King Dominic would not give up power without a fight, and by the tone of Jasmine's voice, she was willing to give him exactly what he wanted.

"The factions are already preparing for a push," Gemma said, resting her forearms on the table. "Having the full backing of Forest's Edge will be immeasurable."

"A push is not enough," Omari retorted, placing a hand on the back of Jasmine's chair. "We need to protect our people now."

"Then why are these two here?" Aeolus jabbed his thumb in Nora and August's direction. "Can they be trusted?"

"Whether they can be trusted or not is still to be decided, at least in Nora's case," Jasmine said simply. "Evelyn trusts August so I do too."

"They have potential to be strong allies," Omari added. "And we would be stupid not to utilise everything we have. Not only do they have insider information on the Alta and King Dominic, but they are skilled in ways that make them more valuable than many of our soldiers combined."

"What are you suggesting?" Gemma asked, raising a brow. "Provoke a war?"

A knock came at the door and Nora turned her head to see a Forest's Edge guard striding into the room. He stopped before the table, his expression forlorn as it rested on Jasmine.

"My lady," he began. "I went to the Healing Centre, but Evelyn was not there."

Jasmine frowned. "She wasn't in Poppy's room?"

He shook his head. "Neither Evelyn nor Poppy were there, but I found this," he reached into his jacket, retrieving a small bunch of pastel blue flowers and a folded piece of paper.

The note was handed to Jasmine whilst the flowers made their way to Will who scrunched his brow once the bunch was in his hand.

"Myosotis, or as they're commonly referred to as… Forget-me-nots," he said, dropping the flowers to the table. "The name speaks for itself."

"Who would—" Florence began.

"Evelyn has been taken," Jasmine said softly, clutching a hand to her chest, and Nora froze in her seat at the announcement. Omari dropped his hand to Jasmine's shoulder, giving it a squeeze. "My sister has been taken."

Nora's stomach dropped. Evelyn had been kidnapped? Chills crept over her skin; she was worried about Evelyn's wellbeing, and the realisation was somewhat shocking.

"What does the note say exactly," Florence asked.

"Your sister has agreed to join me, do not follow or there will be consequences," Jasmine read, throwing the paper to the table. "That's it." She turned to the guard. "Was there anything else? Anyone looking suspicious?"

He shook his head. "No, my lady."

"Who gave you this letter?"

"I found it in Poppy's quarters, my lady."

August jumped to his feet, his chair falling to the floor behind him. "Let me go after her. I can bring her back."

"How can you possibly do that when you have no idea who's taken her or where she's gone?" Gemma's voice was cold. "Unless you know something we don't."

"I had nothing to do with what happened to Evelyn and you know it." August shot Gemma a glare. "I would never put Evelyn in danger."

"And yet you're so certain you can find her."

"Enough!" Jasmine's words cut like a blade. "We need to stop arguing amongst ourselves. Can't you both see that in doing so King Dominic wins?"

August began, "I want—"

"I know what you want, August," Jasmine said calmly, then turned her attention to Gemma. "And I know that the king had gotten so close to what you have built here that you're on edge, but let's not allow him to weasel his way in any further. I will send guards out to search for my sister."

August nodded stiffly, picking up his chair and sitting back down with his arms folded over his chest.

"Zaim," Nora said, her words barely audible as the realisation dawned on her.

"What?" Sage asked, from where she sat on August's other side.

Nora turned to face Sage, her eyes wide. "Zaim took her."

"Who is Zaim?" Sage asked. The rest of the table had fallen still, silently watching the discourse between the two women.

"An Alta," Nora said, suddenly feeling cold all over. "He visited me when I was in the cell and brought me those exact same flowers." She pointed at the blue blooms in front of Will. "He said he was leaving as soon as he collected what the king desired. Some key to the north. Whatever that is."

"That's impossible," Aeolus scoffed. "There is no way you had a visitor. You were under guard the entire time."

Nora's head snapped towards him. "Everyone has their price."

"What is the key to the north?" Florence asked, looking at everyone at the table. "And why would he want to take Evelyn hostage?"

"I don't know what the key is, but I do know that Zaim is a bad guy," August told them, sitting up straighter in his chair. He slammed his fist down onto the table, causing those closest to jump in their seats. "You need to send me after Evelyn now."

"What does he mean by bad?" Jasmine asked, ignoring August's outburst. Her eyes were filled with worry as she focused her attention on Nora.

"As in sadistic torturer who gets his jollies off tormenting people in all manner of gruesome and downright horrific ways." Nora said, clenching her fists in her lap. "You think I'm horrible, compared to Zaim I am mother fucking sunshine."

Jasmine paled. Taking a deep breath she looked to the guard who still stood before the table. "Organise a group to retrieve my sister and leave immediately. I don't care what you have to do to get her back, I just want her home."

"Yes, my lady," the guard nodded, retreating hastily from the room.

"Let me—" August began.

"No," Jasmine said, her tone allowing no room for negotiation. "She is my sister, this is my city, and you will do as you're told."

To Nora's left, Gemma and Aeolus sat back in their chairs, smirking at each other.

"Now, where were we?" Jasmine asked, composing herself.

"I believe you were suggesting war," Gemma replied dryly.

Another knock sounded at the door, but Nora didn't turn her head, assuming another guard had come to speak to Jasmine. With everything that had happened over the last couple of days, what other surprises could possibly come their way?

"If you're looking to go to war, I might be of some assistance," a male voice declared.

Nora spun around to see Felix stopping before the table, folding his arms over his chest. He had never managed to appear as muscular as August, built more for speed than brute strength, but that didn't mean he wasn't equally as powerful. She gaped at Felix as he grinned at her, all confidence and ease, and was barely able to believe he was there. She and August had been following useless leads in search of Felix, and here he was, freely strolling into the home of the Lady of Forest's Edge. She wanted nothing more than to slap that cocky smile off his stupid fucking face. A large spotted leopard with ash grey eyes prowled in behind him, the wild cat surprisingly familiar, but now wasn't the time to try and work out where she'd seen the creature.

"I was wondering when you'd show up." Nora's head snapped to August, shocked at the words that had come out of his mouth.

"That's where you kept disappearing to?" Nora growled at August, baring her teeth. "I thought you were with Evelyn, and she was under the impression you were with me, but you were with *him*." She swung her shackled arms out in Felix's direction. "Your lies are piling sky high! Anything else you want to tell me?"

'Nora—' August began.

"Always the dramatic one, aren't you Nora?" Felix drawled, cutting August off as he casually stuffed his hands into the pockets of his trousers. "I must say, it is *so lovely* to see you again."

# EPILOGUE

## August

August sat before the fire, nursing a glass of Alvish spirits in his hand. He slowly turned the crystal, swirling the blue liquid, staring at it with little interest. His mind was elsewhere, his thoughts torn between the two women he cared for more than anything else in this world.

Nora barely looked at him during the meeting, only acknowledging his presence once—and that was to yell at him. Aeolus had summoned her once the meeting had ended and she'd rushed to follow his command. At first, August thought she'd been afraid of not complying, but when she'd turned to look at him, all he saw was pure emotion swirling in her brown eyes. It wasn't anger like he'd expected… that he could deal with easily.

He'd seen her in a rage before and could easily weather that storm, but what he'd seen reflected in her eyes today was betrayal and that emotion had dug its claws deep into his heart. Nora had only ever trusted one person in this world, and August had let her down.

Fuck. What else was he supposed to have done? Let her continue being the pet of a fucking psychopath? Blindly following each and every whim until it destroyed her soul?

He wouldn't have been able to live with himself. She may never want to speak to him again, but August had set her free and he hoped one day she'd see that. He really fucking hoped she would. Nora was his only family, and he wasn't prepared to let her go.

August took a sip of his drink, savouring the smoky flavour. He shifted in the armchair, resting his head back and looking to the ornate ceiling. Every surface of Evelyn's home was finely crafted from top to bottom.

Evelyn.

She'd been kidnapped right under their noses. Jasmine had said she trusted him but that was clearly bullshit if she wouldn't let him go after Evelyn. He was pretty sure he was falling in love with Evelyn and the idea of her being with Zaim made his stomach roil. August had promised to keep Evelyn safe, and he had failed her.

The door opened and August tilted his head to see Felix striding into the room, a spotted leopard following close behind. Felix grinned as he sat opposite August, and the leopard shifted, a man with dark hair and eyes the colour of his name appearing in its place.

"Brooding, August?" Ashe asked, smirking as he sat on the floor before the fire. He stretched out his legs and laid back, resting his head on his arms. Even in his human form, he had a feline air.

August sent him a scowl, which Ashe laughed at, apparently amused by August's pain.

"About Nora or Evelyn?" Felix prodded, sitting back in his chair, and crossing his legs.

"Both," August grumbled.

"Predictable," Felix chuckled.

August sighed. "Have you come here to talk or piss me off?"

"I've come because I want to know how many times you used your magic on Nora," he said, looking at August intently.

August shrugged. "You know I used it to try and take the tattoos away."

"Then why was I told she was so easy to capture?" Felix pushed.

August didn't look at him, instead downing his drink then placing it on the table next to him. He stared at his hands in dismay. "I didn't know that I was draining her magic."

"You stole magic from your friend?" Ashe blurted, looking at August with wide eyes. "That's cold, man."

"It wasn't intentional," August growled. "On the nights I slept next to her I woke full of magic. The night they captured her? That's when it clicked that she was the source of my power."

"Have you drawn from anyone else?" Felix asked, leaning forward, and resting his forearms on his knees.

"Evelyn, but that was to heal me," he said, then remembered their kiss the other night. "And I think when we kissed…"

"Again," Ashe laughed. "Ice cold."

"Fuck you, Ashe," August barked, jumping to his feet.

Felix darted between the two men, placing his hands on August's chest, his eyes imploring August. "Come with me to the Periculum Mountains."

"No," August replied instantly, his dark gaze narrowed on Ashe behind Felix's shoulder. "I'm staying here where I'm needed."

Ashe chuckled, still lazing in front of the fire. He looked completely unperturbed by August's murderous glare. "By whom? Jasmine doesn't want your help in finding Evelyn."

"You need to learn to control your magic," Felix said, imploring August. "I know someone who can help you. If you don't you'll be a danger to those around you."

"I can't up and leave Nora," August sighed. "Especially in her current state."

"I'll take care of her for you," Ashe offered with a shrug. "I think we'd get along quite well, plus I don't think she wants you around anyway."

August stepped forward, pushing against Felix's hands, but the other man held his ground. "I may be happy to work with you on taking down King Dominic but if you fuck with Nora I will not hesitate to kill you."

"You didn't mind me following her around before," Ashe wiggled his brows, then laughed, his eyes dancing with glee. "I won't fuck with her I promise. Fuck her, on the other hand…"

August ground his teeth, his dark eyes filling with rage. "She's in a vulnerable state at the moment."

"Then maybe she would like a roll in the sheets," Ashe winked. "Pick her right on up."

"You're a dick," August growled.

Ashe flashed August a grin.

"Now that it's settled Ashe will watch over Nora," Felix said, drawing August's attention back to him. "You are free to come with me."

"And who is in Fellbun that can help me?" August asked.

Felix smiled broadly. "I didn't say we were going to Fellbun."

August scrunched his brow. As far as he knew, Fellbun was the only inhabitable place anywhere near the mountain range. "There's nothing else near the Periculum Mountains…"

"Oh, but there is," Felix replied, a sparkle in his brown eyes. "We're going to the Temple of the Faithful to meet with the Mors Alvs."

# ACKNOWLEDGEMENTS

To be an author has always been a dream of mine. To put to paper the worlds that were forever growing in my mind and the characters that traversed them. This book has been a long time coming and, on the journey, it taught me so many things—not just about writing, but about what I want from my life.

I wouldn't be here today without the constant love and support from the people around me. I am so thankful to each and every person who made this book possible.

Thank you to my husband, Mitch, who has always believed in me and encouraged me to chase my dreams. For seeing me as worthy of success and reminding me of it constantly. The continuous support and understanding you have given means the world to me. You are an amazing human and I'm so lucky to have found you.

Thank you to my children, Liam and Zoe, for loving me and believing that I can do anything, especially when I find it hard to see it myself. You are the reason my world is bright and full of love.

Thank you to my mum for introducing me to stories, encouraging my creativity, and for always making sure that I had a book in my hand. Thank you to my sister, Jess, for always having an open ear and open mind to my sometimes crazy ideas for stories; to Pete for insisting that I can do whatever I set my mind to; and my zia Rita, for being there for me always.

Thank you to Georgia for being the bestest friend anyone could ask for. For reading a million versions of my drafts, having countless conversations about the most minute details, and helping me work out how to get what was in my brain onto paper. Thank you to Bird and Michelle for answering my random questions, reading my drafts, and supporting my dreams, and to Emily and Meghan for all your amazing feedback, advice, and general support in the making of this book.

Thank you to my amazing friend and editor Chloe for working with me to not only make the story as best as it can be but also helping me with the entire publishing process. I have grown so much as a writer since knowing you and I am so grateful for all you have done.

Thank you to everyone who has made this book possible, including K.D Ritchie at Story Wrappers for the amazing cover art, and Amy at Imagine Ink Designs for the wonderful formatting.

And finally, thank you to all of you who have read my book. I am so thankful for your time and support!

**If you enjoyed Liars and Light, please consider leaving a review. It would mean the world to me!**

# ABOUT THE AUTHOR

Rebecca Camm was raised in Melbourne by a single mother, who encouraged her passion for reading and all things magical. She has been writing stories since she was a child to help manage her anxiety and make sense of the world.

Rebecca strongly believes in the power stories have in changing lives. Just like her, Rebecca's characters are flawed, yet they are continually learning. Unlike her, they are confident, witty, and just generally more exciting.

Rebecca lives with her husband and two children. When her children allow her free time, she is either writing or attempting to conquer her ever growing tbr pile.

**Stay in touch!**
Website www.rebeccacamm.com
Newsletter www.rebeccacamm.com/contact
Instagram @readingwritingdaydreaming
Tiktok @readingwritingdaydream
Facebook @readingwritingdaydreaming

Lightning Source UK Ltd.
Milton Keynes UK
UKHW012029090223
416719UK00010B/726/J